"A rare treat, and a wonderful journey! ' is wrapped up in a marvelously surprising adventure, where I never knew what to expect from one page to the next. There's an air of enchantment in the pages of this novel, as if we're swept up in a fairy tale–flavored reality. Beautifully drawn, authentic characters navigate this engaging story that is the first in a promising new series!"

Joanna Davidson Politano, author of *The Lost Melody* and other historical novels

"Intriguing, heart-tugging, and romantic—Susan L. Tuttle's latest packs an emotional punch. *The Rare Jewel of Everleigh Wheaton* was a delight to read. I especially loved watching both Everleigh and Niles soften throughout the story, discovering the gift of vulnerability and proving that love is every bit as much an adventure as a quest to find a missing jewel. Kudos to Tuttle for a wonderful read!"

Melissa Tagg, *USA Today* best-selling and Christy Award–winning author

"In *The Rare Jewel of Everleigh Wheaton*, Tuttle infuses a century-long international mystery with her signature style of high-chemistry romance and witty banter. Thanks to the quirky multigenerational cast, every scene is a character study that will have readers captivated long after the last page is turned."

Janine Rosche, best-selling author of *With Every Memory*

"Susan L. Tuttle has a way of hooking you from the beginning and entertaining you to the very end. *The Rare Jewel of Everleigh Wheaton* is a fantastic combination of history, intrigue, and romance that will touch every reader's heart. I look forward to reading more from Ms. Tuttle."

Toni Shiloh, Christy Award–winning author

The
RARE JEWEL
of
EVERLEIGH
WHEATON

Treasures of Halstead Manor

The Rare Jewel of Everleigh Wheaton
The Novel Adventures of Natalie Daughtry
The Hidden Key of Brooke Sumner

TREASURES OF HALSTEAD MANOR

The
RARE JEWEL
of
EVERLEIGH
WHEATON

Susan L. Tuttle

KREGEL
PUBLICATIONS

Cataloging-in-Publication data is available from the Library of Congress.

ISBN 978-0-8254-4859-1, print
ISBN 978-0-8254-7186-5, epub
ISBN 978-0-8254-7185-8, Kindle

Printed in the United States of America
24 25 26 27 28 29 30 31 32 33 / 5 4 3 2 1

To my favorite son,
who started me on one of my best
adventures of all, motherhood.
You are indeed rare and treasured.
Perfectly imperfect.
And I am so thankful God made you mine.
Love you more.

CHAPTER ONE

Archduchess Adelheid, age seven
Vienna, Austria, 1921

FALL ERUPTED OVER SCHÖNBRUNN PALACE, ushering in more than a simple change to the air. Adelheid raced up the stone steps from the gardens, breathless from a victorious game of hide-and-seek. For once, she'd finally bested her older brother. She couldn't wait to share her win with Mama and Papa who always reminded her she was a Habsburg. And Habsburgs were strong.

"Mama! Papa!" Adelheid ran down the long echoing hall, her voice bouncing ahead of her.

One of the servants dusting sconces jumped out of her way. "Slow down, child."

She ignored the reprimand, even knowing that should Mama duck her head into the hall and catch her unladylike behavior, she'd receive a scolding. Papa, however, would encourage her to run faster. Adelheid giggled at the thought.

Reaching their door, Adelheid disregarded another rule and burst inside. "I won—"

Mama's and Papa's stern faces halted her exclamation. Baron Bruno Steiner stood beside them.

Oh. Clasping her hands, she tried for an apology that would keep her from trouble. "I'm sorry, Mama and Papa. I did not mean to interrupt."

Papa shared a glance with Mama, one she hadn't seen before, then returned his gaze to Adelheid. His eyes crinkled at the edges, but not like when he was happy. Her tummy bubbled as it often did before she was expected to greet new people. Mama called it an anxious stomach.

Papa's face relaxed, and for a moment he didn't appear as worried. "It is all right, child."

It didn't feel all right. Something was bothering him.

Baron Steiner cleared his throat. "I will ensure what we've spoken about is handled." Then to Mama, "I'll meet you at Gödöllő."

"Thank you, Bruno." Papa shook the man's hand.

As Baron Steiner left, Mama touched Papa's arm. "You go as well, Charles. You are needed elsewhere. I will ensure this is handled." Her tone held an urgency Adelheid hadn't heard before.

Moving quickly, Papa kissed Mama's cheek, then gathered papers from his desk. This wasn't right. Papa's normal joy had been replaced by worry. As he passed Adelheid, he tugged on her braid. "Obey your mama and help her with your siblings while I'm away."

She nodded at the familiar instructions, given each time Papa traveled. But this time he did not follow it with a promise of chocolate upon his return.

"Papa? Will you still bring me chocolates?" she called.

He paused at the door, no twinkle in his eyes, though he did smile. "Yes, child, I will bring you chocolates." Then he sought Mama's face, dipped his head ever so slightly, and left.

Mama glanced her way. "Please gather your siblings and bring them to the nursery."

She caught sight of the shiny jewels on the desk, Mama's words barely registering. "Why are those here?"

All the sparkling pieces resided in a special room, one Adelheid had only visited once when they'd held a grand party. Mama had allowed her to choose a bracelet, but not the piece she'd wanted most. The giant yellow diamond set in a glittering hatpin.

"No, dear, not the Florentine. You'll wear that on your wedding day," she'd said.

Now the diamond rested on the desk surrounded by several pieces she'd seen that night.

Adelheid inched closer, her fingers reaching for the nearest item—a gold necklace with several thick, large squares linked together. Dangling from the center was what she and her brother called a lazy sheep, because the ewe hung as limp as their cat when it slept in her arms. She'd seen Papa wear it on formal occasions, and he'd told Otto all men in the Habsburg Empire received one. Something they called a Golden Fleece.

Mama stepped in front of her. "Adelheid, did you hear me? I need you to collect your siblings."

She shifted her gaze to Mama's, then to the jewels and the case beside them. A few others already sat inside on black velvet. "But why are you packing them?"

With a sigh often heard when her younger siblings exhausted her, Mama finally replied. "Because I'm taking you along with your brothers and sister to our palace in Gödöllő."

Where Baron Steiner said he'd meet her? "But why all of them? We never do that."

"Because we will be gone for some time."

Her insides tightened, and her skin grew all itchy. She didn't want to go to the other palace. She loved it here. The halls. The gardens. The hill where she and Papa watched over their city, Vienna. He'd tell her stories about their family and other emperors of the Habsburg Empire who came before him.

"I don't want to go." Adelheid crossed her arms.

Mama knelt in front of her and gently brushed a lock of hair from her cheek. "We must leave. There are people who don't want us to stay."

"People can tell Papa what to do?" She thought no one could do that.

"They can try." Mama gently gripped Adelheid's chin. "Papa is strong, as are you and I. We are Habsburgs."

Mama's words reminded her of why she had raced in here. She nodded, trying to recapture that feeling. "I am strong. I finally bested Otto at hide-and-seek."

Warm pride filled Mama's face. "Then, since you are such a champion, think of this as one giant game of hide-and-seek. We shall hide in Gödöllő, and we will take our jewels with us. Won't that be fun?"

"Perhaps." A little of her scratchiness eased. "Will we return here after our game has ended?"

Mama stood, moving her hand to Adelheid's shoulder. The tiny wrinkles beside her eyes deepened. "This is our home. A Habsburg has always lived here. Papa and I do not wish for that to change."

But wishes did not always come true.

CHAPTER TWO

Present Day

"THAT WOMAN'S A THIEF."

It took approximately four words to kill a reputation. Oh, Everleigh Wheaton supposed it could take a few more or a few less, but in all her thirty-five years, four remained the average. This moment lent support to the well-worn fact.

Palmer Quimby, disinherited son of Everleigh's former employer, jabbed his long, manicured finger in her direction. "She stole everything from my mother."

Silence spread across The Corner Café, the lone diner in this small town of Kenton Corners, Illinois, where moments ago the clink of dishes and hum of conversation had filled the air. Now every eye and ear tuned in to the show Palmer put on with an almost gleeful zeal.

Everleigh bracketed her hips with her hands and sized up Palmer. This wasn't the first time she'd dealt with bogus accusations, and she doubted it would be her last. "The only thing I took from your mother was my weekly paycheck. Now, if you're hungry, please have a seat. Otherwise, you can leave."

The slant of his nose created a harsh line practically as severe as his dark eyes. Funny, today they weren't bloodshot. They were, however, narrowed in on her with animosity. "I'm not leaving until you tell me what you did with my mother's money. Her bank accounts have been cleaned out, and our housekeeper said you took Mother for a drive last week."

She didn't bother refuting his words or the housekeeper's recounting. Both were actually true. "Do you want to eat or not, Palmer?"

He encroached on her space, his sickeningly sweet cologne churning her stomach. "I want my money."

"You mean your mother's money?" If they bottled up her saccharine tone, it would rival that scent he wore.

Red blotches marred his neck and cheeks. Before he could respond, Ham-on-Rye, a recent regular who claimed the same booth every day at eleven, stood from his seat. "Everything okay?"

Everleigh glanced across her shoulder to the dark-haired thirtysomething who studied them from behind black, rounded frames. She assured him with a smile. "It's all good." Then blinked to Palmer. "I don't have your mother's money. If you want to know what she's done with it, I suggest you ask her."

"I can't." He practically vibrated. Most likely from a high wearing off. "She hasn't been coherent since you left. I know that was your doing as well."

Everleigh's heart hitched. Taking blame for something she stood innocent of, well, that occurrence she'd grown used to. Losing a patient she'd come to care for? That circumstance she'd never grow accustomed to. Based on Palmer's revelation, Constance Quimby neared the end of the disease that had ravaged her body.

She opened her mouth to seek out more information. The swinging door to the kitchen bumped open and her boss walked out, cutting off her attempt. Palmer latched on to him immediately. "Are you in charge here?"

"I am." Garrison Moore flipped a dishrag over his shoulder, then crossed his arms. At fifty-two, he remained as trim as when he'd been star quarterback at the local community college, the evidence proudly displayed in photos adorning all the café walls. "What's all the racket about out here?"

The greasy, coffee-scented air around them remained strained and silent as diners watched the unfolding drama. They seemed to salivate for another helping of Palmer's show rather than their quickly growing cold meals. Palmer commanded the space like the leading man he'd always hoped to be. "Your waitress is a thief. You don't want her stealing other people's money, let alone yours."

Garrison slowly drew his stare from Palmer to Everleigh. "Care to explain?"

Palmer bristled. "I just—"

With a step in his direction, Garrison silenced him. "You know what? I've had enough of you." He hitched his thumb toward the door. "Time for you to go."

"But—"

"This isn't a discussion." The sizzle of burgers on the grill carried from the pass-through behind him. It was the only noise in the room. "You don't come in here, disturb my patrons, and harass my waitress." Palmer stubbornly stood his ground. The spoiled man was used to getting anything he wanted. Garrison wasn't up for his games. "Leave. Or I'm calling the cops." He pulled out his cell phone.

"Fine." Palmer tossed his hands in the air. "I'm going. But if I were you, I'd fire her."

The café door hadn't even shut behind him before Garrison addressed her. "My office."

He pushed open the swinging door, holding it for her to step through. Behind her, the swell of chatter rose faster than butter melting on hot pancakes, and her coworkers' shoes squeaked as they hustled to refill coffee cups. No doubt they'd also add some salacious gossip of their own to sweeten the brew.

Everleigh stepped into Garrison's small, oak-paneled office and folded into the seat in front of his desk. Garrison tucked his muscled frame into his leather chair, its wheels squeaking as he rolled to face her. "Explain," was all he said.

She offered the little she was at liberty to divulge. Unfortunately, withholding truth could appear incriminatory, and she hadn't provided Garrison with this information when applying to work here. "That was Palmer Quimby. I used to work for his mother, Constance, whom he believes I stole from. He fired me two months ago."

Yep. Garrison's thick, black brows drew together. "You didn't have Constance Quimby's name on your application. You also didn't talk about her in your interview."

"Because I was unfairly let go from a job I loved, and I didn't want the drama to follow me here." Plus, she'd specifically taken a job here rather than in the ER because leaving off her last nursing job didn't feel like quite as much of an oversight when applying at a diner. Well, that, and she hadn't procured her licensure by endorsement to work in Illinois yet. Either way, the omission still bit her in the rear.

"Yet, it just did." Garrison roughed a hand through his hair. "Why does he believe you stole from his mother?"

"Because I was with her when she withdrew money from her accounts."

"Did you take the money?"

"No." Her fingers itched to twist the rows of her Rubik's Cube. Instead, she fiddled with the silver ring she wore that had belonged to Mom. "I did not take the money."

He rocked in his chair. "I want to believe you, Everleigh. You keep to yourself, but you haven't given me any trouble." His fingers drummed on his desk. "Problem is, you weren't forthcoming on your job application, and I get the sense you're not telling me everything now."

"I've always been honest with you."

"Withholding information isn't lying, but it is deceitful." Garrison watched her closely, his silence offering her the opportunity to fill it with explanation. All she had to offer was her track record over the past six weeks. Unfortunately, based on his expression, that didn't appear to be enough. "I'm sorry, but I need to be able to trust my employees, and your silence is making that awfully difficult. Not to mention, I have no idea if that yahoo will show up here again and disrupt things. I can't have that." He rubbed his chin and blew out a breath. "I have to let you go. No need to finish your shift."

Or argue. She'd only worked here a short time, but she knew Garrison well enough to know his decisions were final.

She stood. "Thank you for the opportunity."

He nodded. "I wish you well."

Everleigh made her way to her small locker off the kitchen. There wasn't anyone she needed to say goodbye to here, so she dropped her apron in the laundry bag, grabbed her backpack, and exited through the rear door. Late March and still no buds on the trees. She was tired of the monochromatic scheme of winter, and more than ready for color to burst through the world again. Hopefully soon.

She made it to her beat-up Ford Escape when a silver Tesla pulled up.

The window rolled down and there was Palmer. If his smile grew any wider, it would crack the cheek implants he'd overpaid for. With his prescription drug habit, she'd been surprised he could afford the unnecessary surgery. His poor financial choices and long-standing addiction played into Constance's decisions about her money.

"Appears that Neanderthal's smarter than I thought."

"Go away, Palmer." She stuck her key into the door and unlocked her car.

"All you have to do is return the money, and I'll leave you alone. This doesn't have to go any further."

Because fueling his finances held more importance than any sense of decency. Ruining her would come as easy as breathing and with as little thought. She and Constance had spoken as much when she'd agreed to help her, so it wasn't a huge surprise. In fact, she thought she'd be prepared should this happen. She'd accumulated a lot of practice at her reputation being wrongfully tarnished, and that was one of the main reasons she kept her distance from people. With her safeguards securely in place, she'd assumed herself impervious to any ill feelings should her character be called into question again.

Surprisingly, exhaustion weighed her down.

She tossed her backpack on the passenger seat. "I don't have your money. Bug me all you want. That fact won't change."

"We'll file a civil suit."

Wonderful. "Do what you have to do."

Intimidation tactics not working, Palmer peeled out of the lot.

Everleigh slid into her seat, closed her door against the cool spring breeze, and dropped her forehead to the steering wheel. It hadn't taken long for Palmer to track her here, but she hadn't stopped using her credit cards or changed her phone number. He might not have access to his mother's money, but he still retained plenty of contacts who would be willing to help find her if they thought it would lead to a big payday for them as well.

She probably should have made it harder for them, but it would've only prolonged the inevitable. The changes Constance made to her will wouldn't come to light until her passing. No doubt at that time, Palmer would ramp up his pressure on Everleigh, because he wasn't going to like what he discovered. Still, in spite of any trouble he caused her, she didn't regret what she'd done. Not for one single moment.

Fingers on her keys, she caught sight of her coworker Molly running across the lot, waving something in her hand. Everleigh rolled down her window as Molly approached, her expression sympathetic. "Oh, good. I thought I missed you. Garrison filled us in. I'm so sorry."

"It's all good."

Molly's blond curls bobbed as she shook her head. "It's not, but there's not much I can do." She held out a thick white envelope with Everleigh's name scrawled in black ink across the front. "This was left inside for you."

Everleigh scrunched her face as she accepted it. "Do you know by who?"

"No clue. It was on the counter by the register."

Strange. "Okay. Well, thanks."

Molly walked backward toward the diner. "Wish I could do more. I think Tawny's hiring at the salon if you know how to cut hair."

She didn't. But there were plenty of other things she could do. Her lease ran month-to-month, so moving wouldn't be an issue if it came to that. She purposefully kept her belongings sparse and relationships even sparser. Both only brought unwanted heaviness to her life. Except for Uncle Maddox—probably because their interactions consisted mainly of texting and the very occasional FaceTime. They hadn't been in the same room since Mom passed away. Before that she'd gone several years without physically seeing him, but he stubbornly remained a part of her life. He'd been the one to help her relocate here, and he'd no doubt have an idea of where she could try next.

Her attention returned to the curious envelope she'd been tapping in her hands. It was thick but not heavy, with unfamiliar cursive handwriting calling her name. She ran her finger along the flap at the back, pried it open, and slid out the rectangular card from inside.

Your presence is requested at Halstead Manor tomorrow morning at nine o'clock.

Sincerely,
Caspar

Caspar? She didn't know anyone named Caspar. Everleigh turned the card over. Nothing on the back side. She flipped it once more to reread the invitation. Her curiosity sparked brighter. According to the diners she'd asked after spotting the lone mansion towering in a field, Halstead Manor was a landmark in Kenton Corners and provided the town with its one claim to fame, at least within northern Illinois. Built in the early 1900s, the massive redbrick home could be seen from miles away. It had been owned by the Forsythes, a Scottish couple, who loved the people of Kenton Corners almost as much as they loved their privacy. Everyone here knew everything—and simultaneously nothing—about the husband and wife who'd opened their home for all the town celebrations, annual Easter egg hunt, and just-because potlucks. When they passed away in the 1970s from old age, Halstead Manor had been shuttered.

Tapping the invitation against her steering wheel, Everleigh stared out her window at her now-former place of business. The Corner Café served up rumors as fast as it did its famous fried mush, a panfried cornmeal porridge topped with savory or sweet delicacies. Better than waffles or pancakes in her opinion, the mush was the food of choice for swapping gossip over around here. Until her debacle with Palmer this afternoon, the manor had been the hot topic. Speculation became that the Forsythes willed the home to their grandchildren in Scotland, which is why it remained vacant. For a brief stint in the nineties and another in the early two thousands, the house held signs of life, although the town never saw whoever inhabited it. Then, earlier this year, the doors opened once more. Renovations began taking place. Lights shone through the windows at night. But again, the new owner remained an unknown. Had someone purchased the home? Did it still remain in the Forsythe family? Though theories ran rampant, no one had learned the name of the person behind Halstead Manor's reawakening.

She held up the thick white card, zeroing in on the signature. If she had to guess, the person bringing life back to the manor was named Caspar.

And she had between now and tomorrow morning to collect any information she could on him. She loved a good puzzle, and this invitation presented her with one she had every intention of solving.

CHAPTER THREE

CURIOSITY ALL TOO OFTEN PLACED Everleigh in a world of trouble. She hoped today wasn't one of those times.

With a deep breath, she shut off her engine and stifled a yawn. She'd spent most of the night on her computer, trying to dig up information on whoever this Caspar was. At three this morning, exhausted and desperate, she finally texted Uncle Maddox. If one person existed who could help her, it was him. Literally. Because she didn't have anyone else in her life to ask. Unfortunately, asking for help induced an emotional allergic reaction akin to the physical one she suffered when she ingested seafood. But time grew short, and answers remained elusive.

Plus, the man possessed more answers than Google. She'd yet to stump him, and she had tried. They shared a love for puzzles, constantly attempting to one-up each other. Their current go-round involved riddles, and the latest one she'd sent he'd answered in under a minute. Well, from the fact that he'd provided zero info on Caspar, it seemed she'd finally found a mystery to stymie him. Except this time she hadn't been trying.

Pushing her sun visor into place, Everleigh stared out her windshield at Halstead Manor. With its three-story redbrick towers joined in the middle by a two-story entrance, the manor's pyramid black roofs and straight lines reminded her of an Italianate farmhouse. The land encircling it only enhanced that feel. Grass, crunchy and brown from winter, spread out for the first acre, met by over a hundred acres of dormant cornfields. Even with her windows closed, she could hear the faint rumble of the trucks traveling along nearby Route 66, the semis visible in the distance.

Driving in, Everleigh had bumped along the gravel two-track flanked by dried, colorless wildflowers leading to the circle drive where she now parked. The lone tree on the property, a massive oak that must have been planted by the original owners, grew alongside the west corner of the home.

Her phone vibrated, signaling an incoming text from Uncle Maddox.

> I have no information to
> add to what you've already
> discovered. If I find anything
> new, I'll text you.

She shot off a return text.

> Can't believe you're unable to
> find more information on this
> Caspar. Never thought I'd see
> this day.

> What day?

> The day where I proved you're
> human.

> I AM fully human.

> Maybe if you visited more
> often, I'd believe that.

> ☺ You know if you need me, I'll
> be there in a heartbeat.

> I do.

You're going to the meeting?

I'm about to go in.

Three dots blinked across the screen. Disappeared. Then blinked again. Strange since Uncle Maddox never seemed lost for words. Finally,

Be careful.

I will. There's other cars here. I don't think I'll be alone.

Time would tell if that was a good or bad thing.

Text me when you're done.

Will do. By the way, the answer's a candle.

He'd sent her a riddle during their early morning text session.

That took you entirely too long.

You sent me an easy one to try to make me feel better about being fired and then being stumped on this Caspar. It backfired and I spent the night sulking that you went easy on me.

Point taken. When Everleigh's life is hard, give her a harder riddle.

Exactly.

Goodbye, Sunshine.

Phone in hand, she climbed out and started for the stone steps leading to the massive wooden doors of the entrance. Thick rays of light spilled from a cloudless sky overhead. Everleigh relished the warmth on her face. During winter in the Midwest, the sun acted like an introvert at a party, hiding behind clouds so it wouldn't be seen. While it was an analogy she wholeheartedly related to, she much preferred the sun's personality change to an extrovert come spring—even if temps remained winter-like and the earth refused to awaken fully. One thing at a time, she supposed.

As she walked past the other cars parked in the drive, she stopped and snapped a picture of their license plates, then sent the photo to her uncle.

In case I vanish, here's a lead.

☺

Not something to joke about.

I only partially was.

Gravel crunched under her feet as she placed her phone into her sling bag. Her fingers rubbed the small Rubik's Cube attached to her key ring. Uncle Maddox might reside a quarter world away in the Canary Islands, but since Mom passed, there wasn't anyone else to notice if she disappeared. Definitely not her father who'd never been able to see beyond his own losses and needs. Even his stint in jail hadn't changed him. Still, flying primarily solo was her choice. Relationships historically delivered more hurt than happiness. Now she shielded who she allowed into her life more tightly than the Royal Guard protected Buckingham Palace and the King.

She clanked the heavy metal knocker against the door to announce her presence. Footsteps drew near from inside. The door opened, and Everleigh blinked in surprise.

"Ham-on-Rye?" The words escaped before her manners stopped them.

His dark brows rose over the frames of his familiar black glasses. "Excuse me?"

She stood frozen in place, her mind working to hook together the pieces she currently held of this puzzle. "Ham on rye. It's what you've ordered every day for the past two weeks. You sit in my section. Pay cash. And eat a ham on rye every afternoon at eleven."

His angular face split with a smile that deepened the cleft in his chin. "With a side of fried mush." He leaned against the doorframe and tucked his hands into the pockets of his dark flat-front chinos. A white collared shirt and the knot of a navy polka-dot tie peeked out from his fitted V-neck sweater. His stance looked more relaxed than his attire.

"Everyone orders fried mush. It's what we're known for." The dish was a staple in many small Midwest towns, but Garrison took things a step further. He'd dedicated an entire section of the menu to fried-mush dishes named after the regulars who'd ordered them. Bill's Fried Mush consisted of bacon, cashew butter, pecans, and brown sugar syrup on top. Doris's Fried Mush had wild berries and mascarpone. And the list went on.

"I'd never heard of it till I moved here."

"Not many have." She tossed out the side thought as a more predominant one formed. "You left me the invitation?"

"I delivered it, but it wasn't from me. I would have handed it directly to you, but you were . . . preoccupied." He stepped back, pulling the door open farther. "Come inside and I'll fill you in."

Curiosity might have been the impetus for coming, but common sense eclipsed her inquiring mind when his familiar face opened the door. The situation flipped from temptingly intriguing to possible crazy stalker in the space of a hello.

"I'm good out here, thanks." The cool spring wind challenged her response. She tucked herself farther into her long down coat. "So, you're not Caspar then?"

"I am not." He reached his hand out in a welcoming shake. His left hand now rested on his hip, and a wedding band adorned his ring finger. "I apologize. I know your name, but it hit me that you don't know mine. John Doyle."

Another gust swept her hair like a whirling dervish above her head. She attempted to tame it with one hand while cautiously accepting his handshake with another. "Good to finally have a name for the face."

"You mean instead of Ham-on-Rye?" His gray eyes twinkled.

"Be thankful you didn't order the tuna salad."

He chuckled. "I am. On many levels."

Silence descended on them for a few beats before he stepped away from the door. "I should return to the others and start our meeting. Unless you plan on changing your mind about coming in?"

Her gut shifted toward John not posing a threat, and her intuition always served her well. She lifted her phone and snapped a picture of him. Then she texted it with his name to Uncle Maddox.

"Precautionary?" he asked.

"Yep. I've seen *Dateline*." She stepped over the threshold and peeked inside, leaving an arm's length between them. "Which way are we headed?"

He nodded to the door on the left, just beyond the foyer. "The parlor."

Not too far into the home. "I'll follow you." Because she wasn't turning her back to him.

"I assumed." He started down the hall, his voice drifting to her. "How'd you make out yesterday after you disappeared into the kitchen? That guy who came in was tossing around some inflammatory accusations." His tone, vernacular, and attire created pieces that when fashioned together would most likely form the picture of a lawyer.

"He was."

John didn't press any further. Instead, he slid open the pocket door to the parlor. Everleigh stepped inside and observed two women already in the room—most likely the owners of the other cars. The brunette immediately stood and crossed the room. Her wavy hair fell slightly beneath her collarbone, and her hazel eyes oozed a warmth turned up a notch by her smile. She wore skinny jeans, a white T-shirt, and a golden cardigan. In chunky ankle boots, she stood slightly above Everleigh's five-eight frame yet firmly below John's estimated six foot three.

She offered her hand. "I'm Natalie Daughtry."

Everleigh returned the grasp. "Everleigh Wheaton."

The blond remained against the wall, watching. With her arms crossed and legs slightly braced, her silvery blue eyes cautiously appraised them. She wore black jeans and a black turtleneck under her black leather jacket, each piece fitted to her exact measurements. A few strands of hair fell from the knot she'd twisted them into and lay loose against her cheek. While she didn't move, she did introduce herself. "Brooke Sumner."

So, unless they'd kept their maiden names, neither were John's wife.

He nodded to the couch Natalie had vacated. "Would you all care to have a seat?" Natalie settled again onto her cushion. Everleigh dodged it and claimed the lone leather club chair. Brooke waited a beat before perching on the opposite side of the couch as John continued talking. "We have a few minutes before Caspar calls. How about we get to know one another a little bit."

"Caspar's not here?" Brooke asked before Everleigh could voice the same question.

"He's not." John circled the desk, pulled out a padded office chair, and sat. "Why don't you start? Tell us a little about yourself, Brooke."

Her lips remained in a thin line.

Natalie broke the stalemate. "I'll go." She tugged on the arms of her cardigan, the motion appearing more related to nerves than neatness. "Like I already said, my name's Natalie. I moved back to Kenton Corners in the fall because my husband, Mason, took a job as football coach and athletic director at the high school. I have two boys, Hunter and Reed. Hunter is in his third year at Purdue University and Reed started Cornell this fall. So that's me."

"No. That's your family," Brooke observed. "That didn't tell me anything about you."

Natalie's head tipped as she met Brooke's gaze straight on with a no-holds-barred one of her own. Huh. In the five minutes Everleigh had known the women, she'd assumed that Brooke would be the stronger of the two. That was prior to learning Natalie had raised two boys into young men. As a nurse, Everleigh had worked a lot of places and seen a lot of people, and one truth proved universal: nothing made a woman stronger than motherhood.

"Are you married, Brooke?" Natalie coolly asked.

Brooke shook her head.

"Do you have children?"

Another shake.

"Then I'm not surprised you think I told you nothing about myself." She leaned against the couch cushion.

Brooke's focus landed on the far wall and remained there.

Well, this was a boatload of unexpected fun.

John cleared his throat. "How about you go next, Everleigh?"

"Sure." Except she'd ask a question of her own. "Why are we here?"

The mahogany grandfather clock behind John clanged the quarter hour, the sound of the bells reverberating through the room. He pulled out his phone as the echoes faded away and placed it on the desk. "Seems it's time to find that out."

With one touch, a ringtone filled the silence, then someone answered.

"Hello, ladies. And John." A modulated male voice greeted them.

Natalie, Brooke, and Everleigh shared a glance, then stared down at the phone. John reclined in his chair and clasped his hands behind his head. His relaxed appearance seemed to say he'd officially handed this meeting off to Caspar.

"I feel like I'm in some strange rerun of *Charlie's Angels*. Hopefully minus the guns and stunt requirements." Natalie broke the silence, earning a few strained laughs from the rest of them.

"I can see that," Caspar replied.

The voice resembled a combination of her male British selection on Siri and a robot. The cadence wasn't quite as smooth as today's technology but also not as rough as original computerized versions.

"It's not polite to invite someone to your house and then not be here, Caspar," Everleigh tossed out. "This is Caspar, correct?"

"It is. And I had John there to greet you." A pause. "Is this Everleigh?"

She straightened. "What makes you think that?"

"Intuition. A skill you also have."

How on earth could he know that?

Brooke moved around the room. "Either that or he has cameras."

"I promise you I don't, Brooke."

She stilled.

Had he heard their voices before? How? Or had he been watching them long enough to pick up on their traits? She'd only spent a few minutes with these ladies, but Brooke definitely read as the suspicious type. If he'd already identified Everleigh in this conversation, that left only Brooke and Natalie—who definitely did *not* seem the suspicious type—to choose from. So, yeah, he could be using simple deduction to play his game.

"You're enjoying this." Natalie's voice held a hint of amusement.

"I'll admit, I am. It's a pleasure to finally meet you all." The line buzzed a second. Then, "I've waited some time for this."

Brooke inched to the perimeter of the room, surveying every angle. Everleigh stood and approached the phone. "Which means you've been watching us for a while."

"Not creepy at all," Brooke muttered.

"I apologize. Let me clarify." Something whirred in the background. Everleigh recognized the sound but couldn't place it. "It's a pleasure to finally meet the three of you, yes. But what I've been waiting some time for is finally having three qualified candidates I can possibly hire."

"Excuse me?" Natalie sat up. "This is a job interview?"

Interesting timing. "For what?"

"I already have a job." Brooke squinted up at a vent. She didn't relinquish her suspicions easily.

"I'm fully aware," Caspar responded. "This is something you would do on the side, and I intend to pay you well." A short pause in which the whirring sound happened again. Then, "No interview necessary. I know the skills you all have, and that's why you're here."

Things didn't add up. "If we haven't sent you our résumés, how do you know our skills?"

"Besides the jobs you hold, you've each had some rather impressive accomplishments, be it in historical research, antiques, or puzzles. All information that's available online." None of them interrupted him, but they confirmed his explanation with nods. "Your notable achievements, among other abilities, lifted your names to the top. Think of me like a headhunter offering you a new job opportunity."

Brooke had completed her perimeter sweep. "Why the note then? Why bring us all here for this meeting? Headhunters aren't secretive."

The sound of tapping preceded his automated-sounding response. "I'm not one to do things in a conventional manner."

Obviously, or he'd have put an ad in the paper and hired people that way.

Still seated, John affirmed Caspar's response. "He hired me the same way. White envelope on my doorstep. That was three months ago, and so far everything is legit."

With their leaned-in posture, it was clear Brooke and Natalie hadn't ruled out accepting their positions. Neither had Everleigh, but she needed more info. "Tell us about this job."

"There's an item I'd like you to find for me. I don't know how long exactly this will take, but once it's found, I'll pay you fifty thousand dollars apiece and a percentage of the finder's fee should there be one."

Everleigh suppressed a large gulp. That money would go a long way toward paying off the medical bills and loans she'd accumulated when Mom was sick, especially since she hadn't had life insurance. When she'd passed away, all Everleigh still had to hold on to was a mountain of debt.

"How do we know what we'll be doing is legal?" Natalie asked.

Brooke voiced her own concern. "And that you'll actually pay us."

The phone line crackled, then cleared. "That's where John comes in." Settling forward in his chair, John tuned in to what Caspar was saying—not that Everleigh thought for one second he hadn't been paying attention. Caspar continued. "His reputation as a lawyer is well noted both in Michigan and here. Feel free to look it up. I hired him to handle multiple things for me, one of which will be working with you. I've provided him with access to a bank account with your funds already in it. He's able to get in contact with me should you ever have questions on the job, and he'll ensure no legal lines are crossed—by you or by me."

Though her caution remained, her curiosity continued to grow, and that might win out here. It typically did in a battle between the two.

Brooke's stare met John's as she hauled out her phone. "Let's see what I can find, John Doyle."

He welcomed her challenge, clearly not intimidated by her in the least. "Be my guest."

Everleigh left digging into John to Brooke. No doubt she'd find exactly what Caspar said they would, or he wouldn't have challenged them to do the deep dive. Instead, she pursued more information to fill in their unknowns. "Back to the specifics on this job. You mentioned a finder's fee. What are you having us hunt down?"

"A gem." A faint clicking sounded, almost like someone typing. Then, "But before I provide details, are you interested?"

Brooke held up her phone. "John checks out." Her tone implied that to be her affirmation.

"I am." Natalie nodded.

Everleigh shrugged. "Go ahead."

The air in the room seemed warmer than when she'd walked in. Everleigh unzipped her sweatshirt as Caspar began. "There's a retired FBI agent, Gertrude Levine, who lives there in Kenton Corners. Her needs are twofold. One, she has macular degeneration that's progressed to the point of needing live-in care. She and her nephew have been looking to hire someone, and part of your role in this job, Everleigh, would include filling that position."

"Okay." He must have read her LinkedIn account—not that she'd updated it in the past few years. Bet Natalie and Brooke each had one too. "Keep talking."

Natalie crossed her legs and brushed animal hair from her jeans as Caspar continued. Most likely she had a dog. If it were a cat, Everleigh would already be sneezing.

She forced her attention back to Caspar's voice. "There's one mystery that Gertrude has always wanted to personally solve. It involves a missing gem called the Florentine Diamond. I want you to help her find it."

Brooke's laughter peppered the room. "An FBI agent hasn't been able to find this diamond in years, and you think we will? Sure."

"I know about that diamond"—Natalie nodded at Brooke—"and she's right. People have searched for it since before Gertrude was born. That is, if she's younger than one hundred years old."

Everleigh tipped her head. "It's been missing over a hundred years?"

"Since 1921. It belonged to the last Imperial family of the Austrian Empire, also known as the Habsburg Empire, and was part of their Crown Jewels. Emperor Charles I and his wife, Zita, fled their country when the empire fell apart just after World War I, and they sent their Crown Jewels ahead of them. There's a dispute about what happened after that time, but the Florentine Diamond hasn't been seen since."

As Natalie spoke, Caspar's recounting of their skills played through Everleigh's mind. "You must be the one who's done well with research. What is it you do?"

"I'm a librarian who loves history. Luckily, my job allows for a lot of reading." She shrugged. "And I tend to easily remember the things I read."

Apparently.

Brooke showed them her phone again. This time a massive yellow diamond filled the screen. "Originally over a hundred carats. I wouldn't be surprised if it's been cut down into multiple pieces, because that's what often happens to missing jewels this size. Easier to move."

"There's been rumor of that as well." Natalie lent credence to the assumption.

Tracking all the pieces Caspar had put into play meant, "And, Brooke, that makes you the one who's into antiques."

"And you're the one who likes puzzles," she countered.

"This right here is why I wanted you all together," Caspar broke in. "You each have strengths that I believe will help you succeed in locating the diamond."

Sounded great on paper, but the reality of working with other people that closely wasn't something Everleigh wanted to sign up for. She had no interest in building new relationships. Her track record with friends—with people really—was rather dismal. She'd been let down more times than a blood pressure cuff in the ICU.

Still, she needed the money, and her employment status was even more depressing than her relational status at the moment.

Natalie and Brooke appeared lost in their own contemplations. This entire situation was a lot to take in, and they still knew virtually nothing about Caspar, one another, or even this Gertrude he proposed sending her to live with.

Which begged more questions.

Everleigh started. "This is a caregiver job, not nursing, right? Because I haven't obtained my licensing here yet." She really hoped not to go into why, especially in front of these three in the room.

Natalie added her own inquiry. "And why Gertrude?"

Brooke tagged on with, "Are you two acquaintances?"

"You're correct, Everleigh. It's more in line with a companion, though your nursing skills certainly help."

Caspar waited a long moment as if debating his next answers. "As for the rest. There's a lot of information I'll share with you. In fact, should you say yes, I have a lead to get you started. But one thing you'll all have to accept, if you decide to work for me, is that not all your questions will be answered. That means there's really only one thing to know at this juncture. Do you want the job?"

For the umpteenth time that morning, the women all shared a look. Mirrored in Natalie's and Brooke's eyes were the hesitation and curiosity that swirled in Everleigh's gut. What she couldn't read, however, was their answer. She didn't know them well enough to even guess, and she didn't plan on getting to know them that well. Working with them wouldn't require friendship, though, so she removed that variable from the equation and simply focused on the two enticing factors at play here. An intriguing mystery to solve and a much-needed payday.

With that in mind, her answer came easily. "I'll take the job."

Natalie's response arrived next. "I will too."

After a few seconds of silence, Brooke spoke. "Guess I'm jumping on that train. Sign me up."

John opened a drawer and pulled out a file. He tossed it on the desk as Caspar's computerized voice filled the space. "Welcome aboard, ladies. Let's get started."

CHAPTER FOUR

IF THERE WAS A QUOTA for historic homes within a town, Kenton Corners didn't only meet it but undoubtedly exceeded it.

For the second day in a row, Everleigh peered up at an old brick house. This one stood at the edge of downtown Kenton Corners. Rather than red tones, the façade of this three-story home consisted of a myriad of brown shades, and its rectangular shape produced a decidedly boxlike appearance. The plaque to the left of the glass-and-paneled front door proclaimed this residence to be over a hundred years old as well. She had to admit, there was something comforting in a structure that weathered life as well as this place appeared to have done.

Everleigh climbed five steps to reach the entry. Before she could knock, the door opened, and a tall, trim older man greeted her. "Been expecting you." His silver hair cut tight and slicked in place, the man wore a black button-up tucked into fitted trousers and shiny Oxford shoes. Leaving the door open, he retreated up the narrow hall attached to the entry. He didn't bother to see if she followed. "Glad you're on time. Gertie will appreciate that."

Everleigh snuck a glance around. Seriously. Had the past twenty-four hours been some kind of elaborate prank? Was a reality TV show filming her or something?

"Hurry up. You're early but you're not that early." His admonishment echoed down the hall.

Everleigh stepped inside, closing the door behind her. Once again she'd texted Uncle Maddox all the information on where she'd be. Last night she'd filled him in on the little she knew about Natalie, Brooke, and John, which didn't extend far beyond the few answers Caspar graced them with yesterday. She did uncover the achievements he'd referenced, though.

Natalie had won two librarian awards, her most recent from the Illinois Library Association for her research and preservation skills. Brooke was highlighted as one of the most sought-after antique runners in the country after she'd found and secured for Leonardo DiCaprio one of four movie posters from the 1927 film *Metropolis*. Her budding reputation led to an invite to become Midwest President of the National Pawnbrokers Association—a position she'd turned down. Everleigh had also confirmed they each had LinkedIn accounts citing Natalie's work as a librarian and Brooke's occupation as owner of a pawnshop.

Uncle Maddox took the information and was working to find out more. So far everything seemed legit. Caspar's identity remained elusive, but a measure of ease lay in the old adage that no news was also good news. She ascribed to that motto for the time being.

Everleigh peered around the doorway the man had disappeared through. Inside, she caught sight of him standing beside a woman who must be Gertrude.

"Don't stand there. Come on in." Dressed in a fitted burgundy pantsuit, Gertrude stood. For such a short woman, she maintained a commanding voice and presence. With her gray hair in a stylish pixie cut, thick aubergine rounded glasses, and tiny wrinkles broadcasting that she laughed more often than frowned, Gertrude Levine projected every inch how Everleigh hoped to be when she surpassed seventy years. "I may not be able to see, but I can hear just fine, and your feet aren't moving."

Said with more bark than bite, Gertrude chased the blunt words with the barest hint of a smile that coaxed out Everleigh's. Yep. She had the distinct impression she was going to like Gertrude, which made her job easier.

Everleigh stepped into the room and crossed over to her. She placed a hand on the woman's shoulder. "It's a pleasure to meet you. I'm Everleigh."

"I should hope so." Gertrude chuckled. "Otherwise Burt here is losing his edge."

The man who'd greeted her now held out his hand. "Burt Lancaster, and yes, my parents named me that on purpose."

Everleigh drew her brows together. "Don't all parents name their children on purpose?"

Earlier she'd chuckled. This time Gertrude full-on laughed. "Oh, thank you, Everleigh. Burt often needs reminding of his age."

She bounced a glance between the two, replaying their few comments until she made sense of them. "Guessing Burt Lancaster was a movie or television star?" Because this Burt appeared to be around Gertrude's age. If he'd been named after a sports star, chances were good Everleigh would recognize the name. Mom had been a huge sports fan, and she'd started Everleigh watching all types at a young age.

"Brilliant deduction." Gertrude's tone held approval. She reached out and nabbed Burt's forearm so easily, Everleigh momentarily wondered if her sight was as bad as Caspar had led her to believe. The way Burt protectively placed his free hand on top of Gertrude's spoke of a man tenderly guarding a woman he cared deeply for. Seeing as the room held no physical threat, it was easy to surmise her disease was his foe. One he had no hope of forcing into retreat. Gertrude gently shook his arm. "We'll be all right here, Burt. You can head on home now. See that daughter and grandkids of yours."

"They'll be fine on their own for another hour."

"I'm sure they will be, but they're only here for another two days. Enjoy your time with them because time is notoriously obstinate. Once it leaves, it never comes back no matter how much you beg it to."

"So you're fond of saying." Burt remained stalwartly beside her.

Gertrude gave him a playful shove. "Go on, now, and let me get to know my new helper, since you and my nephew insist I hire one."

Ah. This hadn't been Gertrude's idea. Made sense. Rarely did people want to rely on outside help. Especially those who'd been independent their entire adult lives. Based on the file John provided her with yesterday, Gertrude oozed independence, a trait Everleigh understood and respected. After reading through the thick folder, she held Gertrude in high esteem.

Gertrude had not only received her bachelor's in criminal justice but her master's degree in record time. She worked as a trooper for the Illinois State Police and had often been nominated as Officer of the Year. Her reputation for not shying away from dangerous situations caught the attention of the FBI, and she sailed through Quantico. As an agent there, she held one of the highest records for closing cases. She helped start and run the Jewelry and Gem Theft arm of the FBI until she retired to become a private investigator. A multitude of notations followed each step of her career, outlining her strong work ethic, fierce instincts, and fearless attitude.

"Fine." Burt patted Gertrude's arm, then leaned down and kissed her cheek before leaving. "I'll call you in the morning."

"I'll contemplate answering my phone."

"If you don't, you know I'll show up here."

"Then I'll contemplate opening the door."

He strolled across the room, barely pausing as he ducked into the hall. "Good thing I know how to pick locks." His words echoed behind his disappearing form.

The entire scene completely captivated Everleigh. She'd read much on Gertrude yesterday, but not a speck of information on Burt made the file. And with every current detail supporting her assumptions of the no-nonsense, autonomous woman before her, the last thing she'd anticipated was this soft side she'd displayed with Burt.

"Burt, bless him, is my old FBI partner. I swear he's more protective of me than my nephew, Niles, whom you'll meet later." Gertrude settled onto the sofa she'd stood from. "Tell me, Everleigh, do you know the difference between a hippo and a Zippo?"

Um . . . "No, I do not."

"A hippo is really heavy, but a Zippo is a little lighter."

Oh, boy. This was going to be fun. "Nice pun."

"Thank you." Gertrude patted the cushion beside her as if she'd decided Everleigh had passed her test. "Come on, now. Let's get acquainted."

She took the seat. Caspar informed her yesterday that Gertrude was well aware a part of Everleigh's job would be helping to find the Florentine Diamond. Before they started on that topic, Everleigh had a few questions of her own. Knowing Gertrude only a few minutes, she'd already surmised the woman appreciated directness.

"How do you know Caspar?"

"All right, Everleigh, jump right into the deep end. I like that." Gertrude leaned into the corner of the couch and faced her as if she could see her. "I don't know Caspar. At least I'm not sure that I do. I was hoping you'd be able to fill in my blanks."

Her own hope for impending answers collapsed like every loaf of bread she attempted to bake. "Sorry, but no. I only met him yesterday while at Halstead Manor, and that was via a phone call and computerized voice."

"Halstead Manor?"

"Mm-hmm. That's where our meeting took place. It appears he's the new owner."

Gertrude played with the fringe on the throw pillow beside her. She'd perked up at the mention of the manor and now appeared to be processing that information. Everleigh was about to ask why that location seemed so interesting to her when she spoke. "Well, I'm afraid I don't have much more to offer. Last week a young man, John, showed up on my doorstep inquiring about the caregiver job my nephew posted. During that conversation, we heard from Caspar via phone, using the same computerized voice you mentioned. I'll admit, with my background, my suspicions nearly had me tossing John into the street. But then Caspar mentioned the Florentine Diamond."

"And your suspicions turned to intrigue."

Gertrude nodded.

"But aren't you equally as intrigued about who Caspar is?" Everleigh couldn't let one mystery go for the sake of another. She simply wasn't wired that way.

Gertrude's mouth swished to the side, then she stood and nabbed the bright yellow cane leaning against the couch. "Come on." She jutted her chin toward the door.

"Where are we going?"

Thrusting her arm out, Gertrude nodded for her to take hold. "You're going to help me upstairs. Last door on the right." Everleigh complied, leading Gertrude to the door she'd indicated. The older woman used her cane to feel the floor in front of her rather than for stability, which seemed strong and steady. "Go on," Gertrude instructed once they'd stopped. "Open it."

She did, and it took her nearly a full minute to digest what she discovered. Papers and photos covered three of the four walls with pushpins and red yarn connecting different pieces. A good old-fashioned war room constructed all around the Florentine Diamond. "Caspar wasn't kidding. You have been tracking this for years."

"I have." Gertrude's voice thickened as she continued. "I had a younger sister, Amelia. Niles is her son." The mention of him had her smiling. Or perhaps it was the combination of two people she obviously loved very much. "Amelia made friends everywhere she went, and she was always dragging me along to play with them. She had one friend in particular who loved adventure as much as she did. Those two would come up with the grandest treasure hunts for us to go on. Lost pirate's gold. The Crown Jewels of Ireland. Fabergé Eggs."

"And the Florentine Diamond?"

"That too."

"So you've been searching since your childhood?"

Gertrude laughed. "No. As children we'd race through our back yards, always on a new hunt. But something about that diamond stuck with Amelia and me." What looked like remorse wrinkled her brow. "We grew apart as adults." She swallowed, her memories obviously bitter as her lips pursed like she'd eaten a lemon. Her head gave a slight shake. "It was Amelia who resumed the search as an adult, but she passed away without finding it. I hope to finish what she started."

Things made slightly more sense.

Before Everleigh could ask her lingering question, Gertrude answered. Almost as if she knew what it was because she'd have asked it herself.

"I also come from a line of work where I cared more about vetting the information a source provided than I did their identity. So, with all of that, you can understand why I'm willing to set aside discovering Caspar's identity in lieu of the first possible real lead I've had in years." Gertrude surveyed the room as if she could see every shred of evidence. No doubt she still did in her mind's eye. "I'm not getting any younger, and I'd like to solve this before my time's up."

She'd consulted Gertrude's medical files supplied to her. Besides the macular degeneration, the woman was healthier than most people Everleigh's age. "You're seventy-two, Gertrude. You could easily live another fifteen, twenty years."

"But my patience won't." Even though they were clouded by illness, her eyes sparkled. "Now, this Caspar said you'd not only show up here with a suitcase, but with a clue. I haven't heard any rolling wheels or new leads on where the diamond may be."

"My suitcase is in the car and the lead—"

"Aunt Gertie? Where are you?" The slam of the downstairs door precipitated a deep male voice booming through the house.

Gertrude stiffened, the stance more warrior than fearful. It put Everleigh on the defensive too. She turned as feet clomped up the stairs.

"Time to meet my nephew, Niles." Gertrude faced Everleigh. "I should probably warn you. He didn't want me to hire you."

Everleigh had about three seconds to digest that piece of information before a giant filled the doorway. She'd put him at six-four and all muscle. She quickly catalogued jet black hair grown out to his jawline in messy curls that somehow also managed to appear tamed. Dark, thick scruff covered his upper lip, chin, and cheeks, and ebony eyes studied her with warm approval.

"Niles," Gertrude spoke. "I'd like you to meet Everleigh Wheaton, my new caregiver."

Her words doused the warmth in his eyes. Scratch that, they turned it up several notches to fiery disapproval.

That same heat laced his voice. "Noticed your suitcase was still in the car out front. No need to bring it in, because you're not staying." He thrust his hand toward the hall. "I'll see you out."

Unbelievable. He and Aunt Gertie had talked this through. Agreed that things were sketchy with this Caspar person and the woman he wanted to send to help. Sure, Caspar had baited Aunt Gertie with empty promises about that diamond, but they'd both recognized the entire thing for the sham it was. Or at least Aunt Gertie had led him to believe she had. Instead, she'd gone around his back and hired Everleigh despite all their misgivings.

Maybe more than her vision was growing dim. Her instincts must be too, because the FBI agent turned private investigator who'd raised him—the one who never allowed emotions to get in her way—wouldn't let such a shady figure across their threshold, let alone invite her to move in.

"Niles Samuel Butler, you put on the manners I raised you with." Aunt Gertie stomped her cane on the ground.

Even though he was thirty-seven years old, she still possessed the ability to put him in his place with only his full name. She was a tough woman. Fiercely independent. Growing up he knew he needed her way more than she needed him, and he'd learned to accept that. He'd lay down his life for her as easily as she'd placed hers on hold to take him in and raise him. Watching her lose her eyesight and independence this past year about did him in. And while weathering this disease had softened her into the aunt he sometimes wished for growing up, he'd give anything to restore both.

He absolutely refused to stand by and allow this wisp of a woman to take advantage of his aunt, even if it angered Aunt Gertie in the process.

He'd tone down his voice or risk another repeat of his middle name. But he'd maintain his cross-armed stance and hard stare, which only Everleigh could see. Once again, he motioned to the hall. "Shall we?"

Everleigh nonchalantly tucked a strand of brown hair behind her ear and held her ground. She stood at least six inches shorter than him and wore a pair of jeans that showed off plenty of curves, but not in a way that said she sought attention. Her blue eyes bordered on gray—maybe because a storm currently raged in them—and she had the barest of dents in the middle of her chin. People normally backed down when he set his jaw and hit them with his current glare. With Everleigh, his mood slid off her like rain on his waterproof jacket; she seemed impervious to it all.

Aunt Gertie broke the silence. "We'll head downstairs, but only because I'm hungry and want a snack." Then she took Everleigh's arm. "Lead the way."

Everleigh's lips tipped in a triumphant smile as they moved past. She made it to the bottom of the steps before halting. "Sorry, Gertrude, but I'm actually not sure where your kitchen is."

"Please call me Gertie, and it's at the rear of the house. Go on down the hall, through the dining room on your right, and you'll run smack into it."

Niles followed them, his blood boiling faster than the water she'd undoubtedly want Everleigh to heat for her afternoon tea. Sure enough, as soon as Everleigh led her to the small table in the kitchen, Aunt Gertie noted her teakettle's location. Everleigh crossed to it, but Niles reached there first.

"I've got this." He grabbed the blue kettle before she could.

"Where are the tea bags?" Everleigh asked as if they were old friends.

He pointed to the drawer closest to her. Easier than pushing her aside to reach it himself. "There."

"It's nice to hear you both working together." Aunt Gertie's tone dripped like the honey she'd ask for next.

Niles turned on the faucet and filled the kettle. "Once your tea is made, I'm politely seeing Miss Wheaton to her car."

"No, you are not." That honeyed tone from seconds ago hardened as if someone left the top off the jar. "My house. My rules. That hasn't changed since you moved in here at seven years old."

"Maybe it's time it did," he murmured.

He should know better, because Aunt Gertie had always been able to hear him, even from a room away. Her mouth set in a thin line, but she remained silent. That was worse than if she'd responded. He hadn't crossed the line; he'd launched leaps and bounds over it.

Still, he refused to back down.

Silence reigned in the kitchen until the kettle whistled. Everleigh dropped a tea bag into a mug she pulled from the cupboard. She poured water over the chamomile leaves, their apple scent permeating the air. In the continued quiet, she read the tea bag before glancing at the clock. That tea should steep five minutes. After those minutes passed, she removed the bag, squeezed the water out of it, then dropped it in the trash. "Honey, sugar, or cream?" she questioned Aunt Gertie.

"Honey."

Having found its location as well, Everleigh added a hefty squirt, then delivered the hot drink to his aunt.

"There are gingersnaps in the jar on the counter. I'll take two with my tea, and I'd like to enjoy them in my room, please."

"Sure thing." Everleigh nabbed the cookies and placed them on the saucer that held the mug. "Just tell me where that is."

Once again, Niles followed them as Everleigh balanced the snack in one hand and offered her other forearm for his aunt to hold. She settled her on the settee by the window. Aunt Gertie might not be able to enjoy the view anymore, but she could still feel the sun on her face, and she lifted her cheeks to absorb its warmth. He knew this was one of her favorite spots in the house.

He also knew she was testing him. Aunt Gertie would often lay down the law, then set him up in a situation created to assess if he'd follow it. Retiring to her room had zero to do with fatigue and approximately one million percent to do with seeing if Everleigh still remained here when this sham of a nap was over.

One of them would be surprised. It wasn't going to be him.

Aunt Gertie took her tea as Everleigh handed it off. "You're good people, Everleigh Wheaton. Thank you."

Everleigh's face softened. "Can I get you anything else?"

"A throw would be nice. It's a little chilly today."

Everleigh crossed to the basket at the end of Aunt Gertie's bed. Niles ducked into the hall and waited there until Everleigh exited, softly closing the door behind her. Without a word or glance, she slipped past him straight to the front door. Huh. Not what he expected.

She exited without a word. A twinge of guilt pricked at his stomach. He could have at least said goodbye. Thanked her for not making this more difficult than it already had been. Even ensured her that they'd pay a full day's wages for her time.

Yes. Then at least he could tell Aunt Gertie that some of his manners had surfaced after all.

He started for the front door, but it opened before he made it there. Everleigh reentered with her suitcase. She regarded him casually, as if he wasn't vehemently opposed to her staying here.

"Could you tell me which room will be mine?"

It took him nearly ten full seconds to find words. "None of them. I couldn't have been more clear."

"Neither could your aunt. And I'm fairly sure the 'my house, my rules' trumps whatever leg you believe you have to stand on."

"How about I'm not a man who'll stand by and let his aunt be taken advantage of by a con artist."

If he hadn't been watching her so closely, he would have missed the slight narrowing of her eyes and the tick in her jaw. Yeah, she tried to play it cool, but he'd surprised her with that one. Did she really think he wouldn't do his research on her?

She drew herself to full height. "What makes you think I'm a con artist?"

All right. She wanted to play like her past didn't exist, he'd call her on it. "I'm a PI, just like my aunt. I looked you up. Saw why you were fired from your last nursing job."

"And you believed what you read?"

He crossed his arms with a shrug.

This earned him a slow nod. "Well, your aunt says I'm good people. So I guess I'm staying."

"She's old. She's lost her edge." He hated the words. Hated even more the feel of truth to them.

Everleigh sized him up. "And I suppose you found it?"

Oh, this woman was feisty. So much like Aunt Gertie that it didn't surprise him she liked her. But the similarities stopped there, and he refused to allow her entrance into their lives. "Yes." He bared his teeth.

And Everleigh dissolved in giggles. "If that's your attempt at a look of intimidation, you need to do a whole lot better, Yogi." She patted his shoulder and walked away, dragging her suitcase behind her. "I'll wait for Gertrude in the living room."

Yogi? Had she just compared him to the world's least threatening bear?

The living room pocket door sliding closed snapped him out of his utter disbelief. Getting rid of Everleigh Wheaton wasn't going to be as easy as he'd thought.

CHAPTER FIVE

"I DIDN'T THINK NILES WOULD ever leave." Gertrude placed her cane along the edge of the couch where Everleigh had helped her settle the next afternoon. They'd just finished lunch, but Gertrude insisted Everleigh leave the dishes and come sit in the parlor with her. "My curiosity has about done me in. Tell me about this clue before the stubborn mule decides to come back."

Everleigh laughed. All yesterday Gertie had staunchly refused to let her mention anything about Caspar's lead in Niles's presence. She'd tried to bring it up after Gertie's nap, but the old woman deftly switched subjects. After two more similar occurrences, Everleigh realized what Gertie was up to and completely dropped the subject. Problem was, Niles also picked up on the fact that his aunt didn't want him privy to certain information, and that instigated his transformation into metaphorical glue. He stuck to his aunt for the remainder of the evening and all morning.

Watching the two of them had provided Everleigh with hours of entertainment. Equally stubborn, they'd done their best to outlast the other. The stalemate could have continued, no doubt, but Gertie pulled out her Boss Card and insisted Niles leave to check on a new client.

"Nice move sending him to work," Everleigh complimented.

"Only thing stronger than his stubbornness is his work ethic. Especially when it comes to helping me keep my PI firm afloat. He made me a promise, and Niles always keeps his word even when it irks him." Gertrude tapped the cushion beside her. "Now spill."

Easier said than done. Still in the dark about so much herself, Everleigh wasn't quite sure where to begin, but she didn't think Gertie possessed any further patience to wait while she chose her words. So she dove into the facts she knew. "Something called a gold collar was found inside a cave in Madeira, Portugal. It's supposedly this heavy, chain-like necklace with a sheep hanging from it, and it was given to people within a knighthood called The Order of the Golden Fleece—"

"A ram," Gertrude interrupted.

"Excuse me?"

"It was a ram, not a sheep, that hung on the chain."

"You're familiar with it then?"

"Of course. The Habsburgs were the ones who awarded the chain to a select few. All the men in the Habsburg family also received one when they turned eighteen, and the family's collars were a part of the Crown Jewels that went missing. But how is this one going to help find the Florentine?"

"Well, from what Caspar said, it was found with a contract that appeared to bear the signature of an Afonso Silva and Charles I, who was—"

"The last Emperor of Austria," Gertie finished on a puff of air.

After seeing the room upstairs last night, Everleigh was fully aware Gertie would recognize the name of Charles I.

"Which means," Gertie began, "if we can authenticate the collar and signature, it would prove that Charles lied when he said Baron Bruno Steiner stole the jewels when he was transporting them for him. Instead, Charles and Zita had them all along."

Everleigh nodded then remembered Gertie couldn't see her motion. "Exactly."

They sat in silence a long moment before Gertrude spoke again. "The Steiner family has always claimed their ancestor was wrongly accused of the theft. That he handed those jewels off to the emperor, but things became a giant 'he said, she said' with no tangible proof on either side."

"Until now, possibly."

"Until now." Gertie wiped her palms on her beige slacks. "The location works too. Charles, Zita, and their children stayed in Madeira for a time after fleeing Vienna. It's where he passed away."

"I read about that. Incredibly sad. Zita was pregnant with their eighth child. Just doesn't seem fair."

This pulled Gertie's attention straight to her. "Child, if you are going through life expecting it to always be fair, you're destined for constant disappointment."

"Not fair maybe, but I'd settle for balanced."

"Same thing." Morning sun highlighted the gray in Gertrude's hair. "I'm thankful God doesn't balance the scales where we're concerned, because his grace far outweighs our sins."

"I agree." Because she did. She'd be eternally grateful for God's grace where forgiveness was concerned. She'd simply like it if he extended a little more of himself over other areas of her life. Like when it came to shielding her from other people's actions. Instead, she'd had to take on that protective role herself.

Gertrude narrowed her eyes. Everleigh had spent less than twenty-four hours with her, so there was much yet to learn about her likes, dislikes, hobbies, and habits, but one thing she'd picked up on. While Gertie's natural sight was indeed compromised, the old woman possessed a skilled ability to see inside a person's soul. Probably from her years as an FBI agent.

Everleigh steeled herself for more prodding.

Instead, Gertie clapped her wrinkled hands. "What's next then? How do we get our hands on these items? And has Caspar told you who this Afonso Silva is?"

Apparently, Gertie was also adept at conversational whiplash.

Everleigh took half a second to catch up with the reverse direction of their talk. "He said nothing about Silva, but I did look into him a little."

"I'm not surprised. Can't complete a puzzle without all the pieces." Another clap. "Tell me what you know."

She'd had a feeling Gertie would ask. They both seemed to dislike unanswered questions and sought out their explanations. Everleigh was discovering, however, that with this mystery the answers were few and far between. "Not too much, other than his family is the oldest on Madeira. Also, Afonso and his wife had a son, Tomas, who was about the same age as Charles and Zita's oldest. That could have provided a connection between the families." Children often brought parents together. "Afonso owned a large number of homes along the coast and several family members still reside in them. In fact, his grandson Rafael, will be hosting an auction in one of those homes in just under two weeks from now. The collar will be there. Oh, and it was Rafael's grandson who found the collar."

Gertrude nodded along as she listened. "Thorough work. I assume someone will be attending the auction?"

"Yes. Caspar's offered to send us all there to bid on and authenticate the piece and letter."

Confusion scrunched up the wrinkles on Gertie's forehead. "Us all?"

"Right. Sorry." She completely forgot Gertrude knew zero about Brooke and Natalie. "There were two other women who received the same invitation to Halstead Manor as I did. Brooke Sumner and Natalie Daughtry."

"You don't know them?"

"Nope." Though not for lack of Natalie trying. She'd called with an invite to lunch that Everleigh had politely turned down. "But I have done a little digging on them as well." She'd planned to do more last night, but she'd been more tired than she'd realized. By the time she'd made and cleaned up dinner, dodged Niles's constant disapproval, and helped Gertie to bed, she'd fallen asleep herself. "Nothing nefarious popped up so far on either of them."

"Good. Though people like to hide their faults fairly deep, and not all of them are the kind discovered with a computer search. It might take getting to know them."

Everleigh preferred computer searches. "Yep."

Gertrude sat for a second before nabbing her cane and tapping it on the floor. "All right, I'm in. I've waited years for a break in this case, and this could very well be the one. Tell Caspar to book those plane tickets."

Everleigh highly suspected excitement buzzed under Gertie's skin even stronger than what she heard in her voice. "I can't get ahold of Caspar, but I'll call John who can relay the message." Everleigh pulled out her phone. "If you think Niles will be okay with it."

Gertie smiled. "I'll handle Niles. You go on and make the call."

Everleigh did just that, then she and Gertrude chatted for another hour before Burt arrived. He'd brought Gertie lunch, which allowed Everleigh to sneak out and run a few errands. She'd noted Gertie's cupboards were sparse in places, plus there were a few items she wanted for munching on herself, like potato chips and a carton of ice cream. Then she needed to stop by and speak with her landlord to let him know she wasn't renewing her monthly lease.

In between all of that, she planned to dig deeper into Natalie, Brooke, and John, plus check back with Uncle Maddox to see what he'd uncovered about Caspar. She found it incredibly frustrating that information on him proved so impossible to find. Every puzzle had a solution. Some simply took longer to reach than others.

As Everleigh left her second stop, her eyes snagged on a vehicle in her rearview that raised her suspicion. By the time she pulled away from her apartment, that suspicion was confirmed. Someone was following her. The same silver sedan had been on her tail since she'd pulled out of Kroger. If she had her guess, Palmer had sent someone to watch her. Might as well find out if she was right.

Spotting a strip mall ahead anchored by a coffee shop, Everleigh pulled into the lot. She joined the drive-through line and ordered a toffee nut latte—might as well enjoy the excuse for a midday pick-me-up. The sedan had parked at the far side of the lot, providing whoever sat behind the wheel with a perfect view of the exit. The way they'd parked, however, prevented them from seeing the end of the drive-through line.

Everleigh swung around and approached the sedan slowly. If she thought about it too long, common sense could nix her impulse. Instead, she gunned it, parking at an angle with her passenger door practically touching their front bumper. Taking off her sunglasses, she met the surprised gaze of the person who'd been following her.

"You!"

※ ※

Niles bit back words he no longer spoke. The past twenty-four hours were not going to plan.

First, Aunt Gertie ignored his advice and hired this woman. Then she'd refused to allow Everleigh to share information in his presence, instead kicking him out the door this afternoon to follow a case. She knew good and well he wouldn't refuse her work request.

When he'd called to check in, Burt had answered Aunt Gertie's phone and informed him he was hanging out with her while Everleigh ran errands. A few well-placed questions and the fact there was only one grocery store in town allowed him to easily catch up with her and take advantage of the moment. Never mind how not even twenty-four hours into her caregiver position, Everleigh had already ditched his aunt. If her poor work ethic provided a chance for him to find out more info on her, he'd take it.

Except most of her stops pointed to her actually doing her job. She'd scarfed down potato chips while stowing groceries in her trunk, some of Aunt Gertie's favorites visible in the bags. Then she'd dropped off his aunt's dry cleaning before picking up her prescription—at least he guessed that's what she was doing at the Walgreens pharmacy window. He'd followed her next to her apartment where she'd stopped long enough to chat with her landlord and grab another duffel bag. She'd been fiddling with a Rubik's Cube as she wandered to her car. It now rested on her dash.

How on earth had she spotted him?

His grip on the steering wheel tightened. The moment Aunt Gertie found out Everleigh had made his tail—and she would find out, he had no doubt—she'd heckle him mercilessly. Nope, she'd never let him live it down.

Beyond his windshield, Everleigh's lips kept moving. While he couldn't read them, he easily understood the fire shooting from her eyes. With a sigh, he unbuckled. Time to face this unbearable music.

As he unwrapped himself from his vehicle, Everleigh stood from hers. She scowled at him over the roof of her car. "You've been following me?" Caught between a question and indignation, she flung the words at him.

"I have, and quite honestly, I'm surprised you noticed." A backhanded compliment, but true, nonetheless.

Her scowl turned to disgust. "You're a real charmer, you know it?" As she spoke, she left her post beside her door and stomped toward him. She stopped an arm's length away, not the least bit intimidated. "I'm fine with your disparaging remarks and your misplaced dislike of me, but this crosses a line. My private life is way outside your purview."

"I wholeheartedly disagree."

"Well, you're wholeheartedly wrong."

They stood staring at each other, neither breaking from their stalemate.

Oh, but he had no doubt she was a perfect match for Aunt Gertie in personality. If she'd simply shown up on their doorstep in answer to his ad, no checkered past or questionable references, he would have hired her on the spot. But the manner in which she arrived, along with everything he dug up on her, said she couldn't be trusted. He'd learned the hard way to trust his gut. To dig deep rather than take things at surface level. Personality traits might line up, but that didn't make letting an individual into one's life safe. People were too complex and too skilled at hiding things.

Good thing he'd become proficient at uncovering what they hid, and he had a feeling he'd only scratched the surface with Everleigh Wheaton.

As the silence stretched, Everleigh's stance relaxed, but her facial expression turned cunning. "Seems we need a third party to weigh in. I'm sure your aunt will happily agree to do so."

He already knew Aunt Gertie's response. He also knew there wasn't a way to hide this from her, because Loose-Lips across from him would be sure to share. Taking chastisement from his aunt didn't bother him. He'd already reconciled that they wouldn't be on the same page when it came to Everleigh, her unknown boss Caspar, or the crazy idea that they could search for this diamond. Until he found solid intel to prove to Aunt Gertie that these people couldn't be trusted, their hook would remain embedded in her.

What bothered him was his screwup this morning. Being caught provided Everleigh with ammo to drive the wedge further between him and Aunt Gertie over this entire harebrained scheme that she'd bought into. He, however, wasn't paying a penny for it.

"Go on and fill her in when you see her, but I'm not backing off."

"Fine." In a huff, she returned to her car.

He allowed his voice to remain silky smooth. "Fine."

The look she gave him just before ducking into her seat spoke louder than any hand gesture she most likely held back.

Niles waited until she pulled away before returning to his sedan. It chafed that she'd made him, but it also told him she was observant. Normal people didn't watch for tails. Guilty people did. Just another brick in the case he built against her, and while the stack appeared dismally small, he wasn't about to give up.

Everleigh exited the parking lot, her car aimed in the direction that would return her to the town house. He'd have to face Aunt Gertie at some point, but he might as well finish the assignment she sent him on before he did. No sense giving her multiple reasons to be upset.

Three hours later he had the digital proof the insurance company asked for regarding a claim they were investigating. These types of jobs were their bread and butter, though harder to stay on top of since Aunt Gertie was unable to be in the field anymore, a truth she had to face. He understood she needed a little more time, though. For now, he did his best to close the same number of jobs by himself that they'd once closed together.

He parked on the street, slowly climbed the cement stairs, took a deep breath, and opened the front door.

"Niles Samuel Butler!" Aunt Gertie's gruff voice greeted him.

He'd take his lumps. It wasn't the first time. Certainly wouldn't be the last.

"Coming." He strolled down the hall to the living room where she sat on her couch. "Before you say anything, I'm not apologizing for following Everleigh." Who, right now, was conspicuously absent.

Aunt Gertie snorted. "I wasn't about to ask for an apology I knew I wouldn't get. What I am going to say is stop it."

"I can't give you that either."

"Niles."

"Aunt Gertie." He wasn't a child anymore. His fear of her had morphed into his fear for her. Somehow, somewhere in all these years, they'd formed a strong bond, and he'd fiercely protect her even if it made her mad in the process. "The one thing I can give you is a promise to make sure you're safe. If you want anything contrary to that, then I'm sorry, but it's just not going to happen."

"She's a good girl, Niles."

He tossed his hands up in frustration. "You don't even know her."

"All right, then tell me. What did you see while following her today? Before she caught you, I might add."

Ah. There was the little dig he'd been waiting for. "Exactly. She knew I was there, which tells me two things—like it should you. One, she wasn't about to do anything incriminatory if she knew I was watching. And two, if she was watching for a tail there's a fairly good chance she's guilty of something."

"Or you're just losing your touch if a perfectly innocent woman spotted you."

"That woman is as innocent as Al Capone." He tossed the first gangster name out that came to mind. She'd raised him on a diet of biographies and documentaries of famous criminals rather than cartoons. Might as well use the knowledge she'd imparted.

"Or she's as clean as his vault was when that Geraldo opened it on national television." She pointed her cane at him. "You keep insisting she's dirty, you're going to wind up as surprised as he was when you discover otherwise."

"If it means keeping you safe, I'll take that chance."

He wasn't worried, because he didn't think for one moment that he was wrong about Everleigh Wheaton.

CHAPTER SIX

HER THIRD MORNING ON THE new job and Everleigh decided it wasn't all that bad. Her run-ins with the very bearish Niles remained tolerable, Gertrude proved consistently delightful, and she'd continued to avoid her new coworker's attempts to meet. Things had been busy enough here for her to offer legitimate excuses. She'd helped bake some of Gertrude's favorite treats, watered every one of her plants, read her an Agatha Christie novel, and survived most of her puns. They'd also talked further about all the material Gertrude had collected on the diamond and their lead from Caspar. After dinner last night they'd highlighted and scanned any pertinent information into Everleigh's computer so they could take it with them to Madeira.

Gertrude's excitement over their trip grew daily. Finding concrete proof for one of her theories refreshed her investigation. Even better, it seemed to have refreshed her. Interestingly enough, Niles hadn't said anything to them about the trip. No doubt he had an opinion, but Everleigh didn't mind that he was keeping it to himself. With his gruff attitude, the less they interacted, the better. She still couldn't believe he'd followed her like she was some two-bit criminal. Though his suspicions were misplaced, she begrudgingly couldn't fault him for wanting to ensure his aunt's well-being. Gertie inspired a certain devotion, which was saying a lot coming from this introvert.

Everleigh's phone rang beside her.

"You going to answer that?" Gertrude asked.

The screen showed Natalie's name. After realizing the frequency with which Natalie called, she'd added her contact info for the specific purpose of avoiding her. "It's just Natalie. I can let it go to voice mail."

"What if it's news about our case?"

Holding in her sigh, Everleigh moved to the other side of the room and answered. No new info but another new lunch invite—which she politely declined on the grounds of caring for Gertrude.

She shared a few platitudes, offered hope that perhaps next time would work, hung up, and returned to Gertrude's side.

The old woman's listening skills were on par with a bat's, and she'd employed them to catch Everleigh's phone conversation with Natalie. "I meant to tell you, Friday afternoons I won't be needing your assistance. You can call her back and tell her you're free to meet."

She could. Natalie would be thrilled if Everleigh accepted the third invitation she'd offered to get to know one another. However, she wouldn't. "You don't have to give me an afternoon off. I was hired to be here twenty-four seven."

"No one works twenty-four seven."

"Caregivers can and do." Especially when the job leaned more toward the role of companion.

"That fact doesn't change my fact, which is that I don't need you from eleven till seven on Fridays."

"Then I'll hang out in my room."

"When you don't have plans." Gertrude tapped her cane on the floor. "But it sounds as if you do today. Or at least you don't have an excuse *not to* have plans."

Except she was an expert at coming up with legitimate reasons to avoid gatherings. The skill so honed, she excelled even on the fly. "Honestly, if you're giving me the afternoon off, I'm going to drive to my dad's." Yes, that showed the desperation of the moment, but desperate times called for desperate measures. "I try and see him once a month and with this treasure hunt, who knows if I'll be able to keep that up."

"Does he live alone?"

Her innocuous question didn't mask her curiosity. It was simply a polite way of asking what she really wanted to know—why hadn't Everleigh mentioned her mom?

"He does." She was tempted to leave it there, but Gertrude would only press for answers. "My mom passed away several years ago."

"Oh, Everleigh, I am sorry." Gertrude supplied the world's default platitude to death.

To which, Everleigh supplied the standard response. "It's all right."

"No, it's not." Her muscles tightened, and she sat ramrod straight. "Losing someone you love is never all right. Unless you didn't love your mother. Did you not love her?"

Wow. Okay then. She'd veered from the script. "Of course I did."

Gertrude settled into her chair, the tension slowly sliding from her. "Then don't tell me it's okay. With God's grace you'll *be* okay, but the situation is most definitely not okay." Her hands splayed across the armrests. "Loss hurts bone deep."

While her honest reaction had surprised her, there was something refreshing in it. "You're absolutely right."

"I know I am." This came with a sly smile. "So, you're going to see your daddy today? Where does he live?"

"Kenosha." He'd returned to her hometown after his release from jail last year. The same town where he'd worked as principal at her high school, embezzled hundreds of thousands of dollars from the school, then been caught red-handed her senior year. He'd lost their house as part of reparations and now lived in a mobile home along a river.

"That's a bit of a drive," Gertrude said.

"A little over two hours. Plenty of time to get there and back by seven." In all honesty, she'd return before dinner. Gone long enough to avoid Natalie's invite to lunch, but not so long she had to endure too much time with Dad. "What do you have going on today, anyway?"

"Fridays are my poker days with my old coworkers. They're here until Niles gets home from work, and then he and I have dinner and discuss our cases from the week."

She didn't ask how Gertrude still played poker. No doubt the woman had something rigged up. She did, however, wonder, "Do you need me to do anything before they arrive?"

"Just help with the food."

Several hours later, after a long stint in the kitchen and an even longer one in her car, Everleigh pulled up in front of Dad's mobile home. Natalie had texted her twice more while she drove. Once to inform her that she and Brooke had changed the lunch time, in case Everleigh could make it. The second was to say they'd missed her, and she hoped she could make it next time.

Natalie seemed like a nice woman, she truly did. Someone who had no problems making friends, and it was great that it worked for her. They simply had different personalities. Everleigh was a consummate introvert, and it appeared it would take a little bit for Natalie to realize that fact. Still, eventually she would take her up on one of the lunch invites. Possibly sometime next weekend before they flew out together for the auction. It was a fine line between alienating herself from them and growing too close for comfort.

Dad's golden bullmastiff greeted her with a deep, bellowing howl from behind the screen door. So much for taking a few minutes outside before knocking.

Her dad stepped to the door. Still trim—if anything, he'd added muscle while in jail—with a head full of chestnut hair styled in a crew cut, he wore every one of his sixty-four years on his wrinkled face. "Didn't know you were coming today." The screen creaked as he opened it.

"Surprise." She passed him and entered the trailer, skirting his dog. She'd made a promise to Mom to take care of him, so she visited monthly to ensure he had all he needed. "I took a new job, and my schedule won't be predictable the next few weeks, so I wanted to make sure your freezer was stocked." Dad mainly survived on the batches of heat-and-serve meals she made for him. To fill in, he'd hit the drive-throughs in town.

"I appreciate that. Things were getting low." He followed her to his kitchen where she conducted a quick survey of his pantry and fridge.

"I'll grab groceries and be back."

He didn't offer to join her, didn't inquire about her new job, just returned to his recliner in front of the TV. Not a surprise. Their parent-child roles had swapped before she'd hit her teenage years. He couldn't handle Mom's constant sickness. Someone had needed to step up, and Everleigh was the only other one in the house. She had wound up caring for them both. Mom, physically. Dad, emotionally. She'd even attempted to care for them financially, but obviously she hadn't succeeded well enough since Dad pulled his stunt.

She made it through the grocery aisles in record time and stopped her cart beside a self-checkout. As she left, a flyer caught her eye.

"Kenosha School's 100th Anniversary Celebration."

A celebration for her alma mater, and all alumni were invited. She studied the fine print, reading over each event of the weeklong festivities. Her onetime best friend spearheaded the planning committee. It appeared past class presidents had been invited to work alongside her.

Apparently, Everleigh's invite had been lost in the mail.

Squaring her shoulders, Everleigh walked to her car. There'd been a day they'd been tighter than sisters. She was one of the few people Everleigh let in close. When Dad was arrested, strangers spreading rumors about her hurt but didn't come as a surprise. Then the kids at school started, and it stung. But when her best friend joined in . . . Everleigh slammed her trunk shut.

If she'd been tempted to form relationships with her new coworkers—which she hadn't—this right here served as a timely reminder not to do so.

⇥ ⇤

Niles set his Nikon on the dash of his silver Honda Civic and did his best to stretch in the tiny space. With the blue sky overhead and crisp spring air, the day begged for him to pull out his Harley and head down Route 66. This was his favorite time of year to wander the old road. There was nothing like the first ride after a long Illinois winter. The promise of warm months and longer days ahead revived him better than any jolt of caffeine he could consume.

And he'd consumed plenty in the past six hours.

But work called, and he couldn't ignore his responsibilities if he wanted to keep the doors of their PI firm open. Aunt Gertie's abilities and track record had secured them a good reputation. They didn't lack referrals, they lacked manpower. He'd lost Aunt Gertie and his right-hand man in the space of six months. Her, to this infernal disease. Him, to Niles's former fiancée. Sure, by that point he and Iris hadn't been together for over two years, but Ben had been around for Iris's cheating. Niles still didn't understand how his friend could have watched all he went through and then wind up engaged to her himself. But that was Iris. Cunning. Manipulative. Convincing.

They lived in an age where anyone could be anything. Motives could be easily hidden. Not only had he experienced deception himself, but he documented it on a near daily basis. So maybe he did err on the side of skepticism—but with good cause. Especially when it came to his aunt. She'd given up so much to take care of him, he owed her his allegiance and protection.

Not that they'd been overly close while he was growing up. No one would describe Aunt Gertie as warm and cuddly. If anything, those bearlike qualities Everleigh teased him about had been learned from his aunt. She was gruff and prickly. Preferred her alone time and few words. But she'd opened her home to him without hesitation, and she'd loved him as best she could. They'd developed their own closeness, one that had grown as her eyesight diminished. He didn't quite understand the change in her, and it had taken nearly all year to adapt and trust it. Now, though more rusty than fluid, her words and warmth flowed around him on nearly a regular basis.

Movement in front of him returned his attention to the job at hand. The dad who claimed he couldn't afford to pay child support pulled into his drive in a cherry red Corvette. Niles already had discovered how he was hiding his money, and these pictures would simply add another layer to the information the mom's lawyer requested. Money always left a trail. Sometimes that trail took more digging to find, but it was always there. A theory he planned to prove yet again through delving into Everleigh's past employment.

Work done for the day, Niles pointed his car to the gym. He'd scheduled a round in the ring to help work off some of the tension that had found its way into his muscles these past few days. He'd been coming here since he was eight years old. Aunt Gertie recognized his need for an outlet for his grief and accompanying anger after losing both of his parents. This gym provided a haven for him, especially through his teenage years. What began as a way to keep him out of trouble quickly grew into one of his passions. Then about ten years ago he'd started a mentorship program for at-risk youth. Now he taught them the same coping skills he'd learned.

"Hey, Mr. Niles," one of the kids called as Niles strolled inside.

Niles greeted him, and they spent a few minutes chatting about school. Then he quickly changed in the locker room before making his way to the mat. A sweaty hour later, he felt ready to head home and combat with Everleigh. These nightly sessions between work and home had equipped him to coexist with her in a civil, albeit curt, manner. Meanwhile, he worked to find a way to break her connection with Aunt Gertie. Until that happened, extra boxing sessions would have to suffice.

Twenty minutes later he walked into Aunt Gertie's home. He'd moved back in six months ago to care for her until they hired extra help. The plan had been to move out once that happened, but he'd placed that plan on hold.

Laughter drifted from the parlor as he walked past on his way to the stairs. Typically, he'd stop and speak with Aunt Gertie, but one of those laughs belonged to Everleigh. He already recognized the sound from her chuckling through Aunt Gertie's groan-inducing puns. Either she shared his aunt's humor, or it was further proof of her ability to deceive.

He wasn't sure which was worse.

Intending to scoot on past the room and preserve the calm he'd achieved at the gym, Nile's put his foot on the first step.

Aunt Gertie's voice halted him. "You weren't successful sneaking in as a teenager, and you're not successful now."

Retracing his steps, Niles poked his head into the parlor. "Wasn't trying to sneak in. You sounded busy." The two perched on the sofa with one of Aunt Gertie's photo albums open in Everleigh's lap. "What are you ladies up to?"

"I was showing Everleigh some pictures of your mom and me when we were little."

Intrigued, he walked over and stood behind the couch to peer over their shoulders. Several black-and-white photos spanned the two pages. His mom and his aunt smiled together in every photo, often with their arms around each other. Sometimes his grandparents joined the group. Sometimes other children. These photos were as familiar to him as his own memories. He'd spent hours combing through the albums as a child to learn as much about his mom as he possibly could. She'd been taken from him far too soon.

Everleigh peeked up at him. "I've been describing the pictures, and she's been telling me stories about all their adventures. Seems they pulled in several neighborhood children to go treasure hunting with them." She pointed to Halstead Manor in the background of a photo where a young Gertrude and Amelia played with friends. "I didn't know she'd grown up here in Kenton Corners until I saw this."

Aunt Gertie nodded. "Lived here my whole life. My dad sold insurance and Mom ran the PTA of our school. She loved bringing the community together, and the Forsythes often allowed the town use of their lawn to have get-togethers. Especially when their grandchildren visited. I think they loved having us children around to entertain them." She toyed with the fringe on the throw covering her legs. "There was nothing like a party on Halstead Manor's property. Mr. Forsythe's hobby was beekeeping, and he'd make his own honey. Mrs. Forsythe used it to bake the most delicious treats. She'd put out quite the spread when we all came. Cookies. Biscuits. Cakes. You never left hungry."

Everleigh studied one of the pictures filled with hundreds of people. "That's a lot of treats."

Aunt Gertie nodded. "Mrs. Forsythe loved to bake."

"With honey? No thank you." Niles retreated to the doorway because he found himself enjoying Everleigh's perfume too much.

"You don't like honey?" Everleigh asked.

"After learning how the bees make it?" Thanks, fourth-grade science. "I do not."

"That says a lot, coming from you." Aunt Gertie tracked his movements as if she could see them. "He's a—"

"Man who doesn't need his secrets told to a woman he doesn't know." He made no effort to hide the gruffness in his voice.

Everleigh's brow lifted. "With how much you've dug into me, you haven't learned enough to know if you can trust me with your taste preferences, Yogi?"

Her and that blasted nickname got under his skin. "Right now, Everleigh, I wouldn't trust you with my enemies, let alone my preferences." He paused. "Don't even get me started on my aunt."

Said aunt chose that moment to break into the conversation. "The only thing in life you shouldn't trust are atoms. They make everything up."

"Not the time for one of your puns, Aunt Gertie."

"I thought it well placed." Everleigh patted Aunt Gertie's arm.

"Thank you." She rapped her cane against the floor. "Now be nice, Niles."

It bothered him, seeing those two amused together. "If she doesn't like my personality, she's free to leave." He cracked his neck both ways, a tactic he often employed before stepping into the ring.

"It's okay." Everleigh rose and placed the album on the coffee table. Then she crossed to where he stood. "I'm used to people acting ugly to me, so unfortunately for you, that tactic won't persuade me to leave." She glanced behind her. "I'm going to go make your evening cup of tea. With honey."

Shoulders tight, head high, she stepped past him as if she didn't have a care in the world, and if she did, it wouldn't be him. If she were anyone else, he might admire her steely attitude. Or the way she gentled it around Aunt Gertie. But she wasn't someone else. She was an unknown entity who'd embedded herself into their lives under mysterious circumstances.

All right. Time to switch tactics, because it was painfully obvious, as she'd admitted, this one wasn't working. He'd execute a one-eighty and kill her with kindness instead.

He stomped off to his room with a decidedly bearlike growl that only deepened with the rogue thought that showing Everleigh any hint of affection might not be quite as unpleasant as he initially anticipated.

CHAPTER SEVEN

IF NILES BUTLER THOUGHT EVERLEIGH didn't see right through him, he wasn't the PI his aunt believed him to be.

"Need anything else chopped?" he offered as he slid the green onion he'd diced into the bowl brimming with ingredients for the Mexican corn dip. In the past week since he'd stomped away from the parlor door, he'd become most accommodating. And ever present.

She wrapped the final jalapeño in bacon, then set it into the glass nine-by-thirteen. "I think I can handle the rest. Thanks." Picking up the dish, she double-checked the oven's temp. She slid the poppers inside and moved on to another appetizer.

"You sure? It looks like you have a few more things to prepare." He leaned against the counter, a rogue curl dipping over his forehead. He didn't seem to mind it. Neither did she.

With a hard shake of her head, she returned to her mini assembly line. "I'm sure."

"Because I don't mind helping. I know how much food Aunt Gertie and her friends can put back during one of their card games."

"Niles." She extended his name over an exaggerated sigh. "Your hovering is nearly as bothersome as your feigned hospitality. One of them has to go."

He tossed her a "Who, me?" look that she wasn't buying.

She held up the bread knife she was using to slice through the sourdough. "I don't have a problem with you not liking me. In fact, I found your initial honesty refreshing. Let's stick with that, shall we?" Crankiness was an easier sentiment for her to deal with than kindness. People rarely faked negative emotions like they did the sweet ones. Being candid enabled her to know where things stood between them and manage her expectations for their relationship—of which there would be none.

He studied her. "Maybe I'm a slow-to-warm type of guy."

"Ha." She cut through the end of the bread and arranged the slices around the dip. "I wouldn't buy that even if your aunt hadn't filled me in on your personality." She shot him a quick look. "You aren't fooling her either, so you know."

He pinched his lip between his thumb and forefinger then released it. "Holding your chair at dinner last night was too much, wasn't it."

"Seeing how you're so convinced I'm up to no good that you were tailing me last week? Yeah. It was."

"All right, fine." He nabbed one of the slices. "I don't trust this Caspar that dangled a carrot in front of my aunt and enticed her to throw common sense out the window. Because of that, I already wouldn't have trusted you either. But then I looked you up."

"I recall. And read all about me on the internet, which we all know only publishes complete truths."

She wasn't sure if it was her sarcasm or his inference over her statement that raised his indignation, but his neck grew blotchy like she was learning it did when he was upset. "I am capable at my job. I verified the information I found in the articles."

"Where? Snopes?" She couldn't help it. He was too easy to needle. As he drew to his full height, she backed off. "I'm only teasing." Sort of. First impressions were a very real thing. Unfortunately, people all too often allowed social media or gossip to drive their opinion rather than truly meeting someone first and forming it themselves. Rarely did anyone try to confirm what they heard.

Her acknowledgment that she'd spoken in jest released a bit of his steam, and he settled against the counter again. The scent of bacon and cheddar wafted from the oven. Like a woman who'd caught the sweet smell of a bouquet of flowers, he moved closer for another whiff.

"Mind checking those while you're over there?" she asked.

He inched open the oven door. "Couple more minutes." Then refocused on her as she moved to the final appetizer. "As I was saying, I spoke with

Palmer Quimby. I tried to speak with Constance, too, but she's not doing well."

Again, Everleigh's heart pinched with the news. "Palmer mentioned that."

"There's a lot pointing to you taking advantage of Constance."

"There is." But he'd find no direct evidence. Only circumstantial.

"And your dad served time for embezzlement."

"Ah, yes, a strong genetic trait." She gave him the side-eye.

He replied with a heavy sigh. "A criminal isn't born by nature, no, but they can definitely be made via nurturing."

"Someone's been taking his psychology classes."

His silence captured her full attention. She peered up to find him studying her in a way that made her squirm. Her sarcasm typically deflected people's attention. Niles appeared drawn in, as if for once she was the mystery needing to be solved rather than the one solving it.

He crossed his arms over his chest, the edge of a tattoo on his forearm peeking out from underneath the sleeve of his black Henley. But rather than press her on the myriad of questions in his eyes, he simply stated, "I don't want the same thing happening to my aunt."

"It won't." She barely considered herself acquainted with Niles, yet she knew enough to determine he was nothing like Palmer. Thus, that situation wouldn't repeat itself here.

"I agree. Which is why I haven't moved out again. I plan on helping with this crazy quest for the Florentine Diamond."

She really did not need more of him around. "That isn't necessary."

"Again, we disagree." A buzzer went off, and he turned toward the sound.

After pulling the wings from the air fryer, she doused them with the hot sauce Gertrude requested. Like last week, Gertrude instructed her not to be stingy with the flavoring. The woman had at least twenty bottles in her pantry, so Everleigh could indeed apply it liberally.

And while Everleigh didn't possess a similar amount of warmth toward the man standing across from her, she had plenty of experience dealing with people who didn't care for her. Fighting Niles wouldn't prevent him from hanging around here. It would only make things more awkward.

"Fine. But let's get something straight. He's not *my* Caspar. I don't know him any better than you do." Not for lack of trying, though, which still irked her.

Surprise fanned across Niles's face. "He's your boss."

"And everyone always knows their boss well? Just hired and with only one interaction?"

He shrugged. "True. But you've met him, right?"

"Nope. We've spoken on the phone, and that's it. He facilitated my coming here. Asked me to help your aunt find the diamond and put me in touch with Brooke and Natalie." Not that she planned to engage them any further than Caspar forced her to. She would, however, finally join them for another lunch Natalie invited her and Brooke to an hour from now. "I'm meeting them at The Corner Café while your aunt plays cards." Since they flew out on Monday, she couldn't put it off any longer. Besides, she'd exhausted all her excuses to avoid the two.

Everleigh opened three cupboards before glancing over her shoulder. "Trays?"

"Second cupboard to the left of the stove." He grabbed a bottle labeled Green Machine from the fridge. Maybe he wanted to compensate for all the bacon he planned to eat. "You hadn't met either before Caspar hired you?"

"Nope." She set the tray on the island and retrieved the poppers from the oven. "I hope to find out more about them at lunch."

He slowly nodded. "What about the lead you shared with Aunt Gertie? The one she begrudgingly told me about."

She arranged the food between the trays. "Your aunt and I are working on that. There's really no need for you to help at this point." Better to leave that perceived door of collaboration open. Slamming it would only result in him obstinately forcing himself through. "Once we know for sure what we're dealing with, we can better assess the situation."

"Maybe Brooke and Natalie have new info to add. Mind if I tag along?"

And give him a chance to ingratiate himself further into all of this? No, thank you. He had yet to bring up their trip to Madeira, and she counted that a miracle. She had no clue how Gertrude planned to keep him from joining them, but she wasn't tempting fate by inviting him to a lunch where the topic was sure to come up. "It's a girls' lunch, so yeah, I would."

"Hmm." He pinched his lip again then released it. "All right. You seem to have everything handled here, so I'll leave you to it." He snagged two poppers from the dish as he passed by it.

"Those are hot! Don't burn yourself," she cautioned as he ducked out of the kitchen.

"I have zero intention of being burned."

His deep voice carried his words that hung in the air like a warning to her rather than a response to her admonition.

Whatever the man was up to, she had the distinct impression he'd keep her on her toes.

✦ ✦

Strange to be in The Corner Café as a patron rather than an employee, but Everleigh wasn't one to race off with her tail between her legs. She wasn't guilty of Palmer's accusations, so she refused to act like it.

If only Niles would receive the memo on her innocence and stop following her. Or call Burt off, because it wasn't Niles's silver sedan on her tail anymore. The black Buick had taken her longer to spot, but Burt also had once been Gertie's partner in the FBI. He might have lost a bit of his edge, but she spotted him yesterday and again today on her way here. At least she assumed it was Burt since she'd seen him in the same car when he visited Gertie's.

Niles was smart, she'd give him that. If she mentioned the tail to Gertie again, he could honestly say it wasn't him. And by making Burt do his dirty work, he banked on the fact that Everleigh wouldn't want to rat the old man out to the woman he had an obvious crush on.

His wager paid off because Everleigh had a secret soft spot for the elderly, especially adorable ones like Burt. She wasn't about to sell him out. Which was why she hadn't confronted Niles earlier in the kitchen where Gertie could easily overhear.

Sliding into a booth in Molly's section, Everleigh waved to Garrison as she watched the door. She'd purposefully arrived early so she could pick the seat. Several of her ex-coworkers salivated for any crumb of gossip they could sniff out. They'd spend far too much time hovering at the table for details that wouldn't change their assumptions, only reinforce them.

What she needed was privacy. Molly minded her own business, a trait Everleigh appreciated.

"Here you go." Molly dropped off a plate of Jamie's Fried Mush topped with sliced bananas sautéed in a local maple syrup. A dollop of house-made whipped cream topped the stack. She set a chipped mug of steaming black coffee beside the plate. "To cut all that sugar."

"Thanks." She may have ten years on the girl, but Molly had the distinct advantage when it came to health. If a food wasn't organic, sugar-free, or naturally the color of the rainbow, chances were it wouldn't make it past Molly's lips. Plus, she worked out every day. Everleigh had thought her once-a-week salad and three weekly runs were something to brag about before observing Molly.

"You're welcome." She hustled to her other customers.

The bell over the door jingled as Brooke and Natalie stepped through. Had they ridden together? They appeared chummier since their first meeting. Probably because Brooke had taken Natalie up on one of those other invitations Everleigh turned down.

Their eyes scanned the crowd before landing on her, and they headed over.

"Good to see you again." Natalie slid in beside her. Brooke provided a clipped nod in greeting, then picked up the paper menu in front of her. Natalie shed her cardigan. "Good choice on the fried mush. I typically get Doris's with the berries and mascarpone, but I love that one too. Though today I might try something different. I'm feeling adventurous." She pulled a pair of glasses from her purse, pushed them on, then picked up the menu.

"You two ride together?" The question tumbled out, this strange need to know surprising her.

"My car's broken down, so Natalie picked me up."

"Don't you live like an hour from here?"

"Her shop's a little over an hour from here. She lives forty-five minutes away," Natalie said. "It was no big deal."

Brooke set her menu on the table, leaned back, and crossed her arms, conveying business as her priority, not small talk. She'd obviously had enough of that on the ride here. Which meant that while Brooke played nice with Natalie, her walls remained up. Common ground, not that they were going to bond over it.

"So about this trip," Brooke began. "Are we sure we should take Caspar's private jet? Might be smarter and safer to book our own flights and accommodations. I'd even go so far as to say separate flights and hotels for each of us."

Natalie frowned. "Isn't there safety in numbers?" She drummed her short, pink-painted nails on the table. "Besides, I don't have money for all of that. I need this trip to stay on his dime."

"Me either, but if Caspar is rich enough to have his own plane, he's got enough money to pay for our flights." Brooke pulled the water Molly delivered closer to her. She gave her order, then they waited while Natalie chatted up Molly. She extracted her name, dating status, and career plans in under two minutes and only stopped talking when Brooke obnoxiously cleared her throat.

"Sorry." Natalie handed off her menu. "I'll take Doris's Fried Mush."

Apparently, her adventurous feeling had fled.

As Molly walked away, Brooke continued as if there'd been no break in their conversation. "Caspar's already paying for our hotel. Switching the location shouldn't change that as long as they're comparable." She drilled Everleigh with a hard stare. "Thoughts?"

"Honestly, and I think you know this, if Caspar is luring us to Madeira for some shady reason, neither scenario matters. Either we trust that he's legit, or we don't go."

Brooke's lips curved up in a half grin as if Everleigh passed the test she'd been given. "*You* I trust to have my back." Then they flatlined as she turned to Natalie. "I'm reserving judgment on you."

So much for playing nice.

Natalie perfectly mirrored Brooke's expression but remained silent. It was going to be a quiet drive back to Brooke's place.

Everleigh cleared her throat. "Brooke, I was looking up info on your pawnshop in Chicago, and I noticed you have one right outside Kenton Corners too. Along Route 66?"

Brooke's fingers tightened on her water glass. "You obtained old info then. That shop is no longer mine."

She'd accessed records from the past six months, so the change had to be rather recent. Based on Brooke's body language, most of the questions forming on Everleigh's tongue wouldn't be welcomed. She pivoted. "How long was it yours for?"

"Awhile." A flicker of pain flashed across her gray eyes, momentarily clouding the storm in them.

Her answer prompted another question Everleigh had pondered. "Mind me asking how old you both are?" She'd already discovered Natalie's age, but figured Brooke would be more willing to share if Natalie did.

Natalie leaned back while Molly delivered their meals, thanking her before the waitress stepped away. She picked up her fork. "Just turned forty-two."

Everleigh had found that info with one trip to her Facebook page, though she struggled to believe it. Natalie's youthful face barely held any wrinkles, the dent in her chin deeper than any lines around her eyes.

Brooke met both their gazes before zeroing in on Everleigh. "How about you next? I already found Suzy Homemaker's age along with all her life details online. Not that she hasn't also freely shared them in the lunch you missed out on." She pointed a fry her way. "I also found lots of interesting info on you. Though nothing you put out there on your own, and no birth date. Smart."

"She's thirty-five." Natalie palmed the table on either side of her plate and pressed into her hands. Her focus rested on Brooke, no anger yet no softness either. Just an eerie calm that demonstrated the ability to maintain her cool while expertly shutting down her adversary. "And you're thirty-one." She paused, then, "This *Suzy Homemaker* is used to being under-estimated, but I refuse to be disrespected. We're here to work together. We don't have to be best friends, but we do have to be pleasant."

Everleigh fought a grin. It always made her smile when someone stood up for themselves. Natalie's assessment that they didn't have to be friends made her doubly happy. Maybe she could work with these women.

Brooke seemed to arrive at a similar conclusion. She picked up her olive burger. "The woman can research."

"I'm a mom and librarian. I know how to find information."

"Making more and more sense why Caspar hired you too." Brooke took a massive bite, and a glob of the olive sauce landed on her plate. She didn't even bat an eye.

Everleigh took a sip of her coffee. "Have you found any information on Caspar?" Because if she'd dug into them, she'd certainly tried to dig into him.

Natalie stopped before her berry-laden fork made it to her mouth. "I did a real estate check on Halstead Manor to see if I could find Caspar's full name, but it's owned by a corporation not an individual. No name listed as business owner either. I haven't given up, though."

"I put out some feelers to see if anyone by his name has been asking about the Florentine Diamond. So far, nothing." Brooke finished her last bite of burger then moved on to her fries.

Finished with her own meal, Everleigh pushed her plate away. "Have many people searched for it over the years?"

"Hundreds."

"I'll admit, that doesn't make me too hopeful with our chances." Everleigh acknowledged what she didn't want to say around Gertrude. She genuinely liked the woman and didn't want to see her disappointed.

"Except this new lead could be a game changer." Natalie cut another bite. "If we can authenticate Emperor Charles's signature on that contract, and it's paired with one of the missing Golden Fleece collars that were part of the Crown Jewels, that means Bruno Steiner didn't steal them, and they remained with the Habsburgs while in exile."

"Brooke, will you be making the authentication?" Everleigh assumed so, based on her background, but confirmation of assumptions whenever possible was best.

"I will with the collar. Not sure who Caspar has for signatures."

Natalie held up her hand. "That would be me." Everleigh and Brooke must have worn matching surprised expressions, because Natalie explained. "I've sort of made a side job out of dealing with antique books that are often signed. I needed to ensure I didn't fall for forgeries, so I took a course on handwriting. I'm no forensic handwriting specialist, but I do know how to spot a fake."

Brooke genuinely appeared both impressed and intrigued with their overlapping expertise.

As they spoke of first editions they both sought and ones they'd found, Everleigh surveyed the waning lunch crowd. The only lone diner was the sheriff, but he sat at the counter and every other person stopped to chat with him.

"Are you and Gertrude all packed? I know she's got to be excited for this trip."

Everleigh dragged her attention back to her table and Natalie's question.

"I've set a few things aside, but we won't get out the suitcases till Sunday night."

"I'm not packing until Monday morning." Brooke wadded up her napkin and tossed it on the table. "Do you think Gertrude is up for the trip?"

Everleigh opened her mouth to respond when a deep voice spoke. "Oh, well how about that? I wondered if I'd bump into you here." Niles strode up to their table with an innocent grin she saw through completely.

"Wondered?" Everleigh scoffed. "You knew I was here."

"I knew you were meeting your friends for lunch, but I didn't know the time."

No, she'd never mentioned a time, but he was still there when she left Gertrude's house.

He held out his hand to Natalie. "I'm Niles, Gertrude's nephew. I'm guessing your name's either Natalie or Brooke."

She shook it. "Natalie."

He turned to Brooke. "Then you must be Brooke."

In what Everleigh was coming to know as true Brooke fashion, she gave only a short nod and did not return his greeting.

Natalie, however, motioned to the empty space beside Brooke. "Why don't you join us? I'm sure you'll want to hear about our trip to Madeira as well, seeing how your aunt is accompanying us."

She looked up at Niles, expecting his grin to have morphed from innocent to triumphant with how he'd weaseled his way into their lunch. Instead, he looked like a thunderous storm cloud about to rain down questions.

"What do you mean my aunt is going to Madeira?"

Well, that explained why he'd been mum about the trip. Apparently, Gertrude hadn't told him about her plans. That little oversight plopped

Everleigh smack-dab in the path of his tempest. She supposed she better batten down the hatches, because she was in for a bumpier ride than she'd anticipated.

Buckling in, she firmly met his scowl. "She's going for the auction. We leave Monday."

"Then so do I." He slid into the empty space beside Brooke. "Start talking."

CHAPTER EIGHT

Archduchess Adelheid, age eight
Madeira, Portugal, 1922

ADELHEID PEEKED PAST THE BLACK fabric of her mother's skirts. At eight, she should not still be hiding behind Mama, but her courage was gone. The first bit she'd lost when they'd been forced to flee their home in Vienna. Another piece left when she saw the fear on Mama's and Papa's faces. But then they'd settled on this island, and Papa promised all would be well. They'd even donned coats and shopped in town for little Carl's birthday present.

But then Papa became ill and so quickly was gone. What little of her bravery lingered seemed to have drifted into heaven along with him.

She blinked rapidly, not wanting a tear to fall. Her courage might have left, but she would remain strong for Mama as she'd promised Papa. Her older brother, Otto, and her five younger siblings needed her. Soon to be six.

Adelheid gripped the smooth fabric tighter in her hand, Mama's dress pulling against her rounded belly. She couldn't remember a time when Mama's belly wasn't large. There seemed to always be a new sibling to greet. With Papa gone, Mama said this was to be the last.

"Adelheid, sweetheart." Mama's stern yet gentle voice reached down right along with her hand, nudging Adelheid from her hiding place. "Remember your manners."

She hadn't forgotten, but that didn't make them easy to use. Meeting new people always made her tummy bubble. Even if those new people resembled her in size and age. Papa had known how to help her. He'd hold her hand and be the first to speak. His warm voice would encase her like a cozy blanket. She missed him so very much.

The little boy and girl in front of her peered at each other. Adelheid recognized Tomas, who often played with her and her brothers. He was the son of one of Mama and Papa's friends here on the island. His papa owned the house where they now stayed. Their last name sounded like a color. She chewed her bottom lip in thought. Ah yes, Silva. Tomas Silva. But this little girl beside him was someone new.

Even though she felt shy, something stirred inside Adelheid at the sight of the girl's warm brown eyes, long black hair, and sweet smile. There was a round mark on her cheek with soft edges that gave it the appearance of a flower. Adelheid had never seen anything like it, and her curiosity grew. Surrounded by boys, she'd long wanted a sister. Mama finally had another girl, but Charlotte was only a year old now—far too young to share secrets with. Adelheid willed herself to speak.

But before she could, the little girl smiled and stepped forward. "Hi. I'm Luciana Perez." And then Luciana did something no one ever did when meeting her. She wrapped her arms around Adelheid and hugged. "We're going to be friends."

Adelheid knew they would be bonded for life.

The cool spring gave way to summertime, her favorite months. No boring lessons. Simply freedom to play with her new friends. Luciana and Tomas visited often with their parents, who enjoyed their talks in private with Mama. They'd send the younger children off with the nannies, but she, Otto, Luciana, and Tomas were allowed the freedom to explore. On sunny days, they'd race along the cliffside, exploring caves or sliding to the beach to dip their toes in the ocean. Other times, they'd pick Anona fruit from the orchard to see who could spit its black seeds the farthest, or bite into lemons in a challenge of who could tolerate the sour taste longest.

Then there were rainy days. This particular day they decided to put on a play. The boys went in search of items that would pass for weapons, since they wanted to be pirates. She and Luciana scurried off to Mama's room to find silky scarves, long gloves, and hairpins so they could be princesses.

Mama's heavy door squeaked as Adelheid pressed it open and peered around the edge.

"Is it empty?" Luciana asked from behind.

Adelheid nodded and they snuck in together. "You keep watch," she instructed Luciana. On tiptoes, Adelheid crossed the soft rug to the other side of the room where Mama's chest sat against her bed. With shaking fingers, she opened the top. Several scarves lay inside, and Adelheid pulled out a blue one for Luciana and a purple one for herself. Then she dug deeper for Mama's gloves. Her hand connected with a wooden box. Curious, she pulled it out and set it on the bed. This was the same box she'd seen Mama pack their last day at Schönbrunn Palace. Ever so gently, Adelheid opened it.

Golden necklaces with those lazy sheep rested against black velvet. The Golden Fleeces. But this made no sense. They were to have played hide-and-seek with the jewels, but someone bested them like she'd bested Otto that day. She'd heard Mama speaking about how Bruno Steiner, their friend, had taken this chest then hid himself so well, no one could find him. The story spread over time. She'd even heard the servants talking about how his name made the newspapers.

Luciana's giggle startled her. "That one has a sheep on it." She pointed over Adelheid's shoulder.

Adelheid jerked around. "You're supposed to be watching the hall."

"They're all downstairs, talking." Luciana pressed in closer. "That's such a silly looking necklace."

Adelheid agreed. "It's for my brother. All the boys in my family receive one when they become of age. Mama had several." She pulled one more out and set them aside, wondering what other objects created the bumps under the velvety fabric.

She lifted out the material to reveal another layer of gems.

"Ooh, I want that one." Luciana lifted a sparkling hatpin from the box, a giant yellow diamond the base of the piece.

"No." Adelheid shook her head and reached for it, but Luciana pulled from her reach. "That's not for play." Mama told her how special the Florentine Diamond was to the family. Something she called an heirloom. The gem was so large, it covered her entire palm. Adelheid couldn't ever imagine wearing it, but Mama promised she would on her wedding day. Except, how did Mama still have the Florentine when it had gone missing along with all the other jewels?

Luciana slipped the glittery pin into her hair. "I feel like a real princess. Just like you."

Adelheid's pulse beat fast as sunlight danced off the diamonds holding Luciana's brown curls. So much felt wrong with this moment. "I'm no longer a princess. Not really." Though she loved her new friend, she desperately missed the city sounds of Vienna and her rooms in Schönbrunn Palace. All these jewels had been kept in their rightful place there, and now they sat in this chest for an unknown reason. Nothing in her life seemed to make sense anymore.

Luciana twirled in front of Mama's gilded mirror. "Yes, you are. Mama and Papa remind me of it every time we come to visit."

Before Adelheid could answer, footsteps and voices sounded in the hallway. The door opened and Adelheid's heart leapt in her chest. But it was only the boys.

"We found our weapons." Otto, her eldest brother, swung a sword through the air.

Luciana's eyes widened. "Where did you find that?"

Otto grinned. "From a suit of armor in the hall. There are several. They won't be missed."

Tomas strolled to the bed, his eyes on one of the Golden Fleeces. "Hey. I've seen this before."

The admission yanked Adelheid's attention his way. "You have?"

Tomas picked one up and tapped the sheep, making it sway. "My papa asked me to hide one along with a note bearing both our papas' signatures."

Her eyebrows drew together. "That doesn't make sense. Bruno Steiner stole them along with the rest of our family's jewels. Papa didn't have one to give."

Tomas shrugged. "I promise you. I held both in my hand and hid them in a cliffside. The note mentioned payment for your stay here, but since your papa passed away, mine said he would not keep it. That Luciana's parents would be helping your mama now, and that no one must know about any of your family's jewels being here on the island. Your mama would not take the necklace back, so Papa had me hide it."

"But the jewels were stolen," she repeated, shaking her head with disbelief. "I don't understand."

"He's right, Adelheid. Mama does sell the jewels to Luciana's parents." Otto's soft confirmation landed in the room. The force of its impact reminded her of the time she'd secretly climbed on Papa's prized stallion, and it had tossed her to the ground. Only that landing hadn't hurt quite as much.

All of them looked to Luciana, who held a hand to her hair, her fingertips brushing the pin. "*My* parents?" Her surprise was as great as theirs.

But before any more questions could be asked, voices drifted from the hall.

"Children? Where are ye?" Nanny called.

With a gasp, they all helped stow the jewels just as Nanny opened the door. "There ye be. Come, come before ye catch a scolding for being in yer mama's chambers." She hustled them into the hall. "It's time for Tomas and Luciana to return home, and for ye children to dress for dinner."

Adelheid nodded, though she would not eat tonight. All she hungered for was answers.

CHAPTER NINE

TWELVE HOURS INTO THEIR THIRTEEN-HOUR travel day and Everleigh could take it no longer. She reached over and placed her hand on Natalie's, stilling the noise of her nails clicking together.

Natalie peeked at her. "Sorry. Nervous habit."

"I figured." She'd also figured it would stop after about the first hour. She'd been sorely mistaken. "Snapping gum seems to be Brooke's tell." Though Brooke sat behind her, so short of leaning over the seat and expectantly holding her hand under the woman's chin, Everleigh saw no way to stop that habit. Besides, she had a sneaking suspicion that rather than spit her gum into Everleigh's palm, Brooke would stare her down and snap it several more times.

"Yours is playing with that thing." Natalie nodded to the Rubik's Cube in Everleigh's lap.

Everleigh smiled. "Guilty." Since she'd first been gifted one by Uncle Maddox at twelve years old, she'd rarely been without the toy in reach. "I keep them stashed in several places."

Natalie held her page with a bookmark, then closed the cover. She'd spent the first half of the flight seated beside Brooke. Then she'd moved to take the fourth seat in this configuration where Everleigh, Gertrude, and Niles sat, engaging them in conversation. After Gertrude and Niles dozed off, the conversation dwindled and Natalie had pulled out a book instead.

She stowed it away, apparently to leap on Everleigh's break in silence. Talking was a small price to pay if it meant no more nail clicking.

"I'll admit to some nerves on this trip." Natalie's half smile was sheepish. "I've never actually been out of the country before."

"Neither have I." Everleigh cocked her head. "Well, as long as you're not counting Canada."

Natalie chuckled. "I can't even make that exception."

"Your husband didn't mind you going without him?" Everleigh couldn't imagine that being the case. Dad didn't know how to function without Mom. He'd faded away through the years right along with her. That's what had ultimately led to his embezzling from her school. His last-ditch attempt to save them both by paying for Mom's kidney transplant that insurance had denied. She'd been too sick, but he'd been determined to make it happen. All he'd succeeded in doing was losing his job—which lost Mom her insurance—earning a lengthy jail sentence and being absent when she passed. Everleigh had buried her mother completely alone.

"Mason barely batted an eye." Natalie tapped on her phone, illuminating a family photo. "That's Hunter. That's Reed." It was obvious who Mason was. "We've been married twenty-two years. His biggest concern was if the parking was paid for at the airport."

"Seriously?"

She nodded. "I drove myself and Brooke there. She needed a ride, and Kenton Corners High has a baseball game the night we get home, so Mason couldn't pick me up anyway."

"I thought he coached football."

"He does. He's also the athletic director, and they need to hire a new baseball coach, but he hasn't liked any of the candidates. He's filling in for the season." The plane jostled as they hit minor turbulence. Natalie gripped her armrest. "That's Mason, though. He takes his job very seriously, especially when it comes to those kids. His best years involved high school sports, and he hopes to provide the same experience to the students he interacts with."

Natalie's tone, more than her words, spoke to a longing inside. For what, Everleigh didn't know. But if she had to guess, it involved desiring more from her marriage . . . or maybe her husband.

"How did you and Mason meet?"

This brought a tender smile. "High school sweethearts right there in Kenton Corners actually. Mason was two years ahead of me." That sweet expression transformed like someone who sucked on a candy whose coating wore off to reveal a sour center. Interestingly, her soft voice never changed. "I followed him to college, and we were going to wait to marry until I finished my degree, but then he graduated and took a job that required him to move. So we got married and I followed him to Ohio. Then we moved three more times after that, so it's nice to be back where we started."

Seemed like a lot of following on Natalie's part.

Sunshine streamed through the window by Natalie as the pilot banked the wings, and Everleigh shifted to keep it out of her eyes. "Based on your job, you eventually finished your degree." Many people figured librarians didn't need degrees when, in fact, most library systems required their employees to have one. The position wasn't simply stocking books alphabetically on shelves.

"I did, but it took a little longer than I planned." She released her armrest and reached for a bag of Jelly Bellys in her backpack. Tipping it toward Everleigh, she offered, "Want some?"

"Jelly Bellys? Sure." She held out her hand, and Natalie poured a few into it. Everleigh popped one in her mouth and savored the coconut taste. One of her favorites.

Across from them, Gertrude opened her eyes. Everleigh suspected she hadn't been sleeping but rather listening to every word of their conversation. Proving the point, Gertrude extended her own palm. "I'll take a few, too, if you don't mind."

Natalie reached over and dumped several into Gertrude's wrinkled hand. "Not at all."

Gertrude tossed three into her mouth. "Oh, my. Nothing like cinnamon and lime together."

"Oh! Sorry, Gertrude. I should have picked through the flavors I gave you. I forget you can't see them."

Gertrude waved her off. "My dear girl, I'd eat them the same whether I could see them or not. I love the unexpected. Keeps me on my toes."

Everleigh looked her way. "Niles said you hate surprises."

"That's because he equates frustration with animosity, when in reality you can be upset with something and still love it." She dropped two more sugary beans into her mouth. "Look at any relationship. You can adore someone and still have grievances with them. In fact, it's typically the people you love the most who hold the greatest ability to disappoint you, but even in the disappointment, you still care for them." Now she reached for her water. "So, no, I don't hate surprises. In fact, they've brought far more wonderful moments into my life than bad ones."

Natalie tapped Gertrude's now empty hand with her bag, and when the woman opened her palm, she poured more beans into it. "You make some good points, Gertrude."

"Life teaches a lot of lessons the more you live it."

Their captain spoke from the cockpit. "We're thirty minutes outside Madeira. You'll need to stow anything you've taken out and prepare for landing."

Natalie sealed up and stored her Jelly Bellys.

Gertrude nudged a softly snoring Niles. "Time to wake up, Sleeping Handsome."

Natalie laughed. "Great nickname."

"Oh, that's not his nickname. It's—"

"Not to be shared." Niles blinked awake, somehow managing to not look or sound groggy.

Everleigh perked up. "Now you've sparked my curiosity, and I love a good mystery."

"I thought it was puzzles you liked." He nodded at the Rubik's Cube on her lap.

She fiddled with it. "Puzzles are an element of mystery solving."

Natalie buckled her seat belt. "I read that you're actually pretty well-known in mystery-solving circles. You won the MIT Mystery Hunt."

"Twice." Niles added.

Brooke leaned forward, finally participating in the conversation. "And Western Washington University's Great Puzzle Hunt once."

That win she was particularly proud of. "Like Caspar said, we all have achievements that snagged his attention. Let's keep our focus on the task at hand. Figuring out the validity of this lead."

"Right, because until we know if this collar and contract are real, we won't know our next step," Brooke said.

Everleigh turned to face her. "What does your gut say?"

But it was Natalie who answered. "After everything I've read, I really believe the jewels stayed with the royal family. I think Bruno Steiner took the fall for something he didn't do to keep suspicion off them. Especially after Emperor Charles died, leaving Empress Zita alone in exile, pregnant, and with seven other children to provide for. Many remained very loyal to the Habsburg Empire, Bruno included, and would do whatever they deemed necessary to help ensure the safety and protection of its royal family should they ever regain the throne."

"Even lose his own reputation?" Brooke questioned.

Natalie nodded. "If necessary, yes."

Everleigh couldn't fault Bruno if that were the case. She definitely felt for him.

Ten minutes later, they bumped to a landing and their lone flight attendant dropped the stairs to the tarmac. Niles helped his aunt disembark first while Everleigh grabbed Gertrude's carry-on along with her own. They descended into a day not unlike the one they'd left behind in Chicago, except in this cool, cloudy weather a hint of salt scented the air and dusted their lips. Not surprising, seeing how Madeira Airport occupied a cliffside along the ocean's edge.

"John said there'll be a car waiting," Brooke mentioned as they headed for the entrance.

Within half an hour, they were checked into the hotel. John had arranged for each of them to have private spaces close to one another. Everleigh's room connected to Gertrude's, and she led the older woman down the hall.

Niles followed. "My room's on the other side of yours, Aunt Gertie."

"I'll help you get settled," Everleigh said as she swiped Gertrude's card for entrance. Niles stepped behind them, and Everleigh glanced over her shoulder. "I've got this. You can head next door. I'm sure you're tired."

"I'm good. I slept on the plane, remember?"

"Oh, right. Sleeping Handsome." She smirked at him as she set Gertrude's suitcase on the small bench at the foot of her bed. "Gertrude, would you like anything?"

"Just some rest. I don't handle the time change like I used to. Don't plan on me for dinner tonight." They'd all agreed to meet in the lobby around six. "I want to be rested for tomorrow."

"Want me to lay out a change of clothes for you?"

"Yes. My navy joggers and sweatshirt. And then I want you both to head out of here. I don't need anyone hovering."

Everleigh quickly retrieved the requested clothing, placed them on the bed, and gave Gertrude a quick tour of the space. Then she and Niles exited.

"See you at six?" Niles pulled his own key card from his pocket.

With a nod, Everleigh slipped into her room.

⟶ ⟵

Everleigh subscribed to the tough-it-out theory on jet lag. As such, she'd dropped her bag in her room, then searched out an adorable café within walking distance. She'd made the short stroll, ordered a cappuccino and water, and settled into a corner seat with her computer as her phone dinged a text from her uncle.

> I speak without a mouth and
> hear without ears. I have no
> body but come alive with the
> wind. What am I?

Setting her phone on the table, she fiddled with her Rubik's Cube. How did one speak without a mouth? Except it wasn't a person. "What" constituted a thing. She twisted the rows of color, her mind working along with her fingers. Speaking and hearing meant sound. What kinds of things moved sound? Two more minutes of fidgeting, and she straightened. Grabbed her phone. Typed one word.

> Echo.

His reply was immediate.

> Under five minutes. I guess it
> was still too easy.

☺

83

How was your flight? Get to
know your new coworkers any
better?

A little. Gertrude is a hoot. I
think you'd like her.

Even after spending thirteen hours traveling with Natalie and Brooke, she hadn't learned anything new. Well, anything worth noting. She'd become well acquainted with their nervous habits. And while she'd yet to discover more about those two ladies, one thing had become abundantly clear—you couldn't put anything past Gertrude Levine. She had a feeling that woman was about to give her a run for her money.

Her phone pinged again.

If you need me, you know I'm
close by.

The Canary Islands were only an hour from here.

I do. <3

Goodbye, Sunshine.

She texted her own goodbye, then clicked open the file she'd started on the Florentine Diamond. She pulled up the information from the walls of Gertrude's room that they'd scanned into her computer.

Connecting to the Wi-Fi, she further researched Silva's family line and reacquainted herself with photos of any relatives she might meet tomorrow. Before they'd departed Kenton Corners, John had provided them with a packet of information from Caspar. It contained their hotel and rental car info, a map to the auction site, and credit cards bearing each of their names, along with cash. Also tucked into the envelope was a picture and bio on Rafael Silva, Afonso's grandson who was hosting the auction at his villa. So while she knew what Rafael looked like, there were Afonso's great-grandchildren and great-great-grandchildren to familiarize herself with as well. Everleigh studied their faces and did her best to commit their names to memory.

"Mind if I join you?"

She glanced up as Niles's deep voice broke her concentration. He stood beside the empty chair across from her, his own coffee in hand.

"I thought you stayed with your aunt."

Without waiting for her response, he settled into the chair. "You heard her, all she wants to do is rest, and she doesn't need me watching her while she does that."

"Oh, I heard her. I simply didn't think you'd listen."

"I prefer to save my fights for the ones I really need to win. Keeping tabs on her while she sleeps isn't one of them."

Stopping Everleigh from being hired had been, though. She understood to a degree. Yet, he hadn't won that one, and she wasn't about to rehash it. "Can you blame her? No one likes being watched." She arched a brow. "Or followed."

"Rather sure any teenager on TikTok would disagree with you on that last part." He stirred sweetener into his coffee, the edge of his lip curving ever so slightly.

The man had attempted a joke.

"I'm impressed you even know what TikTok is."

"Why? I'm hip and cool."

She picked up her phone and aimed it at him. "One more time, for the camera."

"I don't want to break the internet."

With that stinking dimple, he could. "I was actually hoping the internet would break some of your ego."

He sipped his warm brew, the cup covering up that devilish smirk. The breeze blew his hair into his eyes, and he set down his coffee to dig a rubber band out from his pocket. He tamed his mass of loose black curls, giving her a much better sight of his scruff, which approached beard stage. A look she appreciated more than she ought to.

"Drives me crazy when my hair blows in my face."

"Then why not cut it?"

"Aunt Gertie. She hates when I grow it out." He leaned close. "Teasing her is part of why I do it. Every time she sits by me, she reaches out to check."

Everleigh had seen that play out a few times. "You're giving her something else to ruminate on besides her eyesight."

His brown eyes warmed and a moment of shared understanding stretched between them. It felt a little too . . . enticing.

Everleigh leaned away and crossed her arms with a shrug. "I barely know her, but my guess is if you don't cut it soon, she'll handle it while you're sleeping."

His laugh came easy, right along with his navigation of the conversational turn she'd taken. "You're probably right." The patrons who'd glanced their way resumed their own conversations. Niles tapped her computer. "What are you working on?"

"Research."

"About the diamond or your new friends?"

He was as intuitive as his aunt. "Right now? The diamond." She slid her computer sideways so he could see. Sharing this wasn't a big deal since it was all information he'd be familiar with. "It's intriguing to think that all these years people believed Bruno Steiner stole the Crown Jewels, and if we're able to authenticate the pieces tomorrow, it'll prove otherwise."

"He was the last one seen with them, so it was a logical deduction to make."

"Logical, but not conclusive. Big difference. One that's colored their family name for years." She clicked on a photo of the couple. "He was a baron whose life changed greatly due to unfounded accusations."

He slowly nodded. "Why hide if he wasn't guilty?"

"Because he was either unable or unwilling to prove what was being said about him wasn't true." Everleigh swiveled her computer toward herself. "People are all too eager to believe indictments without actual evidence. I prefer to lead with believing the best in someone until proven otherwise."

He ran his finger along the edge of his mug. "Interesting."

"How so?"

"You're pretty closed off for someone who believes the best in others."

"I'm cautious, yes, but I wasn't talking about that. I was talking about simple kindness. Extending someone the benefit of the doubt."

"Just not extending friendship." He must have read her surprise at his comment because he continued. "You're not exactly becoming best friends with your new coworkers."

She tipped her head. "Because we're women, we should be BFFs?"

Her sarcasm didn't stop him from making his point. "No. But it couldn't hurt to be less standoffish."

"Says Yogi."

"I'm protecting my aunt, not myself."

"So it's okay for you to guard another but not for me to guard myself?"

He absorbed her words. "Touché." He didn't seem to mind his viewpoints being challenged, but he wasn't quick to change them. There was merit to such a personality, because once on a person's side, he wouldn't be easily swayed from it.

His fingers drummed along the edge of the wooden table they shared. Everleigh resumed scrolling on her computer. After a few minutes, he leaned forward again. "You made the point that you believe Bruno was either unable or unwilling to clarify the truth about himself. I'm intrigued by the unwilling portion of your statement. Mind expounding on your thoughts?"

"They're not fully formed." She'd been chewing on possible reasons since reading up on the Crown Jewels.

He reclined and placed his ankle over his knee, then rested his laced hands together on his lap. "Maybe you'll find clarity through talking them out. I mean, why would someone allow their name to be tarnished if they had the ability to clear up the facts?"

They weren't talking about Bruno. Niles was digging for info on her current situation with her past employer. Well, he could keep on digging.

"Perhaps he presumed the people who knew him would believe the best of him, and he didn't care about what everyone else thought."

"His reputation didn't matter?"

She leaned in. "Reputation? No. Truth? Yes. But truth isn't swayed by people's opinions. It remains unchanged no matter what is said, printed, or believed." With that, she resettled into her chair.

As was growing typical between them, a long swath of silence lingered. This time, it was broken by her phone announcing an incoming text. She glanced down and grinned at Uncle Maddox's name.

"Boyfriend?" Niles asked.

That elicited laughter. She picked up her phone to respond. "Nope." Typing away, she kept talking. "You really need to gather more intel before making assumptions."

"Maybe that's exactly what I was doing."

Her hand stuttered on the keyboard. Head still down, she peeked up at him. He'd been waiting for her. He tipped his head and flicked his eyebrows up in a challenge that bordered on flirtatious. Oh, this man was trouble. She had no doubt his plan started with keeping her off-kilter and ended with obtaining answers to every question he held about her.

That wasn't about to happen.

She met his flirt head-on with a saccharine grin lined with steel. "Flirtation works much better when the object of it believes there's authenticity."

Only his slight straightening belied his surprise. He didn't continue the ruse, however. But he also didn't seem bothered that she'd called him out. If anything, it appeared she'd raised his respect of her a notch.

He twisted his arm to glance at his watch. "We should probably get back if we want to be ready for dinner on time."

She caught the time on her computer. "I'm not sure how long you need to get ready, but I'll be fine for another half hour at least."

He stood. "Suit yourself." He took a step away, then turned. Palm on the table, he leaned over her computer, his face inches from hers. "And, by the way, the jury is still out for me over a lot of things where you're concerned, but being attracted to you isn't one of them."

Then he straightened and walked out without another look her way.

Everleigh grabbed her water and guzzled the last sip.

Trouble, indeed.

CHAPTER TEN

"OH, WOW. IT'S LIKE SOMETHING out of a movie." Natalie's awed voice filled the leather interior of the black BMW Caspar provided for them while on the island.

Everleigh couldn't argue with her. For the third time in the past two weeks, she found herself at another impressive home. Arriving at the Silva estate, they submitted their names to the guard, then waited while he swung open the black iron gate. They rolled past, their tires crunching over white gravel as they drove through a tunnel of lush island vegetation. The palm fronds and purple flowers gave way to a wide expanse of thick green grass that spread toward a creamy stone villa towering about a hundred yards from a rocky cliffside. Sunlight bounced off the ocean below.

Brooke stared out her window. "I'm more interested in the antiques inside."

"We only came for the one," Gertrude reminded.

Niles navigated them to the circle driveway where other cars were parked. "Seems we're not the only interested party."

"How many are here?" Tension threaded through Gertrude's voice.

Reaching forward, Everleigh gently squeezed the woman's shoulder. "According to Brooke, most are here for other items." She'd overheard her and Natalie talking last night.

Rafael Silva, the current patriarch and owner of the estate, had recently celebrated his seventy-second birthday. It was during that party when his grandson, exploring the caves below, found the collar of The Order of the Golden Fleece and accompanying contract tucked into a crevice. Rafael believed the timing providential. He hosted an annual auction for close friends who worked in the antiques world. Usually, he didn't have any of his own pieces to add. This year proved different.

Not turning from the window, Brooke snapped her gum. "Yep. Most of what they're auctioning are pieces that belong in specific collections. Those are far more valuable to collectors than the collar."

Natalie leaned forward from her rear seat. "Except this isn't any old collar from The Order of the Golden Fleece. Its implications help shape where we search next, and while I know we're interested in one specific piece, what happened to the Austrian Crown Jewels is a mystery that's enticed lots of people."

"I didn't say we wouldn't have anyone bidding against us. Just that not every one of them will be," Brooke said as the car rolled to a stop. "Besides, Caspar gave us a high ceiling for our bid. We should be fine."

They all climbed from the car. As they approached the front door, an elderly gentleman stepped out to greet them. He wore head-to-toe white that highlighted his matching hair. His blue eyes sparkled as he held out his hand. "Welcome to my home." His rich, deep voice reminded her of that guy on that old 1970s show . . . *Fantasy Island*. In fact, he even resembled him minus the black tie. "I am Rafael Silva." His wide smile and warm greeting only enhanced the likeness. "It's so good to have you here. Please, join the others inside. Feel free to enjoy the food while you peruse the items up for bid this afternoon."

As they offered him warm smiles and thank-yous in return, Rafael moved to Gertrude's side. His perceptive eyes scanned the cane she held in her right hand while also noting how her gaze took a moment to track to the current speaker. Bending his arm, he bumped it against hers. "Might I escort you inside?"

Her chin dipped ever so slightly before she accepted his offer. "I'd appreciate that very much."

Gertrude stepped away, and Niles filled the space she vacated. Leaning down, he watched Rafael and Gertrude—now laughing—as he spoke. "Apparently, I'm not the only one getting Mr. Roarke vibes."

Everleigh jolted. "That was his name! I was thinking the same exact thing."

"My aunt obviously is too. I'm fairly confident she had a huge crush on Roarke when I was little. The reruns were on at our house all the time."

"He does kind of look like him." Natalie joined in. "But Gertrude can't see him."

"It's the voice," Niles said. "I'd hear her and her friends chatting about how it was smooth like butter. Not that the saying makes any sense. Butter's greasy."

Brooke strolled past them. "I have no clue what any of you are talking about. I'm going to check out what we came for."

Everleigh lifted her shoulders then followed. Natalie and Niles trailed behind. Stepping into the home, Everleigh held in a gasp. Natalie, however, released hers quite audibly. This place belonged on Pinterest. Warm white walls met light wood floors. The plush furniture and rugs in the space created a monochromatic feel, allowing the outdoors to serve as the art of the space. A direct line of sight traveled from the entry to the back of the villa where an accordion wall of windows spread wide open. Beyond that bloomed a garden brimming with more tropical flowers than were planted at the botanical gardens in Kenton Corners. Food stations stood on the stone patio and several people milled around, stopping to chat at tall tables draped in white linen.

A long hallway extended to their right, most likely leading to living quarters or a kitchen. To their left, an archway opened to an expansive room set up for the auction. The items were already displayed, many in glass cases, and Brooke approached what appeared to be the piece they'd come for. Gertrude and Rafael weren't far ahead of her.

"I think that's where we need to be." Natalie stepped toward the room.

Everleigh slowed to walk with Niles. "Your aunt may be smitten with Rafael's voice, but she sure stays on task."

He clipped a nod. "You have no idea."

"I have a feeling it runs in the blood."

He didn't deny it. Not that he could.

They caught up with Brooke, who'd found someone from Chapman's—the auction house Rafael had hired—to unlock the case around Lot 27. She studied the piece. Rectangular gold sections connected to what reminded Everleigh of sunbursts, the two shapes repeating to form a pattern. This created a necklace of sorts, chunky and long enough to reach midchest, with a ram for the pendant on the end.

Brooke addressed the man. "Could you turn it over?"

He did, and she leaned in again. Her eyes wrinkled around the edges, her full concentration resting on the shiny item. Then she straightened and nodded at Natalie. "You're up."

Natalie stepped close to observe the signed contract. She consulted something on her phone, glancing back and forth between the two.

Everleigh tilted her head toward Brooke's. "That ram looks like a limp noodle hanging there. You'd think they'd want something more powerful since these things were given to males of noble birth in the Habsburg Empire."

The edge of Brooke's lip lifted slightly in response.

After a long moment, Natalie pocketed her phone. "Thank you," she said to the attendant from Chapman's. Then she turned to them, "Shall we head outside?"

"I'll leave you to your discussion," Rafael said.

But Gertrude's hand still rested gently on his arm, and her fingers tightened their hold. "Actually, could you join us? We'd love to hear more about where your grandson found this piece. And, of course, stories about your father and how he knew the emperor and empress."

Rafael's thick brows lifted. "You would?"

"Of course we would," Gertrude assured.

"I apologize for my surprise." Rafael scanned the room, his focus latching on to a young man whose mannerisms, dark hair, and thin posture captured a younger version of himself. That must be his grandson. "My family stories, passed down by my father and grandfather, are not appreciated by many these days."

Natalie followed his stare, taking in the young man. "I can relate. Though I'm told children eventually come back around."

Rafael glanced at her, understanding etched into the lines of his face. "They do. And we must be patient in the process." After a brief hesitation, he rubbed his hands together. "Let's go to the patio where it is quieter."

Falling into line, they strolled through the open living area, heels clacking on the polished wood floors. As they dodged yet another group,

Brooke pulled up short. Everleigh couldn't see her face, but her stiff shoulders conveyed the displeasure she obviously felt.

"Hello, Brooke," a deep voice greeted seconds before a tall man stepped from the crowd. He towered over her and had a head full of chestnut-brown hair. His high forehead, sculpted cheeks, and square chin created a striking profile, and the hint of whiskers he wore worked well for him. Especially with his attire. He sported a bow tie along with a tweed jacket, which gave off a devilishly handsome history teacher vibe right down to his smirk that held a hint of swagger. Though whoever this man was, his relationship with Brooke didn't seem amicable. At least from her side.

"Storm." Her cool tone adequately portrayed his name.

Everleigh surveyed the room. Other than Natalie who'd also stopped, no one else seemed to notice the awkwardness unfolding around them.

Storm studied Brooke, taking in her black jeans, boots, and leather jacket. "I see you've moved on from your Flower Child stage."

Brooke didn't acknowledge his comment or move out of his way.

He thrust a hand in his pocket, lifting the edge of his suit coat. "Aren't you curious why I'm here?"

"I can guess."

He chuckled. "I'm sure you can." His gaze landed on the others. "Care to introduce me to your friends?"

"Coworkers. And no."

This caused his eyebrows to arch. "You don't do coworkers."

"I made an exception this time."

"Funny. I thought you swore off those."

If possible, the air between them grew frostier.

"If you'll excuse me, I'm needed elsewhere." The rest of their group had continued on to the patio. "It was *not* a pleasure seeing you."

Brooke strolled away, Natalie on her heels. Everleigh followed but not before noting Storm's cocky expression softened to one of regret as he watched her retreat.

Everleigh caught up in time to hear Natalie's urgent whisper. "Who was that?"

Brooke stopped and they encircled her. Some would see it as emotional support. Brooke didn't seem the type to need it, and Everleigh wasn't the one to give it. Curiosity, however, kept her rooted in place.

"That"—Brooke bit out—"was Storm Whitlock. Aptly named."

"And you know him how?" Everleigh pressed.

Her stare penetrated his back as if she envisioned using it for target practice. "He's a competitor. Always bidding against me. I have no doubt he's here for Lot 27. For himself or someone else, I haven't a clue, but I will find out." With a blink, she refocused on Natalie. "What did you think of the piece?"

Natalie slipped her hands to her hips. "The signatures match, best as I can tell. Otherwise, it's one of the best forgeries I've seen." She nodded at Brooke. "You?"

"The mark used for the insignia included an orb and scepter. That places it as something the Austrian Crown would have added to the collection pre–seventeenth century. After that, they changed the insignia to the archducal hat."

"And pre-seventeenth is good?" Niles's voice from behind her shoulder startled Everleigh. "Sorry," he said. "Aunt Gertie wondered what was keeping you. I said I'd check."

Natalie stepped out of the way of a couple. "Pre-seventeenth is very good. The collar that is missing was thought to have originally belonged to Emperor Joseph I who ruled the Habsburg Empire until his death in 1711."

"So we think this is real?" Everleigh questioned.

"I do." Brooke's gaze snagged again on Storm. She pulled out her phone. "You go hear those stories. I'm calling John and asking him to up our limit with Caspar. Then I'm going to figure out exactly why Storm is here. I refuse to lose to him." Phone to her ear, she took off in the opposite direction.

Niles released his bottom lip. "This ought to be interesting."

Everleigh studied the group waiting for them on the patio. "Hopefully, so will Rafael's stories." Because she needed more pieces of this puzzle.

CHAPTER ELEVEN

Rafael Silva proved to be a charming storyteller, spinning the tales of his father and friends with such animation that Everleigh nearly forgot she was listening for clues. He recounted the day Luciana and his father, Tomas, met the Habsburg children. Told about how his father hid the very golden collar they'd come to bid on. Detailed how the children played together, racing along the cliff's edge or creating plays to stage in the room where they'd viewed the auction items. But it was one recollection in particular that arrested her attention.

"Wait." Everleigh held her hand in the air, interrupting Rafael. "Your dad actually *saw* the Florentine Diamond when he was a child?"

The elderly man's eyes blinked to hers. "Yes. Though I cannot promise you it remained in the Habsburgs' possession."

"Because, by Otto's admission, their mother sold jewels to Luciana's parents," Niles recounted. "But it's *your* grandfather's name on the contract."

"That is true." Rafael nodded. "When the Habsburgs arrived, they needed a place to stay."

"And your grandfather provided one?" Natalie asked.

"My family is the oldest on the island. We've always owned several homes here and as such had a place for them. A contract was drawn up and the collar exchanged for housing." The crinkles around Rafael's eyes smoothed. "Family is everything to us. It broke my grandfather's heart that while Charles shopped for his son's birthday present, he caught a chill and eventually passed. Afterward, Grandfather felt it his responsibility to see Zita and the children taken care of."

"Which is why he tried to return the gold collar to her," Gertrude surmised. She leaned heavily on her cane. The day had tired her out. Everleigh hoped this quest wasn't too much for her after all.

Rafael nodded. "Then he introduced the empress to Luciana's parents."

Dragging her attention from Gertie, Everleigh sought one of the pieces still missing. "Who were Luciana's parents?"

"Matias and Camila Perez. Old family friends of my grandfather." He took a champagne flute from a passing waiter. "I have few memories of them and also Empress Zita. Most are from stories my grandfather shared rather than actual interactions of my own. But Luciana and Archduchess Adelheid I saw often at my home as they were close friends of my father."

Natalie shifted. "I thought the Habsburgs left this island right after the empress's husband died, then moved to America in 1940."

"They did." He nodded. "But Empress Zita and her children returned frequently for visits. At least until their move to America. Then several years passed before our families saw one another again." He sipped his drink. "By that time, I was born."

"And you remember seeing the empress?"

"Once or twice. However, as I said, Luciana and Adelheid came by often during my childhood and teenage years. They'd sit with my parents and tell stories of when Papa and they were children. Luciana's son and I were captivated by their recounting and often tried to find the golden collar ourselves."

"Not the other jewels?" Brooke, who'd rejoined them, questioned.

"No. Because of the stories, Jerrick and I knew those were not on the island. But Jerrick did love to make up his own tall tales of where they might have gone."

"Jerrick? Luciana's son?" Gertrude's posture shifted with interest like it had earlier when Rafael mentioned Luciana's parents. Of course, if she'd searched for the diamond, she'd be familiar with any family who had interacted with the empress. Was that all it was?

"Yes," Rafael said.

Brooke crossed her arms over her chest. "But you also knew where the fleece was because it was your father who hid it. So why did you go searching for it?"

"Ah, yes. Well, when Papa brought his friends to show them its hiding place, the fleece was gone. He never knew if someone had taken it or if the tides in the caves swept it away. Until my grandson found it, the question remained one my family dearly wanted to solve."

Natalie cleared her throat. "Much like the Steiner family wants to put final answers to the question that has plagued their ancestors. This lot proves Bruno Steiner's innocence." She pierced Rafael with an intense look. "As does your story."

"It is my family's story. I am simply its keeper."

Everleigh tapped her lips. While she found this conversation immensely interesting, her curiosity was sparked more by Gertrude's straightening spine and Brooke's narrowing eyes when Rafael spoke of Luciana's family.

Everleigh refocused on Rafael. "Were Luciana's parents"—she fumbled with her words, unsure if there was a plural form but opting to try it—"fences?"

Brooke glanced her way, but it was Gertrude who responded. "The Perez family were notorious for fencing items. What made you ask?"

"You stiffened when Rafael said their name, like you were familiar with it. Brooke inclined her head and narrowed her eyes, like she'd heard it before, too, but couldn't place it. Between the story he told, Brooke's line of work, and your former profession, I pieced together what appeared to fit."

Gertrude faced Everleigh with a smile. "You don't merely listen, you observe. I knew I liked you." Then she turned back toward Rafael and focused in with a shrewdness that would convince anyone she could still see. "No one's heard from the Perez family in decades. Do you maintain a relationship with Jerrick?"

Everleigh's phone buzzed an incoming text, and she silenced it. This was the second message within the past minute, but what transpired in front of her was far more important. Niles's penetrating gaze in her direction, however, showed his interest also extended to her buzzing phone. Yes, well, he could wait as well.

Rafael pulled in a deep breath and motioned for a refill on his drink. He paused until a waiter arrived at their private circle. "Anyone else?" he asked as he received a fresh glass. While they all politely declined, Rafael drained his flute. He handed off his empty glass, waved off the waiter's offer of another, and placed his full focus on their tiny group. "Jerrick and I have remained in contact, but he will not be here tonight, if that is what you are hoping. In the past we had many items from his family in our auctions, but I'm afraid it has been years since that was the case, and I no longer believe that will change."

Gertrude pursed her mouth. "Why?" Her gravelly voice held something more than curiosity, but Everleigh couldn't place exactly what she heard.

"Jerrick is retiring, and he has no one to take his place." Rafael cast a glance out over the ocean. "Though I doubt he desires for an heir to follow him. For generations both our families passed our traditions from parent to child. That season is changing." He paused, as if searching for his next words. "Not all children want to follow the ways of their parents. Jerrick believes that to be a good thing."

"And you don't?" Everleigh asked.

"I do not."

The group fell silent for a moment before Rafael clapped his hands together. "Thank you for entertaining this old man by listening to my stories. I must go and see that everything is ready for the auction. I hope you win the bid you came here for."

"Might I ask one more thing?" Gertrude halted him with a question.

"Definitely. I will answer if I can."

"Could you tell me what Luciana and her family looked like? In all my work, I never came across a picture of them."

His grin gave his response before his words. "They were not a family who posed for pictures, and I do not remember Luciana in great detail other than her deep black hair and eyes to match. As for my dear friend, Jerrick, it has been years since I have seen him. Most likely his hair is as white as mine now."

They were the most basic descriptions, and Everleigh had no doubt that was done on purpose.

With a kind tip of his head, he turned to leave.

Brooke's voice followed him. "Where does Jerrick live? We'd love to speak with him."

Rafael paused his retreat. "Lekeitio, Spain. Though I doubt he would meet with you. As you might guess, he's a rather private person."

With that, he strolled away.

⇥ ⇤

Their group remained on the patio rehashing everything they'd learned thus far. Everyone, that was, except Brooke. She'd grown pensive and silent in the past few minutes. Natalie hadn't missed Brooke's mood shift, either. She tugged her a step away, but still close enough that Everleigh could hear her ask, "What are you thinking?"

Brooke snapped her gum, looking out across the garden. She seemed to be fighting herself. "That Lot 27 would mean more to the Steiner family than to us."

Natalie straightened. "Wow. Okay. That's a huge switch from earlier."

"I know. Especially since I discovered that Storm is indeed here on their behalf, and it chafes me to even suggest we let him outbid us." Another snap. "But setting aside my competitive nature"—more like her heated emotions—"I can admit this lot connects with their heritage in a strong way. It's a missing piece of their story. They've sought answers, and we can give them that."

"So you're saying we let Storm win?" Natalie still sounded surprised.

Brooke looked like a child forced to take a spoonful of medicine. "Yeah, I guess I am."

Not that they asked, but Everleigh added her two cents. "Truth is truth no matter what people say. The Steiner family doesn't need this lot to change what really happened. They either believe in their ancestor's innocence, or they don't. They shouldn't need a necklace or piece of paper to make up their minds."

Brooke sucked in a deep breath. "And we don't need the pieces for our next step either. We only needed to prove their validity, which I feel we've done." She turned to Natalie. "Don't you?"

"Yes." Natalie's voice hitched up on the end of the word, as if she wasn't sure she wanted to pick sides in this discussion.

But Everleigh clearly saw where Brooke was—unbelievably—directing things and refused to let that happen. They'd come for the fleece, and they'd leave with the fleece. She needed this job. Needed the paycheck. She did not need the friendship.

If she upset Brooke, so be it.

"We came for Lot 27. We're going home with Lot 27."

"We got what we came for." Brooke pushed back.

Seriously. Who was this woman? Not even an hour ago she'd sung a completely different tune.

"Caspar tasked us with validating it *and* bringing it home."

"Brooke is right, Everleigh." Gertrude laid a staying hand on her. "That family may not need the items, but they're far more valuable to them than to us. I'm sure Caspar would understand."

Everleigh tightened her forearm muscle but didn't remove Gertrude's grip. "You've never even met the man."

"I've spoken with him, and I'm a good judge of character." She patted her. "As I believe you are."

Everleigh's phone buzzed again in her pocket. One glance at everyone's faces in their small circle showed she stood alone. Even her familiarity with the position didn't stop the situation from rankling her. "Fine. Make whatever decision you feel is the right one." She pulled out her phone and waved it. "I have messages I need to respond to. I'll meet you by the car."

"Everleigh." Natalie spoke as if trying to reel her in.

But she needed distance. Needed to maintain it. Partnerships, friendships, relationships . . . all the ships. They weren't her thing and every time she tried, she'd receive another dent from them. This small moment served as a huge reminder of why she maintained surface level with people. Offering her abilities was one thing. Herself? Another entirely. If she didn't desperately need the money Caspar would pay them, she'd hightail it out of here. Oh, the joys of adulting. Wisdom came before emotions, so she'd do the responsible thing and stay the course.

She wandered to the cliff's edge, a cool breeze buffering her. Crossing her arms around her middle, she kept her eyes wide open and inhaled the salty air. Beautiful didn't serve as an adequate description for this place. She'd never been anywhere that felt as if she stepped into a movie, and this place seemed just as surreal. For that, she was thankful. The rest? Well, she couldn't change the parameters of the job, so she'd keep sucking it up and taking breathers as necessary.

Looking down, she noted her flurry of texts was from Uncle Maddox. Not too unusual. He liked to send small bursts of information rather than anything long and rambling. He'd always been straight to the point, while also maintaining his caring demeanor. She never wondered where she stood with Uncle Maddox. He'd cemented his place in her life long before she'd built up her necessary boundaries. As such, he lived on their inside territory. Since Mom passed, he was the one "ship" she did maintain, and the only person she truly trusted.

As she read the first text, another appeared.

> You haven't responded. Just
> checking in on you. Remember
> I'm only an hour away should
> you need me.

His home in the Canary Islands put him temptingly close. But he was already doing so much, and there was enough comfort in simply knowing he kept tabs on her.

Her fingers typed quickly.

> It's all good.

> How's the puzzle you're
> working on coming along?

> Which one?

They'd talked in depth about her seeking answers on the Florentine Diamond, the women she now worked with, and whoever this Caspar was.

> I'll take updates on any and all.

> Had an interesting conversation
> with the man who lives here.
> I'll fill you in later. The piece we

came for seems authentic but
the team no longer wants to bid
on it. They believe someone
else needs it more.

Who?

The Steiner family. Look them
up. They have ties to the
diamond too.

I've read about them.

Not surprising. Anything interesting to her became interesting to him.

I can see how they'd want the
piece as well.

Not you too.

He sent a smiling emoji but otherwise left it alone. She'd learned through the years that Uncle Maddox reserved challenging her on things to moments he strongly felt she needed to reconsider. And when that occurred, she had better watch out, because his stubbornness and logic far outweighed hers. Plus, he was often right . . . though she'd never admit that to him.

Three bubbles appeared before his next text popped up.

How are things going with your
new patient and her nephew?

Everleigh's hand hovered over the screen. Niles made fifty percent of that question impossible to answer. He readily admitted to being attracted to her while also not trusting her. How did she interpret his stance?

She shook her head. Didn't matter. Civility was all she had to offer him.

She typed:

> It's all good.

His response time said he pondered her reply and was debating if he'd ask further questions. In the end, he simply stated:

> I was actually hitting you up
> to let you know that Palmer's
> lawyer has been fishing around.
> Won't be long until they trace
> the money here.

Everleigh expelled a long breath. She'd scanned his earlier texts as they'd been chatting. This wasn't a surprise on many levels. It was, however, a much easier topic of discussion.

> We knew it would only be a
> matter of time.

> Just wanted to give you a
> heads-up. Will keep you
> posted.

> Thanks.

> And you keep me posted on
> how your new job is going.

> Will do.

> Goodbye, Sunshine.

Pocketing her phone, she reached for the small Rubik's Cube attached to a carabiner at her waist and began rotating the pieces. A throat cleared, and she turned to find Niles watching her.

"You said you'd meet us by the car."

"Everyone's ready to leave? I thought they'd at least stay to see if Storm won his bid."

Niles shook his head. "We got what we came for and Aunt Gertie is tired."

A pang of guilt hit her. Yes, they'd come for a specific purpose, but she'd also been hired as Gertrude's caregiver. "Sorry. I shouldn't have stalked off."

He shrugged. "I don't disagree."

The man was direct. She'd give him that.

They started for the car, opting to follow the garden path around the house rather than return inside.

Hands in his pockets, he watched her as they walked. "Whoever you were texting has you nervous."

His casual stance belied the curiosity she'd already spotted on him earlier. Their "ship" wasn't one of shared confidence, however, nor would it become such. And it needn't be for him to simply believe in her. She'd done nothing to him or Gertrude to earn his distrust, but he easily gave it based solely on what he read rather than what he'd encountered.

They rounded to the front yard, where their car idled in the drive. Everyone sat inside, waiting for them. She reattached the cube to her belt loop. "Thoughtful, not nervous."

"Care to share those thoughts?"

"Not particularly."

The muscle in his jaw tensed beneath all that dark scruff, but he maintained his relaxed stance. As they reached the car, he paused. "You know I'll figure you out eventually. Might as well come clean before I do."

"I'm already clean, Niles. Maybe you better wipe off the lens you're viewing me through so you can see that." She opened the door, tired of his suspicions and exhausted by the dynamics with Brooke and Natalie. "But that would require extending me the benefit of the doubt, which is about as likely to happen as me becoming less standoffish."

She ducked into the car, popped in her earbuds, and did her best to tune everyone out.

CHAPTER TWELVE

EVERLEIGH COULDN'T EVER REMEMBER A time when someone younger than her had scolded her. Yet here she sat in a small conference room of their hotel early the next afternoon under the disapproving stare of John Doyle. Amazing how the strength of his glower transferred astoundingly well through the video screen of this conference call.

"I'd like to state, for the record, that I disagreed with the decision." Everleigh fought the urge to hold her right hand up in the air.

John's brow furrowed. "This isn't a court of law, Everleigh."

"Sure feels like it," Brooke mouthed off before glaring at her. "And way to throw us under the bus."

"Kind of like you did by unilaterally making the decision that has us in hot water?"

"It wasn't unilateral." Natalie jumped in. "Again, just because you disagreed doesn't mean we didn't take your opinion into account."

"Really? Because I don't even recall a true discussion about it."

Brooke looked at Everleigh like she was from another planet. "Were you not there? Because *I* recall you standing right in front of me and words coming out of your mouth."

"Oh, you heard them then? It sure didn't seem like it."

"Honestly, Everleigh, you sound like my children." This from Natalie.

That did it. Sweet Jesus better hold her back because she was about to come unglued. Everleigh opened her mouth—

"Ladies." Caspar's computerized voice filled the room. "That's enough."

They all looked at John who sat nonchalantly behind his desk at

Halstead Manor, hands clasped on its smooth mahogany top. When had he added Caspar to this call?

"I assume by your silence that you're all settling down?" Caspar continued.

Everleigh held Brooke's and Natalie's stares in some unspoken stalemate.

"Good." The slight British edge to his computerized voice softened his words. He must be using a synthesized voice rather than his own because one—or possibly all—of them would recognize his real one. But she'd yet to find a connection between any of them and Caspar.

"Now, John explained that you verified the authenticity of the piece, yet you didn't return with it?"

Pink colored Brooke's cheeks. Good. Let her squirm since she'd been the initial weak spot in their wall.

Brooke leaned toward the phone. "Did John also explain why we made that choice?"

John nodded even as Caspar answered. "He did. And I happen to agree with it."

"What?" Everleigh practically exploded.

John shifted uncomfortably in his chair. He'd been on her side, making it known the moment he'd joined the meeting. No doubt he was as surprised as she was right now.

"I'd planned on mailing the collar to the Steiner family. They do need it far more than me."

Everleigh caught a gloating glance from Brooke, but Natalie just studied the wood floor. Huh. She possessed a backbone, but no desire to revel in her wins, it seemed.

John drummed his fingers across the desk. "Still, I should have been a part of the decision. A simple phone call would have been nice."

"Also agreed," Caspar noted. "Ladies, I appreciate your ability to think on your feet, and your confidence to make decisions. However, in the future, both John and I need to be kept in the loop."

That wiped the smile from Brooke's face.

Natalie was the one to answer. "We can do that."

"More importantly, I don't want you fighting over decisions. You're to work as a team or this won't work at all."

Sunshine streamed in from outside, and Everleigh shifted in her chair to avoid squinting. "Not every part of this requires teamwork."

Caspar caught her mumbled words. "This next part does," he countered.

Brooke brushed lint from her black jeans. "Which is?"

"Figuring out your next step."

Right. Because she was stuck with these people until they found this diamond. Still, "I don't think that requires all three of us. I can figure something out, and if I need help"—which she wouldn't—"I know where to find them."

"Sounds fine by me," Brooke agreed.

Natalie said nothing, her eyes flitting between Brooke and Everleigh.

A pause, then, "None of you see the value in working together?" Caspar asked.

"Honestly? Not really."

"Not if it means working with her," Brooke added.

John remained silent.

"I see the value," Natalie spoke up quietly. "No team is perfect, especially at the start, but I think we're making a pretty good one. Given time, we'll only get better."

"Anyone else?" Caspar prompted.

Natalie's expression implored them to budge. To say something.

A whirring sound extended through the line. Finally, Caspar's synthesized voice offered a lifeline. "I certainly don't want to force you to work together. We can most definitely rectify that."

The tension in Everleigh's shoulders released. Brooke's stiff posture softened as well.

John removed his glasses and set them on his desk as if awaiting instructions.

Caspar provided them. "I'll need you to decide which one of you three will remain in my employ. John made a private lunch reservation for you in the hotel restaurant. Discuss while you eat, then let me know."

"Excuse me, what?" Brooke's confusion represented all of theirs, judging by John's and Natalie's parted mouths.

"If there's no value in working together, then I only need one of you. So chat together over lunch. You have an hour." The line went dead.

"Uh . . ." Everleigh straightened in her chair.

Brooke turned on her. "Nice job."

"You were in the same boat with me two minutes ago."

She deflated at the reminder. "Because I didn't think it was going to sink." She slumped against the conference room table, her palms covering her face.

Natalie spoke in a calm voice. "You can take me out of the equation."

But Everleigh shook her head. "You need the money as much as we do."

"How would you know?" Natalie's hazel eyes found hers. "We've never talked about it."

Because they hadn't talked about much more than surfacy things. Yet, she'd seen the hopeful expressions on both Natalie's and Brooke's faces when Caspar informed them of how much he paid.

"Then maybe we go eat lunch and do that."

Brooke nodded. Wishing them luck, John disconnected the call.

They moved through the decadent lobby of the hotel, its white marble floors gleaming in the afternoon sun that streamed through the overhead atrium. The concierge nodded from behind her walnut podium. Between her and the general manager, their stay here lacked nothing. Was that Caspar's doing? Was he known here or did his money simply pave the way? She'd tried to bring his name up to both people, but they were trained in maintaining the privacy of their guests. Their responses revealed nothing.

They reached the glass entrance to Bom Apetite, but before they went in, Natalie confessed, "I can't eat a thing."

"Me either," Brooke said.

Well, looked like they *could* all agree on something.

The mid-April temps had risen into the low seventies, and the sun shone bright in the clear sky. "How about we sit out on the patio?"

Retracing their steps through the lobby, they exited onto the white marble patio that overlooked the ocean. As was characteristic for small islands, the breathtaking views expanded in all directions. With the unusually warm spring day, most people had flocked to the beach, leaving this space quiet. They settled at one of the green iron tables. The metal bent in soft curls and scrolls, creating an intricate art piece.

For the first few minutes, they remained quiet while staring at the surf rolling in to the beach below. Children's laughter rose on the air as parents chased them into the water. One family worked to build a sandcastle, but each new wave washed their work away.

Brooke turned from people-watching. "The way I see it, Everleigh and I were the ones who got us into this predicament. We should be the ones to bow out." She glanced Everleigh's way, seeking confirmation.

"I agree." No, she hadn't wanted to work with them, but this outcome she liked even less. "Natalie, you keep the job."

"No." Natalie shook her head. "I at least have another half bringing in income." She tapped her nails. "Sorry. That's not a jab at you both being single."

"I didn't take it as such," Everleigh responded. "But you also have two sons to put through college." And who knew what other bills. Everleigh remembered overhearing Mom talk about the stress of not being able to afford her tuition after what Dad had done. The next day Everleigh applied for loans to remove the burden from her. Life was too short to worry about money. There was no way she'd contribute to another family feeling the same way.

Natalie's mouth opened like she planned a rebuttal, but it never came. Her head dropped forward, her hair draping her face. "If I'm being honest, things have been difficult lately." She shrugged. "Caspar's offer arrived at a really good time. But can you two honestly tell me you don't need the money too?"

When both she and Brooke remained silent, Natalie sighed. "You guys remember I'm the researcher of this little trio, right? I might not know everything about you both, but I do know that your shop is struggling, Brooke. And you"—she turned to Everleigh—"have loans from nursing school. At least that's what I'm guessing after reading about your parents." Her features softened. "I'm sorry about your mom."

Everleigh swallowed past the lump in her throat. "Thank you."

A furrow creased Brooke's forehead. "Your mom passed away?"

Everleigh nodded. "Several years ago of kidney failure after a lifelong battle with lupus." She hesitated before adding the rest. After all, Natalie already knew most—if not all—of her story, so there was no guarantee she wouldn't share with Brooke. The two seemed to talk a lot. "While she was sick, my dad went to jail for embezzling money from my high school, so

I took out loans to help with her medical bills along with paying for my tuition. I'll pay them off, though."

Both ladies studied her. Their compassionate looks stirred an unfamiliar feeling inside. Desperate to ignore it, she poked at Brooke. "Your turn." A gust of wind practically stole her words.

"Not much to share." Brooke pulled her long hair into a knot, securing it at the nape of her neck. "I opened a business, then lost that business. Things have been a little tough since then, but I've started from nothing before. I'm already doing it again with my place in Chicago."

Natalie lifted her water, and condensation slipped from the glass. "But you don't have to. Not if you keep the job with Caspar."

Everleigh faced her. "You have as much of a need, Natalie."

"As do you." This from Brooke. "So now what?"

They all leaned back, falling silent again. Everleigh twisted all the moments of the afternoon around in her mind. Slowly, the pieces of the puzzle began connecting. She straightened with a laugh. "Now we go tell Caspar his plan worked."

Brooke and Natalie tipped their heads in her direction.

"You really don't see it?" She lifted her palms. "Rather than arguing with us, Caspar gave us what we thought we wanted so we could see that it wasn't what we really wanted after all."

"You're hurting my brain." Brooke squeezed her forehead.

"She's absolutely right. If Caspar pushed, our backs would have gone up." Natalie crossed her arms, nodding her head as if impressed. "Instead, he banked on our hearts being bigger than our stubborn pride."

"Pretty big risk where I'm concerned." Brooke's self-deprecating laugh coated her words.

"Same here," Everleigh added. "I mean, I do my best work alone, but I don't want you two to lose your jobs because of it."

"Or maybe," Natalie started, "you work really well as part of a team, but you don't know it yet."

Doubtful.

Everleigh smiled at her. "Maybe." Better to agree than stoke a fight that could eventually wear out Caspar's generous patience. It didn't matter if she was a team player or not. This job required her to act like one, and she would. She knew what it meant to struggle for money, and she refused to be part of that equation for anyone else. Instead, she'd be part of the solution.

She pressed to her feet. "What's our next move, then? Because Caspar asked us to return with a plan, so let's give him one that includes all three of us."

✈ ✈

A half hour later, they sat around the conference room table on another video call with John. They'd revealed their decision to him, and he'd dialed Caspar's number. Now they awaited his answer. The ring pricked at Everleigh's nerves. Judging by Brooke's snapping gum and the way Natalie tapped her nails, she wasn't the only one struggling.

"Hello." Caspar's computerized voice answered.

"Caspar, it's John and the girls. They finished their meeting."

"You have an answer for me then?"

John peered at them.

Natalie spoke. "We do." She swallowed, though her voice held strength. "We'd like to all continue working for you."

"But you convinced me that I only need to retain one of you."

"Because we were shortsighted." Everleigh took the reins now. "We spoke based on our emotions rather than the facts."

There was a pause before Caspar spoke. "Which are?"

Brooke jumped in next, almost as if this whole conversation had been carefully choreographed. Demonstrating today's lesson that, when necessary, they could band together. "There remain multiple places the diamond could possibly be. Together, we can search for answers in less time."

"Tell me more."

He wasn't shooting them down. Not that they thought he would, but hope didn't offer the same guarantees as reality.

Natalie and Everleigh nodded at Brooke, who stood to pace. "With what we discovered here in Madeira, we know the jewels remained with Empress Zita. We also know she sold pieces to the Perez family."

"That has long been a theory based on the fact that no one knew how she supported herself and her children." Natalie pushed glasses on her face and consulted her iPad. "She did collect some income from their private properties, but not nearly enough to provide the schooling and royal preparation her children still received, let alone their travel to the United States."

Everleigh picked it up from there. "What we can't know is when or if she sold the diamond." That was the wall they had kept hitting ever since the auction. "However, in chatting with Gertrude last night, she mentioned the heaviest rumors support the idea that Zita retained possession of the diamond and had it with her when she came to the United States."

"Rumor isn't strong enough to stand on," Brooke countered.

Everleigh held in her scoff. Barely. "Trust me, people have built entire cases and life choices on rumor alone."

"I don't." Brooke offered a one-shouldered shrug, as if her stance were so simple to keep and even easier for Everleigh to believe in. Unfortunately, Everleigh had encountered enough situations to know that even people who didn't want to be swayed by rumor all too often were.

"So what do you think you should do next?" Caspar asked, bringing their focus back to center.

Natalie stood and moved to the window, perching herself along its wide edge. "We also know Zita took the children to Spain then Belgium until Hitler invaded the region in 1940. That's when they fled to the United States." She leaned against the glass, the sunshine streaming through and casting her in a shadow. "I think with as close as we are to Spain, we should check there first. Maybe see if Rafael would place us in touch with Jerrick since he mentioned Jerrick lives there. His mother, Luciana, was Archduchess Adelheid's best friend, so he might know more than Rafael."

"I agree." Brooke swung her gaze to Everleigh. "Because we need more than rumor to go on."

Her point of view bolstered Everleigh. "I agree as well."

Caspar's automated voice filled the space. "It sounds as if you've decided that working as a team does have merit after all."

"We have." Their voices mingled, much like their attitudes had started to do.

"Good. So can we put this idea of working solo to bed and move forward?"

"They're nodding their agreement," John spoke.

"All right. John, you handle the logistics of their travel, and all of you please continue to keep me informed." He quieted, and there was the sound of someone clearing their throat on his side of the line. Was someone there with him? Before she could ask, Caspar continued. "Good luck, ladies. And remember you're working toward a common goal. Keep your focus on that, not on your differences, and you'll do fine." With a goodbye, he disconnected.

Caspar was a unique boss, and she still wasn't sure what to make of him. But he was right. They needed to set aside differences and continue to be civil toward one another.

She drummed her fingers on the table. "I'll have to check with Gertrude and make sure she's up for extending the trip."

"My guess is Niles will have something to say as well." Brooke grabbed her small backpack from the floor.

"Most likely." He'd been mostly silent since the auction yesterday, only speaking when necessary, which was fine by her. Fewer words meant fewer complications, and she couldn't shake the feeling that—if she let him in— Niles would definitely complicate her world. "I can handle him, though."

Brooke assessed Everleigh with an almost encouraging look. "I have no doubt you can."

Playing her mothering role that seemed to come so naturally, Natalie added, "Now you say thank you, Everleigh."

Ugh. These two. She didn't want to be friends with them, yet for some unknown reason, she couldn't seem to stay mad at them either. She made a show of sighing. "Thanks."

John chuckled and murmured low. "Women. I'm not even going to try and figure you all out."

Everleigh faced him down with a chin tilt. She had a sneaking suspicion that Natalie's and Brooke's expressions mirrored hers.

"You were saying?" Brooke did the talking.

John threw up his hands. To his credit, he owned his comment. "A cautionary tale to myself, is all."

"Smart man," Everleigh said.

He grinned. "Would have been smarter to wait until you hung up."

This pulled a snort from Brooke, laughter from Natalie, and an eye roll from Everleigh. They bid their goodbyes to John, disconnected the call, and vacated the room. Now to face the real battle of convincing Niles that this trip wasn't over yet.

CHAPTER THIRTEEN

OPENING HIS LAPTOP, NILES PULLED up the pictures Burt had emailed him. His aunt's old friend held down the fort while they were gone, seamlessly picking up the open cases Niles had. With Burt's FBI background, surveillance wasn't an issue. In fact, Niles suspected he was happy to come out of retirement. A good thing, too, because they couldn't afford to put clients' cases off, and Aunt Gertie wasn't ready for him to hire anyone new. Burt slipped through her stubborn stance due to their well-established relationship and her desire to gallivant off on this crazy treasure hunt. After this, she might even be okay with adding him to the payroll. But at Burt's age that solution only served as a bandage to Niles's hemorrhaging schedule.

He tried exerting patience and understanding with his aunt. So much had been taken from her, it made sense that she didn't want to let go of her place in the PI agency she'd started. No, she didn't serve much of an active role currently, but placing someone new into her position wouldn't force her to accept all that had changed in her life. He'd wait until she was ready and be thankful for Burt in the meantime.

Niles enlarged the photos in front of him, clicking through to study the incriminating evidence. Burt had sent a short video clip, too, and Niles played it. Movement on the open second floor motel landing caught his eye. He zoomed in closer. "Gotcha."

He paused the video. The screen in front of him proved that the man cheated on his fiancée, breaking not only his commitment, but her heart. Better now than after they said their "I dos." That was the only thing he remained thankful about when it came to Iris. Ben could happily have her. Their relationship would last only as long as the fun did. *Commitment* wasn't a word in her vocabulary. She'd never given Niles her heart, which made it all too easy for her to walk away.

Seemed as if the man in this video had the same issue.

Niles picked up his phone, his stomach churning. This was the part of his job he hated most, but he couldn't put it off on Burt. The woman didn't know him—she'd hired Niles. And he understood firsthand the heartache coming her way.

"Hello?" A soft, feminine voice answered.

Ten minutes later he hung up and hit Send on the evidence in front of him. One short phone call had radically changed her entire future. He offered up a prayer because it was the only thing he could do to aid in her healing. It would take time. A fact he knew all too well, as God still worked on mending his own heart.

He glanced down at his watch. Everleigh had some meeting with Caspar, and she had no idea how long it would last. Aunt Gertie had decided to nap, but it was now two o'clock. If his stomach was growling, he bet hers was too. He knocked on their adjoining doors.

The knob twisted and the door opened. Everleigh's wide eyes greeted him. Awkwardness fell like a cloak over them. They hadn't spoken more than a few words since their last encounter at the auction.

"Hey." She provided a wide berth. "Come on in."

"Thanks." He stepped past her, not that he needed an invitation into his own aunt's room. "I didn't figure you'd be here. I stopped by to see if Aunt Gertie was hungry."

"She is," Aunt Gertie answered from where she sat on her lanai. "Which is why Everleigh ordered me room service."

He brushed his hands together. "Good. I'll head on out then."

"To grab your own food?" Aunt Gertie called.

"Yeah." He refused to lie to her even if he had a pretty good idea of what was coming next.

"Nonsense. Join us."

Yep. That's what he thought.

Before he could decline, Everleigh stepped in. "I'll leave you two to enjoy lunch together."

"Oh no you don't." His aunt bristled. "You have to finish telling me all about how Caspar nearly fired you today."

Niles's gaze swung to Everleigh. "You were almost fired?"

Her cheeks reddened. "It was a misunderstanding. It's all good."

He got the misunderstanding part. Ever since she'd shown up on their doorstep, he felt as if he was operating under a giant one he couldn't clear up. "You're continuing forward on this treasure hunt?"

"I am." She nodded. "In fact, I was just speaking with your aunt about it."

Something in her voice gave him pause. "Then why don't you stay while we eat and fill me in too?"

The nervous way she nodded and attempted a smile only put him on further alert. "Sure."

They settled with Aunt Gertie around the small table outside her sliding patio door. "Everleigh says I have quite the view out here."

Her room was housed in a corner of the hotel, and her deck covered the entire rounded area. To her left, the ocean rolled. To her right, mountains soared. She had the best of both worlds, and his heart ached that she couldn't see it. He wished he could fight this disease for her. He couldn't. But he could protect her in other ways.

"So, what were you and Aunt Gertie talking about?"

"Our next plans." Aunt Gertie sat with her hands clasped over her abdomen. She remained as trim today as she had been all his life. Her hair was styled in the pixie cut she'd always worn, only with more gray to it. She wore the same aubergine glasses—though now simply for style—and no-nonsense clothes. And her mind remained as sharp as a tack. So much hadn't changed, which made the last few weeks nearly impossible for him to understand. He never imagined she'd fall for some fantastical plot of a stranger. Yet here they sat.

He had no clue what this Caspar's endgame was, how Everleigh played into it, or what truly occurred with her last employer. Every day he struggled a bit more to believe she could be a dishonest person, but she refused to open up, and he had yet to find concrete answers. Until he could figure everything out, he planned to remain by Aunt Gertie's side. It sure beat trying to follow Everleigh at a distance, something he didn't feel right about anymore. He hadn't tailed her since leaving on this trip, and he didn't plan on revisiting that method when they returned to Kenton Corners.

"And those plans are what, exactly?" he asked.

"It seems that instead of going home, we'll be flying to Lekeitio, Spain, tomorrow."

That development silenced him. They had work waiting for them at home. He'd already given the better part of a week to this craziness. Not to mention, Aunt Gertie seemed tired. They needed to stick with the plan to fly home overnight.

He faced Everleigh. "Can't you go without my aunt?" Because there was no way he'd send her on without him.

"Your aunt is sitting right here." Aunt Gertie straightened in her seat, her tone edging toward frustration.

"Yes, you are," he answered, "and I don't think you're up to extending this trip."

Though he'd tried to maintain an evenness to his words, they still sparked her old temper.

"How about you let me decide what I'm up for?" She stomped her cane.

No, temper wasn't the right word, though as a child coming from his mother's soft-spoken words to Aunt Gertie's curt ones, her stern tone certainly felt like anger at first.

Another stomp. "And while you're at it, get it through your thick skull that my eyesight is the only faculty I've lost."

He pointed a look at her cane.

Everleigh shook her head vehemently, stopping any further comments from erupting from his mouth. Probably a good idea. He could concede that this wasn't an argument he'd win. "I'll need to see if Burt can cover for me a few more days."

"No one says you have to tag along." Aunt Gertie huffed. "You can go on home."

Her words shouldn't punch him. He'd spent a lifetime with Aunt Gertie holding him at arm's length. At first he thought it was because she hadn't wanted to be saddled with him. As he grew older, he wondered if he reminded her too much of the beloved sister she lost. But as an adult he realized she maintained distance with everyone.

He grew accustomed to her fiercely independent ways and clipped speech. The two of them had found their footing and a rhythm to their days—and their relationship. To hear her push him away, even though he knew she didn't mean it, still stung.

"I'm not going home until you do."

"That's your decision, so no complaining about it."

There was a knock at the door. Everleigh rose. "I'll grab it."

He and Aunt Gertie sat in silence. After a long moment, she spoke. "Like I've told you, Niles, she's a good girl. If you can't trust your gut, would you at least trust mine?"

Interesting that his aunt thought his gut was telling him Everleigh could be trusted. He studied Everleigh, who was smiling at the bellhop who brought them lunch. Not gonna lie, the woman proved a dichotomy. On one hand, mystery shrouded her appearance in his life. There remained too many questions for which she refused answers. On the other hand, she intrigued him. She possessed a soft side he'd seen in her care for his aunt. She also had a dry sense of humor that played well with his, making it too easy to flirt with her. Then there were moments her own insecurity or hurt would peek out from behind her confident façade, and a protective urge welled up inside him.

All right. Maybe Aunt Gertie did know him better than he knew himself, because his gut did seem to want to trust Everleigh. But Iris had done a number on him, so trusting himself when it came to women was an issue.

Aunt Gertie, however, had never steered him wrong.

"Niles?"

"I can only agree to trying."

She smiled. "That's all a body can do."

The bellhop served them from the silver cart he'd rolled into their room. After he finished, Everleigh walked to the door, no doubt to tip him.

"If you do need to get back to work, Niles, I understand."

"Burt should be able to keep things under control."

Everleigh rejoined them, taking her seat. "I heard he had a pretty successful stakeout last night. Caught a man red-handed. He called and told Gertie all about it."

Niles turned to Aunt Gertie before remembering she couldn't see the censuring stare he bestowed on her. She knew him too well, though. "Don't give me that look. I didn't mention any names to her."

"First, you can't see me to know I'm giving you a look—"

"He is." Everleigh's grin showed pure amusement, so he leveled his frustration at her instead. To which she added, "It's very Yogi-like."

A growl escaped his lips before he could stop himself.

Everleigh lifted her hand to her mouth, no doubt attempting to hide her snigger, but her jiggling shoulders gave her away. At least the awkwardness from earlier had passed.

He stabbed at the bowl of rice and seafood in front of him, dumping a healthy portion onto his plate. "How about we focus on our next step here. You mentioned Lekeitio, which is where Jerrick lives, right?"

"Yes," Everleigh said. "It's also where Zita and her family moved shortly after her husband's death, so it's a strong bet that the diamond was still with her. What we don't know is if she sold it there or if she had it years later when she moved to the US."

"What's the plan for answering those questions? Have you gotten in touch with Jerrick?" He tossed out the questions around bites.

"Not yet." Her lips pursed in a frustrated pout. "Natalie and Brooke haven't heard from Rafael yet. In the meantime, they've been trying to track different Jerricks who live in Lekeitio, but he seems to keep a low profile, and we don't even know his last name."

"You assume his mother married, and it's not Perez?" Gertrude asked.

"They're working both angles, though they've gotten no hits on a Jerrick Perez, so yes, we believe she married." She fumbled with her ever-present Rubik's Cube.

It seemed Brooke and Natalie's joint specialty was research while Everleigh's was puzzle solving—only there hadn't been much of that for her to do yet. That bothered her, but he wasn't sure why. Did she feel left out?

There remained plenty she could help with, though. "While they're working on that, we could check further into where Zita and the children stayed. See if there are any families still connected and on the island." It would be a long shot but chasing down even remote possibilities had led him to valuable leads. He'd learned that from Aunt Gertie.

Everleigh perked up. "I'm good with that."

Gertrude placed the napkin from her lap onto the table. "First, I'd like to walk off my lunch. Then we can reconvene here. I'll call Burt and ask if he can continue covering business at home while you two work on things."

"Sounds like a plan."

One, he noted, Everleigh didn't question. She seemed to naturally understand Aunt Gertie had doled out those assignments because a phone call didn't require eyesight. Yet, being in the same room kept her privy to their findings and nearby to offer her own thoughts. Every step of this process, she effortlessly accepted Aunt Gertie's contributions in whatever way they were offered.

Everleigh's phone dinged, and she glanced down. Smiled.

Who warranted that soft response?

"Boyfriend?" he asked.

Her attention blinked to him. "Why is it that every text I get you assume is from my boyfriend?"

He lifted a shoulder. "Because you lit up. Whoever it is, the person is special to you."

"He is. And he's not a boyfriend. He's my uncle."

Something akin to relief unknotted his gut. Following that thought through to its source knotted it back up. His attraction to Everleigh wasn't ebbing. If anything, it was growing. But he didn't know her and what little he did, he wasn't sure he could trust. That didn't exactly create building blocks for a healthy relationship. He refused to repeat the mistakes he'd made with Iris.

Which meant he had two options. Keep more distance from Everleigh or get to know her better. As she stood to help Aunt Gertie, laughing at one of his aunt's crazy puns, clarity and captivation hit him in equal waves, promising only the latter of those two options was viable.

⇒ ⇐

"I think your aunt really likes Burt." Everleigh joined Niles in his room after she helped Gertrude to bed that evening. They'd spent the afternoon walking a portion of the island, though not as far as Gertrude hoped to go, before returning to her room to work. After a few hours, they'd taken a break for a late dinner with everyone. By the time they finished, fatigue weighed heavily on Gertrude. Her eyes closed nearly the same moment her head hit her pillow.

Niles glanced up from his computer, where he was reviewing cases Gertrude and Burt had spoken about earlier in the afternoon. Seemed Niles not only worked the PI angle, but he handled all the billing as well. "They've been friends as long as I've lived with her. He was married, but his wife died when their kids were little. He did a really great job raising them, and now he's reaping the rewards as a grandpa."

"As he should." Nabbing a water bottle from the small fridge in his suite, she held it up. "You want one?"

He shook his head.

She leaned against the wall, tired but not ready to return to her room. "I think it's more than friendship between the two of them."

"I do too. But for their own reasons, they've never acted on it." He rested his hands on his thighs. "I mean, for a long time Burt was grieving and trying to be a single dad. And Aunt Gertie, while a great friend, wasn't so natural at parenting. I think he recognized that." Moonlight streamed across the wooden floor. "I always thought, though, that once they had all of us kids raised, they'd get together."

"Friendships are tough enough to maintain. If you're lucky to have one like theirs, you don't want to risk losing it."

He studied her. "You really are quite cautious with people, aren't you."

She squelched a laugh. "Again, says the guy who thinks everyone is out to get him."

"I do not."

Her turn for the disbelieving expression.

"What?" He held his palms up. "Just because I exercise caution in a different way than you do doesn't mean I think everyone is evil."

"Just untrustworthy."

He shrugged. "I've seen a lot. It's made me protective of myself and those I love. But I'm no pessimist."

"The jury remains out on that one." Though it was sweet how he watched out for his aunt.

He chuckled, leaning back and crossing his arms over his chest. His T-shirt pulled against his biceps. "What's the plan for Spain?"

She yanked her attention from his muscles, chastising herself for letting it snag there, and settled in front of her computer. "John emailed the lodging info." Clicking to her email, she read, "We're staying at the hotel that once was Uribarren Palace. That's where Zita and the children lived until around 1929 when they moved closer to Brussels. Depending on what we find there, we may travel to Belgium afterward."

That last little bit was an addendum added today. Brooke and Natalie still hadn't heard from Rafael. This trip to Lekeitio might be a bust. Even if by some miracle they found Jerrick, they had no clue if he'd share info or where that info would lead. Huge question marks loomed in front of them, which necessitated their plans remain fluid. When it came to Gertrude, flexibility wasn't Niles's strong suit.

He pulled on his lower lip, a habit she observed that seemed to accompany his deeper thinking.

"You're worried about your aunt, aren't you?"

He released his lip, his skin pink where his fingertips had been. "Doesn't she seem tired to you?"

"No more so than anyone else her age." His feelings weren't unusual. It tended to be extremely difficult for family to watch their loved ones grow old. To see them transition from vibrant, able-to-do-it-all parents to visibly slowing down and needing help. And Gertrude was his parent, even if he did call her *aunt*. She'd raised him, and now that caretaker role was reversing. The shift often felt seismic at the onset. Things shook until they finally settled into their new place. "She's doing all right. I promise. Your aunt's health is my first priority, even over helping her find this diamond. If I feel, even for a second, that all this travel is detrimental for her, we'll return to Kenton Corners and allow Natalie and Brooke to do the rest."

"We'd have to hog-tie Aunt Gertie and carry her to the plane if it comes to that."

"I know some good knots." She grinned. "Seriously, though, right now this is the best medicine for her. So much better than sitting at home, thinking about how much her life has changed."

Behind him the curtains shifted in the evening breeze, carrying the scent of the ocean on it. "She does seem happier than I've seen her in months. I think she'd convinced herself that the macular degeneration wouldn't get to the point where she'd be legally blind. When it finally did . . ." He shrugged. Sniffed. Swiped a hand under his nose before fortifying himself with a deep breath. "You're right. This is good for her."

"I think for you both."

He tilted his head.

She continued. "Everyone needs a break sometimes. Having me come in to help care for your aunt takes a little of the pressure off you." It was one of her favorite things about working in a home rather than the ER. She hadn't anticipated this aspect but recognized it early on. "You get to enjoy being her nephew again. Working with her on a case. Letting that be your main focus and her health the secondary one."

Slowly, he nodded. "Are you always so spot-on with your analysis of situations?"

"Careful." She smirked. "Sounds like you're suspiciously close to trusting me."

He chuckled. "I wouldn't go that far."

They chatted for a few more minutes before returning to their computers. She should head to her room, but for once, the idea of a quiet room didn't hold its normal appeal. While Niles worked, Everleigh checked her other email. One message caught her eye, and she winced at the sender's name: Palmer Quimby.

Well, it was better than a phone call. She clicked it open.

> Mother has taken a turn for the worse. Hospice tells us it could be a matter of days. If you'd like to say your goodbyes, now would be the time to visit.

Oh, Constance. Everleigh swallowed away tears. Her old friend would be fully healed. Her body restored. That didn't make grief any less of a companion, however. It simply allowed for hope in the midst of it. Hope that one day she'd see her again.

That day wouldn't be this side of heaven. First, Palmer's invitation stemmed from his desire to corner her. She refused to have that kind of confrontation and stress play out in front of Constance—even if she could make it there. As things stood, she had no idea when she'd return to the

States or if Constance would hang on until then. It sounded as if she wouldn't make it in time. Everleigh would have to hang on to the goodbye they'd already shared.

Pulling out her phone, she fired off a text to Uncle Maddox to keep him in the loop.

Seconds later, he responded.

I'm sorry, Everleigh.

I'm fine.

He sent a meme meant to make her laugh, but all it did was well up more tears in her eyes. Communicating with Uncle Maddox had always been enough. So why did she feel so lonely?

"Everything okay?" Niles peered at her over his computer.

Her stomach flipped at the warmth in his tone. This was the second time tonight he'd aimed his concern her way, and both times it stirred a feeling she wasn't ready for.

"Yeah. It's just that a past patient of mine is coming to the end of life."

Wrinkles bracketed his frown. "I'm sorry, Everleigh. When was the last time you saw them?"

His caring response reached further inside than even Uncle Maddox's. Maybe it was because he sat across from her, and she could see the concern in his brown eyes. That compassion coaxed her to open up to him, but providing that information would tip off which patient she referred to. His mind would dredge up all his unanswered questions about the Quimbys, and that could erase the calm that had settled between them. Still, she refused to lie.

She squared her shoulders. "Right before coming to Kenton Corners."

He tugged on his lip. "Constance Quimby?"

Everleigh nodded. "Palmer emailed me that she's taken a turn for the worse, and mentioned I should come see her."

Understanding dawned on his face. "Because then he could push you for answers."

"It's certainly not out of any concern for me or his mother."

"He's not exactly the most upstanding of citizens."

Palmer and his ex-wife both were addicted to pain meds, though she suspected they'd moved on to even stronger drugs.

"No, he is not." Everleigh straightened. "Wait. You dug into him?"

Niles shrugged with that nonchalance he enjoyed portraying. "You told me to wipe off the lens I was viewing you through. I figured learning more about him would be a solid first swipe."

"And?"

He crossed his arms, pushing his chair onto its rear two legs. "Jury's still out." He recycled her response from earlier. "But it's leaning toward you. If you'd like to fill in some of my blanks, you might swing the verdict your way."

"I'm not one who's into trying to convince people of my innocence. You'll have to arrive at that conclusion all on your own. Once you do, then maybe we can talk."

His chair dropped to the ground. "I've always liked a challenge."

CHAPTER FOURTEEN

THE NEXT MORNING, THEY ALL sat down for breakfast at Bom Apetite in the private room intended for their lunch yesterday. That meeting felt like weeks ago, not merely half a day. A waiter dressed in black trousers, a white shirt, and a black tie served them a delicious spread that ensured Everleigh wouldn't be hungry again until dinnertime.

"You know, a boiled egg in the morning is hard to beat." Gertrude tapped the hard-boiled egg Everleigh had placed in front of her while everyone groaned.

"Too early for jokes, Aunt Gertie." Niles reached for the coffee carafe. "I need caffeine first."

"Laughter feeds a soul better than caffeine any day," she quipped.

"But caffeine feeds my brain."

Everleigh snagged the creamer. "And his attitude." She figured that one out in the first week.

He shrugged his shoulder. "True."

Conversation lulled while they all ate. When Gertrude had only her tea remaining, she reclined in her chair. "What time does our flight leave?"

"Three o'clock," Brooke answered.

A plume of apple-scented steam rose from Gertrude's mug. "What's everyone doing until then?"

Natalie pulled out her phone. "I thought it might be fun to go swimming with the dolphins. I checked before coming down. They have enough spots open for all of us on the morning excursion. We'd be back in enough time to make it to the airport."

Leave it to her to find a way to utilize every spare moment and keep them all together in the process.

Niles darted a glance toward Gertrude that Natalie caught. She quickly added, "I spoke with them about your sight restrictions, Gertrude. They're fully equipped to work with them, and they promise you'll have an amazing time."

That didn't seem to assuage Niles, but Gertrude spoke before he could get a word out. "I'm in. I've always loved the ocean."

Everleigh reached over and squeezed his arm, leaning closer to him. "She'll be fine," she whispered. "And she'll have fun. We'll be right there beside her."

He looked like a new parent preparing to drop his child off for their first swim lesson. With a sigh that bordered on a grumble, he gave a nod.

That was as close to him being fully on board as they were getting.

Everyone headed to their rooms to change, then reconvene in the lobby. Everleigh dropped Gertrude in her room, laid out her swimwear, and promised to return once she'd donned her own suit and grabbed a beach bag. She was ducking back into Gertrude's room when her phone rang.

"Hey, Gertrude," she greeted as she glanced at the screen, fully intending to let it roll to voice mail. But Uncle Maddox's number showed on the screen. He never called. "I need to take this."

"Feel free." Bathing suit and cover-up on, Gertrude settled against the pillows on her bed.

"Uncle Maddox?" Everleigh answered.

"Who's tall, charming, a puzzle-champion extraordinaire, and standing in Madeira as we speak?"

"You?" she squeaked out.

"Yep. I caught a flight this morning. Thought we could meet up."

She couldn't be more surprised if he'd said he'd solved the Kryptos sculpture at Langley. Thirty years on the CIA grounds and no one had cracked the puzzle's code.

She shook her head. "I can't believe you're here." Her excitement dimmed as her gaze caught on Gertrude, reminding her of plans already made. "But I'm not sure I can." She nibbled her lip, an idea forming. "Do you possibly want to join me and the group I'm with? We're going swimming with dolphins."

His familiar chuckle warmed her from the inside out. "I didn't exactly pack for an ocean excursion. I have a flight out this afternoon." Cars honked in his background. "Listen, it's fine that you're busy. I should have texted before hopping a plane, but you sounded like you could use a shoulder last night. I was an hour away, so I thought I'd offer one."

"And I'd really love to take you up on it."

"Go play with your uncle." Gertrude, always listening, broke into the conversation. "Between Niles, Brooke, and Natalie, I'll be fine. You can take the afternoon off as my companion."

She'd taken to calling her a companion rather than caregiver, and Everleigh hadn't corrected her. She covered her phone speaker. "You're my first concern, Gertrude."

"Then it's a good thing you've made sure I have people to watch over me today."

Always with an answer, that one. Uncle Maddox jumped on the bandwagon. "Sounds like you're free."

Between the two of them, she wouldn't win the argument. Honestly, she wasn't sure she wanted to. "I suppose I am."

She and Uncle Maddox made plans on where to meet, after which Everleigh walked Gertrude to the lobby. The rest of the group stood waiting for them.

"There's a van out front to take us to the catamaran." Natalie motioned to the vehicle parked beyond the glass doors.

"I'm actually not coming. My uncle called while we were upstairs, and he just landed here. He wants to catch up."

Confusion crinkled their faces. Brooke was the one who spoke. "Your uncle flew in? Here?"

She supposed that did sound funny seeing as they had no clue of his proximity. "He lives in the Canary Islands, so it's not quite an hour flight."

Her explanation erased their concerned looks, all except for Niles's, which remained skeptical. "You're not coming?"

His first concern was for his aunt, as it should be.

Everleigh shook her head. "Your aunt assured me she'll be safe in your capable hands, then instructed me to go see my uncle."

Standing beside Niles, the top of her gray head barely reaching his shoulder, Gertrude landed a look on him that no doubt he'd seen countless times over as a boy. Her eyesight may be gone, but her grit wasn't. "After all, if you hadn't seen me in years, and I showed up on your doorstep, would anything stop you from meeting with me?"

His jaw cocked slightly to the side. "No, I suppose not."

"Then don't stop Everleigh from seeing her uncle." She wrapped her arm around his. "Now, let's go swim with some dolphins."

The rest of the group headed for the van. Niles spoke to Everleigh over the top of his aunt's head. "All right, then. Have fun with your uncle."

She smiled. "And you have fun with your aunt."

⇒ ⇐

Uncle Maddox's wavy hair still dropped a curl over his wide forehead, only now the dark strands held more silver than the last time she'd seen him. His deep green eyes still sparkled with gold specks, bringing a familiar merriment to his face. He engulfed her in a hug that spoke of home.

"I'm so glad you're here." She relaxed into him, needing this hug more than she realized. Tension melted from her, and she held on for an extra beat. "I can't believe you showed up."

Rushing water cascaded down a waterfall in the distance. Uncle Maddox released her. "Your response to my text yesterday was 'I'm fine,' not 'It's all good.' That's like sending up a flare for you."

She laughed. "I didn't even realize I said it."

"I did."

Two simple words that made her feel seen.

They'd decided to meet here at the Monte Palace Tropical Garden, a tropical paradise filled with exotic plants, ivy-covered stone bridges spanning curving rivers, and birds of brilliant colors. She'd hoped to see this place before leaving Madeira.

Sunshine spilled from a cloudless sky, warming the day once again with the perfect temp. They strolled along one of the stone paths. "I guess the last few weeks have been a tad stressful."

Uncle Maddox slipped his hands into his pockets. He wore his usual, flat-front black pants with a white button-up tucked in and sleeves rolled. Tall and trim, he often received double takes from women, much like the ones passing them now. Yet he never allowed their attention to pull his from her. "It's for the best that you're here. Palmer wants you in that house, and there's no telling what he might do."

They'd talked this through before. Neither thought Palmer posed a physical threat to Everleigh, but he liked to play dirty—as evidenced by the stunt he pulled at the café—and stepping foot into his territory only left her more vulnerable.

"I know." And she did. As she'd already determined, Constance didn't need to witness any further trouble caused by her son. One gift she could give her now was to stay away. "I'm glad I'm here too. The distraction has been good for me."

A drip of water from a palm frond overhead dampened his shirt. "How has it been going?"

"Honestly, I haven't done much other than taking care of Gertrude. Brooke and Natalie have had more to do with finding the diamond. I'm just tagging along at this point."

He lifted one bushy but well-trimmed black eyebrow, an expression he'd given her since childhood. Typically, her self-pity elicited the look. "Wasn't your care of Gertrude one of the main reasons Caspar hired you?"

"Yes."

"But?" he coaxed.

"But I feel like . . ." Her voice trailed off because she couldn't put her finger on what unsettled her. Everything about this situation was poking at the bruised places inside of her.

Uncle Maddox stopped. "You've never made friends easily, Everleigh. You are amazing at caring for people without actually caring for them."

She crinkled her forehead.

Watching her intently, he continued with his thought. "One is something you do. The other is something you feel. You tend to people's needs, and you treat them kindly, but you don't form attachments. You offer them your talent or skill and receive their interaction, and you've convinced yourself that's a relationship. It's not. It's a transaction."

"I'm attached to you," she argued.

His green eyes warmed to the color of a Christmas tree, the feeling of home and happiness in them as strong as memories of those mornings with her mom. "You are," he acknowledged. "But who else have you allowed close? You need more than your uncle in your life."

"I'm an introvert."

"Even introverts have friends, Sunshine." He resumed strolling. "It's not about a number, it's about a position. You've closed yourself off, and that's why you're lonely."

"I'm not closed—" Except she couldn't finish her sentence because he was right. But was it really so bad that she guarded her heart? God certainly hadn't been protecting it.

They reached one of the bridges and paused to take in the view. Standing side by side, they rested their forearms along the railing. The waterfall they'd heard crashed from the rocks above into the river. "I understand it feels safer to only allow relationships within the parameters you've set, but you're cutting yourself off from so much. People will love you for more than your abilities if you let them close enough to truly know you." He faced her. "God too."

That little addition surprised her. "I've never questioned if God loves me."

"No. But have you questioned if he's secure?"

She wanted to say no, but the word wouldn't come out. Not when the denial felt more like what she desperately desired to be true yet didn't believe.

Uncle Maddox took her hand. "Your silence is a pretty loud answer."

"I'm tired of being hurt by everyone, including God." She swiped at a tear. "I just don't know why he stays silent on so many of the big things in my life."

"Just because he's silent doesn't mean he isn't there or that he's not working."

"Then why haven't I seen the evidence?"

Uncle Maddox smiled. "Not everything in life is a puzzle with concrete answers, Everleigh. Faith is not only the confidence in what we hope for but the assurance about what we do not see."

"I have plenty of assurances from the things I *have* seen. They're why I keep my distance from people."

"Then you're choosing to look only at certain pieces of your life, and it's creating a distorted picture that's holding you back from what could be some pretty amazing relationships." His gentle squeeze offered comfort.

"Maybe." Conceding the point wasn't hard. Changing her mindset and actions would be.

"The crazy thing about life, Sunshine, is that you can't stop bad things from happening, but you can stop the good." A pair of birds flew overhead, their wings a rainbow of colors. "Instead, choose to see the good, too, because it is there. I promise you."

They stood in silence for several minutes, both lost in their own thoughts while nature sang around them. Their conversation had been difficult, but the moment still felt peaceful.

"How about some ice cream before we head back? I saw a stand when we came in." Uncle Maddox offered her his arm right along with a temptation he knew she couldn't resist. That's often how he was, serving hard truth but ending on a sweet note.

"Sounds good."

Uncle Maddox steered them around a cloud of mist from the waterfall. "I have a riddle for you."

"Of course you do." She glanced up at him. "Make it a good one, because the last few have been way too easy."

"I think it's a good one."

"Let's hear it."

"What is both unsolvable while also being the only solution?"

Everleigh twisted the words in her mind while they walked. Like the sides of a mixed-up Rubik's Cube, she worked the riddle, searching for the answer. They arrived at the ice cream stand before she reached one.

Uncle Maddox smiled. "I've stumped you, haven't I?"

"Momentarily."

He ordered her Rocky Road and himself Mint Chocolate Chip. By the time they threw their cups away and headed to the car, she still hadn't figured out his riddle. When he stopped beside her car, she still had nothing. It both drove her crazy and made her deliriously happy at the same time. He'd offered her a much-needed distraction to all the emotions he'd dug up and asked her to inspect.

"Thanks for coming." She hugged him goodbye. "It was really good to see you."

His chin rested on the top of her head. "Even if I pried a little?"

She peeked up at him with a grin. "You pried a lot."

"Because I love you and care about you."

"I know."

132

He stepped from their hug and opened her car door. After she was seated, he leaned in. "Let me know when you solve that riddle." Then he shut her safely inside.

She waved and pulled off, watching him grow smaller in her rearview mirror as their conversation lingered in her mind. For years she'd told herself that Uncle Maddox was enough. He was right, her small circle did feel safer. It was easier to interact with others based on what she could contribute to the relationship. People accepted her help far easier and more often than her friendship, so she'd learned to lead with that. Manage her expectations. Even with God.

But lately that small circle also felt a whole lot lonelier. The fear holding her back more suffocating than safe.

Seemed that maybe, just maybe, her heart expected more.

CHAPTER FIFTEEN

Archduchess Adelheid, age fifteen
Lekeitio, Spain, 1929

ADELHEID PULLED HER CLOAK CLOSER around her shoulders. Clouds covered the sky overhead and a cool, sodden wind blew. She wiped the mist from her cheek, the dampness mingling with a few tears sliding down her face.

Her dearest friend, Luciana, took her hand. "Don't cry, Adelheid. We'll still see one another. I promise."

"But it won't be the same." Belgium might as well be on the moon.

When Mama first moved them to Spain only weeks before Elisabeth had been born, Adelheid was quite convinced she'd never be happy. She'd lost so much in such a short time, Papa's death being the hardest. But then they'd eventually moved to Uribarren Palace, with the ocean in front of them and the mountains behind. She had hours to race and explore with her brothers, the sunshine and fresh air doing exactly as Papa always promised it would—heal her heart. It was as if within the silent brush of the wind carrying the sparrows he'd told her about, she could sense God knitting her tender places together again.

Then, a year after they arrived at the palace, a wonderful gift arrived. Luciana's family returned to their family home in Lekeitio, and she and Luciana's friendship, sustained by letters, flourished. She was the sister Adelheid prayed for. Oh, she loved Charlotte and Elisabeth dearly, but they were so much younger. With Luciana, she poured out her secrets, hopes, fears, and yes, laughter. Yet because Mama wished them to have better schooling, hundreds of miles were to separate them once again. She couldn't envision a return to only letters with her dearest friend.

"We shall write each other every week." Luciana smiled and leaned her head close. "Who else will I tell about how Angus kissed me?"

Adelheid's breath caught. "He did not!"

Luciana giggled, her eyes sparkling with a bright cheerfulness. "It was only on the cheek, but it still counts as my first kiss."

"Oh, I cannot wait for mine. Mama doesn't allow any boys close enough to me for it ever to happen." She released Luciana's hand. Happiness for her friend dimmed the ember of envy glowing inside. "When will you see each other again?"

"I don't know." Another smile filled with wistfulness. "But it cannot be soon enough."

The mist changed to droplets, and they raced inside, still chatting breathlessly about that kiss. They hushed their voices as they dashed into the wide, echoing entry of the palace. Luciana's parents met with Mama in the front parlor, its massive mahogany door closed. Still, voices carried in this hall and neither wanted their parents to know about Luciana's secret.

"What are you two carrying on about?" Otto, Adelheid's older brother, stood on the stairway landing, eyeing them.

He used to race along the beach with them. When the tide was low, they'd scurry across the open sand to San Nicolás, the tiny island across the sandbar. They'd spend the afternoon collecting seashells and swimming in the small tide pools. As they'd float in the salt water, gazes fixed on the blue sky above, they'd spin stories filled with adventures that would have them reclaiming their home in Vienna—and, of course, moving Luciana into Schönbrunn Palace with them. Over time, however, Mama hired tutors for Otto and separated his education from her and the other children's studies. Now the adventures they used to imagine and the tales they used to spin, Otto believed would really happen. He would regain the empire their family had lost.

She watched him standing so regally on the steps with a letter in his hand. "Nothing that you need to concern yourself with."

"I will always be concerned with your welfare." Warmth filled his eyes as his gaze settled first on Adelheid then Luciana. He descended to their level and strolled over to them. "We will miss you greatly, Luciana. Should you ever need anything, please don't hesitate to call on any one of us. You truly are a sister of our hearts." He tapped the letter in his hands and addressed Adelheid. "Do you know where Mother is? I have news for her." A line pressed between his eyes.

"What is it?"

He hesitated for a moment. There was a time they shared secrets without pause. As Otto assumed more leadership within the family, those days stretched fewer and farther between. After a moment, he straightened his shoulders. "Baron Bruno Steiner has passed away."

Adelheid absorbed the shock. She hadn't known Baron Steiner well. As a child she'd met him only a handful of times, the last being the day they left Vienna. Then there'd been all the rumors circulating about him stealing the Crown Jewels—which remained in her family's possession. That subterfuge helped maintain secrecy around the true location of the jewels. In the game of hide-and-seek, some may call that cheating, but Adelheid realized years ago they played no game. She may very well never understand what transpired between Bruno and her parents or why he allowed his reputation to be soiled, but she did know this: Mother quietly ensured Bruno was acquitted, and she'd never allowed anyone to speak poorly of him within these walls.

"She is in the parlor with Luciana's parents."

"Ah, yes. I'd forgotten that was today." It wasn't unusual for Luciana to visit without her parents. "Then I shall wait in the library until they are finished." With a dip of his chin, he turned on his heel and headed that way. No doubt he'd work on his studies while there.

Luciana watched him go. "He's changed much in the past few years. Still, I will miss him dearly. He is the brother I never had."

Adelheid looped her arm through Luciana's. Her friend had four younger sisters and often asked her parents to provide her with a brother. "Well, you may borrow one of mine anytime. You did promise we'd still see each other often. They can accompany me on my travels, and I will leave them here." She chuckled and tugged her friend along. "Come. We had ensaïmadas for breakfast, and I know there are some leftover." The sweet bread was a rare treat, but Mama was trying to make their final days here special. Adelheid shook away the looming sadness. She promised herself to make this time with Luciana filled with happy memories, and she'd nearly broken that promise outside.

As they headed for the kitchen, the parlor door opened, and their parents stepped into the hall. Mr. and Mrs. Perez glanced at their daughter. "Come, Luciana, it's time for us to leave." They strolled toward the entrance, a small case in Mr. Perez's hand. He carried it with him each time he came to speak with Mama. They thought she and Luciana didn't know what was inside, yet they did. Ever since they'd learned about Mama giving Luciana's parents pieces of jewelry, they watched their encounters closely. Recently, Mama had brought Otto into her confidence in case anything ever was to happen to her. While he reverently held the responsibility, he never divulged that she and Luciana knew more than their parents were aware.

Luciana leaned in close, twisting slightly so they couldn't see her moving lips. "I'll check the book tonight. If it was the diamond this time, I'll send word right away."

Several years ago, they'd discovered that Luciana's parents kept careful records, and they made no exception for Adelheid's mother. After each visit, Luciana would return home and wait patiently until she found a secret moment to peek at the black journal to see what had been sold.

They'd grown especially fond of the yellow gem set inside a hatpin. "I don't think she'll part with it. Mama speaks often to Otto of how I'll wear it one day for my wedding when he retakes the throne." Hope unfurled inside as it always did with the thought of returning to Schönbrunn Palace. To her home, Vienna. Though at the rate Mama sold their treasure, there might not be any Crown Jewels remaining when they finally arrived. "I wonder which piece she parted with."

"Luciana," her mother called from the doorway.

Luciana wrapped Adelheid in a hug. "I'll sneak downstairs tonight and peek. Then I'll come tomorrow and let you know."

Her friend dashed after her parents, and Adelheid swallowed at the sight. Here they lived close enough to see each other daily. All too soon their parting would be in letters, not in warm hugs. She'd hear about Luciana's next kiss weeks after it happened rather than hours. She'd be surrounded by only her brothers as confidants and playmates once again. While she loved them dearly, that would not do for a young woman such as herself.

Adelheid straightened with steely conviction. Life would change, as it often did, yet her friendship with Luciana would stand the test of time.

CHAPTER SIXTEEN

EVERLEIGH WASN'T QUITE SURE WHICH universe she'd been dropped into recently, but it once again felt like an alternate one.

"Seriously," Natalie said on an awe-filled breath. "Is every place we're visiting going to be so gorgeous?"

They stood outside the Hotel Silken Palacio Uribarren, nestled inside a fishing village along the Bay of Biscay with the slopes of Mount Lumentza and Mount Otoio towering behind. To the south a more industrial style of buildings and a busy street ran along the hotel's perimeter. But to the north, a tiny island peeked out of the ocean and waves bobbed between its shoreline and this beach. Oranges and pinks streaked through the darkening sky as dusk began to give way to night.

In front of them, the hotel remained walled in what appeared to be the original brick and stone masonry of the palace. Several terraces in dark wood had been added along the front and sides, providing amazing views from the rooms above. And down the street a little way stood an old cathedral with flying buttresses of stone connected to a spire patinaed with age.

"Probably. I mean, we are following the route of a royal family." Brooke slipped aviator sunglasses over her eyes, her blond hair lifting on the warm, salty breeze.

"I know, but still." Natalie spun to take in the full view. Her enthusiasm with each location was sweet to see. Back in Kenton Corners, despite her extroverted nature, a weariness had clung to her. Each stop along their journey seemed to breathe more life into her. It was like watching someone awaken. "It's all a bit much to take in."

Everleigh snagged her bag from where Niles unloaded them out of the black SUV John had waiting for them when they landed at Bilbao Airport. "Honestly, my head is spinning a little too. Two weeks ago I was taking orders at a diner. Now I'm standing in Spain on a modern-day treasure hunt."

Gertrude leaned on her cane, her face to the awakening stars. "Take it all in, girls. Life moves fast. Be careful you don't let a second of it slip by unnoticed."

Niles shut the hatch and picked up his and Gertrude's suitcases. He motioned to Everleigh. "You've got her?"

His aunt's face turned in the direction of his voice. "You make me sound like a sack of groceries."

He kissed her cheek. "Never. Groceries don't talk back." Then he snuck away before her swat reached him.

Everleigh offered Gertrude her free arm. "Don't worry. I'll get him for you later."

"See that you do." She grabbed on with glee.

While the exterior of the hotel maintained its old-world charm, the inside mixed gold, white, and black in a modern design. They crossed dark hardwood to the reception desk, the wallpaper behind it filled with sharp angles. A set of glass doors to their left led to a winding staircase. Brass and black iron fixtures adorned tables and hanging lights, and sleek but comfortable white couches provided plenty of places to rest.

"Not how I anticipated this place to be decorated." Natalie waited while Brooke checked them in.

Brooke turned from the desk, obviously listening. "I like it."

"Never said I didn't," Natalie replied.

The clerk tapped away at her computer, then handed keys to Brooke, who passed them out. Rafael had finally called as they boarded the plane. Jerrick would meet them tomorrow evening.

"There's a town hall that opens by nine tomorrow," Brooke noted. "Want to visit there first thing?"

Gertrude didn't even hesitate. "I'm in."

Everleigh swallowed her standard refusal. She wasn't typically one for group outings. "I'm in, too, then."

Once again the parameters of this job were challenging the boundaries she'd placed for herself when it came to relationships. Come to think of it, all this forced togetherness was probably why her talk with Uncle Maddox this morning caused her to question if those borders remained necessary.

They all agreed to meet in the lobby for an early breakfast, and then headed to their rooms. Everleigh ensured Gertrude had everything she needed before they both retired for the night. After a sound sleep, they rose, got cleaned up, and enjoyed a delicious meal that Gertrude downed with speed. She was ready to start their day here.

Bellies full and caffeine ingested, they headed out the lobby doors, taking it slow for Gertrude. Brooke navigated for them, and after a short walk along cobbled streets, they reached the town hall. The creamy stucco structure with flower boxes underneath its windows stood near the marina, with a wide stone courtyard along its southeast side. Here arched entries led to the lower level, but those doorways remained locked. To the left stairs climbed, delivering patrons to another entrance off the main street. Both the Lekeitio tourist center and town hall resided inside.

They climbed the steps to enter one of two arched green doors. A woman with dark hair secured at her nape peered up from the counter and greeted them warmly. "*Kaixo.*"

Um. She'd brushed up on her high school Spanish on the flight here, but that wasn't a word she ever recalled hearing. It sounded like *kie-show*, not *hola*.

"*Kaixo.*" Natalie returned the greeting, albeit with a little less polish. "*Ba al dakizu ingelesez?*"

Brooke's wide eyes pinned on Natalie with a look of surprise that matched Everleigh's. Niles simply seemed amused. Gertrude, meanwhile, leaned over to Everleigh and whispered, "Pretty impressive. The only other language I know is sign-language, but it's typically pretty handy."

Everleigh bit her cheek to stop her laughter. Gertrude and her puns would be the end of her.

Natalie turned their way. "They speak Basque here, not Spanish, but I asked if she speaks English. I don't know many Basque words."

The woman came from behind the desk and held out a hand. "I do. As well as Spanish." Her warm smile never dimmed. "I am Esmerelda." A thick accent encased her words.

Everleigh took her turn shaking Esmerelda's hand. "I'm sorry. I just assumed everyone spoke Spanish here."

"Ah, some do, but we are in Basque Country." She stopped in front of Natalie. "As it appears your friend knows."

Natalie shrugged. "I enjoy research and learning about new places. I've read a lot about Basque Country, and Lekeitio is a very unique place. Where else can you find a Gothic cathedral, mountains, and an island you can walk to all beside a fishing village?"

Esmerelda laughed. "You know all of our secrets."

"Not quite." Natalie's sincere kindness and interest put the woman at ease as they seemed to do with every person she met. "We've come to discover whatever we can about Empress Zita and her time here. We're staying at the Silken, and we even plan to meet with one of her old family friends, Jerrick Perez." Her brows pulled together. "Although we believe his last name is different because it was his mother who was a Perez, but we never learned her married name."

"You truly do love our history." Esmerelda returned to her counter and motioned for them to follow. While Natalie had teed Esmerelda up perfectly to fill in their missing blanks, the woman remained mum about Jerrick. Either she didn't know him, or she did but the fact that they were strangers kept her silent.

They all hung back, allowing Natalie to maintain the lead she'd so easily taken. Her warm personality might not immediately win someone over, but they'd all learned it proved hard to resist.

Gertrude's cane knocked against the wood floor as Everleigh guided her. She didn't need her eyesight to remain a part of this conversation. Her eyebrows tightened over those milky eyes, a sure sign she concentrated on every word spoken.

Natalie placed her hands on the smooth cement counter. "We absolutely love the history of this quaint town, especially me." A pane of glass separated them as Esmerelda moved to the opposite side. Natalie leaned in. "I'm a librarian who's also a history buff of sorts."

"Oh! You must visit our library. I give you directions, and you must walk there next." She pulled out some paper from a drawer. "There is ice cream along the way as well."

"We only just had breakfast," Niles said. "It's too early for ice cream."

"Says who?" Gertrude responded.

Esmerelda held the paper in her hand as she regarded Gertrude. "You are a lover of life. This is good."

Gertrude rapped her cane on the floor. "If I would have become one sooner, maybe he wouldn't be such a stick-in-the-mud."

Niles's mouth opened.

Everleigh squeezed his bicep. "She teases because she loves you."

"I'm not so sure." But his expression said otherwise.

Esmerelda slid the paper she held to Natalie, but she did not release it. "Why your interest in the empress?"

"Her life was one filled with many stories to tell."

"Of which you can read in a book, no?" Esmerelda lifted a brow.

Brooke stepped up. "We're trying to track down her jewels. Specifically, the Florentine Diamond."

"I am not surprised. You are not the only one." She released the paper.

Natalie took it and turned it over. A map of Lekeitio with tourist spots highlighted. "Oh." Natalie blinked. "I thought . . ."

"That I hand you a map to the Florentine Diamond?"

"No," Natalie quickly responded. "Though maybe some information on when Zita stayed here."

"That is on there." Esmerelda pointed to the number seven.

They bent their necks to look. "That's our hotel."

Esmerelda nodded. "Yes."

Well, this was not going as planned.

In their silence, Gertrude stepped forward. "It's true we're searching for the diamond. In fact, I have been for thirty years, but not because I want to keep it for myself." Somehow she held Esmerelda's gaze even though she couldn't see her. "My sister, Amelia, and I, along with many of our friends, loved to pretend to treasure hunt as children. The Florentine Diamond captured our attention, and she and I collected every bit of information we could. We'd work on theories until late in the night."

"You were close." Esmerelda, fully focused on the story, surmised.

"Yes. Until she married and I didn't. I'll confess to some jealousy being involved, especially as the years passed and she had a son." She reached for Niles, and he took her hand, squeezing it. "She was my younger sister. Not that the explanation gives me any excuse."

"It's all right, Aunt Gertrude." Everything about Niles in this moment portrayed strength and assurance.

As if his words soothed not only what she'd said, but what was to come, Gertrude continued. "I allowed that envy to create space between us, so I didn't know she continued the hunt. One day she called and asked me to take a research trip with her to Belgium. It was her way, once again, of trying to connect like she had over so many years. And like always, I turned her down. So she took her husband." Her fingers tightened on Niles's hand. "They died in a car crash on that trip."

Everleigh sucked in a breath.

Gertrude paused, then, "Finding the diamond has always been about finishing what my sister and I started. When I succeed, I intend to bring the gem home to Austria where it belongs, which is exactly what Amelia would do. I failed her when she needed me most. I don't want to fail her in this."

Oh, Gertrude. Everleigh's heart ached. The importance of this task shifted even as her thoughts did too. She blinked to Niles's emotionless face. This story, though he was obviously familiar with it, couldn't have been easy to hear. Yet it shed new light on so many intricacies of their job. Finding this diamond didn't only help the woman who raised him, but the woman who'd given birth to him. Rocked him as a child. The one he must still miss to this day.

Esmerelda sniffed, and her eyes glistened. "It seems that you *were* there for her when she needed it most. This is her son, no?"

"I am," Niles answered.

"And she raised you?" She nodded toward Gertrude.

"Without hesitation."

Esmerelda scanned the group, then refocused on Gertrude before bestowing a quick nod. She dug into a drawer, pulled out an old photograph, and turned it so they could see.

Wrinkled lines of time creased the black-and-white portrait, but it didn't diminish the joy captured in the photo. Two young girls with their arms wrapped around each other's waist smiled at the camera. One short with slightly darker skin and black hair that reached to her hips. The other, pale and tall, with her hair captured into a soft bun.

Natalie held the picture. "That's Archduchess Adelheid." She spoke in a hushed tone as she pointed to the other girl. "Is that . . . Luciana Perez?"

Esmerelda nodded.

"Gertrude." Everleigh's breathy voice held awe.

"It's her? Tell me what you see. Please." The wistfulness in her voice spoke to the years she'd wondered what someone, anyone, in this family looked like. If Gertrude hadn't raised the inquiry with Rafael, Everleigh would never have known of her desire. Now with the long-awaited photo in reach, her eyesight failed her. Everleigh would do her very best to describe it in detail.

"It's black-and-white but I can tell she has glossy black hair like Rafael said. And it's long. To her hips with a slight bit of curl on the end. She's shorter than Adelheid, so maybe five-three? Five-five at the most, I'd say. And she has the prettiest eyes. Almond shape and they look dark like her hair. But the most interesting thing is she seems to have a birthmark on her cheek. Unless . . ." Everleigh gently rubbed her thumb against the photo then held it up close to her face. "Nope. It's not a smudge. It's definitely a birthmark. It's ovalish and then it's almost like it feathers out along the edges."

Eyes closed, Gertrude remained silent as if trying to envision the description Everleigh provided.

"I wish you could see this, Gertie," Everleigh said.

Eyes still closed, she smiled. "I can. Quite clearly." She reached her hand out and when Everleigh took it, she squeezed firmly. "Thank you." Clearing her throat, she opened her eyes and turned to where she'd last heard Esmerelda. "And thank you. You didn't have to share that with us."

"Many people are interested in our history, but most people do not deserve to know it. That is not so with you." Esmerelda accepted the photo back from Natalie. "You say you are to meet Jerrick, and now I believe you. He will tell you the rest of what we know."

Natalie hugged the woman. "Thank you."

They all repeated the words, though with handshakes instead. Until Gertrude's turn. The two elderly women embraced.

"I pray you find what you are searching for," Esmerelda whispered to her. If Everleigh hadn't been standing by her side, she wouldn't have heard it. Or Gertrude's response.

"I believe I already am."

In that moment, Everleigh silently promised to do whatever it took to help her finish this quest.

⇢ ⇠

That afternoon, after spending the remainder of the morning exploring the city, Gertrude retired for a nap. She said that she wanted to be well rested before meeting Jerrick that evening. Everleigh ordered her a snack from room service, ensured she ate, and then safely tucked her in bed before slipping from her room.

Sunshine filled the sky, the spring air reaching for summer warmth. The attendant at the front desk said that would soon change, but her idea of cold and this Midwestern girl's idea varied greatly. Everleigh quickly changed into shorts and flip-flops, then headed to the beach mere steps away. Moving across the brick patio, she encountered Brooke and Natalie enjoying what appeared to be their own afternoon snack.

"Everleigh!" Natalie spotted her at the same moment and waved her over.

She shut down her knee-jerk reaction to keep moving as if she hadn't seen them. Changing course, she strolled over to their round table. Natalie nudged an empty chair, its black iron leg scraping against the stone. "Sit with us."

The woman could make friends with a serial killer. Even Brooke was beginning to lose her sharp edges. Natalie smiled up and added, "Please."

Everleigh cast a longing glance toward the footpath now evident between this beach and the small island, San Nicolás, which was only reachable at low tide. Once upon a time only a sandbar had connected the two, but the town had since added rocks on either side and paved the way. She really wanted to check out the island, but her conversation with Uncle Maddox still churned like a paddle trying to make milk into ice cream. She hated milk, but she loved a bowl of Rocky Road. Which quite possibly would always be what navigating relationships felt like to her—rocky but sweet. She wouldn't know until she trusted them—trusted God—and tried. "Okay. But only for a few minutes. I really wanted to check out the island."

"We just came from there," Brooke said. "We passed Niles on his way out."

"Definitely worth the walk," Natalie added. "But be careful. It's slippery in spots." She nodded to the rough cement path, wet and covered with swaths of green algae along the edges.

"Did you hike to the top of the island?" She'd read the view more than made up for the short climb.

Both women nodded. Then Natalie's forehead creased as her brows dipped over her hazel eyes. "Sorry. We should have waited for you."

"No." Everleigh waved her off. Natalie's persistent kindness in the face of all the times she'd turned her down no longer felt cloying. She'd started to find it sweet in a good way. "You had no idea how long I'd be with Gertrude, and she's my first responsibility."

"That story about her and her sister. Whew." Brooke motioned to some sort of fresh shrimp salad. "Help yourself, by the way. I ordered while Natalie was in the bathroom and apparently she's allergic."

"To lobster," Natalie amended. "So I figure I better stay away from shrimp, just in case."

"Well, I am actually allergic to shrimp as well, so I'll pass." She noted another dish nearby. Some bright red sausage-looking meat on top of a fresh slice of bread. "What's that?"

Natalie pushed it over. "Chistorra. It's delicious."

Everleigh's stomach growled, and she picked up a piece. Garlic and paprika played against a salty background, the taste perfectly paired with the sourdough slice under the meat. "That *is* good."

A waitress filled an extra glass at the table with water, and Everleigh took a sip. Natalie circled the conversation around to earlier. "Did you know the reason behind Gertrude's search for the diamond?"

"She shared a little with me the day I met her." In the distance, colorful fishing boats bobbed against their docks.

Brooke lifted her hair off her neck and secured it in a loose bun. "It's sad, how she and her sister grew apart."

"Yeah. Their lives took them in opposite directions." Something Everleigh understood. Mom had been all that connected her and Dad, and even that link had been weak. Now, duty was all that remained. "Being family doesn't always mean you stick together for life."

"Well, this new empty-nest mama sure hopes it does for mine." Natalie zipped the pendant on her necklace along the chain. "I've threatened both my boys that if they don't come home for visits, I'll show up to visit them."

Amused, Everleigh filed the ploy away to use should she ever become a mom.

"With that incentive, I have no doubt they'll both be home." Brooke tipped her face to the sun and closed her eyes.

The palms swaying on top of the rocky San Nicolás island captured Everleigh's attention. She stood. "I should get moving so I have enough time to explore before the tide changes."

"Plus, we have plans tonight," Natalie reminded.

As if she would forget. "I'll be back in time."

With a wave, she slipped her sunglasses on and started walking to the island. Natalie hadn't been lying. As expected, the pathway remained wet and slippery, which slowed her down. Rocks jutted out on either side of the footpath. The last thing she needed was to tumble onto their sharp edges.

Ten minutes later, she reached the sandy shore of San Nicolás. People milled about, hunting for shells the tide deposited. The beach didn't extend very far before rocks led to lush green soil and a trail to the top of the island. She started up it.

"Fancy meeting you here." A familiar deep voice pulled her gaze off the path.

Niles stood a few feet in front of her, backlit by the sun. She squinted even though she had sunglasses on. "Hey. Brooke and Natalie mentioned you were out here."

"You came for me, then?" His sly grin bordered on wolfish, and his eyes glinted with an equal predatory glint—in a way that flipped her stomach.

She cleared her throat, refusing to fall for his flirting. "I came for the view." As the lines around his mouth deepened in a widening grin, she realized the fault in her response. "Of Lekeitio. Not you."

His deep chuckle affected her even more than his look. "I'm just your bonus."

"Bonus headache." She started past him, doing her best to hide her smirk.

He turned and kept pace. "Mind if I come with you?"

"Aren't you on your way back?"

"I was, but I don't have any plans, and it's a beautiful day."

"Suit yourself." Her pulse raced, but that was due to the uphill terrain. Not because of the man walking beside her. She snuck a side glance at him. He'd tied back his curly hair, which showed off his strong jaw covered in thick black scruff. With only one day in the sun, his skin already leaned toward golden. He'd changed into a pair of black shorts made for trekking and a black T-shirt with a white outline of a mountain on it. The outdoors suited him. He wasn't at all what she typically found attractive, and yet her keen awareness of him continued to grow.

"My aunt asleep?"

"She nodded off as soon as she'd finished the snack I had her eat."

"Thanks for taking such good care of her."

"It's what you pay me for."

He looked across his shoulder at her. "There's a difference between politely doing your job and truly caring. You care for my aunt."

"I do." Everleigh nodded. Her foot slipped on a rock, and Niles's steadying grip was on her with lightning speed. "Thanks." She righted herself.

He didn't immediately release her, but rather waited until her feet were firmly planted on the ground. "Anytime."

Her skin warmed beneath his firm grip. His eyes settled on hers for a long breath before he let go. And that's when Everleigh saw it.

"What is *that*?" she asked on the breath of a giggle, her gaze focused on his arm. Because the shape of his tattoo was perfectly clear, but she wanted to hear him say it.

Red mottled his neck. "Nothing." He pulled his arm close to his abdomen. No wonder he always wore long-sleeve shirts around them. No doubt he planned on changing back into one after this little hike, but he hadn't anticipated bumping into her.

"Oh, that's most definitely something." She yanked his arm out and straightened it to show off the incriminating evidence. "You have Winnie-the-Pooh tattooed on your arm." A realization hit her. "I was right when I nicknamed you for a bear. I just called you the wrong one!"

He extracted himself from her grip. "I already own the nickname Pooh Bear."

She wanted to laugh. She really did. But she desired an explanation even more, and she knew if she broke out in laughter, he wouldn't give it to her. "So that's why you cut your aunt off before she could share it."

"That's why." He remained unamused.

"And why she teased you about not liking honey."

"Yep."

She clasped her hands in front of her. "You have to explain. Please."

"It's not one of my finer moments."

"We've all done things we're not proud of, so I won't judge. I promise." She held out her pinkie.

He stood there and stared at it. "Am I missing something?"

"Have you never heard of a pinkie promise?" She sighed at his bewildered look. "We clasp pinkies and it's a bond that can't be broken, so when you tell me your story I am sworn to secrecy."

"Ah. Well, I'm a guy. We spit in our palms and shake."

"We will not be doing that."

He chuckled but wrapped his pinkie around hers. "Fine. Pinkie promise it is then."

"Good. Now start talking."

She waited him out a full minute before he finally spoke. "Let me preface this episode of my serious lapse in judgment by saying that my mother used to read me Winnie-the-Pooh. It was kind of our thing." Sadness touched his features, but love oozed in his voice. "Anyway." He dragged his hand through his hair, his tattoo smiling at her. "When I turned twenty-one, I made the unfortunate decision to get drunk at a bar beside a tattoo parlor. I'm convinced the guy made most of his money off intoxicated kids."

"Smart businessman."

He glowered at her. "I got thinking about my mom, got incredibly sad, and tried to chase that emotion away with too much tequila."

"Yikes."

"Yep. And the rest is history." People passed by, momentarily quieting him. "I did think about getting it removed, but it has stopped me from ever touching alcohol again." He gave her a lopsided grin that slowly disappeared as he grew somber. "Plus, it's kind of like having a piece of her here with me. Every time I'm about to react emotionally to a situation, I catch sight of this and can just hear my mom telling me to stop, think, and pray before acting."

His voice cracked on that last part, and Everleigh couldn't help it. She reached out and took his arm again, her fingers tracing over the adorable character. "Niles, that is the sweetest thing I have ever heard."

His disbelieving chuckle drew her eyes to his. As her thumb brushed over his tattoo, his pupils flared.

Releasing her hold, she rubbed her hands together. "Your secret's safe with me." Her voice felt shaky, but not as shaky as her insides.

He cleared his throat. "Thanks. But if it does get out, remember, I know where you live." Then he scooted past her to resume their walk.

She stood still in the space he sweetly gave her, breathing deeply to restore her equilibrium. Heart rate calming, she hustled to catch up with him. They reached the top within a few more minutes. Natalie and Brooke weren't lying. This view was worth every step. Everleigh turned in a circle. The ocean to one side, and the Basque fishing village of Lekeitio to the other. The panoramic view stretched from the red-roofed buildings in the marina to the tall stone buildings near her hotel. Sandy beaches raced toward the water while lush green mountains lifted behind the city. "It's gorgeous."

Niles *hmm*'d. "It is."

She inhaled the briny scent of salt water and watched a seagull glide along the warm breeze. All the talk about Niles's mom had her thinking of her own. Mom would have loved this place. She'd have loved even more that Everleigh was able to visit here. And with how she always said God didn't mean for a person to go through life alone, she also would encourage her to take a chance with making new friends . . . or possibly something more. Everleigh glanced at Niles before looking out over the water. Shedding her introverted ways still felt scary. So much of what she knew said she'd get hurt again, but she'd never build a different track record to look back on if she refused to move forward.

After exploring the top of the island, Niles spoke. "The tide's starting to change. We should probably head back." He tipped his head. "Unless you enjoy swimming."

"Um, that's a negative."

They retraced their steps. "You *can* swim, though, right?"

She nodded. "But I prefer to do so in places where I'm not possibly on the menu. I'm not a fan of big bodies of open water where sharks roam freely."

"Ah. So your uncle showing up created the perfect excuse to miss our dolphin excursion." He slipped his hands into his pockets, his casual stance only making him more attractive.

"I would have gone in if needed."

"I wouldn't have let a shark get you." A simple confidence underscored his jesting declaration, as if defending her would come naturally to him. Did he realize that stood in stark contrast to the first day they met, when he declared his intent to defend his aunt *from* her? She sensed a change happening between them, and this walk only solidified that feeling. Could she let go of past hurts and trust it? Trust him?

The warmth curling inside her at his easygoing tease said she wanted to.

She shook her head and reached for her Rubik's Cube.

He tossed a lopsided grin her way. "What're you thinking about?"

There was no way on this green island that she was sharing that with him. So instead, "About meeting Jerrick tonight."

He studied her. "Not buying it."

She shrugged and continued walking, not breaking pace. As the dirt path wound through trees, the air filled with an earthy, fruity scent met by the salty ocean breeze. They reached the footbridge, the gently rolling water flowing over it at times as the tide rose.

Everleigh slipped off her sandals to walk barefoot. "I didn't know your parents had passed away while searching for the Florentine Diamond."

"Yep." He, too, removed his flip-flops.

She skirted around a puddle of algae. "Is that why you were so adamant about Gertie not going on this trip?"

"Because of my parents' death?" They stopped to allow other people past, snorkel gear in hand. Niles shook his head as watched them. "They, apparently, do not share your fear of sharks, because they'll be swimming back." She laughed and he continued. "And no. My dislike of this treasure hunt had nothing to do with fear over losing Aunt Gertie. I never really blamed Mom and Dad's death on their search for the diamond. It was a terrible accident."

"That's pretty well-adjusted for a man who lost his parents so young."

He tugged on his lower lip for a moment. "It's no different than me not blaming all cars for their death. Just because something awful occurred in one situation doesn't mean I have to live in fear of it happening every time I'm in that same situation again. I've learned to trust God in spite of my past. Make him bigger in my life than my fear. Otherwise, I'd never leave my house, and I don't think that's what my parents would want for me." A wave hit, spraying their legs with foamy water. "It's certainly not what I wanted for my life."

His words offered plenty for her to chew on regarding her own life, while also growing her curiosity over his. "Then why are you so cautious with people?"

He wagged a finger between them. "Pot. Kettle." But then he grew serious. "Cautious isn't closed off. There's a difference." They reached the beach, their toes digging in the warm sand. "Between what I've seen in my line of work and experienced in my personal life, I've learned to be vigilant when it comes to people. But that doesn't mean I don't eventually let them in."

They stood there, sunshine beating down on them, sandals in hand, the ocean rolling waves against their ankles. The moment stretched, becoming one she felt the need to mark in her memory. Because in it, she heard both their hearts creaking open.

"Hey you two!" Brooke waved as she called from the steps leading to their hotel. "We're leaving in thirty."

"Ready?" he softly asked.

She slipped past, her response containing as much double meaning as she heard in his question. "Almost."

Niles fell in step behind.

CHAPTER SEVENTEEN

Brooke tapped the heavy brass knocker against the wood door. As it hammered their arrival, Everleigh gave Gertrude a quick scan. Her fingers gripped her cane, and she leaned heavily on its support. She'd been uncharacteristically quiet on the walk here. Normally, Everleigh would play it off as lingering fatigue, but she couldn't shake the feeling that the old woman wrestled with something.

Everleigh shifted her gaze and caught Niles studying her assessment of his aunt. With raised brows, he silently inquired her thoughts. She gave a slight shake of her head, and the lines deepening on his forehead promised he'd press for answers later.

The door opened, revealing a young woman with black hair trailing to her waist and wide umber eyes set in a round face. She greeted them with a smile. "Kaixo," she said as she waved them inside. Her accent encased the words, making them slightly hard to understand. "I am Rosa."

She closed the door after them, and they made introductions, then she motioned them to follow her down the hall. Her yellow skirt swished around her ankles as she crossed the terra-cotta floor. The short hall opened to a large room with white stucco walls and dark wood trim. Colorful pillows adorned creamy cushions on sofas with rattan frames. Two matching chairs anchored the sisal rug under the furniture. She pointed for them to sit, so Everleigh helped Gertrude into one of the chairs and stood beside her.

"I have cider and water. Which do you prefer?" Rosa headed for the small kitchen at the far side of the room.

"We're fine," Brooke said.

Natalie dropped a mom look on her. "Cider sounds amazing." She leaned toward Brooke seated next to her on the sofa. "It's impolite to turn down your host's offer."

Brooke's mouth opened on a sigh as she rolled her eyes.

"Anyone else?" Rosa asked from where she stood at the blue tiled counter.

"Cider sounds good for us all," Niles answered.

Rosa poured out the drinks into tall, thin glasses, then delivered the traditional Basque drink to them. Seemed everywhere they'd gone today offered a variation of cider. Everleigh wasn't a fan of apple drinks, but she'd force it down.

After Rosa handed them each a glass, she settled on a stool she brought from the kitchen counter. "You enjoy Lekeitio so far?"

Again, with her accent it took a moment to process her words. Natalie seemed to catch them the fastest. "It's a beautiful town. We've loved being here."

"You go to the island?"

Everleigh answered this time. "We did. A fun walk with a lovely view."

Rosa nodded. "I go often. When I am not needed here." Her eyes tracked to another hall that led to the rear of the house. "I am Jerrick's nurse."

Gertrude straightened. "Everleigh is sort of like that for me. I've recently gone blind."

Deep lines furrowed Rosa's forehead. "I am sorry." She didn't offer why Jerrick needed a nurse, likely the info Gertrude was fishing for by revealing her own need. Instead, Rosa explained, "Jerrick had hoped to meet with you today, but he had an appointment that has made him very tired. He now is asleep."

"We can come back," Gertrude offered.

But Rosa shook her head. She stood and opened a drawer on the nearby desk. "No. He told me I must show you this." In her hands she held out a black journal. The frayed leather edges held paper yellowed by age. Brooke slid on gloves and reached for it. "You do not need gloves," Rosa said, her own hands free of them.

Brooke shook her head. "I do." Her respect and care for antiques no doubt dictated she must, and this was definitely an antique. "Can we take it with us?"

"No." Rosa's answer landed quick and firm. "But you may take all the time you need with it."

"What about pictures?" Natalie asked.

"No flash," Brooke spoke before Rosa could.

Rosa nodded her agreement. "*Sí*. Though you may take pictures." She backed away. "I need to check on Jerrick. Please enjoy more cider if you like."

Brooke eyeballed them. "Not around this journal."

Rosa left the room, and they congregated around the book. Except for Gertrude who remained in her chair. Everleigh stepped closer to her. "Doing okay?"

"Just fine, dear."

Her words and tone matched, but something niggled at Everleigh. Niles's stare collided with hers, his eyes questioning her again. She lifted her shoulder, still equally confused as he about what Gertrude was thinking.

"Here." Brooke's triumphant voice lifted. Her gloved finger pointed to something in the book. "It's the first entry of a transaction between the Perez family and Zita." She traced the line, reading as she did. "For a star-shaped hair clip made of diamonds. Could this be the Florentine?"

"It specifically says star-shaped?" Natalie questioned as she leaned in closer to read the line Brooke's finger marked, her voice heady with excitement.

"Yes."

"Then that's not the Florentine. Sissi wore those!" Natalie stood straight. Her excited look changed to surprise at their blank expressions. "Sissi? Empress Elisabeth of Austria before Charles and Zita?" When they all stared back cluelessly, she continued. "She was a bit of a rebel, very strong-willed. Some people thought she was crazy, but she didn't care. Oh, and she was assassinated."

"She was my kind of lady," Gertrude said. "Minus the assassination."

"I can see that, but she was also known to be obsessed with her appearance and often depressed. Neither of which describe you." Natalie spoke as she tapped away on her phone. Finding what she searched for, she turned the screen for them to see. It displayed a painting of a young woman in an off-shoulder white gown, her chestnut hair falling to her waist and a dozen glittering diamond stars tucked into her curls. "There's lots of stories of what happened to these hairpins, and while they weren't considered part of the Crown Jewels, it's not unlikely to think Zita would have had one in her possession. Sissi had twenty-seven of them made."

"That's a lot of hairpins," Brooke said.

"Her hair actually went to her ankles. It took hours to work it into the braids you see here."

"Okay. Maybe that's not a lot of hairpins." Brooke consulted the book again. "There's several more entries in here." She flipped pages, scanning as she went.

Natalie observed from over her shoulder. "I wish I had something to compare this handwriting to."

"It definitely looks old," Everleigh said.

"Looks can be deceiving." Brooke turned another page. "But I do agree. There's a feel and scent to this journal that newer objects can't duplicate."

"What are you, a bloodhound?" Niles joked.

Brooke spared him a glance and a grin. "More like a mutt."

After another few moments of paging through the book, she flipped backward in it. "The final entry I can find between Zita and the Perezes is dated 1952."

"That would make sense." Natalie nibbled on her thumbnail. "Zita moved to Luxembourg to care for her mother around that time. Most of her children were married by then, and once her mother passed away, she lived in a residence provided by the Bishop of Chur. She wouldn't have had a need to sell any more pieces."

"How do you know all of this?" Everleigh asked.

"I researched the family when we started this job." She said it as if everyone magically remembered every detail they read. Everleigh had researched, too, but not as thoroughly or with the same amount of retention.

She watched Brooke and Natalie. Those two, heads bent together as they consulted the journal once again, worked effortlessly as a team. Dare she say they'd even formed a friendship?

A small ache began inside.

"No mention of the diamond?" Gertrude asked.

"Nope." Brooke shook her head.

Natalie straightened. "What does that mean for our next step?"

Everleigh sorted through the information, finally feeling somewhat useful. "No record that she sold it, at least to the Perez family. There's no indication that she ever worked with anyone else, and the fact that she didn't want word to get out that she had the jewels means it's doubtful she ever did use other buyers. The more people who knew, the more likely the information would leak."

"True." Niles stood and paced. "So did it go with her to Luxembourg?"

"That seems like a logical deduction." Though nothing even hinted at where they should start there.

Rosa reentered the room, several additional small leather books in her hands. "Jerrick asked me to give you these. He say they might help as well." She placed the stack on the table. "They belong to his mama. She write in them."

"Luciana's journals?" Gertrude spoke from her chair.

"Sí. Yes." Rosa nodded.

Natalie started paging through one, completely enraptured. "We could be here all night."

"I make coffee?" Rosa asked.

"Yes, thank you." Everleigh nodded. "Strong and a lot, please." Then she took a few books from the top. Across the way, Gertrude's forehead wrinkled in frustration. Of course! Without her eyesight she was missing out on a huge moment in her search. Everleigh's heart twisted. She nabbed a wicker chair from the small dining table and settled beside Gertrude. "I'll read to you from mine."

The defeat on Gertrude's face morphed into delight. "Thank you."

"Of course." Such a simple thing to bring joy into this woman's life.

Across from her, Niles silently mouthed his own thanks. The warmth and gratitude carried in his expression reached out like a hug she'd happily sink into if the room wasn't full of other people. Since—regrettably—that wasn't a possibility, Everleigh cracked open the journal and gingerly smoothed out the yellowed pages. "It's dated 1929."

Natalie lifted the glasses she'd donned to read. "Adelheid would have been fifteen. I haven't found anything online about Luciana yet, but I'm guessing based on the picture we saw, she'd be around the same age."

Everleigh nodded and began reading. Rosa moved in and out of their space, filling their mugs and bringing snacks when she wasn't checking on Jerrick. Over an hour passed in relative silence other than Everleigh's whispered words to Gertrude. They made it halfway through their slim journal, she and Gertrude giggling like young girls themselves over Luciana's crush on a boy named Angus. "Oh!" Everleigh gasped. "He was her first kiss."

Gertrude straightened. "Don't stop there. Keep reading."

Niles watched them, amusement softening the lines around his deep brown eyes. In moments like this, he reminded her of a teddy bear, not a grizzly or even Yogi. Perhaps his tattoo wasn't so far off after all. Her lips wiggled against a laugh.

"What?" He set the journal he'd been reading on his lap, one finger holding his spot. The interest he'd poured into its pages now rested fully on her with an intensity that claimed he found her far more intriguing.

"Nothing."

His unrelenting stare challenged her.

"Fine. I was imagining you with a bow tie." A half-truth, as her favorite teddy bear as a child wore one, but that was as much as he was getting out of her.

Gertrude cleared her throat.

Niles shook the confusion from his face with a promise that, "I'm going to want the genesis behind that thought a little later."

Too bad for him, he wasn't receiving it.

Everleigh turned to the story in front of her and dove into Luciana's first love. She and Gertrude were two pages farther when Brooke stretched and yawned. "There's a lot in here but nothing much about the jewels."

"It does seem like their friendship remained strong. I have several entries in mine about letters she received from Adelheid," Niles said.

Brooke nodded. "Me too. I'm getting bits and pieces of her time in the United States."

"You guys must have ones dated later than mine," Everleigh said. She cracked open the other two she held. "These are all from the 1930s."

Brooke and Niles confirmed theirs were from the 1940s.

Natalie, who'd been sitting silent in the corner of the couch, held one finger in the air. "I think I have something."

The room hushed.

"Go on," Gertrude nudged. "Don't keep us in suspense."

Pressing her frames up on the bridge of her nose, Natalie's warm voice read Luciana's words.

"How terribly tragic to have lost so much in her life. Will. Her father. Vienna. Her sorrow is unparalleled. It is a small comfort to know that the diamond remains near her heart even as her home is now elsewhere."

Everyone in the room straightened. It took a moment, but then their voices eclipsed one another's.

"Adelheid had the diamond?"

"Who's Will?"

"Where was she when that was written?"

Natalie held her hand up again. "I'm only reading what's here. Based on the time frame of this and other things Luciana mentioned, I'd say this was when Zita and her family were in Royalston, Massachusetts. I have no idea who Will is or if Adelheid had the diamond while there, but it sure reads like it."

Niles shook his journal in the air. "May I?"

They nodded, and he dove into an entry from his.

"Received a letter today from Adelheid. She sounds so in love. Who would have thought that this Will would capture her heart? They are unlike each other, yet in her words I hear the admiration I feel when I think of my Angus. One day I shall marry that man. It seems, however, Adelheid will be first to marry. I admit to feelings of jealousy, though not over her taking a husband. I envy her taking a new friend, Marie. Still, knowing now that Marie brought Adelheid her precious Will and, as such, happiness, how can I maintain any ill will toward her?"

"What year is yours?" Natalie asked.

"Fall, 1943."

"Mine's late 1944," she noted.

Brooke voiced what they all must be thinking. "Which means at some point that year, Will passed away."

"Before they were married, since everything I've read on Adelheid says she never married," Natalie added.

"How sad." Brooke shook her head.

Gertrude tapped her cane on the floor. "Better to have loved and lost than to never have loved at all."

The sentiment carried a heaviness to it, as if personal experience burdened the words with a weight the older woman no longer wished to carry.

Niles squeezed his aunt's hand. "Something you don't have to worry about since you are loved and have loved me well."

Moisture built in Gertrude's eyes, and she blinked it away with obvious embarrassment.

Everleigh stood. "So, we need a trip to Royalston next." She stepped toward the kitchen. "But before we go, I'd like to see if Jerrick will let us take his mom's journals with us. I have a feeling there's lots more to read."

⇀ ↽

Niles closed the door to Aunt Gertie's room, shutting out her soft snores. She'd slept through breakfast. Everleigh had peeked in on her before joining their table, and he'd agreed to check on her after they'd finished their meal. An hour later, she still hadn't stirred. Their flight home wasn't till the afternoon, and he had a sneaking suspicion they'd rouse her long enough to eat and board the plane, then she'd doze off once again.

All this treasure hunting was exhausting her, that fact never more evident than in her emotional moment at Jerrick's home. In all the years he'd lived with Aunt Gertie, warm and cuddly weren't words he'd ever use to describe her. There were no bedtime hugs even when he woke from nightmares. She'd hand him a glass of water, tell him God didn't believe in ghosts so neither should he, then turn on a night-light in the hall. If he fell and scraped a knee, she'd spray alcohol on it, add a bandage, and tell him to keep moving because life was full of scrapes and if he let that stop him, he'd never get anywhere. When a bully had set his sights on Niles, she taught him to fight rather than cry. One well-placed hit meant his opponent fell rather than Niles's tears.

The skills she'd taught had turned him into the man he was today, and he was thankful for those tough lessons right along with her more recent softer ones. He'd needed both. After Iris he'd been in danger of becoming bitter and harsh. Long talks with Aunt Gertie about God, love, and forgiveness, along with the hugs she'd learned to give—though still infrequent—steered him in another direction.

So no, Aunt Gertie hadn't been perfect, but she had loved him in her own way. Which made it hard to watch her emotional and physical fatigue grow each day they continued this hunt, especially since there wasn't a chance she'd turn back when new information continued to pull her forward.

Too restless to sit in his room, Niles exchanged his shorts for a bathing suit and jogged down the steps to the lobby. He crossed the creamy marble floor to exit onto the patio facing the ocean. A gentle breeze carried the scent of fish and salt from the marina as fishermen unloaded their catches in the warm morning sun. He headed for the stone steps that led to the beach but stopped when his eyes landed on Everleigh.

She sat at the table closest to the stone railing, her feet propped on it as she scrunched down in her chair. The journal in her hands absorbed her full focus, and as she read, she paused to jot something in the notebook on her lap. Then she tucked her pencil into the knot she'd pulled her hair into. A few loose strands blew against her nape, their movement tickling her, based on how she scratched what he was sure was soft skin. His lips curled with a thought of brushing his fingertips against the same spot to elicit a similar response, and his feet carried him over as if the thought had a power of its own.

She heard his approach, and her blue eyes blinked up, her face lighting as she saw him. His fingers curled into his palm. "Hey," she greeted.

"Hey, yourself." He pointed to the empty chair beside her. "Mind if I join you?"

"Be my guest."

He settled into his chair and ordered a sparkling water from the waiter who magically appeared. As the man strolled away, Niles motioned to her reading material. "I still can't believe Jerrick allowed you to take that."

They'd been given five of the journals to read, all of which covered the years Adelheid would have been in Royalston. Jerrick requested everything else remain with him. They didn't test his generosity but rather accepted his offer and left before he reconsidered.

"My dad always said, it's not the fool who asks."

"Wise man."

"Well, except for that part about him embezzling hundreds of thousands of dollars."

"Right. Except for that."

Mirth filled their words, and as the hint of laughter played out, they shared a look. Where her voice held a lightness, her eyes zeroed in with an intensity that cut through him, as if probing to see if he still viewed her through the lens of her father. He didn't.

And she must have caught the change, because something shifted in her face. In her entire demeanor, really. Like when the first hint of spring sunshine hit the ice covering Aunt Gertie's small pond, her ever-present frosty barrier was starting to melt. Oh, he'd discovered her a pro at appearing as if she connected with the people around her, but she only allowed them so close. Superficial didn't create the same relationship as knowing someone bone deep. That took vulnerability. They weren't there yet, but this was a step in the right direction.

"Anyway"—she did her best to bridge what was dangerously close to becoming an awkward silence—"there's a lot of good stuff in here, but nothing more about the diamond." She scooched up in her chair and settled the journal in her lap. "I'm not an overly emotional person, but I'll admit that Adelheid had it hard. She lost her home and her father at such a young age. Was bounced around Europe and then America. Fell in love. Lost love." Everleigh shrugged.

"She had Luciana." Niles reached for his water. "Their friendship lasted through all those losses, time, and distance."

Watching the ocean waves roll toward shore, Everleigh reached for the Rubik's Cube always attached to her waist. She didn't play with it, but her fingers did rest there. "I've never had that."

"Have you ever tried to?" He kept his voice low, hoping to encourage her contemplation rather than her defenses.

For a long moment, he thought she wouldn't answer. Then, "A few times. None ended well."

"Hmm." His turn for contemplation because he needed to be very careful with his next words. "How was nursing school for you?"

Her forehead crinkled. "Nursing school?"

"Yes." He nodded. "You know. Did you pass every test you ever took?"

She chuckled. "Not by a long shot. In fact, I had to retake organic chemistry because—" She abruptly stopped. The puzzle pro no doubt connecting the pieces. "I think I'll start calling you Yoda instead of Yogi."

"I am quite wise."

"I hear that happens in old age," she replied, rather drolly.

"Hey!" Now he straightened. "I only have two years on you."

"In years. Personality, however . . ." She swished her lips to the side as she offered a shrug that came off way more adorable than sassy. Especially with her scrunched nose.

"You know what else age brings?" he asked.

"What?"

"Experience." With one hand, he yanked her chair close, turning it as he did. Before she could react, he had both hands on the arms of said chair, effectively trapping her. He leaned in, his eyes flicking over her freckled cheeks. Taking in her steely blue eyes. Dropping to the curve of her lips and that dent in her chin. This close, he didn't miss her fast inhale or the way her breathing quickened. He leaned in, letting his scruff rub against her skin as he brought his mouth close to her ear. "And my personality is a man who goes after what he wants. Do you know what I want, Everleigh?"

Her head barely moved in a shake, but it was enough to deliver another press of her cheek against his. He pulled his lips into a smile, knowing she could feel the movement, and he deepened his grin when she shivered.

"To go for a swim." And just as abruptly as he had tugged her into his space, he stood, releasing her from it. He took a step toward the beach. "You should come with me. You look a little overheated."

Her expression morphed from dazed to dangerous in under a second.

Then she shifted to disinterested, swiveled her chair around, and propped her feet up on the ledge. "No thanks. I'm good."

"Suit yourself." He didn't even attempt to hide how entertained he was by her. Turning, he jogged down the steps.

Her voice halted him as he hit the bottom. "Oh, and Niles?"

He glanced over his shoulder. "Yeah?"

"You should have asked what I wanted." Then she stood, graced him with a look that slid a bead of sweat down his back, and walked inside.

CHAPTER EIGHTEEN

THREE DAYS LATER, EVERLEIGH SAT in the front parlor of Halstead Manor. Outside, the sun worked hard to raise the frosty morning temperature. Inside, the fireplace ran, creating a toasty atmosphere. Mid-spring in Illinois bounced from frigidly cold to unseasonably warm, sometimes—as predicted for today—all within the span of twenty-four hours.

The familiar oaky scent of worn leather wrapped around her from her usual perch on the lone club chair. John manned his desk while Brooke and Natalie held down the couch. When they'd landed in Kenton Corners, they'd each gone their separate ways to catch up with their daily lives and allow John time to secure their next travel plans. Though they'd already filled him in on their discoveries, they had a meeting with Caspar today to talk through their upcoming trip to Royalston.

On their plane ride home, they'd created lists of locations to visit and who they should speak to, dividing the tasks. In between work these past few days, Brooke located contact info, Natalie called ahead to coax appointments from strangers, and Everleigh continued to pore over the journals for any nuggets they might have missed.

"Lekeitio seems to have proved very helpful." Caspar's computerized voice buzzed through the open line.

"Very much so," Natalie agreed for them all.

"And everyone's ready to hop on that plane again?" John sat behind his desk, tapping his pen against it. "Even Gertrude?"

"Especially Gertrude." Everleigh had struggled this morning to convince her to rest. The woman thought they should already be on a plane to Massachusetts. Luckily, Burt stopped by to fill her in on their open cases he'd been working. The distraction seemed to momentarily prove successful, and Everleigh left Gertrude in his care while she drove to this meeting. She'd half expected to see Niles join Gertrude and Burt, but he'd been gone when she'd awoken this morning. Not a bad thing. He was currently on her list after she caught Burt tailing her again yesterday.

His obvious remaining lack of trust only made her more embarrassed that her reckless side decided to blatantly flirt with him in Lekeitio. Her face flamed thinking about her teasing response and how she'd joined in his game. The heat in his eyes when she had. It had seared through her with a sudden awareness. Flirtation required nothing of her but could lead to more. The "more" had terrified her.

She didn't need to worry about that now.

"And Niles? Is he coming to Royalston?" John had stopped tapping his pen and now scribbled on the legal pad in front of him.

"Yes." Unfortunately. He'd made that clear when they'd boarded the plane home. Everleigh suggested in passing last night that he stay in Kenton Corners, to which he reiterated his determination to accompany them. Resigned to the fact that he'd remain in her sphere, she'd headed to bed for some restless sleep.

Clicking drifted over the phone line before Caspar spoke. "Natalie, your family is okay with you being gone again?"

A mirthless laugh escaped her. "My boys won't be home until the semester ends, and Mason is fully focused on his baseball season. I highly doubt they'll even notice."

"We'd notice if you didn't come." Brooke reached out and squeezed Natalie's hand.

It confounded Everleigh how she and Brooke had started out in a similarly standoffish place, but Brooke had made headway where Everleigh struggled. As a result, Brooke and Natalie had formed a bond, and she stood on the outside. Like the chemical equations she'd studied in nursing school, the bond remained open in case she wanted to join herself to them. She worried, though, that doing so would create something combustible. Just because elements appeared to belong together didn't mean they equaled healthy mixtures when combined. Sometimes what you ended up with was toxic.

John resumed the tapping of his pen. "All right, I have you scheduled to fly out Monday at ten in the morning. That gives you all the rest of the week to rest or catch up on work, whichever is needed. Sound good?" They all nodded and he continued. "Who's on the list for people to meet when you're there?"

Pushing her glasses onto her face, Natalie consulted her iPad. "So we believe we figured out who Marie was. Zita and her family visited a home called La Bastille that was owned by Calvin Bullock. He had a son Hugh who would have been a little older than Adelheid. Hugh's wife, however, was close to Adelheid's age and her name was Marie."

"Good lead," Caspar acknowledged.

Brooke picked up the conversation. "Hugh and Marie are deceased, but they had two daughters, Fair and Fleur, who were around through the years Zita and her family stayed with and visited the Bullocks."

"Fleur claims to remember Adelheid and even have some pictures. She's willing to speak with us," Everleigh added.

"Any idea who Will was?" Caspar asked.

John's brow raised as if he was telegraphing Caspar's facial expressions.

Outside, the barely budding tree limbs swayed on a light breeze. Natalie stood, pulling her cardigan close, and walked toward the fireplace. Flowers and scrolls were carved into the gray stone mantel, its massive size nearly as tall as Natalie. "I'm combing through county birth and death records for men who'd be a similar age to Adelheid and who passed away in 1943 or 1944. It's slow going. Will was a popular name. My hope is that when we get there, something will help me narrow down the search."

"I'm sure something will spark for you," Caspar said.

"And I'm waiting to hear from Jerrick on the other journals. He hasn't been willing to part with any more of them." Everleigh had given it one last-ditch effort prior to their departure. Rosa posed the question to Jerrick who still wasn't feeling well, and his response hadn't changed. The remaining journals stayed with him. "We did ask if he'd be willing to read them himself and let us know if he sees any more about Adelheid or Will."

"Which Rosa said he agreed to do once he felt better," Brooke finished.

Some clicking and then Caspar spoke, "Hopefully he'll come across something helpful."

They covered details such as where they'd stay near Royalston and how long they intended to be there. Caspar commended them on the job they were doing, and then left for an appointment. After he hung up, John stood and used a remote to turn off the fireplace.

"I have a meeting, so we should head out." John had yet to leave them in the house alone, and that fact piqued Everleigh's curiosity. Were there clues to Caspar's identity hidden somewhere in these walls? She'd yet to unearth who purchased this place from the Forsythe family. The county only listed a corporation as the buyer, and even Uncle Maddox couldn't figure out who owned the corporation. A little bit of time alone inside these walls might answer a whole lot of her questions.

They picked up their belongings and headed for the front door.

"Anyone else hungry?" Natalie asked.

Brooke slipped outside first. "I could go for some fried mush from The Corner Café."

Both their gazes swung to her as John locked up. "I should head to Gertrude's."

Her excuse was legit, even if she had over an hour before Burt left.

Natalie and Brooke firmed up their plans to meet, and they all waved goodbye, climbed in their cars, and drove down the long drive. Everleigh lagged behind, turning right when they all turned left toward town. She drove a mile before making a U-turn and doubling back to Halstead Manor.

Digging in her purse, she pulled out a bobby pin. Not ideal, but she'd picked a lock with less, a skill she'd acquired, thanks to the multiple puzzle games she'd played and won. Granted, she had never tried out this skill in the real world, but it should work the same.

Jogging up the stone steps, she knelt in front of the ancient door and examined the oval brass knob attached to a rectangular base. Yep. She had this.

She unbent the bobby pin and jammed it into the lock, wiggling. Her concentration zeroed in on the task in front of her, so much so that she didn't notice the approaching car until it reached the circular drive. Crud! She yanked on the bobby pin, but it wouldn't move. Great. The thing was jammed into the pinhole lock.

Behind her, the car engine cut and a door slammed. She jumped to her feet and turned as a familiar deep voice oozed over her.

"Thought I'd have to convince you to join me for lunch but looks like you need my help." Niles dropped one of his grins on her. "And my silence."

⊷ ⊶

"It's jammed in there good." Niles straightened, his shoulder bumping her chin from where she'd leaned in close to examine his attempts. He turned, the warmth of his breath providing sudden awareness of their proximity. "Did you honestly think this would work?"

"It has before." She stood, needing space for all the wrong reasons. Especially since she was still mad at him.

"Where? On a Barbie house?"

She ignored the dig, thankful that he filed this under amusing rather than suspicious. He didn't need any more reasons to distrust her since he seemed incapable of releasing the ones he'd originally had. Not that it mattered what he thought of her. At least that's what she told herself— though she'd always been a terrible liar.

His head tipped as he studied her. "I thought that'd at least garner a smirk. I mean, come on. Barbie house? That's funny."

She shrugged. "Guess I'm not feeling humorous."

A gust of wind lifted his curls, but he didn't let that distract him. "You weren't last night either. Things were good in the morning, but when I came home for dinner, you were closed off. Care to share what happened that still has you upset?"

No sense beating around the bush. "I spotted your tail again."

A deep line carved between his eyebrows as he jammed them together. "Someone was following you?"

His surprise seemed so genuine, she straightened. "Yeah. Burt. You had him following me before our trip, which I didn't like but understood. But I never expected to see him yesterday."

"Everleigh"—he spoke her name slowly, with a hint of confusion and concern—"I never asked Burt to follow you. Not before we left and certainly not since we've returned."

Now she was confused, and yeah, maybe a little concerned. "You're being serious right now?"

He nodded. "What was the car following you?"

"A black Buick."

"Model and year?"

She snorted. "You're lucky I knew it was a Buick."

Niles pulled out his phone and tapped. After a moment, he turned the screen toward her. "Did it look like this?"

Everleigh studied it. "It was an SUV like Burt's, yes."

"So this one specifically?"

"I think so?" She tugged on his hand, pulling the phone closer. "Wait. That's not the same grill. The one I saw wasn't like that, it was smaller. Simpler."

"Then it wasn't Burt because this is what he drives." He scrolled through a few more pictures to see if she recognized any of the models. She stopped him on the Encore. "You're sure?" he asked.

"I'm not even one hundred percent sure it was a Buick now that I'm looking at the pictures."

He practically growled as he scrubbed a hand through his hair. "Fine. Did you see them today too?"

"Not yet."

"If you do, call." His dark brown eyes latched on to hers. "With everything you have going on between Palmer and searching for this diamond, someone following you is at the least suspicious. At the most, dangerous. So please, do not pull what you did with me and approach them." When she hesitated, he followed it up with, "Promise me."

His earnest request was more enticing than that cologne he wore. "Fine, I promise. If *you* promise to help me get this door open."

His turn to hesitate, as if he wasn't quite ready to release the subject. She was, however, and the look she gave must have convinced him, because he sighed. Another gust of wind had him pulling a rubber band from his pocket to secure his hair. "Do you really think you're going to find anything in this place?"

"Pretty sure you can answer that based on my bobby pin's current location."

He side-eyed her before kneeling at the doorknob again. Another minute and he triumphantly tossed the misshapen pin at her. Then, without a word, he pulled a tool from his back pocket and resumed his work. In under thirty seconds, the doorknob clicked. Niles stood and turned around, blocking her path. "You haven't actually done anything that could get you in trouble. Yet. You sure you want to go inside?"

"I'm allowed. It's my place of business."

"To which you haven't been given a key."

She crossed her arms. "You're the one who agreed to pick the lock, and now you're having second thoughts?"

"I needed to fulfill my part of our deal. I helped you get the door open. You said nothing about helping you enter."

"It was assumed."

"But not stated. Therefore, not a part of our arrangement."

Her turn to growl, especially with the impudent grin he added. "Never assume with Niles again. Point taken. Now if you'll excuse me." She made to go around him.

He remained a solid wall in front of her. "How about we grab some lunch and talk over the merits of this decision."

"Or how about *you* go have lunch while I satiate my curiosity. It's far hungrier than my stomach."

Which, of course, decided to noisily defy her at that exact moment.

Niles grinned. "I'm finding that hard to believe." When she refused to allow her own smile to break, he leaned against the door. "What do you say? I know a really great burger place on Route 66." He spoke into her hesitation. "I don't see cameras out here, but it's a good bet he has them inside."

"He's already told us he doesn't. Brooke looked for them on the first day." She wouldn't be trying this little stunt otherwise.

"Follow that through, Everleigh. If Caspar had something hidden here, would he leave it sitting around? With this flimsy lock and no cameras?"

Okay. That hurt on two levels. First, the lock hadn't proved flimsy to her. Second, Niles was one hundred percent right. Darn it. In her over-zealousness to put together who Caspar was, she'd overlooked obvious pieces. She never missed connecting such evident dots.

"You know what will help that feeling of defeat?" Niles's voice held too much cheer.

She fisted her hands on her hips and nailed him with a perturbed look.

He chuckled as he cracked open the door, pressed something on the handle, then closed it again, effectively erasing their work. Well, her attempt and *his* work. He tugged on her forearm as he headed for the steps. "A burger. Come on." They hit the gravel drive. "Want to ride with me, and we'll come back for your car?"

"I'm good, but thanks." She separated from his hold and headed for her beat-up Ford.

"You sure? Place is called Nelly's and they have the best burgers around." He tempted her from over the roof of his silver Honda, a perfectly nondescript car for tailing and spying on people. She shivered at the reminder that someone was following her—someone not sanctioned by Niles—and he caught it. He gave her an appraising glance. "We can brainstorm who might be the owner of that black SUV. Maybe even nail down the make and model."

She nearly gave in until she noticed the time. Enough to do a quick look-see inside, but not nearly enough to grab that burger. "I appreciate the offer, Niles, but I promised your aunt I'd be back by one." The typical rush of relief that flooded in when her busy schedule provided a legit excuse from socializing didn't appear. Instead, she felt something akin to disappointment.

Niles didn't seem to register the same feeling. "Next time then, minus the attempt at B&E." He ducked into his car and sped off before she had hers turned on.

Strange. The word encompassed the entire past fifteen minutes.

She started her car and headed for Gertrude's. She'd gone from upset with Niles to navigating these weird feelings his concern evoked. They'd even dipped their toes into flirting again. And since when did she feel let down about not having lunch with someone, especially a guy? Or affronted when the other person wasn't upset at her refusal? She was as messed up and inexperienced as a teenage girl with her first crush.

Honestly, what she saw as flirting, he probably wrote off as simple communication. Underneath his bearlike ways, Niles had an easiness about him. A light, teasing tone that pulled the same from her. The playfulness didn't mean anything, but with her rusty people skills, she misconstrued things. Sure, she excelled at providing care for her patients, but this entire peer relationship phenomenon was so not her thing. Be it with men or women.

Everleigh parked by the curb outside Gertrude's, entered the house, and hung her jacket on one of the hooks. "Gertrude? Burt?"

"In here." Gertrude's voice came from the small eating nook off the kitchen.

Everleigh joined them. "Hopefully your morning was more productive than mine." She grabbed a soda from the fridge and settled at the round table. Pink roses took up the center of the tabletop. Burt had arrived with them this morning and arranged them in the milky white vase. It wasn't the first time, and judging by how much Gertrude loved their scent, it wouldn't be the last.

"Burt's been taking good care of our clients." Gertrude's hand rested on a teacup in front of her. "I'd hire him full-time if he didn't have those grandkids to play with."

"You know I'd take you up on it in a heartbeat, Gertie."

Everleigh didn't doubt it, what with the way his gaze always held complete adoration. Had that gleam been in his eyes a long time, or did he feel free to bestow it now that Gertrude couldn't notice?

Gertie tsked. "Your memories should be with those kids, not taking pictures of cheating spouses."

"How about you let me decide what memories I want to be making." His gruff voice held no debate.

Huh. With the blush creeping up Gertrude's cheeks, maybe she was a whole lot more aware of his adoration than Everleigh suspected.

"Always have been a stubborn mule," Gertie mumbled.

"Guess that makes us a good pair." He stood and took his own mug to the sink and washed it. Turning, he addressed them both. "You don't leave until Monday?"

"Correct," Gertie replied. Hopefully, she'd use this week to catch up on her rest. "We should only be gone a few days."

"Don't worry if it's longer. I'll keep everything covered here." He placed his mug in the cupboard, squeezed Gertrude's shoulder in a goodbye, and headed out.

Everleigh settled beside the old woman. "What would you like to do with the rest of your day?"

"Hop on my Harley and ride up Route 66. Kayak Lake Orion. Play pickleball." Her fingers tightened on her teacup. "But I suppose I'll finish my tea instead, then take a rest."

This was the first time she'd witnessed even a hint of self-pity in Gertrude. The woman's pervasive strength in the face of all she'd lost always pushed to the forefront. But even the strongest of people had their breaking point. While she wasn't sure what had brought Gertrude to the edge of hers, Everleigh had no intentions of letting her wallow there.

"Come on." She took Gertrude's tea from her and slid it out of reach before pulling her to her feet.

"Hey!" Gertrude protested. "I said I was going to finish that first and then rest."

But Everleigh refused to let go. She didn't know how to drive a Harley, had no clue where Lake Orion was or how to play pickleball, but this small town contained plenty of other things to do.

She led a protesting Gertrude to her car.

"Kidnapping's a federal offense," the woman grumbled.

"Lucky for me, you're retired and can't arrest me."

"Honey," Gertrude said as Everleigh pushed her into the passenger seat, "I may be retired, but I know people who can make you disappear and ensure no one asks questions."

Everleigh slammed the door on Gertrude's bad mood. No idea what had triggered it, but the rareness of this moment prevented Everleigh's own mood from sinking to meet Gertrude's. Something obviously bothered her, and the last ten minutes suggested that Burt's presence somehow created the catalyst to Gertrude's sour attitude. Everleigh didn't need any more pieces. The heart was a mystery no one solved, they simply tried their best to understand.

Everleigh climbed into the driver's seat and took off. Gertrude remained petulant beside her, but she also remained silent. After a few turns and a brief stint on Route 66, Everleigh pulled into the parking lot of their destination. She climbed out, circled the car, and opened Gertrude's door.

"Come on." She tugged.

Gertrude didn't budge.

Leaning down, Everleigh gently gripped her arm. "My mom always taught me that the best cure for a bad mood was laughter."

"I'm not in a humorous mood."

"I know." And it was understandable, but not irreversible. The thing was, Gertrude had allowed her sullen mood to take root, and now they'd need to battle it off. Bad moods didn't disappear on their own. One had to work at removing them. Attitude often boiled down to a choice, but sometimes a person needed help finding the joyful option. "But I'm hoping to change that."

Gertrude sighed and allowed Everleigh to help her from the car. "Where are we?"

"Freddy's Fun Zone." The family entertainment center had go-karts, a seated zip line, and bumper boats. All of which offered two-person options. She clapped her hands together. "You up for some fun?"

Joy-filled screams mixed with the screech of tires as go-karts raced around the track on the other side of the fence. The scent of burning rubber, hot dogs, and chlorinated water from the unnaturally blue pond permeated the air. Gertrude unfolded her arms and her attitude. "Okay. Let's go. But I want a slushie before this is over."

Everleigh smiled. "Deal."

CHAPTER NINETEEN

"Thanks, Everleigh." A worn-out Gertrude offered the words as Everleigh helped her from the car. They'd spent the past three hours in the fresh air and spring sunshine. Gertrude couldn't see any of what they did, but she participated with the gleefulness of a child. Watching her bad mood slide off felt better than when she'd finished the KGB Interrogation at Indianapolis's The Escape Room in record time. A record she still held for a room with less than a five percent success rate.

"My pleasure." And it was. Caretaking had rooted into her heart from a young age. Her predominant memories of Mom were ones spent sitting beside her while she battled recurring illnesses. Doctors questioned why a disease typically so manageable instead raged against her body. Everleigh stopped questioning it years ago. Why repeatedly ask something there was no answer to? She never figured out if God's lack of response was because he preferred silence or if he was simply indifferent to her. Either way, her relationship with God became another one where she'd added distance. It was easier to focus on the things she could solve rather than questions that stumped her.

So while she couldn't change Mom's reality, she could often change her situation, and she threw herself into doing that. Seeing Mom's pain abate even for a brief moment became all the reward she needed.

Gertrude squeezed her arm gently, bringing her back to the present. "I'm sorry for my melancholy earlier. Sometimes it hits me, how fast time goes. That realization can punch harder than some of the hits I took when chasing a runner." A wistfulness lifted her cheeks. She turned toward

Everleigh, an earnestness to her movement. "You remind me of myself. Strong. Independent." They climbed the porch steps. "You think those are good qualities, and in some ways they are, but if I had it all to do over again, I'd—" The front door swung open, interrupting her. Niles looked at her then Gertrude, his gaze landing on the giant purple giraffe Gertrude held.

"Fun afternoon?" he asked.

Everleigh ignored him and focused on Gertrude. Whatever she was about to share felt like words Everleigh needed even worse than the hot dog she had scarfed down earlier to quiet her empty stomach. Because, truth was, her heart felt even emptier, and Gertrude seemed poised to feed it. "You'd what, Gertrude?"

But Niles opening the door had shut down whatever she was about to say.

"We had a wonderful day," Gertrude proclaimed as she scooted past him into the hall. "Now I'm exhausted and going to bed."

He met Everleigh's eyes over the top of his aunt's head. She answered his unspoken question. "We went to Freddy's Fun Zone."

"Everleigh won me the giraffe by besting the magician at the card table. He underestimated her."

Niles grinned. "I have no doubt." He followed them toward the stairs. "You already ate?"

"We did," Everleigh said as she followed Gertrude with a hand between her shoulders.

With her cane, Gertrude felt for the first step and started up. She reached the landing and tapped down the hall, the path familiar. Her free hand trailed along the wall, and she stopped outside her bedroom. "If you'll get me my pajamas, I'll be all set."

"Sure thing." Everleigh opened her door.

"Niles?" Gertrude asked as she stepped inside her room.

"Yes?"

"You fire up the Harley and take Everleigh on a ride. She told me there wasn't a cloud in the sky, which means a beautiful sunset and gorgeous view of the stars. That was always my favorite time to ride."

Everleigh put the brakes on. "He's got too much work to take me on a joyride."

"Actually," Niles started, "I already planned on taking one. I could use a breather, and a ride always rejuvenates me."

"There." Gertrude had settled herself onto the edge of her bed. "Sounds like you'll be helping him."

"He doesn't need me tagging along." Everleigh handed her pj's to her.

Gertrude grabbed Everleigh's wrist. "You didn't let me sit in this house all day. I'm not letting you sit here all night. You're young. You need some adventure." Her words functioned like hints pointing toward the wisdom she nearly shared earlier. It was her next sentence, however, that she could have happily left off. "Get on that Harley with my handsome nephew and enjoy this beautiful night."

Heat rushed up her neck, and she cut her eyes to Niles, who leaned against the doorframe, arms crossed, entirely amused by the moment. His shoulders lifted in a shrug. "She is your boss."

"It's past work hours."

"Aren't you the one who tried telling me caregivers work twenty-four seven?" Gertrude tossed out.

Of course she'd remembered that.

Outside the sun dipped lower in the sky, and soft pastels blended with the blue edges of early evening. She hedged. The offer sounded enticing. What was it about Niles that tempted her to lean in when she normally ducked out?

He read the indecision on her face and waited for it to play out as if he were totally confident of the outcome. So it didn't surprise her when she sighed and gave in with, "All right, I'll go," that he pushed off the door-jamb with a grin.

"I'll dust off your helmet and start her up."

Everleigh made sure Gertrude had everything she needed before leaving her for the night.

"Have fun." Gertrude slipped the expectation-laden words in as the door shut.

Niles waited for Everleigh in the entryway.

"I thought you were starting the motorcycle."

"Wanted to be sure you grabbed the right stuff." He held out a leather jacket several sizes too big for her. No doubt it was his.

"That's not my size."

"Doesn't have to be. Just needs to protect you should we take a spill."

She wrinkled her brow. "You planning on that?"

He leaned in and wrapped the jacket around her, motioning her to slide her arms into the sleeves. All the while, she felt his warm gaze on her. "There's lots of things in life you don't plan on happening, Everleigh. You just do your best to prepare for them." The man didn't need his mouth to smile with, because his espresso eyes conveyed more than enough emotion. Though, she had no doubt his lips would be expert communicators if she ever indulged in their conversation. He tugged on the collar, sending her even farther off-balance. "All set?"

She swallowed. Nodded.

He turned to open the door, waving her past. "Let's go." He closed the door behind them. "I followed you back to my aunt's from Caspar's today, but didn't see anyone tailing you."

There went that swirl of warmth through her middle again. "How did I not see you?"

"Because I'm good."

She stopped beside his bike and gave him some sass. "And yet I spotted you before."

"One, I'd underestimated you—"

"Your first mistake."

He tipped his head at her interruption. "Finished?"

"Maybe."

His light snort conveyed more amusement than frustration at the sauce she was slinging his way. "Second, I knew where you were going so I could hang back. Now, if you're nice, I'll tell you what else I discovered."

She tapped a finger against her chin.

"Well?" he prodded.

"Just trying to decide if what you've discovered is something I haven't already uncovered myself."

"That's it." He handed her a helmet and reached for his.

"I'm kidding. I promise. I'd love to know everything you know."

He stuck the key in his ignition. "Not possible in one night. Not even two. Maybe three, but I don't think you can sit still that long."

She groaned. "A regular comedian."

His grin twisted those ribbons dancing in her stomach even tighter. "Better than a bear. We're making progress."

She patted his chest. "You do actually know who Yogi is, right?"

He leveled a salty look at her, but his eyes still danced. The moment stretched until his gaze flickered to where she touched him. When he blinked back to her, she read his intentions and quickly removed her hand. There went her mouth and hormones taking her places she wasn't ready for yet.

"So." She cleared her throat. "You were telling me what else you found out."

He one hundred percent caught her diversion tactic but was gentleman enough to respect it. "Palmer doesn't own a black SUV that I can find. I've put out feelers to see if he's hired a PI to follow you."

"How can you find that out?"

"I have my ways." He tapped her helmet. "Strap that on and let's get going."

Gladly.

Once they both had their helmets fastened, she situated herself behind him. Wrapping her arms around his waist, she inhaled his peppery scent, made even stronger since she wore his jacket. She might be the one holding on to him, and yet somehow he'd managed to surround her.

"Ever ridden before?" he asked.

"Nope."

"Okay. All you have to do is relax your body into mine and lean with me. Think you can do that?"

"Sounds simple enough."

His shoulders shook with what she guessed was laughter.

"What?" She replayed her words, not seeing any humor in them.

"Nothing." He shook his head as if her missing the punch line didn't surprise him. Turning the key, he called over his shoulder, "Hold on."

She tightened her grip and rested her chin between his shoulder blades. As they took the first curve, she felt Niles's body shift. Instinct told her to stiffen and hold herself upright, but she fought the feeling, instead forcing herself to fluidly move with him. His back rumbled under her chin again, and she fought another urge—to swat him.

They headed out of town, turning onto Route 66. Fields bathed in the golden glow of twilight passed on either side of them. Not awakened yet from winter, the dry rows fanned out in a perfect symmetry that created a hypnotic feel as they flickered along. Old wooden power poles dotted the landscape in even proportion, and in the distance a John Deere kicked up dust as it plowed along.

Her muscles slowly relaxed, and she loosened her hold around his waist, turning her head to better see all of nature flowing past. Night air rushed against her cheeks, cool but not cold. She burrowed into Niles's leather jacket and stared into the distance where the moon began its rise. The purring engine revved as Niles navigated a corner, and this time she moved lithely with him. She could see why Gertrude loved this.

A half hour later, when the sky held only a whisper of light, Niles coasted into a dirt lot toward the top of a forested hill and cut the engine. "Careful," he said as he stood. "Your legs will feel a little wonky."

She swung off then grabbed the seat to balance herself.

"Told you." He smirked. After nabbing a wool blanket from a bag over the rear wheel, he motioned toward a trail marked by two log posts jammed vertically into the ground. "Come on. I'll show you one of Aunt Gertie's favorite spots."

The place had to be popular because other cars and motorcycles filled the lot. They passed the log entrance and darkness cloaked them. Niles reached for her hand—not in a romantic gesture, but to help guide her.

Though her pattering heart wanted to argue that thought.

"It's only a few feet through here. Well worth a walk in the dark," he reassured.

True enough, she could already see moonlight pressing through the opening ahead. She also heard voices. They stepped from the trees into a wide-open rocky area overlooking a valley below. Above, stars blinked alive in the night sky. The nearly full moon bathed everyone in a milky glow, making it feel as if they were inside a black-and-white photo. People spread out blankets around them, watching the show. Some shoulder to shoulder, some cuddling.

Niles spread the blanket out for them to sit on. "Thanks for taking my aunt out today." He waited until she sat, then settled beside her. He removed his leather jacket, the toes of Winnie-the-Pooh sneaking out past his rolled-up T-shirt sleeves. He caught her staring and shook his head but didn't try to hide his tattoo.

They both stretched their legs in front of them and reclined on their palms. Everleigh crossed her ankles and peered up at the sky. This was better than any TV show she would be in her room watching. "She needed it. Most days she handles the progression of her disease in a way that makes her seem superhuman. Today something seemed to slip past her defenses. Could be because she's tired from all her travel. Or could be that we all have down days."

"Even you?" He nudged her with his shoulder.

"Sure." No sense lying when he wouldn't believe her anyway. Better to offer truth but keep it simple so he didn't drag the conversation into deep waters.

Apparently, he wanted to go swimming though.

"What were you and my aunt chatting about when you came home earlier? I opened the door in the middle of your conversation."

She frowned in pretend thought. "Pretty sure it was just about our day."

Like any good PI, he wasn't buying what she was selling, not when it was rotten. "Really?" he pressed. "Because she was saying something about if she had to do it all over again . . . like she was talking about her past." Before she could answer, he held up his hand. "And I don't mean the past few hours with you."

Darn it. The man was good.

"Honestly, I'm not sure exactly what she was going to say, but if I had to guess—"

"Please do," he coaxed.

"She thinks I'm too independent, and I remind her of herself. At least that's where the conversation seemed to be headed."

His head tipped. "She's not off base."

"No, she's not." At least with her observation, not her supposition. "But independence isn't a bad thing."

"You sure about that?"

"Absolutely."

He eyed her. "Even when it keeps all your relationships at a distance?"

"That's quite a leap to make. Independent people still have relationships."

Beside them someone called, "Anyone know how to jump a car?"

They both turned. Two teenagers stood a few feet away. Niles stood. "I can help." Relief flooded their faces. He turned back to her. "You okay here? Or do you want to come?"

"I'm fine."

"All right. I'll be back."

He trudged off with the teens, leaving Everleigh alone with the night sky and her thoughts. She really only wanted to entertain one of those two things, yet her thoughts still crept in. Ever since this entire crazy detour started, she'd been forced to take a hard look at what she'd always considered her personality traits. Introspection was never fun.

She lowered from resting on her palms to her forearms and stared at the moon. Tonight it glowed in a near perfect circle. In a few weeks, it would be barely a thumbnail. Even the moon went through phases. Question was, the phase she now lived in, was it full or only a hint of what it could be?

Niles's challenge poked at her. Mentally wiggling away, she started picking out constellations in the sky. She counted five—okay, three she'd made up herself—by the time he rejoined her.

"Everything all set?" she asked as he settled onto the blanket.

He brushed his hands against his jeans. "Yep. They'll even be home in time for his date to make curfew."

"That's one thankful young man."

Niles chuckled. "You have no idea."

"You kept a girl out beyond curfew before?"

"One time. That's all it took." He reclined, his arm pressing against hers. "You ever stay out with a boy after curfew?"

"One time. That's all it took." She repeated his words lightly, though they pressed against her with the weight of a bad memory. The very next day after that date, she'd been accused of stealing someone's boyfriend. There'd been no stealing involved. The boy willingly issued the invitation while withholding the fact that he already had a girlfriend. The moment Everleigh realized it, she broke things off. Unfortunately, that's not how the story went—not when he tried to save face and his relationship by providing his girlfriend with an alternate narrative.

Niles studied her. They sat close enough that even in this dim lighting, she could see the crinkles around his eyes. After a moment, he swung his gaze to the stars overhead.

Released from his intense scrutiny, Everleigh let out her breath. Relaxed.

"Let's circle back to your response that independent people have relationships."

Only to tense when she realized he'd simply changed direction. But just because he went there didn't mean she had to join him. "Oh, you mean my response to your off-base comment?"

"How are you getting along with Natalie and Brooke?"

He sure enjoyed curveball conversations. She was learning to navigate them at a faster rate. "Fine."

"Why weren't they helping you with your B&E this afternoon?"

"We never made it to the E part, you recall." When he dropped a "be serious" look on her, she sat up, crisscrossed her legs, and wiped her palms on her jeans. "Fine. Because I didn't invite them."

"Why would that be? If you're supposed to be partners?"

"If you're trying to get me to admit that it's because I work better alone, that's not groundbreaking news. I do."

"And that attitude hasn't affected your relationships with them?"

She said nothing.

"Look, Everleigh, you've mentioned how you want people to believe the best about you. But that's a pretty tall order if you don't also let them get to know you." When she still didn't respond, he continued. "You want to be trusted, but you don't want to be known. Yet, those two things go hand in hand."

"It's good to be guarded."

He nodded. "True. It's important to know how to create healthy boundaries. Not everyone deserves the right to your heart, especially when they've proven to be untrustworthy." His words scratched over that last part, as if emotional memories captured the words on their way out. "But there's a difference between putting walls up to protect yourself versus walls that hold you captive."

"I'm not a prisoner."

"You make relationships freely then?"

His question echoed her own internal debate from these past few weeks. She still hadn't arrived at any solid answers in the whole relationship conundrum, but recently solitude wasn't as comfortable as it had once been. Had she outgrown it?

When she didn't answer, he let the conversation settle. No doubt it was so she could keep chewing on his advice much like she'd chewed on her earlier dinner at Fred's Fun Zone. The beefy hot dog had been pleasantly palatable. His counsel, however, reminded her of brussels sprouts. Nourishing, but it went down with difficulty.

After a few minutes, he stood. "How about we head home and put together a puzzle. Aunt Gertie has several of them on the shelf."

"I've seen."

He offered her his hand and pulled her to her feet. "Ready?"

To hop on the back of the Harley and ride? Yes. Tackle a puzzle? Absolutely. But to take on the change his words attempted to provoke?

Not even close.

CHAPTER TWENTY

Archduchess Adelheid, age twenty-six
Royalston, Massachusetts, 1940

How MANY TIMES WOULD HER life be uprooted?

Adelheid gazed at the white colonial home in front of her and forced her smile not to wobble. Mother, dressed in her ever-present black since Papa's passing, shook Mr. Calvin Bullock's hand.

"Welcome to La Bastille." His deep voice boomed warm and friendly.

"Thank you for having us here." Mother responded in kind.

Their host waved his hand out for them to move in front of him. "Please, come inside."

She and her siblings followed, stepping into the home and what Mr. Calvin Bullock referred to as their reception room. By far, it paled in comparison to the rooms they'd maintained at different palaces, but the atmosphere held the promise of safety. The assurance of such a hope had been decidedly absent ever since the first bombs from Germany hit their home in Belgium. Hitler himself seemed to chase them to France and then on to Portugal. Now an ocean separated them from the atrocities happening throughout Europe. Two years ago, she'd mourned Hitler's acquisition of her Vienna, hopeful his thirst for power would dry out, but his spread of evil remained unquenched. Waves of relief and guilt banded around her heart as she now stood secure on American soil when so many others couldn't escape.

"You made it." Her brother Otto had come ahead to ensure they had refuge here. He placed a kiss on Mother's cheek before embracing each of his siblings. When he reached Adelheid, he whispered in her ear. "I have a letter from Luciana. It arrived this morning."

"She is safe?"

He nodded. "Her entire family returned to Madeira for now."

As he spoke, something tugged on Adelheid's skirt. She glanced down. No, not something. Someone. Two giant blue eyes sparkled up at her from a tiny blond-haired cherub.

"Oh, goodness." A woman scurried near and grabbed the toddler's hand. "Fleur, stay by Mother." The brunette nervously glanced at Adelheid. "I'm sorry, Archduchess."

"Please," Adelheid ruffled the little girl's curls. "It's Adelheid. And please, do not apologize. She's precious."

A twinge of sadness that she remained unmarried and childless washed over her. Yet another outcome of the constant upheaval in all their lives. Neither she nor any of her siblings had found their match. "How old is she?" Adelheid asked the child's mother.

"She's three." She took a step backward, Fleur's hand still in hers, and stood beside a man holding a baby.

Mother continued in conversation with Mr. Bullock and his wife. Otto stepped over to the young family. "Adelheid, this is Calvin's son Hugh, Hugh's wife, Marie, and their daughters." He motioned to the toddler. "You've already met Fleur, and Hugh is holding Fair."

Fleur and Fair. What unique names.

Adelheid joined them and peered down at chubby-cheeked baby Fair in Hugh's arms who couldn't have been more than a few months old. She glanced at Marie, who nervously nibbled her lip then caught herself doing so and blushed. Oh, how this young woman made her miss Luciana even more. It had been too long since she'd been with anyone her age, and her heart yearned for a daily companion to confide in. No one could replace Luciana, but perhaps her heart could expand to include another friend.

Adelheid touched Marie's arms and shared a smile with her that spoke of companionship. "Your daughters are beautiful."

"Thank you."

The next week proved she'd read Marie's desire for friendship correctly. They saw each other daily, sometimes with Fleur and Fair, sometimes without, always with a building affection between them. They shared their dreams. Well-educated, Marie enjoyed the arts. While gifted musically, her love of poetry was her true passion, and she wished to someday help poets become as well respected as other writers. Adelheid, in turn, spoke of her desire for a home she didn't need to move from. One shared by a loving husband and overflowing with children . . . a family she could one day return with to her beloved Vienna. Marie listened with understanding nods and reassurances.

Their growing friendship granted the burgeoning ability to read each other's expressions. So it was that during her second full week at La Bastille, when a commotion pulled them from their afternoon tea, Adelheid easily recognized what Marie had planned.

"William!" Marie stood from the couch and called to the young man who'd burst through the front door. The wind and rain outside had blown it against the wall, the smacking thud arresting their attention. "You came. Even in the rain." Her face shone with sweet intention as she flickered her gaze from her wet friend to Adelheid. "William's been in New York, visiting family. He arrived home only yesterday evening, so I wasn't sure if he'd accept my invitation."

William removed his dripping hat and hung it on the hall tree along with his overcoat. Ducking into the parlor, he smiled at Marie. "You mentioned it was of great importance." His eyes scanned the room as if seeking clarification.

She slipped her lip between her teeth as she continued to furtively glance from Adelheid to William. "Yes. I did, didn't I?" Standing between them, she made introductions. "This is my new friend, Adelheid."

Romantic arrangements weren't unheard of in her world, though tradition imparted the parents designed them. Here, it seemed, her new friend constructed this "chance" meeting. Politely smiling, Adelheid stood and offered her hand to William. "Pleasure to meet you."

His grasp was warm, in spite of the rain he'd run through, and he enchanted her. "The pleasure is mine." The sweetest caramel coated his deeply voiced words, the sound reverberating through her with the power to set her heartbeat into a new rhythm. One that played out a song she instinctively knew would always belong to him. His eyes, the color of her favorite flowers in Schönbrunn Palace's garden, bloomed with a matching interest.

Years ago, Luciana spoke of when she'd first met Angus, how her entire world changed in one breath. While excited for her friend, Adelheid couldn't understand how one's heart could belong to another so quickly.

Now she knew.

Without releasing Adelheid's hand, William glanced warmly toward Marie. "You were right. Coming today was of utmost importance."

And, it seemed, William knew it too.

CHAPTER TWENTY-ONE

THE SMALL TOWN OF ROYALSTON, Massachusetts, nestled itself along the border of southern New Hampshire. It boasted historic buildings, a town common, and plenty of natural beauty. One lake, a small pond, three waterfalls, and miles of hiking trails through thick forest all gifted the town with plenty of reasons to visit. Sufficient lodging within its city limits, however, was the one thing Royalston lacked. Thus, John had secured them rooms at Cranberry Meadow Farm Bed and Breakfast situated in Peterborough, New Hampshire, only forty minutes north. They'd flown in last night, slept in cozy beds, and enjoyed a homemade breakfast before heading out for a full day.

"Now I can check both these states off my list." Natalie watched the passing countryside as Niles drove them to Royalston, where they'd split up for their appointments with various people. "Mason and I always talked about traveling out East." An idea must have hit her because she straightened and pulled her phone from her purse. "Do you guys mind if I FaceTime him?"

"Not at all," Brooke responded, her answer matching their nods.

Honestly, Everleigh was curious to see her husband. Natalie rarely spoke about him, let alone to him. She'd attempted to call Mason several times on their trips, but he never answered. Though, maybe they found time to catch up when she was alone in her room at night.

The phone continued to ring and after nearly a minute, Natalie sighed. "He's probably busy at school. I'm sure he'll call back later."

Seated behind her, Brooke leaned forward and squeezed her shoulder.

"You should book a stay at Cranberry Meadow Farm before we leave, because once he sees that place, he's going to want to come here with you. I have no doubt."

The edge of Natalie's lip curled up in a half-hearted attempt at a smile. "Yeah. Maybe."

"No maybe." Brooke cast a pointed glance at Everleigh. "That place is incredibly romantic. Any husband would want to whisk his wife there, right, Everleigh?"

She knew nothing about cheering up friends. It was like a language she'd never taken, so she had no clue how to speak it. As if sensing her awkward cluelessness, Niles's eyes crinkled along the edges as they met hers in the rearview.

"I'm not a husband, but I concur with Brooke's assessment." Niles navigated around a curve, forest and fields on both sides of them. "Only with one small caveat. Guys don't think of places as romantic. We don't really think of anything as romantic. But if it's important to you, it's important to us." He paused. "Maybe don't bring up all the history in this place, though. I'd lead with all the hiking trails and outdoorsy stuff."

Natalie mulled his words over. "Mason does like being active."

Gertrude swiveled in her seat. Her lifelong habit of facing people when she spoke to them hadn't changed simply because she couldn't see any longer. "That's all great advice, but it's even more simple. If you want to come here together, tell him. Only the good Lord is a mind reader, so speak yours clearly or don't be upset when someone doesn't hear what you're thinking."

That silenced them all, until ever so slowly, laughter broke out between them.

"And that, folks, is what I got to grow up with." Niles stopped at a four-way. His eyes filled with tender adoration as they swept over his aunt. "The amazing wisdom of my Aunt Gertrude."

Gertrude turned toward him, her thin brow arched, the movement accentuating the wrinkles across her forehead. "Only works if you listen to it." Their shared tenderness permeated her voice, even as she teased.

He flicked on his blinker and turned right. "Then good thing I always listen to you."

It was Gertrude's turn to laugh.

They finished the remaining twenty-minute drive with ABBA blaring from the speakers and Gertrude demonstrating her knowledge of every single lyric. Brooke's voice rang from behind as "Dancing Queen" played. Then Natalie's as the strands of "Mamma Mia" began. But it was when "Take a Chance on Me" started that Niles's baritone joined them.

It was like their own little version of *Carpool Karaoke*, and she was watching their episode.

"Come on, Everleigh, join us." Gertrude broke from the lyrics long enough to state her request.

"I'm good, but thanks."

They only sang louder.

Blessedly, Royalston Common came into view as Niles navigated a bend in Fitzwilliam Road. They drove past the library to their right, and Natalie pressed her nose to the window. "I would work there in a heartbeat."

A small redbrick building with blooming hydrangea bushes flanking white stone steps that led to an intricate wooden door, it was one of the most adorable libraries Everleigh had ever seen. Every detail added to its appeal, from the gingerbread trim along the eaves to the arched window tops. Even the picnic tables set outside invited patrons to enjoy their lunch and a good book.

"I can see why," Everleigh agreed before describing the building in great detail to Gertrude.

Continuing down the street, they passed Royalston Town Hall. Victorian in nature with a black mansard roof, the building shared a circular drive with First Congregational Church. Mature trees wrapped around the classic white, steepled church, creating a postcard-perfect moment one would expect to find in every small-town America. Across the street from these stood La Bastille, the home they hoped to tour later today. Natalie had a call in to the current owners, but she hadn't heard from them yet. Niles slowed as they drove past.

"It must have been hard on Adelheid, coming here." Natalie's contemplation wasn't surprising. She always seemed tuned in to how others felt. "She had to leave so many places, but at least she remained in Europe. Here, there's nothing familiar. I mean, it's beautiful, but this isn't a castle. Our customs were different. And the ocean is nowhere near."

Niles sniffed. "But I bet we can still get some good lobstah."

Everleigh groaned. "Even if I wasn't allergic, I'd still be turned off by your awful attempt at a Boston accent."

"Awful? I think you meant amazing."

"Yeah. Let's go with that." She bathed her words in thick sarcasm.

Picking up speed, Niles continued down the street. The Old School-house sat in a triangular patch of grass at a Y-intersection. Another white building, this one in Greek Revival style with a square tower rising from the center, it housed both the Royalston Post Office and the Royalston Historical Society.

"That's where our meeting is this morning." Niles nodded to the building as they passed it. They planned on dropping Natalie and Brooke at the town clerk's office first, then circling back to meet with the woman in charge of the historical society. She claimed to have several pictures and articles from when the Habsburgs stayed with the Bullocks.

A few minutes later, they reached yet another white building.

"I'm noticing a trend in this town," Brooke said from the back seat as she nodded to the small church next door. "White clapboard buildings."

"Suits the time period most of this town was built in." Natalie opened her door and climbed out.

Those two would work here to comb through information Natalie had found on several Wills, Williams, and Bills who could be the mystery man Luciana wrote about in her journal. Edna Bullock, the town clerk, said she'd meet them at ten. Not only did she hold access to some of the vital records they hoped to see, but her last name was Bullock, which meant she might know something about La Bastille and its royal guests.

"We're a little early," Niles noted.

"That's okay. I need to stretch." Gertrude reached for her door handle.

Everleigh hopped out and rounded the SUV to help her. A cool wind buffeted them, and she zipped her sweater. "It's definitely not any warmer out here than it is in Illinois."

"Feels good to me." Brooke turned her face into the wind. She strolled toward the church. "I wonder if it's open."

Her desire to explore all old things never waned. Wired similarly, Natalie followed her. "It's got to be full of history. This entire town is like a gold mine." She turned to Everleigh. "You coming?"

"I'm going to enjoy the fresh air."

With a shrug, Natalie hustled to catch up to Brooke who was already pulling open the church door.

Niles's phone rang. "It's Burt, I better take this." He stepped away.

Next to Everleigh, Gertrude leaned on her cane. After a few minutes, she spoke. "Think they found anything interesting in there?"

"I don't know. Maybe." Honestly, with each minute they remained in the church, her curiosity grew. So did a crazy left-out feeling.

"Then how come you didn't go with them?"

"I wanted to stay by you." A legitimate excuse, though the edges of it felt a little worn.

"Hmm." Gertrude might be blind, but she could read a person just fine. "When a door's opened and you don't walk through, you'll always be on the outside looking in. But you can't complain, because then it's your choice."

Across the lot, a small red sedan pulled up to Town Hall, the arrival stopping Everleigh's response but not her consideration of Gertrude's words. They'd take some time to digest. Seconds later, a short woman with a gray chin-length bob, round face, and pear-shaped middle climbed from the car. She smoothed the front of her cropped pink pants, her navy and white floral top fluttering in the wind. Reaching in, she grabbed a canvas bag from her SUV then straightened. As she did, her gaze finally caught on them.

"Oh, hello!" she called across the lot. "You must be my ten o'clock."

Brooke and Natalie scurried from the church as Edna spoke. "Yes, we are." Natalie met her halfway and shook her hand before making introductions.

Edna repeated all their names as if mentally filing them into the cabinet of her brain. "Come on, then. Why don't we take this inside. I'll brew some coffee because I'm already sure—based on our phone call—that we have lots to speak about." She waddled toward the door. "My husband's great uncle Calvin owned La Bastille, and I've heard stories at every holiday and family reunion since I married into the family. I can't wait to share them." She unlocked the building and led them inside, her commentary continuing. In fact, Everleigh hadn't even seen her take a breath yet. "I always wanted to be a storyteller. I have lots of books in this head of mine should I ever have the time to write one. Until then, working here provides me the opportunity to tell them. Though I don't get people through as often as I used to." She dropped her bag on the counter, momentarily pausing as she did.

Niles leapt on the opportunity. "Everleigh, Gertrude, and I actually have an appointment up the street at the historical society. But I'm sure Brooke and Natalie look forward to hearing all your stories."

Natalie actually did appear interested, but Brooke resembled a deer caught in the headlights of a Mack truck.

Everleigh managed a twinge of guilt, momentarily contemplating if she should stay and provide a bit of a diversion. But then Edna picked up her ramblings once again, and the situation became clear—it was every man for himself.

So when Niles opened the door for her to scoot past, she grabbed Gertrude's arm and made her escape.

➤ ◆

"That was a close one." Niles pulled out of the lot and drove toward the Old Schoolhouse where Betsy Middleton planned to meet them.

"I have no doubt Brooke is already planning her retribution." Everleigh clicked on her seat belt.

Niles slid his sunglasses on. "Whatever it is can't be worse than what we just dodged."

Everleigh wholeheartedly agreed—until she met Betsy Middleton. As gray as Edna with a similar affinity for bright pants, floral shirts, and storytelling, Betsy greeted them with the verve of a former starlet stepping into the spotlight after a decade's absence.

"I've been so anticipating your arrival!" Betsy tugged on the purple pendant she wore on a long gold chain. "After we spoke, I went through all my pictures and every article from when the Bullocks entertained the empress and her family." She leaned in close. "My mother was a housekeeper at La Bastille, and I often accompanied her to work. Fleur and Fair would watch me for her. I don't think that was typical, the help bringing their children in, but the Bullocks were so kind. And Fleur and Fair took a liking to me, at least that's what my mother told me." She showed off

195

the pendant. "This is an amethyst the Bullocks gave my mother. She was convinced it came from Zita herself. Can you believe that? Royalty here in our small town? And then to have a piece of them? This is a treasure right along with all the stories my mother told me."

The Habsburgs had no amethyst in the royal collection, so the chances of that pendant being from them were slim to none, but it definitely made a good story. Which Everleigh now worried there may be more fiction than fact in anything Betsy said, even if she believed every word herself. Words that still flowed in a constant stream. She took fewer breaths than Edna did. Everleigh turned to Niles, holding an entire conversation with their features alone.

Everleigh: It's Edna on steroids.

Niles: We dodged nothing.

Everleigh: Can we still make a break for it?

Niles: No. We're stuck.

Everleigh: Not all of us are needed.

Niles: If you leave, there will be payback.

In the midst of her contemplation, Niles arched his eyebrow even higher. When that didn't stop the hesitation on her face, he shifted to block the door and nailed her with another look that clearly said: You're not getting past me. We're in this together.

All the while, Betsy continued her ramblings.

"Oh, here it is." Her voice lifted nearly an entire octave. She thrust a faded black-and-white photo at them. Two teenagers sat with their arms around a toddler. "This is me with Fair and Fleur when I was four. I must admit, I was a rather cute child, wasn't I?"

"I can't say since I can't see it," Gertrude deadpanned. "But I will take your word for it."

Niles leaned in, rubbing the scruff on his chin. "A safe thing to do, Aunt Gertrude, because she's telling the truth. If anything, she's being incredibly humble, because I'd say she's the most adorable child I've ever seen."

Betsy blushed. And, blessedly, stopped talking.

From behind Betsy, Everleigh conveyed another silent message to Niles: You are a suck-up.

Which she just might be thankful for in this situation.

His innocent shrug accompanied the equally innocent spark in his eyes.

Then he refocused on Betsy. "You seem to have organized everything so well"—he flipped over one of the photos from her stack—"and even wrote notes on the back of each photo."

"Oh, I take my job at the historical society very seriously."

"I can see that." Niles nodded solemnly as he took in the weathered newspapers beside the photos. Most places only stored old papers on microfiche, but Betsy Middleton maintained physical copies as well. She'd pulled only the ones containing articles about the royal family. "Which is why we don't want to keep you from such important work. Do you mind if we take these items you've so carefully curated and sit down over there?" He motioned toward a small table in the window up front. "If we need anything, we know right where to find you. Here, keeping everything in order."

Her blush deepened right along with the smile he flashed her.

Gertrude coughed. Except it wasn't a cough. She was hiding laughter. Her fingers covered tipped-up lips, and a sparkle resembling Niles's lit her eyes.

"I suppose I do have plenty of work to do today." She handed off the paperwork and photos. "I'll check in on you in a little bit to see if you have any questions."

"Thank you, Betsy. You're even a lovelier gem than your amethyst."

Hand to her chest, Betsy fluttered off to her desk. Their heels clacked against the old wood floors as they moved across the room. By the time they settled, Betsy was on the phone.

"I bet she's calling her friends to tell them all about the handsome young man who flirted with her," Everleigh whispered to Gertrude.

Niles, of course, overheard. "You think I'm handsome?"

"No." Everleigh stuck her chin in her hands and mustered a stance of indifference. "But Betsy does."

This time Gertrude didn't even bother to hide her laughter. "Oh, Niles. As helpful as your flirting can be, it's refreshing to meet a woman impervious to your charm."

"You're welcome." Niles sat. "And Everleigh is not impervious to my charm. If anything, I'd say she's more affected than most women."

"I concur." She allowed him his satisfied smirk before finishing her thought. "It's like a burr under my skin that I can't get rid of."

He tossed the newspapers her way. "Hey, Funny Girl, how about you read?" His words landed with the same thud as the papers.

Another peal of laughter from Gertrude. Everleigh slid the stack over, located the first story, and started reading quietly to Gertrude while Niles worked through the photos. He seemed to have some sort of system, because he separated them into right and left piles. By the time she started the fifth article, he had finished his perusal.

"Find anything?" he asked.

Gertrude straightened, blocking the sun streaming through the window. "Not really. At least nothing we didn't already know. The Habsburgs arrived in the summer of 1940, and Calvin and his wife greeted them. His son and daughter-in-law, Hugh and Marie, were there too."

"Marie as in the Marie mentioned in Luciana's journal?" Niles questioned.

Everleigh ran her fingers along the edges of the papers in front of her. "We assume so."

Niles pulled on his lower lip. "Nothing on Will?"

"No." Everleigh shook her head.

"At least not yet," Gertrude added, frustration in her voice.

Niles tapped a photo on the table. "Then you'll be really interested in this."

Everleigh studied the image. Two happy couples, captured in black and white and preserved in time. One of the women was Adelheid.

"You want to know what it says?" he asked.

"I want to know what it looks like." Gertrude harrumphed.

Twin lines deepened between his eyes. "Sorry, Aunt Gertrude." He cleared his throat. "It's a photo of two couples, and Adelheid is in it."

Interest sparked, Gertrude smacked the table. "Now I want to know what it says. My guess is that one of them is named Will?"

"You'd be correct."

"Oh, I wish I could see his face."

Eyes on the photo, Everleigh described the young man standing beside Adelheid. "He was tall and thin, but not skinny. More like trim. And he has a long face with a square jaw. Clean-shaven with kind eyes. My guess is they were brown because they're dark in the photo and so is his hair."

"And he's standing beside Adelheid?" Gertrude questioned.

Everleigh wished Gertrude could see this. "Yep."

"Do you think they were in love?"

This time, Niles answered before Everleigh could. "Definitely."

Everleigh's attention swiveled to him. "What makes you say so?" Not that she disagreed with him, but she was curious how he arrived at his deduction.

He tapped Adelheid's face. "She's not focused on taking the photo. She's focused on him like he's the most important thing in the room. That's the face of a woman in love." He glanced at Everleigh. "Don't act so surprised. A man recognizes that look on a woman's face." Next he tapped Will. "And here? How his arm's around her. That isn't a buddy grip. He's holding her close, tucking her into him like he doesn't want to let her go. Like he treasures her."

Everleigh worked on two things simultaneously. Holding her mouth closed and holding her feelings closer. Both had plenty to say about Niles's observations, and neither needed to be said.

Gertrude pointed their way. "Is there a last name on there?"

Niles was watching Everleigh with a narrowed stare that promised he was trying to read her thoughts—and was succeeding. He pulled his gaze from her to answer his aunt. "Unfortunately, no."

Everleigh gave herself a mental shake and refocused on the photo. Clearing Niles from her head gave her the space to lock in on clues they did have. The two couples stood on a porch, white if she had to guess. There were three steps leading to the railing they leaned on, a window behind them to the right, and a screen door to their left. Three rosebushes lined the front of the porch and lilacs bloomed on either side of them.

"But," she began, "the house this was taken at wasn't La Bastille. My guess is it belonged to Will or his family. If we find the house, we can have Brooke and Natalie pull the township records and see who owned it."

"My thoughts exactly."

Gertrude stood. "Let's roll then."

Niles pulled together the copies Betsy had made them. "You heard the lady. We're rolling."

CHAPTER TWENTY-TWO

They began their search with the homes along On The Common. When that proved futile, they expanded along side streets. Halfway down Warwick, Everleigh called out, "Stop!"

Niles hit the brakes, pulling them off to the side. He surveyed the home that caught her attention, a slow smile spreading over his face. "By George, I think she's found it." Holding up their copy of the photo, he glanced between it and the home's porch.

Hand on the window, Gertrude squinted as if with enough desire, she could see what they were seeing. "Everything matches up?"

"Right down to the rosebushes." Everleigh reached forward and squeezed Gertrude's shoulder. "They're pink."

"I love pink roses." Gertrude's voice was wistful.

Niles's head tipped, no doubt linking the same pieces together as Everleigh had a week ago. "Did that love start before or after Burt began bringing them to you?" he asked.

"Who says he's done it more than once?"

Everleigh wasn't letting her friend off the hook so easily. Not after all the times Gertie had pressed her on things. "The fact that he knew exactly which cupboard held your vases."

"I told you we should hire her," Gertrude said to Niles.

"We already have."

"I mean for our PI firm."

Niles scanned her face, that lazy smirk of his growing. "She'd definitely be fun to take along on stakeouts."

"Niles, dear, remember she doesn't swoon under your flirtatious ways."

"Her blush says otherwise."

Everleigh bristled and opened her window. "That's flush, not blush. It's hot in here."

He tugged on his T-shirt. "Sorry. My fault. I shouldn't have worn one so snug."

"Oh my word, please switch back to the grumpy man I first met. He's much easier to handle."

Niles didn't release his visual hold on her. If anything, it became more intense. "They say there's a fine line between love and hate."

"True." Everleigh pulled out her phone. "Good thing I feel neither."

"No?" His chin dipped in challenge.

"I'm the very definition of indifferent." She tapped Natalie's number and held the phone to her ear as she turned toward the window. The challenge in his eyes had deepened, and she'd heard him as loud and clear as she had when they'd silently communicated about Betsy.

Niles: You're lying, and I can prove it.

Everleigh refused to respond to that dare. There was no way she'd win.

"Hello?" Natalie answered, her voice tossing a lifeline she had no clue she threw.

Doing her best to steady her own voice over her racing pulse, Everleigh returned the greeting before launching into why she'd called. "We have an address we want you to check. We think it's either Will's house or at least his family's. Maybe we can get his last name."

"Oh! We were about to call you! We've narrowed it down to a William Hayes and a William Warner. Both of them were an age that made sense, and both passed away in '44 in the war."

Now her pulse raced for different reasons. She rattled off the house's address. "Check the records and call us back."

Niles started the car. "We can drive there before they have the answer. Tell them we're heading their way."

Everleigh passed on the info. Less than five minutes later, Everleigh guided Gertrude up the stairs of the clerk's office while Niles held open the door.

"You know, you should never trust stairs. They're always up to something," Gertrude said as they reached the top step.

"Really, Aunt Gertie?" Niles groaned. "A pun right now?"

"The only bad time for a pun is 6:30. Hands down."

Laughter sprang from Everleigh. "Nice, Gertie."

"Thank you."

Niles shook his head. "Don't egg her on."

"As if she needs it." Everleigh patted his chest as they passed him and entered the room.

Brooke and Natalie glanced up from the counter where they stood. Judging by their beaming faces, they'd found out which William connected to Adelheid.

"William Hayes." Brooke held up a sheet of paper. "That home belonged to his parents, and he was their oldest child."

Edna joined the conversation. "I remember the family. They were friends of my grandparents." She slowly shook her head. "Terrible how they lost William. He was their only son. Our town lost so many boys in the war. I never knew any of them, that was before I was born, but we remember them and their sacrifices annually."

"Do you know anything about William's relationship with Archduchess Adelheid?" Niles held the photo out to Edna.

"Why that's Hugh and Marie with them." Her pink lipstick cracked as she smiled. "They're my husband's aunt and uncle. Out of all the stories Aunt Marie told, I wish that would have been one of them. A duchess and one of our boys? I bet it was a doozy." She took the photo. "Just look at them. I'd say they were madly in love, but that's the romantic in me."

Outside, a truck beeped as it reversed to empty the recycling beside the building. Gertrude spoke over the noise. "You never overheard any family conversations that could shed some further light on William and Adelheid's connection?"

"Not that I can recall." Edna swirled her wedding ring around her finger. "Though, you know, seeing Aunt Marie with them does support my belief that romance was involved."

"How so?" Natalie questioned.

"The family would often tease Aunt Marie about how she set up all her friends. Practically every couple they knew, my in-laws included, could trace their marriages to Marie introducing them. She'd do it rather quietly too. Some of the couples didn't even know they were being set up at the time." Edna giggled. "She was quite the matchmaker."

"Between that photo, your recollections, and Luciana's journals, I'd say we can be confident that this was Adelheid's Will and they were in love." Everleigh looked at the group who all nodded their agreement.

Brooke's watch beeped. "It's almost noon. Edna set up lunch for us with Fleur. She lives in a retirement home a little south of here."

"Did you want to accompany us?" Gertrude asked.

"I'd love to, but my grandkids are coming for a visit."

"That definitely takes precedence." Natalie shook Edna's hand. "Thank you for all the help you've been today."

"It was my pleasure." Edna took turns shaking everyone's hands. "It's not often that I get to recount all those sweet family memories. You two made this old lady's day. I know I gave you more stories than you even asked for."

Brooke slid her backpack on her shoulders. "You truly should write them out. You are a natural-born storyteller."

Smiling, Edna returned to her desk behind the counter as they all stepped out into the cool afternoon. Sunshine spilled through the trees, and they descended the steps to the gravel lot. Everleigh inhaled the scent of lilacs that carried on the breeze as she helped settle Gertrude into her seat.

"I texted you the address of the retirement home Fair and Fleur live in." Natalie scooted herself to the third-row bench, leaving one of the captain's chairs open for Brooke. "Edna said Fair has memory issues, and speaking with her might cause some anxiety, but Fleur would be happy to meet with us."

"The sisters live in the same retirement center?" Gertrude asked.

"They do. They shared an apartment until Fair started needing more care. Fleur moved her to the assisted living section but kept their apartment so they'd still be near each other. Sounds like the two have always been close. Even when they were married, they lived beside each other."

Brooke picked up the tale of their history. "Then when Fleur's husband passed away, Fair had her move in with her and her husband. Those sisters really love each other." Her tone carried a wistfulness.

"It's not often that relationships work so well. Issues crop up, then people give up." The statements escaped all on their own. Everyone glanced at Everleigh. "Wow, sorry. Not trying to bring down the mood." Or hone their attention in on her.

"Is that why you work so hard to avoid us?" Natalie leaned forward until her head was parallel to Everleigh and Brooke.

"What?" Across her shoulder, she met their stares. "I don't—" Except she did. She wasn't a liar, and they weren't oblivious.

"You do," Brooke contradicted.

They merged onto the highway, picking up speed as they traveled the two-lane road through woods. Niles caught Everleigh's eyes in the rearview, then returned his gaze to the street in front of him. He might not be offering help, but he also wasn't tossing her under the bus. He certainly could, because she already knew that his thoughts on how she handled friendship matched up with theirs.

Still, she waited another half mile before speaking. "Sorry, guys. It's nothing personal."

"So it's not us, it's you?" Brooke crossed her arms. Dark green pines flickered past outside her window.

"Something like that." Everleigh fiddled with her Rubik's Cube. "I have been trying, but I'm a total introvert, and I've learned I tend to do best on my own." Old habits did indeed die hard. Especially when they were ones developed to keep a person safe. That didn't mean she couldn't change, but it sure was hard—particularly when she wasn't yet convinced she needed to.

"Well, that's a complete lie. No one is best on their own." Gertrude turned around. "You ever gone on a safari?"

In the rearview mirror, Niles's cheeks twitched.

"We're not animals, Gertrude." Everleigh sighed.

Gertrude nearly growled. It sounded so much like Niles that Everleigh swallowed her own laughter while Gertrude's wrinkles smoothed as her lips flattened. "Fine. Then have you ever been in a foot chase with a criminal?"

Brooke and Natalie covered their mouths, no doubt holding in laughter.

"Can't say that I have." Everleigh maintained an even voice.

"I have, and whenever I tried doing it alone, it only led to me losing them or being hurt. When I let my team help me, that's when we found our successes. We're not meant to chase down bad things alone, whether it's people, thoughts, habits, you name it." Her hand gripped the armrest as she remained facing backward. "We need others, Everleigh. In fact, the Good Lord said that right from the beginning. It's why he created Eve. Relationship is at the core of his creation. You plan on telling him he's got it wrong?"

With her slanted eyebrows and pursed lips, Gertrude wasn't posing a rhetorical question.

"No, I do not." Everleigh swallowed. "But am I allowed to possibly disagree with him?"

Gertrude let out a long sigh and turned toward the windshield. "You're allowed to do whatever you want, but that doesn't make you right."

❧ ❧

Meeting with Fleur had proved sweet, but the only stories she recounted brought nothing new. While she remembered Will and Adelheid, there wasn't anything that stood out about her recollections that would help lead to the diamond. Still, she was a charming old woman, and Everleigh greatly enjoyed their time together.

Especially helpful were the moments Fleur spoke of her sister. All Fleur's memories included her younger sibling. The two truly had done life together, to the betterment of them both, it seemed. Everleigh desperately wanted to inquire if they'd ever fought or lost faith in one another, but even if they had, clearly they'd made up because Fleur saw her sister every single day—and not out of duty, but out of love.

Everleigh continued to ponder that fact. From a young age, caring for her parents was how she interacted with them. Without question, she loved Mom and Dad—though she still struggled with forgiving him for landing in jail—but could she say her interactions with them centered on that love? Or did everything circle around what she needed to do for them?

Consumed with her thoughts, Everleigh tripped on a root and caught herself before she stumbled. Overhead, birds called to one another, and a slight breeze rustled through the canopy of tree branches. After speaking with Fleur, their little group returned to the bed and breakfast with an exhausted Gertrude who immediately settled in for a nap until dinner-time. Brooke and Natalie retired to their rooms as well. Seemed Brooke was dealing with some issues at work, and Natalie hoped to finally connect with Mason. Niles promised his aunt he'd deal with some client emails, which left Everleigh alone. A familiar condition that lately wasn't nearly as comfortable as usual. Like someone had taken her favorite sweatshirt which she'd spent years breaking in and shrunk it.

With everyone busy, she'd taken off on a solo hike. Long ago she'd learned her mind processed best when her body was moving. Each time she struggled with a puzzle or riddle, she'd often find the answer while on a walk. Almost as if her brain needed stretching right along with her legs. After checking for nearby trails, she'd grabbed the keys to the rental car and returned to Royalston and the Tully Lake Trailhead. She planned to hike from Doane's Falls to Spirit Falls, which should take just under two hours. That left her just enough time to return to their B and B, shower, and meet the group downstairs for dinner.

Hopefully, it would also provide her the time she needed to solve this enigma now in her head. Was she truly a loner, or did her heart desire the vulnerability of friendship? To be known and loved for who she was, not what she could do?

Her mind replayed all the times she'd tried to show people who she was and been rejected. She alone was never enough, but her abilities had granted her access to places where she'd felt shut out. It had become so much easier to lead with doing rather than simply being. But when she spent time really recalling all those relationships, they'd never satisfied her heart. Even when she'd been around those who called themselves friends, she felt alone. And feeling alone among "friends" was much lonelier than simply being by oneself. It was in a crowd where loneliness touched a heart more keenly.

Uncle Maddox had been right in Madeira. Somewhere along the way of growing up, she'd decided to stop offering her heart to people and instead offered her abilities. The change had occurred so subtly, she only saw the growth, not the root. What she claimed was all about not being trusted really boiled down to fear. Fear that she'd give herself to others and be met with rejection. Fear that if she admitted she did desire rela-tionship, she'd wind up hurt all over again when no one accepted her offering. Truly left holding her heart in her hands. And at the core was the worry that God would allow it all to happen rather than protect her.

Back in Madeira, she'd begun to feel suffocated by that fear. Now it simply exhausted her. But she'd operated with it for so long, thinking it was protecting her, that shedding it felt scary and huge. She didn't like unknowns, and God offered her no guarantees that any of these relationships would work out.

Which brought her right back to faith being what she couldn't see . . . and being scared to step out in that blind faith.

She reached Spirit Falls and plopped herself down on a boulder. Taking out a granola bar and her water bottle from her backpack, she watched nature's show. Rather than leaping off a high ledge, here the water stair-stepped down a rocky path through the woods. Little by little, gaining force and growing as it flowed, the water moved from a higher elevation to a lower one. It carved its own path through the hard stone, stopping and resting in small pools along the way before taking another tumble down its path.

And perhaps this wild environment provided the key to her heart's mystery. Maybe God wasn't asking her to change all at once, but in little moments that flowed together, eventually bringing her to a new destination. The steps didn't have to be large ones. Even the tiniest of movements added together covered large distances over time.

Nibbling on her snack, she smiled. When God said his qualities could be seen in his creation, he hadn't been lying. He spoke through people, but he also spoke through the world around her. And sometimes he used both.

It was up to her to decide if she'd listen.

Mind and heart feeling more settled, enough at least to concentrate on something else, Everleigh pulled one of Luciana's journals from her backpack. The other reason she'd hiked out here was the hope of deducing the next step in unraveling the actual mystery she'd been hired to solve. Yes, they'd uncovered Will's identity, but knowing who he was didn't help them know the diamond's location. For all their travels and discoveries, they remained as far from answers as they had nearly a month ago.

Perhaps it had been a tad ambitious to believe they could actually locate the diamond no one—including Gertrude—had been able to trace in all these years, but her gut said Caspar held the key. That he'd set this ball in motion long before he'd hired them and had already mapped its path. They were simply following along to his planned destination. She held no concrete evidence of that fact, but her gut had never steered her wrong. This felt like one giant escape room created by Caspar.

Which was why she had been convinced this trip to Royalston would net them their next clue to point them on their way. Instead, she was further along in figuring herself out. Another puzzle that on the outside appeared unsolvable, yet here she was encountering answers.

She inhaled the scent of loam, pine, and fresh water as she cracked open the journal in her hands. Tiny slips of paper marked pages where Luciana mentioned her friend Adelheid. Everleigh turned to one.

> *Adelheid's visit was much too short. I did my best to bring joy to my dear friend. We spoke often of how she misses Vienna and hopes to one day see her again. I sense the sadness in Adelheid over all her losses, but that one seems to prove hardest. Yet, there is nothing I can do but listen as she shares her heart. May her travels help bring more healing.*

Several things struck Everleigh. One was how much Adelheid missed her home. It seemed all her losses began at that point, and for whatever reason, she desired to return there. Like if she could make it back to Vienna, time would rewind and she could regain all she lost. Yet, it seemed she'd never returned to Austria after she'd grown.

The second thing was how much Luciana loved her friend. She truly worked hard to share Adelheid's burdens and be a shoulder she could cry on. For all Adelheid's losses, she'd gained a friend who never left her side.

That was what made the third thing stand out so brightly. Everleigh flipped to reread one of the final entries in this journal. It was dated July, 1946.

> *Adelheid returned for another visit today. While she still travels here a few times a year, a permanent distance has grown between us. Oh, not the distance of anger or broken relationship, but a protective distance built with each block of loss. Her words still flow, even her*

laughter—though not as often as it used to. But the light in her eyes no longer shines, and she no longer shares the matters of her heart. I have come to believe that is because she has none to share. She's closed herself off to everyone, including me. She believes it keeps her safe, yet all I see is danger. For instead of losing another, this time she has lost herself. I pray I can help her find her way back.

The words sunk deeply into Everleigh as if she could hear Luciana's voice speaking them directly to her heart. Jerrick still held so many of the journals, and Everleigh's fingers itched to call him and beg to read more. Yes, in hopes for more clues to the diamond since they seemed to be at a standstill. But another desire began pressing into her. Had Luciana been able to help her friend? And, if not, would she be happy to know that her words were helping another girl—sixty-five years later—find her own way back?

CHAPTER TWENTY-THREE

Niles watched for Everleigh's return from his perch on a lounge chair by the pool. She'd been gone for nearly three hours. Mapping out the route she'd mentioned taking in the note she'd left, the length showed four and a half miles. A leisurely hike with stops to enjoy scenery or indulge in a snack break could put the loop at two hours. The round-trip drive clocked in at eighty minutes. Which meant he had another half hour before he officially could start worrying that she'd gotten lost—or injured—on her solo hike.

He hadn't liked that she'd decided to take off on her own. He'd thought maybe today's conversation had penetrated the stubborn independence she liked to cloak under the label *introvert*. Not that a person couldn't be an introvert, but healthy ones still recognized their need for people. It wasn't that they traveled through life alone, but rather they cultivated fewer—and often more intimate—relationships. Selfishly, he'd hoped for a breakthrough so that he could become one of those relationships in Everleigh's life. Her heading out alone didn't leave him feeling very optimistic.

"Mind if we join you?" Natalie asked as she and Brooke hesitated beside the other open seats.

"Not at all."

"Everleigh still isn't back?" Brooke settled herself crisscross on the end of her chair, facing them.

"Nope. Though I expect her soon."

Natalie watched a few birds soaring overhead. "She took the journals with her. Maybe she'll find something we all missed."

"Doubt it." Brooke sounded resolved, not disappointed. "We seem to have hit a brick wall. We've all read through the journals. There's nothing more there that can help." She played with the fringe on the hem of her jeans. "How's your aunt going to be if we can't find this diamond after all?"

"She'll be all right." Aunt Gertie had no other setting besides perseverance. She'd wired him for the same, and he was thankful for it. While he fully believed she wouldn't allow the outcome of this treasure hunt to affect the quality of her days, he deeply desired to bring about the conclusion she sought. She'd done so much for him, this was the least he could do for her. "But I'm not ready to give up yet, and I know she's not either."

"Then let's hope we see something we've missed." Natalie pushed her sunglasses up on her nose. "Or that Caspar has some new idea for us to follow."

Brooke's fingers tapped against her knee. "Does anyone think he knows more than he's letting on?"

Niles scoffed. "I've thought that since the day my aunt first mentioned him. Everleigh's suspicious of him too."

"Problem is, he tossed us all a mystery we want to solve for our own reasons, and it's created a strong diversion from solving our lingering questions about him." Natalie clicked her nails together. "Though I'll admit I've done a little digging myself."

Brooke grinned. "Me too."

"Keep hitting a brick wall there as well?" The way Natalie spoke the question said she already knew the answer.

"Yup."

Niles started to add in his thoughts when Everleigh pulled into the parking lot. She exited and hustled toward the house, not noticing them on the patio beside the pool.

"Everleigh!" he called.

Her head turned at his voice, and she quickly changed direction. Crossing the grass, she smiled at them. "What're you all up to?"

"Talking about how we can't seem to find solid answers on this diamond or Caspar." Brooke stretched her legs out then scooted to make room on her lounge.

Surprisingly, Everleigh settled beside her.

"I can't help with Caspar—though I do think we should circle back around to that—but I think I found something in here." Cheeks filled with color and blue eyes lit with adventure, Everleigh waved the journal in the air. "I mean, I know I did. At least something helpful to me, but we can save that for a later time too."

Curiosity piqued, Niles held up his hand. "We're all ears for all of it." Especially the part that had wiped the wariness from her eyes. When she'd approached them just now, she'd done so with an air of openness. As if she'd dismantled some of her protective walls, or at least opened a doorway through them.

That tiny dip in her chin deepened as she smiled. "Thanks, but we should focus on one thing at a time."

He agreed, so he rested his full focus on her. Happily.

The blush in her cheeks expanded.

Brooke and Natalie suddenly seemed way too interested in the sky.

Everleigh cleared her throat. "I reread this journal today. There was a lot in there I missed the first time around." She paused as if savoring her own words. "Anyway, when I was driving here, something struck me." She flipped open to a page she'd marked and held the journal out to them.

"Go ahead," Natalie motioned to Brooke.

Brooke took it and glanced down. "I remember this passage." Then, she read it. "'How terribly tragic to have lost so much in her life. Will. Her father. Vienna. Her sorrow is unparalleled. It is a small comfort to know that the diamond remains near her heart even as her home is now elsewhere.'"

Three sets of expectant eyes turned toward Everleigh.

She answered their anticipation. "Luciana talks a lot about how much Adelheid loved and lost, specifically her home in Vienna and then Will. I think the first loss shaped her and the final loss broke her. Almost like they were connected in some way. When we read that entry, we thought Adelheid kept the diamond close to her heart, as in physically with her. But what if she kept it close to her heart as in what she loved?"

Natalie straightened. "You mean like she buried it with Will?"

"Or do you mean it's in Vienna?"

Everleigh lifted her hands, palms up and out. "I think it could be either."

Niles dropped his feet to the ground and sat with his elbows on his knees. "Makes sense. The problem we'll run into is we'll need a court order to exhume Will's grave. We'd have to ask John, but my guess is he'll tell us that's going to be nearly impossible when all we basically have is supposition for evidence."

"And where in Vienna could it be? We can't even find where Adelheid returned there after the war."

"Again, I don't know, but it at least provides a direction for our research." Everleigh accepted the journal from Brooke, noticing the time on her watch as she did so. "I need to take a quick shower before dinner and then grab Gertrude. We'll meet you all by the car." They had reservations at The Waterhouse, a local restaurant recommended by the owners of the B and B.

Niles stood. "I'll walk you up."

"You don't need to." Everleigh stood as well.

"No, but I'd like to." Especially when his offer brought about her smile rather than a refusal.

"All right." With a wave to Brooke and Natalie, they headed inside. Niles held the door for her, and they crossed to the staircase that led to her and Gertrude's rooms on the second floor.

"You seem lighter."

"Thanks?" She chuckled. "I did just walk nearly five miles."

"You're a laugh a minute, you know that?" He side-eyed her. "I meant—"

"I know what you meant." Her fingers wrapped around his bicep with a gentle squeeze that she released far too quickly. "I had a lot to process today, and oddly enough, Luciana's words played into that. I think I've discovered more about myself than I have about the diamond."

"And what are those discoveries?" he asked as they climbed the stairs. "If you don't mind sharing."

She didn't respond until they were beside her door. "Nothing too surprising to you, I'm sure." Her fingers fiddled with her room key. He itched to still the movement if only for an excuse to hold her hand. "Let's just say there might have been some merit to your words the other night about not wanting to be known. I do keep people at a distance, and I'm not so sure I want to continue doing that."

"Huh." He leaned a shoulder against her doorframe, facing her. "I sound pretty smart."

"Or perhaps observant."

"Or maybe both." He tipped his head and studied her. Unable to resist, he reached out and grasped the hair that had fallen loose from her ponytail. The silky strands brushed her collarbone, and as he swept them between his fingers, he skimmed his thumb over her skin. "In fact, right now I'm observing how your pulse is picking up."

"Really." Her voice poured the word out slowly, like the rich molasses he'd drizzled over his French toast this morning.

He'd never had a more deliciously sweet breakfast. It left him craving more. He had a sneaking suspicion kissing Everleigh would produce the same result.

He nodded, moving in closer. "Mm-hmm." His fingertips lingered along her neck. "And I'm smart enough to ask if I can kiss you." When her eyes closed but no response left her lips, he chuckled. "Everleigh?"

She blinked them open, a tease there. "Must not be as smart as you thought if you don't recognize my answer."

Smart enough to not miss this opportunity.

He tugged her to him, his mouth zeroed in on her parted lips. Something about her smiling at his kiss before it even began clenched his gut. In his line of work, he'd seen enough men going after their own needs with no regard to the woman satisfying them—or the one they cheated on. Relationships to him were a sacred thing. Kissing, the start of a connection meant to build into something more. He didn't take the act, or the woman engaging in it with him, lightly. Knowing that Everleigh anticipated him—wanted him—sealed something deep inside his heart.

Kissing her might not be something he came back from.

Beside them, Aunt Gertrude's door opened. "Everleigh? Did I hear you out here?"

Lips brushing his, she turned so fast he nearly lost balance. His forehead pressed against her temple as she answered his aunt. "Yep." She cleared her throat. "Did you need something?"

His aunt inhaled as if breathing in a clue. Then she grinned a devilish grin. "Nope. But I do believe I interrupted something, otherwise that nephew of mine would have announced his presence too." She stepped back into her room. "Carry on. It's taken long enough for you to make your move. Don't let me stop you." Her door clicked shut.

Laughter burst from Everleigh. "Perfect timing."

"I wholeheartedly disagree," he growled.

"Calm down, Yogi." Everleigh patted his chest, her hand still there from when she'd leaned into him for their now nonexistent kiss. "It's probably for the best. We don't want to complicate things. I mean, yes, we're really good at flirting, and I won't even try to deny I'm attracted to you, but do you really see this going anywhere?"

Was she serious?

Oh, wait, her straight face said she was. Which actually lent to her point about his aunt's timing, because while he wasn't taking their kiss lightly, it might be premature. There was a lot she didn't know about him if she thought he'd kiss her without intention.

"Yes, Everleigh, I do." He reached out and cupped her face, his thumb brushing her jaw. "I can't promise where we'll wind up, but I don't do impulsive kisses."

Her chin dipped.

He grinned at her silent challenge. From their first meeting it seemed they could communicate without words, and that ability had only grown. It had been one of those unexplainable things that snagged his awareness of her and hadn't let go. "Don't confuse unexpected with impulsive. I hate to be predictable." Her expression morphed into a challenge of another kind, but he held his ground. What he needed to say was so much more important than what he wanted to do. "There is thought behind my actions, especially when it comes to you. I'm not going to toy with your heart or mine. I may flirt—and let me be clear that flirting with you has been one of my favorite pastimes—but crossing that line only happens because I want to pursue this. Pursue you." He paused, letting his words sink in. "The fact you don't know that about me yet says we have some more steps in front of us first."

Her brow wrinkled. "Are you angry?"

"No, I'm not angry. I'm determined." He softened his voice. "To give any possibility between us the best shot we can, we need to build an actual foundation. I may not be impulsive, but I can rush things I really want, and I don't want to rush this. So"—he took her key and opened her door—"go get ready for dinner, and I'll meet you downstairs."

"Now you don't want to kiss me?" Confusion lined her words.

He brushed his lips against her forehead. "You have no idea how much." Pressing her key into her palm, he turned. "But maybe let's try sharing more of our hearts before we share our first kiss." His words hit his ears as he said them, and he groaned. "That sounded a whole lot less flowery in my head."

"Sounded like an exploding rosebush out here." She stepped into her room and peeked out at him right before she latched her door. "Lucky for you, I love flowers."

Grinning, he turned on his heel and headed to his room. The florist in Kenton Corners, an old client, owed him a favor, and he was about to call it in.

CHAPTER TWENTY-FOUR

THEY'D BEEN HOME IN KENTON Corners a little over a week. Two days after they'd arrived, Everleigh walked in to an attack of flowers in her room and Niles's humor-tinged innocent words, "You said you love flowers," delivered from behind. Over the past few days, she'd gifted several of the arrangements to the retirement home here in town as well as to Brooke, Natalie, and Gertrude, and still one remained on every surface of her room. So in between revisiting all of Gertrude's information collected through the years and rereading the journals for a third time, she plotted sweet revenge on Niles.

She'd had to set aside those tasks for a meeting this afternoon at Halstead Manor. Entering the parlor, Brooke and Natalie laughed at her armful of flowers.

"You still haven't unloaded them all?" Brooke asked.

Everleigh set a large vase of wildflowers on the coffee table. "Nope. But I refuse to give up." She walked over and placed the other vase she'd arrived with on the console table between the windows.

John watched from his perch on his desk. "You recently acquire a florist shop?"

"Something like that." Hands now empty, she settled on the couch. "You should take one home to your wife."

"Happily. Thanks." He brushed his hands together. "All right, then. Other than Everleigh's new flower hobby, how's everyone's week been?"

"Good." Natalie.

"Busy." Brooke.

"Aromatic." Everleigh.

Shaking his head, John set his iPhone on his desk. "Caspar is going to call in, but he's running a little late. He texted for us to start without him." He grabbed some papers and scanned them. "I heard from the caretaker of the Royalston Cemetery. He took our request before the Select Board who've denied it. Will Hayes is a World War II veteran and out of respect, they don't want his grave disturbed. Especially when we have no actual proof the Florentine Diamond is buried with him."

"That doesn't surprise me," Brooke noted. "Have we found any family members who might be willing to override the decision?"

Natalie held up her iPad. "His family was small. I tracked down two second cousins . . . or maybe first cousins twice removed?" Her face twisted in thought. "I never understood how that all worked, but basically, it's the sons of his cousin. Both served in the military as well, so the second they understood what I was asking, the answer was no."

Disappointed but not surprised either, Everleigh reached for her back-pack as John's phone rang. He answered, and they quickly caught Caspar up on recent happenings. Everleigh finished the update with her own thoughts. "I figured on the answers we received, but part of me hoped the draw of the diamond might change their minds."

"Not everyone is a treasure hunter or cares much about history, especially the history of another country." Natalie clicked her nails together. "Even if the diamond is found, it'll be returned to Austria. No finder's fee is guaranteed—though we're hopeful—and bragging rights don't mean anything to people who didn't even know the diamond existed until our phone call."

"True." Caspar's automated voice filled the room. "But that doesn't mean we shouldn't be careful who we share our suppositions with. There's still plenty of people who do know the diamond exists and would love to find it. And they're not all as honest as this group."

"What's next then?" Brooke asked. "Because we have zero leads when it comes to where Adelheid might have hidden it in Vienna. If she even went back there. And if she did, why wouldn't she have simply returned the piece to the government?"

"Because there wasn't much of a government to return it to. Not until the midfifties, and even then, they didn't reinstate her family's rule." Natalie's love of history spilled out. "Maybe Adelheid carried some hurt. Maybe she loved her homeland but not what had become of it. Hitler had done quite a number on that entire area, and for a decade after the war, France, Britain, the Soviet Union, and the United States jointly occupied Austria. When they finally became their own power again and still didn't want the Habsburg family, perhaps she decided she didn't want them."

"We may never know." John paced beside his desk.

Everleigh couldn't accept that answer. "I put another call in to Jerrick to see if he's come across anything in the other journals. I wish he'd allow us to read them."

"It's understandable that he hasn't," Caspar said. "If it's all he has left of his mother, you're lucky he allowed you to take the ones you have. Have you mailed them back yet?"

"No," Brooke answered. "I've been making copies of them. Once that's done, I'll package them and return them to him."

"You're being careful?" Caspar asked.

Brooke narrowed a glance at the phone as if offended he'd asked. "My reputation and career would tank if I didn't know how to carefully handle an antique."

The room quieted. After a long moment, Caspar spoke. "I appreciate your care, then. There's a lot I can help you purchase or replace should you need it in this venture, but some things are irreplaceable."

"Understood," Brooke responded. She turned her focus to Everleigh. "Have you heard anything back from Jerrick?"

"Just his standard response that if he comes across anything, he'll contact me."

"So, what now?" Natalie asked, a hint of frustration in her voice.

Did she worry they wouldn't get paid if they didn't succeed? It was a legit thought, and as much as Everleigh needed the money, she knew Natalie needed it too. As did Brooke. Maybe what they all could use was a little break. Sometimes when she stared at a puzzle too long, it all began to blur together. When she took a break, much like her walk the other day, she'd suddenly make connections she hadn't seen. Her mind continued to work the problem in the background, and day-to-day tasks sometimes created the conduit for new answers to flow.

"Now, we take a breather," Everleigh suggested. "Set this aside for a littlc bit and catch up on some of the other things in life." When Natalie's forehead wrinkled and she opened her mouth to reply, Everleigh continued her thought before she could protest. "Aren't your sons moving home again soon?"

Her mouth closed and she tipped her head. "Week after next. They want to celebrate the end of the semester with friends first."

Everleigh addressed Brooke next. "And I know you've been slammed at work." Though she hadn't really spoken much about what kept her busy. Her friendliness had definitely ramped up, yet she remained a closed book with the details of her life.

"I could use a few more days for a project I have going." She acknowledged.

"And Gertrude and Niles are behind too. Burt did what he could while they were gone, but they already were short-staffed since Gertrude isn't able to be out in the field." They'd arrived home to several messages and an immediate meeting with Burt. Everleigh hadn't seen much of Niles since then. "Today's Thursday. How about we meet Monday and see if any of us has come up with anything new?"

Brooke nodded. "And who knows, maybe by then Jerrick will have read something in one of the journals that will help."

John settled into his chair and jiggled his mouse. "Are you good with that, Caspar?"

"I am." His automated voice responded along with that familiar faint whine in the background. Everleigh had yet to place it. "I hate to lose momentum, but I agree that sometimes a break can help. We'll reconvene next week."

His goodbye filtered over the line, and they all collected their things. John remained at his desk. "I have a few items that I need to take care of here before I go. I'll see you all Monday."

Everleigh followed Brooke and Natalie. As they descended the stone steps to the gravel driveway, Natalie stopped. "Do you both have plans this weekend?"

"I plan on hitting the Kane County Flea Market on Saturday." Natalie swirled her key around her finger. "Want company?" Brooke's lips tipped as her eyes widened. "Uh, sure. That could be fun." They both turned toward Everleigh, expectantly.

"It does sound fun." At least that's what she told herself since she was attempting to turn over a new leaf. "But I can't leave Gertrude all day."

"So bring her along. She's always up for an adventure."

She hesitated, her old self begging her to take her excuse and run with it. Her new self challenging her to accept their offer. To take that first cascading step like the waterfall. "I suppose I could always ask her."

Natalie pointed her key at her. "I'm texting you tonight to hold you to that."

"You do that." Everleigh stepped to her car. Brooke and Natalie followed suit. Ten minutes later she pulled up beside Gertrude's house. Burt's black SUV was parked along the curb. Last time he was here, Everleigh had taken a closer look at his vehicle. Definitely a Buick. Definitely not the one that had been following her. After pouring over multiple pictures with Niles this past week, she'd narrowed the other car down to either an older Encore or a Chevy Trax. If she saw it again, she'd snap a picture . . . and call Niles like she'd promised.

Everleigh hopped out, and her phone rang. Noticing the name, she smiled as she answered. "This is a nice surprise," she greeted Uncle Maddox. "I get to hear your voice rather than read a text."

"Hey there."

Because she knew his tones so well, it only took those two words to understand something was wrong. "What happened?"

"I'm surprised Palmer hasn't called you." For once, Uncle Maddox did sound truly baffled.

"Why?"

"Their lawyers have tracked down Constance's money."

Surprise burst through her. "I thought it was untraceable."

"Nothing's untraceable, but it wasn't easy. He hired someone who knows their way around a computer and offshore accounts. Probably a forensic accountant or computer hacker. Maybe both." He sighed. "They can't do anything about it, though. Her money is completely protected, but they have my name."

Her stomach coiled. "I didn't want to get you into any trouble."

There went his familiar laughter. Deep and low, it always wrapped comfortably around her. "I'm not in any trouble. Legally there's nothing they can do to me. I'm simply surprised by whoever they have in their pocket. And I fully expect they'll come hard after you now with intimidation tactics. Honestly, I'm surprised they haven't already. It can't have taken them this long to find out our connection, which means now they are certain you're involved."

She paced. Her mind told her to worry, but her heart remembered all the conversations she'd shared with Constance. The promises made. "It's okay. You said I'd be safe, too, right?"

"Yes." One word. Firm. "That doesn't mean they can't drag you through the court of public opinion."

"They've already tried that, remember? It's why I'm now employed by Gertrude instead of still at the diner." Not that she minded that trade-off any longer.

"I'm leery of the fact Palmer hasn't contacted you with this new info. He's working on something."

"But it's nothing that can touch me," she reiterated.

His pause stretched her nerves. "Legally, no. Your name isn't on anything, so the best they can do is link you circumstantially to her transfer of funds to the offshore APT I set up for her. They may try to make a case of duress since you were her personal nurse, but they don't have any legal standing for it. It's an irrevocable trust and as her third-party trustee, I control all the assets. Since it's here in the Canary Islands, and I'm not a US citizen, the buck stops there like we talked about." Another pause. "Just watch your back. I've seen people cause a lot of harm over a whole lot less money than this. Once Palmer realizes he has no recourse, he might want revenge."

Which brought her back to her concerns about a recent tail. While Niles had determined Palmer didn't own a black SUV, he still hadn't heard back from some of his connections with the PI world. Their silence could mean Palmer hadn't hired anyone to bother her after all. "He doesn't have the money or the mental capacity to come after me."

"He still has access to his mother's accounts there in the States. And his lack of brain power is what makes me most worried."

"I'll be fine," Everleigh stated for herself as much as him. Still, worry niggled at her, and Uncle Maddox would be upset if something happened and he found out later she hadn't brought him up to speed. "And I promise to watch my back. Though I think someone else has been recently too."

"Palmer?"

"Probably." She recounted the entire situation. "So far Niles hasn't connected the vehicle to Palmer, but he's also checking into if he's hired a private investigator."

"Let me know what he finds, or if you spot them again."

She'd never heard that note of concern in Uncle Maddox's voice. "You really think he's going to do something?"

"I don't know what I think right now." He sounded like she did when she was knee-deep into a puzzle that wanted to best her. "I'll look into it too. In the meantime, you be careful."

"I am. I promise."

"Good." He sounded marginally less worried. "Call me if you need anything."

"I always do."

They hung up and Everleigh headed inside. Niles, Burt, and Gertrude all sat in the parlor watching *Monk*. Snacks littered the coffee table in front of them.

"How'd it go with Caspar?" Gertrude paused the show as Everleigh joined them. The episodes were so familiar to her, she could listen and remember what was happening on the screen.

"Good. We decided to take a break for the weekend. See if anything pops."

"Gertie and I used to take breathers too. Typically, it was me forcing one on her, but she always returned stronger." Burt looked right at home sitting by Gertrude on the sofa.

"That's the hope." Everleigh nodded to Niles. "Good to see you, stranger."

"You too." He propped his socked feet on the coffee table. "Have plans this weekend?"

"Funny you should ask. Natalie invited Brooke and me to the Kane County Flea Market on Saturday." She drizzled queso on her plate then added salsa beside it. "They want you to come, too, Gertrude."

"I would, but Burt asked if I'd accompany him to a jazz concert that afternoon at the park. They'll be featuring Ella Fitzgerald songs."

"Sounds like a perfect date for you."

Gertrude hit play on the show rather than answer.

Everleigh turned to Niles. "You want to join us?"

"As much as a spin around a flea market entices me, I'll be gone this weekend on a job."

"You don't sound disappointed to miss out."

Something she'd not only noticed about Niles but had grown to love was how his eyes smiled brighter than his lips. "Don't I?"

"Not particularly. And here I thought you'd jump at the chance to spend time with me."

"With *you*. Not you, two other women, and a field of old tchotchkes."

Her hand went to her chest, and she dropped her jaw. "You're saying the lure of my company isn't strong enough to overcome your dislike of shopping with a group of women?"

"Honey, your allure can get you most things where I'm concerned, but a man has to draw his line somewhere."

Burt watched them as if they were his evening entertainment rather than Monk's crazy antics. They'd even captured Gertrude's attention. When had they grown so comfortable in their flirting that they no longer cared if they had an audience?

"All right, fine. I concede it's a pretty unsurprising place to draw that line."

"How generous of you." His voice was soft, teasing. He set his feet on the floor and leaned forward, arms draped across his thighs. "But since I am rather drawn by your *allure*, what would you say to lunch Sunday after church?"

"I'd say that sounds great."

They all talked while the episode played out in the background, then Niles stood. "I should pack my bag and hit the road."

Everleigh joined him as he started for his room. "What's this job you're heading out on?"

"One of our clients thinks his wife is cheating on him."

"And you're going to follow her for the entire weekend?" That seemed a tad excessive.

He reached the landing and turned down the hall. "She told him she has a work trip this weekend. He was slightly suspicious, but then he ran into one of her coworkers. Turns out there is no conference."

"Oh, man."

Niles opened his door. "Exactly." He crossed to his closet and pulled out his duffel. "These are some of my least favorite jobs."

"You mentioned it's shaped your propensity toward the suspicious side of life." Everleigh leaned against the doorjamb. "I'm constantly reaching a better understanding of why you took so long to warm up to me."

He didn't laugh. Instead, his shoulders pulled up, and he expelled a heavy breath.

"Niles?"

Turning, he strolled to her. "It's not only my job. I mentioned I've had some rough relationships. One of those was with my fiancée. I was engaged."

That sucker punched her. She straightened. "When?" Because she refused to be his rebound. Suddenly she was thankful he hadn't kissed her.

"Three years ago." His hands went to her arms, and he gently squeezed. "And yes, I've dated since then, but I quickly realized I wasn't ready for another relationship."

"But you are now?"

He nailed her with that half grin that weakened her knees. "Yes." Firm. Confident.

Still, she needed to know. "Did you break it off or did she?"

"She broke her commitment. I broke our engagement." There didn't remain any animosity in his voice. His jaw didn't clench, and those gold lines in his eyes didn't flash. If he harbored any ill will toward her, he hid it well.

Everleigh studied him a moment longer, but all she saw was his desire to let her fully into his world. To share what had been his burden with her so she could understand him better. She slipped her arms around his waist and hugged him, pressing her cheek against his chest. "Thank you for sharing that with me, and I'm sorry she hurt you."

His chin rested against the top of her head. "It's okay. My heart healed a long time ago, but it did shape who I've become."

"Understandable."

"You're helping me see there's a middle ground in there, though."

His shirt warmed under her breath. "I'm a helpful kind of gal."

He ran his hand through her hair, resting his fingers along the base of her neck and gently massaging those muscles. "Yes, you are."

They stood there for a long moment until she felt as if she could melt into him. He'd opened a part of his heart to her without asking for anything in return. He'd been hurt before, and yet he took the first step here. He trusted her.

And that realization created the combination to the lock fastening her heart. All she needed to do now was open the door to him.

Her hand touched the doorknob, but she couldn't make herself twist it. Yet. But for the first time in a long time, she held on to hope that soon, she would.

CHAPTER TWENTY-FIVE

The Kane County Flea Market boasted over six hundred dealers, and it appeared Brooke intended to visit every single one.

"Anyone ready for a snack break?" Everleigh asked after vendor one hundred and eleven. All right. Maybe she was exaggerating. Not by much, though.

Natalie held her hand up to shield her eyes from the sun, even though she had on sunglasses. "I could use something cold to drink." This first weekend in May touched mideighties and without a cloud in the sky or any breeze, they might as well be standing on the sun. Natalie wiped a bead of sweat from her temple. "Then maybe we could hit some of the indoor vendors?"

"It'll be hotter inside. There's shade, but no AC. All those bodies and the air gets trapped." Brooke led them toward what Everleigh hoped was something for her parched throat. "I did tell you guys to dress for heat and bring a water bottle."

Everleigh shared a disgruntled sigh with Natalie, whose tank top and athletic shorts matched her own attire. She wiggled her now-empty water bottle in the air. "We did both of those things, and we could still use a break."

"Fresh squeezed lemonade is right ahead." Brooke weaved past a couple with wheeled baskets. "We can grab one on our way to the next aisle. There's a vendor there who always has great items."

Natalie leaned close to Everleigh and spoke in a low tone. "So . . . we're not stopping then?"

"Did you have any idea she loved shopping this much?"

Brooke halted at the end of the lemonade line and turned on them. "This isn't shopping. I loathe shopping." She gripped the straps of her backpack. "This is like a treasure hunt. Only, unlike the one Caspar sent us on, I'm actually finding things."

True. She already carried a sugar bowl made from cherry blossom depression glass, some sort of green vase she claimed was from the nineteenth century, and a brass candle snuffer with strange etchings on it—all pieces she collected for clients. It had been interesting watching her, because when they stepped into a booth, all Everleigh saw was junk. Brooke, however, could scan the tables then zero in with laser precision on exactly what she needed.

"I bet you played a killer game of hide-and-seek when you were little." Everleigh stepped forward to allow a mom and her stroller past.

Brooke's attention fixed over Everleigh's shoulder and a far-away look drifted across her face. "I preferred hiding as a kid." With the tiniest shake of her head, she seemed to catch what she'd allowed to slip past her lips, and her countenance smoothed over. "Now I love the seeking. I find I have a knack for it."

"Agreed." Natalie nodded.

Three more people stood between them and relief from severe dehydration.

Everleigh stepped into the sliver of shade provided by the lemonade stand's signs. "Is that why you chose your job?"

"No. I sort of fell into this career because I love working with antiques. Every piece has a story. A history. And the people seeking after it have some sort of connection they're trying to reestablish." She shrugged. "I like helping them with that, because I haven't had a lot of connections in my own life."

Their turn finally arrived, but Natalie stood there facing them. She leveled her firm gaze at Brooke first. "Well, you have connections now. With us." Her finger made a circle between them before she landed that unwavering gaze on Everleigh. "So do you. We might not find that diamond, but we've found each other. And I'm sorry to tell you two, but when I make friends, it's for life."

Brooke's face softened. She swallowed and nodded, her voice a bit wobbly as she answered. "Good to know."

And through it all, Everleigh stood there. Is this what it was like? Sharing hearts. Making friends. Belonging? She desperately wanted to trust what these two offered, but allowing them in necessitated a vulnerability she hadn't exercised in years. But Niles was right. If she wanted them to trust her, she needed to return that trust and allow herself to be fully known.

"Everleigh?" Arms crossed and toe tapping, Natalie waited for some sort of response.

"I don't typically do friends." The honest words blurted from her.

"Excuse me," the woman at the lemonade stand called. "But can I help you three?"

Digging in her pocket, Natalie took out a twenty and placed it on the counter. "Three iced lemonades please." She stepped to the side and waved for Everleigh and Brooke to follow. "Are you saying you don't *want* to be friends? Because I kind of hoped when you came today that we were making progress."

So she'd recognized that Everleigh wasn't an open book. "No, I'm saying I don't know how to be a friend, but I'd like to try."

Natalie's cheeks lifted, and a warmth not born of the temperature around them rolled off her. "We'll help, won't we, Brooke?"

"As much as I can. I'm not exactly a pro at this myself."

The server slid their drinks over the counter, and they each reached for one. Natalie sipped hers as they moved out of the way for the next customers. "Honestly, I'm a bit rusty myself." She shook off what sounded like encroaching melancholy. "Which is another reason I needed this job. I feel like I'm not only finding friends but a bit of myself again." A tiny breeze kicked up and they all sighed. "Shall we keep shopping?"

Brooke motioned them toward the aisle she sought. They walked side by side, rehydrated, a new bond forming between them. It felt unfamiliar but not uncomfortable. Just . . . different. Even good things, when new, took time to grow accustomed to. Especially when a lifetime of negative thoughts still wanted to have their say. If she kept focusing on the good, like Uncle Maddox suggested, eventually the balance would shift.

They stopped at a blue-clothed table filled with bangles, necklaces, and rings. A few 1940s hats perched on display poles beside a bin of men's gold watches. Brooke picked up a piece. "This is an antique Rolex." She held it out to Natalie. "You should get it for Mason."

"He only wears his Apple watch."

"One of your boys then?"

She shook her head. "Like father, like sons."

Brooke flipped the watch over and squinted. "It's engraved. Someone's name." She held it closer. "Adam." She slid it on her wrist, holding her arm in the air to admire it. "I can't imagine selling something like this. It's an heirloom. Someone in this person's family should have wanted this."

Natalie dug through the basket of gold bracelets. "Not everyone is sentimental. Mason tosses everything. The only thing he saved from our wedding is his ring, and I stopped giving him cards years ago because they wound up in the trash."

Glancing in the mirror to check out a necklace she held up, Everleigh asked the question she'd held in for weeks. But if listening and sharing were part of this friendship thing, then she determined to try to do her part. "Are you two okay? You and Mason?"

It took Natalie a moment to answer. When she did, sadness lined her hazel eyes. "I don't know." Her shoulders lifted then drooped. "I don't know if my husband still loves me."

Brooke moved in close. "Do you still love him?"

Another shrug. "I want to say yes."

"But?" Everleigh prompted.

Natalie sniffed back tears. "But I don't want to be the only one in love in our marriage." She dropped the bracelets she'd been sifting through back into the basket. "That's crazy, right?"

"No," Everleigh assured her. "Honestly, it sounds like the most relatable thing you've ever said to me." It was comforting to know that she wasn't the only one struggling with risking vulnerability. Another stitch that sewed them closer.

"Yeah?" Natalie peeked up at her.

"Yeah."

Brooke nodded beside her.

With both hands, Natalie shoved her hair off her face and blew out a deep breath. "I guess we're all a little messed up when it comes to relationships, aren't we?"

Like one of those old wooden box puzzles, the kind you had to knock just right to open, Natalie's words hit the spot, exposing a new thought. Their ages, stages, styles, and personalities might all be different, but they were more alike than different when it came to their struggles. And, possibly, their hearts.

She remained unconvinced on that last one yet, though willing to continue in her contemplation of it.

After a second, Brooke straightened with determination. "I'm buying this watch."

"You going to try and figure out where it came from?" Natalie asked.

"Nope." She glanced around for whoever owned the booth. "Strangely enough, I know someone named Adam. He was just in town helping me out, and I'm going to get this as a thank-you for him."

"Sounds like it was meant to be."

Brooke walked farther into the booth, and they followed her. They spent the remainder of the afternoon in easy conversation as they weaved through close to half of the flea market. Brooke good-naturedly moaned that she wasn't able to see it all, while Everleigh felt relief they weren't able to see it all. Natalie remained their neutral ground, mollifying them both as they strolled to the car, sunburned and laden with trinkets and treasures.

"What's everyone's plans for the rest of the weekend?" Brooke asked as she stowed her items in the hatch.

"Nothing. Mason typically watches sports all day Sunday. I'll maybe work in my garden." Natalie stood, hands on the car door. "You?"

"I was thinking of biking the Kankakee trail."

"Is it paved?" Natalie asked.

They climbed into the car, and Brooke started it up. "Most of it. About three miles is gravel." She navigated around pedestrians. "Why? You want to come?"

"Sure. If you wouldn't mind me crashing your plans again."

"Not at all." Her eyes met Everleigh's in the rearview mirror. "You want to come too? I know it's two days with us, but conversation will be a minimal while we're biking."

Brooke highlighting that perk proved they were getting to know her better, and that fact wound around her heart with a feeling suspiciously like comfort. If she didn't already have plans, she might actually take them up on the invite.

"I would, but I'm meeting Niles for lunch."

Brooke pushed up in her seat while Natalie turned completely around. "You have a date with Niles?" Natalie's voice lifted to a pitch previously unheard.

"And you spent the entire day with us but said nothing?"

Natalie nodded at Brooke as if in agreed disbelief over Everleigh's obvious faux pas. "Right?"

Except she had no clue not talking about her lunch plans constituted a misstep of any kind. "I didn't think it was anything necessary to share."

"Everleigh," Natalie said with the immense patience a person used when teaching another a new skill that they were slow in acquiring, "friends always share when they have a date. One *leads* with any information that pertains to a man. In fact, if we hadn't been getting together today, this would be news you'd text us."

That wasn't the kind of friendship she'd ever experienced. Plus, "I don't even know if this will go anywhere, so it doesn't really feel like news at this point."

"A date is always news." Brooke navigated around a slow-moving van. "Then after the date you fill us in on how it went." She glanced in the mirror. "And yes, that includes if there's a kiss. Though the details can happily stop there."

Yeah, this all felt a little awkward, and she highly suspected Brooke and Natalie were going slightly overboard with the whole this-is-how-friends-act thing, but she appreciated what they were doing. Their exaggeration allowed her to maintain her subdued response and still make progress.

"I appreciate that, but I'm not expecting a kiss." Though she wouldn't turn one down should Niles offer.

"Understandable," Natalie said, facing forward again. "We'll expect one for you since we have the benefit of no emotional entanglement."

Everleigh wished she could respond with an honest argument that she had none either, but her mouth refused to form words her heart implicated as a lie.

✦ ✦

After church on Sunday, Niles and Everleigh climbed on his Harley and spent the afternoon cruising Route 66. She was quickly becoming a motorcycle enthusiast. They drove back to Kenton Corners for a late lunch at The Corner Café.

Molly had seen them come in and told them to pick any seat in her section. Niles chose a table along the back wall with no one else around them. He held out her chair. "You're sure this is where you want to eat?"

He'd asked twice already and still seemed perplexed at her affirmative response. "Yes," she replied for a third time. "I'm hungry for fried mush."

That craving must be what he struggled to wrap his brain around. "I can't believe anyone would name a dish that and then people actually order it, let alone crave it."

Everleigh's hand stilled on the plastic menu in her hand. She didn't need to peruse it. Her focus instead rested on Niles as she replayed the last meal they'd shared here, when he'd inserted himself into her lunch with Brooke and Natalie—and then into their trip to Madeira. He'd ordered a burger that day.

"Have you ever tried the fried mush here?"

"I've never tried it anywhere. And I don't plan to."

She slowly raised the right edge of her mouth. "I bet I could change your mind."

He crossed his arms over those tight abs and reclined, the humor on his face signaling what he thought of her challenge. Or, quite possibly, he was simply amused by her. Either one she'd take when it brought about that expression on his face. Unguarded. Focused. Captivated.

She couldn't remember someone ever looking at her as if they were captivated by her, as if she were a subject he wanted to devour every detail on. Made her want to throw open her pages and allow him to read every line—and that freaked her out just a little.

Because Niles wanted every facet, even the works cited page in the back. He'd been honest in his expectations but seeing the desire so clearly on his face made it real in a way she had yet to experience. Plus, her feelings for him had grown.

Those emotions put her into unchartered territory, but honestly, she was tired of being stuck in her past. Which was why she'd moved forward in her friendships with Natalie and Brooke. Surely, she could do the same here. Though a relationship with Niles would be nothing like a relationship with them. It would burrow deeper into her heart. Consume more of her mind and soul. Require more vulnerability.

Create a bigger risk.

"For someone who laid down a gauntlet, you've grown awfully quiet." He unclasped his arms and leaned on the table, his forearms reaching across half the space. "Everything okay?"

"Yep." She navigated away from her pounding heart to safer territory. "Just waiting to hear what you're ordering."

His eyes narrowed slightly, but Molly chose that moment to show up at their table. "You guys know what you want?"

Niles slid the corner of his mouth up, answering in that nonverbal way they easily fell into. He one hundred percent knew what he wanted—her. But he wouldn't move forward until she admitted what she wanted was him. And that she'd let him fully inside her walls.

When she remained silent, he sighed and spoke. "The Jamie is your favorite, right?" He obviously had paid close attention the last time they were here, because when he joined them, she'd only had a few fried bananas and smeared whipped cream left on her plate.

Everleigh nodded, a little awed once again by how Niles absorbed everything in his orbit, yet his attention didn't feel claustrophobic.

She felt seen. Known.

He handed off his menu. "Then that's what I'll have."

She cleared her throat. "Me too."

Molly snuck a glance between them as she took their menus. "Coming right up," she said as she turned and headed to another table.

"So," Everleigh began before Niles had time to hijack the conversation, "how was your stakeout? Is she cheating on her husband?"

Niles waited a beat. His chin dipped, and he tugged on his lip. He recognized her diversion. In the end, he played along. "No, she is not."

Relieved, she continued. "Have you told him yet?"

"I haven't."

"Why on earth not?"

"Because the situation is more complicated than his wife not cheating."

"How is telling the truth complicated?"

He arched a brow, but blessedly did not verbally challenge her on how she'd dived into this entire line of questions to avoid talking out the truth with him. Or herself. "Because," Niles said, "she *is* hiding something, but it's not an affair."

Molly brought their plates heaped high with fried mush smothered in bananas, maple syrup, and whipped cream. She set down a side of sausage patties for them to share and topped off their coffees. "Anything else?"

"Nope." They both responded.

Everleigh used the side of her fork to cut off her first bite. She ensured she had a piece of mush, a banana slice, and a dollop of the whipped cream. Before shoving it in her mouth, she showed it off to Niles. A drip of maple syrup fell to her plate. "The perfect bite, at least in my opinion."

He followed suit and took his first taste, chewing slowly, thoughtfully. Niles was a man who took his time to savor moments, ensuring he made the most of each experience. Kissing him wouldn't be rushed. Her gaze slipped to his lips. She'd never been one to daydream about kissing a man, but she couldn't seem to escape the thought when it came to him.

"You were right." He dug in for another piece, his fork scraping against his plate. She dragged her attention from his mouth and the images her imagination conjured. It was painfully obvious he'd caught her staring, yet again he didn't call her on it. "This is actually really good."

"Did you think I'd steer you wrong?" She scooped another morsel.

"Not necessarily wrong, just in a direction I wouldn't like."

"And instead you find you like where you're headed?"

He paused, his flirtatious grin more enticing than her sweet meal any day. "I like where I'm headed very much."

She reached for her water and took a long gulp. Then another. Niles continued demolishing his plateful, kind of like he was with her walls.

Setting down her glass, she moved to a safer topic. "Are you going to tell me what the wife is hiding?"

"You hate not having answers, don't you?"

"It's taken you this many weeks to reach that conclusion?"

Niles laughed and took a bite of his fried mush, then settled in his chair and sipped his coffee. "She has a child. By the looks of it, she had her when she was a teenager, because she's thirty-one and I'd place the girl somewhere between thirteen and fifteen."

"And how long has your client been married?"

"Eight years."

Everleigh drew her brows together. "If her pregnancy was before they met, why would she hide it from him?"

"I don't know." Niles scanned the restaurant before returning his attention to her. "From what I can gather, she's trying to reconnect with the daughter she gave up for adoption. I don't know how long she's known about her, but it's apparent her husband has no idea this girl exists."

"Wow." Everleigh pushed aside her unfinished meal. Something buzzed inside like it did when a solution sat at her fingertips, but she hadn't quite fit the pieces together. "So what are you going to tell her husband?"

"That she's not cheating on him."

"And if he asks what she was doing all weekend?"

"I'll tell him to ask her. The news is hers to share, not mine. He only hired me to see if she was cheating on him. She's not."

Everleigh fiddled with the handle on her mug. "She has a daughter he knew nothing about . . ." A child she wanted to reconnect with badly enough to risk her marriage. She hadn't stopped loving her daughter simply because she'd given her up. A love like that wrapped around a person's heart and didn't let go. It was a bond not easily broken.

She sat up straight, pieces suddenly clicking into place in a new way that changed every word they'd read. Her eyes slammed to Niles's. "What if Vienna isn't a place, but a person? What if Adelheid had a baby?"

CHAPTER TWENTY-SIX

"See, look at this." Everleigh pointed to a passage. She and Niles sat hip-to-hip on the parlor floor, the journals scattered around them. After Everleigh's suggestion at the diner, they'd quickly paid their bill and headed for Gertrude's house. Burt and Gertrude were attending another concert. Brooke and Natalie were biking the Kankakee trail. Rather than call them all in for what might be another dead end, she and Niles decided to chase down this idea and see if it led anywhere. If they found anything concrete, she'd bring it to her meeting at Halstead Manor tomorrow.

Niles leaned over and reread the lines they'd first seen weeks ago. "We spoke often of how she misses Vienna and hopes to one day see her again."

"I can't believe I didn't see it before." Everleigh leaned against the sofa behind them. "Several times when Luciana mentions Vienna, she uses a feminine pronoun. My brain read that as her speaking about the city." She rubbed her forehead. "I missed something so obvious."

Niles took her hand, stopping the motion. "First, we still don't know that it doesn't mean that. Second, even if it does—"

"It does."

He silenced her with a look. "Even if it does, we all missed it."

"But I'm the puzzle person. I'm the one who's supposed to catch these clues." It was part of her contribution to this team.

"Everleigh"—Niles spoke her name slowly and filled with care—"just because—"

Before he could offer his argument to her warring thoughts, her phone rang. She picked it up from the floor beside her. "It's Fleur!"

They'd placed a call to the older woman on the way home from the restaurant. Everleigh had left a message on what sounded like an ancient answering machine. The hunger for more clues she could successfully string together rumbled with a voracious appetite.

"Hello, Fleur?" Everleigh answered and put her on speaker.

"Yes, this is me." The woman's voice, shaky with age, held a note of curiosity. "You mentioned you had a few more questions about Adelheid?"

"I do. Is now a good time?"

"It is. Our evening movie won't start for a half hour. They're playing *Charade* tonight with Cary Grant. Have you ever seen it?"

"I have." She'd enjoyed it greatly, especially since she'd guessed the twist her first time watching it. "It's a wonderful movie."

"Anything with Cary Grant is. He's my favorite actor."

"He was pretty great." She fumbled with the small talk when all she wanted was to dive in to her questions. "I don't want to take up too much of your time since your movie starts soon, so do you mind if I begin?"

"Oh, please, go ahead." Fleur didn't seem bothered in the least by Everleigh's transition.

"I'm calling to see if it might be possible if—" She paused, suddenly hit by how this sounded. Having a child out of wedlock was a huge deal for Fleur's generation, and she didn't want her to think she was tarnishing Adelheid's reputation. Yet, there was no way to ask this delicately. "We've been reading through some journals written by another friend of Adelheid's, and some of the entries have led us to wonder, well, if perhaps . . . Could Will and Adelheid have had a child together?" The last part came out in a rush of words.

Thick silence filtered over the line.

Everleigh met Niles's gaze and widened her own. Her grip on her phone tightened. He whispered, "Give her a moment."

She had no other choice.

Finally, Fleur responded. "I suppose it's possible." Another beat of silence. "I was only seven at the time, but a memory does stick out in light of your question. Every summer Mother would take Fair and I to her parents' beach house in Rockport. We always anticipated that time with her and our grandparents." She paused as if captured by her memories. In the background, voices lifted and lowered. After a moment Fleur continued, sounding more vexed than nostalgic. "The spring after Will passed away, Mother took Adelheid but had us stay home. Fair and I were bothered by that. And jealous. Mother had been spending more time with Adelheid than with us, and we were too young to understand the grief Adelheid faced."

"I can only imagine," Everleigh said.

"Mother spent the entire summer in Rockport. That fall she and Adelheid returned. Adelheid brought us gifts. I'm sure she felt bad for taking Mother away from us for so many months. Mother had me hug her as a thank-you, and when I did, I commented on how squishy she'd become." Fleur chuckled as if amused by her childish antics. "I don't think I'd recall the hug or my words if I hadn't been scolded so by Mother. She told me that young ladies never comment on a woman's figure. I still remember her and Adelheid's faces. At the time I thought her red cheeks were from embarrassment. Now I wonder . . ."

"Was anyone else in the room with you?"

"Only Father, Fair, and a maid," Fleur recounted. "But the help had a way of spreading news that moved faster than our telephone lines. If Adelheid had given birth, she wouldn't want that news traveling."

Everleigh mulled over Fleur's story. "And they'd been in Rockport all summer?"

"Yes. That was the only summer where Mother traveled there in spring and remained until fall. I know because Fair and I always tried to convince her to extend our trips, but we never stayed longer than one month, typically July."

"So it's possible Adelheid wasn't only grieving, but that she had a child?"

"It's possible."

"Especially with you noticing how . . . squishy she'd become." She swallowed her own laugh at the thought of how that scene played out.

Fleur, however, giggled again like the child she'd once been. "Every time my own children said something out of turn, I'd remember that moment. But, yes, Adelheid's body had changed. In my mind it was because Mother had taken her for all the ice cream she wanted. There was an ice cream store by the beach that Mother would take us to but never more than once a week. I was sure she'd visited with Adelheid more often.

Now I know how a body changes after giving birth, and looking back, I'd say it's quite possible that could have happened."

"But you never heard them speak of a baby?"

"No." Fleur dropped the word with mild disappointment. "Though in those days, no one would have spoken of it. Unwed pregnancies happened, but they were hidden."

So it was a strong possibility, which only created more questions. "Do you have any way of knowing what might have become of the child?"

"Unfortunately, no," Fleur said. "Although, Mother and Father did have a doctor friend who also vacationed there. I remember because one summer Fair broke her arm while playing on the rocks along the water. Dr. Fairchild set it. He and his wife were always around, but I wouldn't have known he was a doctor if not for that."

Niles grabbed a pad of paper to scribble on. "Do you remember his first name?"

"Warren. Warren and Tabitha Fairchild. They stayed in the house beside ours." Then she rattled off the address of her family's beach home. "We no longer own it, but I do know it's still there. Some of my grandchildren have rented it."

Everleigh glanced at the clock. Nearly twenty minutes had passed. "I should let you get to your movie. Thank you so much for taking the time to speak with me again."

"Of course! I don't have much excitement around here anymore. Helping on a treasure hunt is quite the adventure, and it provides me with fodder for coffee time." Something shuffled on Fleur's side of the line. Most likely she stood to leave for her movie. "If you think of any other questions, you can call me again."

"I will." Everleigh said her goodbyes and hung up. She turned to Niles. "Now what?"

"Now we wait until you have time to go over this info with Natalie and Brooke. They might be able to help track down this Warren Fairchild or his family. Hopefully the town of Rockport or the good doctor will have records that prove Adelheid gave birth."

"My guess is the doctor, because if they were hiding her pregnancy, they wouldn't have recorded her birth in the town records."

"No. Not with Adelheid's name." Niles wrapped her hand in his and settled them on his lap. He rubbed the back of her hand with his thumb. "But if we have a time frame, we could see if any other families had babies within that window and check into those. If she gave the child up, another family might have recorded the birth as their own."

Everleigh tried to concentrate beyond Niles's distracting touch. "That would have brought about a lot of questions. A couple can't go from not being pregnant to suddenly having a child."

He slid his feather-light touch along her forearm. "They can if there's money involved and someone who'll happily exchange their services for that money."

"As in creating a false birth certificate."

"As in exactly that." Still shoulder to shoulder with her, he turned his face to hers. Gold glittered in a circle around his deep brown irises. "But let's not jump straight to that. It could be entirely possible that there's a legitimate birth record at the town hall."

She huffed. "When did you become such an optimist?"

His grin sent shivers through her middle. "Wednesday, March 30, at three-thirty in the afternoon."

It took only a second for the date to land. "The day we met?"

He nodded.

"You tried to toss me out on the street."

Another nod. "I was incredibly optimistic that I'd be able to stop you from working with my aunt."

"You didn't succeed."

"I did not," he agreed. "But I then remained optimistic that I could prove you weren't as squeaky clean as you claimed to be."

"You didn't succeed in that either." This close, the pepper-and-pine scent of his cologne filled her every breath. He hadn't shaved today, his scruff only enhancing the wildness of his curls. The black Henley he wore pulled across muscles that outwardly defined a strength she knew he internally matched. He had the appearance of a man who couldn't be tamed, but she'd seen a gentleness inside him too.

"I did not." His deep voice rumbled over her in a most delicious way. "I remain optimistic where you're concerned, though."

"You do?" Her words came on a near squeak. She cleared her throat.

His grin deepened in a way that curled her toes. "Very much so. I'm rather optimistic that you'll let me kiss you." His eyes shifted to her lips then back to capture her full attention. "What do you think my chances of success are this time?"

Heart pounding, she barely had "One hundred percent" out of her mouth before he answered with his all-consuming response.

She'd been right. There wasn't an ounce of meekness to his kiss. It was fierce and powerful. Passionate and intense. But as she cradled both sides of his face in her strong grip, she also felt his restraint. When his mouth softened against hers, she noted his gentleness.

He shifted so his body leaned into hers, his hands moving so his palms braced the floor on either side of her hips. This allowed him to explore her jaw as he pressed kisses along it, moving until his lips reached her ear. "Success never tasted so sweet."

Smiling, she dug her hands into his thick hair and tugged him closer, taking over the kiss. She moved her mouth along his scruff until she reached his lips, then she dove fully in, delighting in his muffled groan.

The moment drew out in a way that pulled breath from her, and yet she didn't care. Kissing Niles was well worth the lack of oxygen. Her fingertips drew across his shoulders, his muscles pulled tight as he supported his weight above her. Wait. When had she laid down?

Every nerve hummed. She struggled to control what was dangerously close to becoming out of control.

Niles must have sensed her shift because his kisses slowed. He pulled away enough to see her eyes. His pupils were dilated and hazy, no doubt mirroring hers. With a slow grin, he dropped a kiss to her forehead then sat back, tugging her into a sitting position too. He dragged his hand through his hair. "I'm rather glad I've become such an optimistic man."

Laughter poured from her still-swollen lips. She had no words to add because he'd stolen them all.

Niles stood. "I should probably head on up."

It was only seven o'clock. Yet, she understood his reasoning, so she nodded. He made it to the door before she finally found her voice. "Niles?"

He turned. "Yeah?"

There was so much she wanted to say, but all she got out was, "Good night."

That line formed between his eyebrows, but he still managed a smile. "Good night, Everleigh."

CHAPTER TWENTY-SEVEN

"Didn't sleep well last night?" Gertrude asked from her perch on the window seat in the parlor. A thin blanket covered her legs, and she kept her face toward the sunshine streaming in the glass panes. Her weathered fingers held her morning teacup, and the scent of apples lifted on the steam rising from the warm liquid. It still amused Everleigh that such a tough old woman sipped such a delicate drink.

She settled onto the chair across from her. "What makes you say that?" Working for a client who couldn't see meant that Everleigh didn't try to hide the bags under her eyes. Or smooth her hair into submission. Or put on matching pajamas. And since Niles had left before dawn to collect a bail jumper he'd nabbed a late-night lead on, she most definitely had no one around to impress.

"That's your third cup of coffee. You typically drink one."

"How do you know it's my third?" She'd strategically poured cups two and three when Gertrude sent her for a blanket then for another biscuit.

Gertrude settled her cup against her leg, the blanket and her pajamas buffering her skin from its heat. "Why is it that people assume I've lost all my senses along with my eyesight? If anything, they've only grown stronger. I thought I'd proven that to you by now."

She had, which was why Everleigh had cloaked her refills. "I do know that, so I'm genuinely curious about what tipped you off."

"Ah." Gertrude perked up. "You tried to throw me off."

"I did." Taking care of Gertrude went far beyond ensuring she made it from room to room safely or donned coordinating clothes each day. This hunt had revived her, which allowed Everleigh to see how important it was for Gertrude to still use the skills she'd honed for years. Those moments, small or large, helped lift the depression that lurked around the edges of Gertrude's days.

"If I tell you, that gives you an advantage." She sipped her tea, remaining frustratingly quiet.

"All right." Two could play at this game, and it seemed to be one Gertrude was enjoying. "I propose an information swap."

"I'm listening."

Yeah, she bet. "There's more from last night that I didn't tell you."

"About Adelheid?"

No. She'd filled her in on all her Adelheid information last night. This was about the kiss. "That's all I'm currently saying."

Gertrude took another sip of her tea, then set her cup on the small table beside her. "You kissed Niles."

She couldn't be more surprised if Gertrude had whipped the Florentine Diamond from her pocket and revealed she'd had it all along. "What? How on earth . . . ?"

"Your extra coffee tells me you didn't sleep, but your chipperness this morning tells me it's not because you're upset about anything. You and Niles were alone here working, but when Burt dropped me off at eight, Niles had already gone to bed. My nephew never retires that early. You fumbled over your words when I asked about him and paused each time you heard his footsteps over us when you were telling me about Adelheid." Gertrude was enjoying this way too much. "But the most incriminating piece of evidence was that you smelled like his cologne."

Unbelievable.

"Well, you're wrong."

"Don't even try to sell me that answer, because I'm not buying it."

"No. You are." She leaned in toward her old friend. "*He* kissed *me*."

Gertrude slapped the cushion she sat on. "That's my boy."

Her joy brought about Everleigh's. She couldn't have imagined a month ago how much her life would change in such a short span of time. Her lifetime of lonely habits was slowly changing. It felt scary and thrilling and enticing and dangerous all at once.

She reined in her own laughter. "So, will you tell me how you knew I had three cups?"

"Will you be kissing my nephew again?"

"I hope so." There was no use trying to pretend with Gertrude.

"I listened, Everleigh. It's as simple as that." Gertrude softened her tone, cuing Everleigh into the fact that the words she spoke were important to her. "Every day you have one cup of coffee, but that doesn't mean that every day you're going to have one cup of coffee. We can get fooled by our expectation that things don't change. But if we choose to listen in each new encounter rather than assume it'll be the same as it's always been, we won't be as prone to miss change when it occurs."

She'd be chewing on that wisdom all morning.

"And here I thought I'd be the one doling out all the help." The grandfather clock in the corner rang out nine clangs, and Everleigh stood. She cleared their dishes. "I need to get ready. The crew is meeting at Halstead at ten."

"When do you think we'll head out to Rockport?" As they'd talked last night, Gertrude was adamant that she'd accompany them on their return trip to the East Coast.

"My guess is the end of the week. We'll need to see if we can track down this doctor's family too. If they're not still in Rockport, then we may split up."

She made sure Gertrude had her phone beside her, topped off her tea, and cleaned up from breakfast. Burt would be arriving as Everleigh left. Niles had sent a sweet good-morning text, and he'd invited her to lunch since they both had full mornings. She'd happily accepted and promised to fill him in on any progress the group made.

At ten she pulled up to Halstead Manor. A car she didn't recognize sat in the circle drive beside Brooke's, Natalie's, and John's vehicles. Her heart rate picked up. Could Caspar actually be here? Was he ready to reveal his identity to them?

Everleigh hustled up the steps. As she entered, voices reached her, and her anticipation soured to dread.

"You should know who you're dealing with." Palmer Quimby's characteristically nasal voice escaped from the front room.

"We do." Brooke spoke low and firmly. "What we don't fully know is who you are."

He laughed. "I'm not surprised she hasn't used me for references, even if I am a past employer." A stack of paper smacked the desk. "I brought you some enticing reading. It'll snag your interest, I'm sure."

"How about you give us the highlights." This from Natalie.

Everleigh stepped into the room before he could continue. "You need to leave, Palmer."

A cold smile slithered across his face. "There she is. The woman who stole my mother's fortune."

"I did no such thing." Everleigh crossed her arms over her chest. "Leave. Now."

Natalie and Brooke stood sentry on either side of her.

"You heard her," John said from his spot only a pace away from Palmer.

Unfortunately, Palmer had nothing more to lose and revenge seemed to be the only thing he could gain. He slid a business card on top of the papers he'd dropped on John's desk. "I'll leave, but I'm also leaving you a way to contact me and the lawyers helping build a civil suit against her. You'll want to join in once she steals everything from you too."

"We trust her." John picked up his card and handed it to him. "Can't say the same about you."

Palmer refused to accept it. He stepped to the door. "My mother made the same mistake." He paused, one foot in the room, one in the hall. "Now everything she worked for is in a trust in the Canary Islands being managed by a man Everleigh introduced my mother to. Has she mentioned a Maddox to any of you?"

The air seemed to leave the room. Brooke and Natalie did their best to maintain neutral expressions, but Palmer felt the shift.

"Keep my card," he said with near glee. "I have a feeling you'll need it."

No one spoke a word until the front door closed. Even then, silence held strong as they stared at one another. It was John who finally broke it. "Someone care to tell me what shifted when he mentioned this Maddox?"

Brooke and Natalie shared a glance weighted with uncertainty. Brooke clasped her hips, her pointer finger tapping against black denim. "Maddox is Everleigh's uncle. She met up with him when we were in Madeira."

Natalie's forehead wrinkled. "He was visiting from his home in the Canary Islands. Can you explain any of this, Everleigh?"

They'd gone from her staunchest allies to cross-examiners, even though what they knew of her hadn't changed. All Palmer had to do was drop what appeared to be incriminating evidence and their faith in her wavered.

"I shouldn't have to." She straightened and placed her own hands on her hips.

Brooke bristled at her fighting stance and the tension in her voice.

Natalie held her hand in the air. "Hold up. I sense you're getting defensive."

"Oh, you do?"

Rather than matching her biting reply, Natalie remained calm. "We just want to hear things from your point of view. Right now we have a lot of confusing information, and we'd love if you could sort it out for us."

Everleigh studied their faces. All three portrayed a wariness that hadn't been there the last time they'd stood together. "I shouldn't have to sort anything out for you." This was exactly why she kept her walls in place. People wanted her to let them in, but they never remained by her side. "You should know I'm innocent of what Palmer's accusing me of."

"Exactly. Palmer. Not us," Brooke said. "So why not explain your side of things, because while he might not be telling the full truth, there is truth in some of the details he provided."

Everleigh shifted toward the door. "The only truth you need is that I'm innocent. Asking for more than that says you don't believe me."

"You're kidding, right?" Natalie took a step toward her. "Friends share, Everleigh. They let each other into their lives. It's asking a lot to expect us to know you when you hold so much back."

John picked up where Natalie stopped. "It's like you're testing us, but you haven't given us all the answers. We're bound to fail."

Brooke unclenched her arms. "Let us in."

She had. Maybe not all the way, but she'd been more open with them than she'd been with anyone in years. Still, when rumors rose and sides were picked, they didn't stand with her. They held the center line, indecision on their faces, and asked her to defend herself so they could make a choice.

She'd make the choice for them.

Shaking her head, she exited the room. The house. She descended the steps. Climbed in her car. Drove down the driveway.

She didn't look back.

She was too busy resurrecting her walls she'd allowed to crumble. Gertrude's words from this morning pressed into her. She *had* listened though, but what she heard only reinforced what she'd expected. Being vulnerable with people wasn't the cornerstone to relationship, it was the catalyst for pain.

⇒ ⇐

Niles slowly unfolded himself from his Civic, wincing as his sore muscles protested the movement. Unfortunately, his bruised face didn't care for the wince, and he stifled a groan. Clive Bowens had a mean right hook, which he'd expertly wielded in protest of his return to jail. Niles had him by three inches, thirty pounds of muscle, and a lifetime of boxing. Even so, Clive landed a few punches before Niles had taken him down.

He was getting too old for this.

Entering Aunt Gertrude's town house, Niles hung his jacket on the hook and shuffled to the kitchen. Caffeine and an ice pack before his afternoon plans with Everleigh. He grinned at the memory of last night, the pain in the movement well worth the enjoyment of the replay. He'd kissed several women through his years but kissing her had been different. He suspected two things.

Everleigh was an expert kisser.

This was a connection he hadn't experienced before.

The careful way she tended to his aunt. Her easy banter with him. Her strength. She didn't back down—from confrontation or his kiss. And she was brilliant. Her mind worked connections others didn't see. He enjoyed chatting over his cases with her or quietly working together on a puzzle at night. Quite simply, he enjoyed her presence.

Which is why he looked forward to lunch even though every part of him hurt.

He grabbed a soda, swished down two ibuprofen, then took an ice pack from the freezer and headed upstairs. With an hour yet until they had to meet, his bed called his name. He paused at the top of the steps, confused. Someone was moving around in Everleigh's room. She shouldn't be home yet. Curious, he diverted in that direction.

A suitcase lay open on her quilted bedspread. Everleigh exited the adjoining bathroom, hands full, and crossed to her bed. He rapped his knuckles on the doorframe, and she jerked her gaze to his. Her eyes widened.

"What happened to you?" She dropped the items onto her bed and crossed to him. Her hand reached out, but before she touched his face, she pulled away.

Something was off. He'd like to think she was worried she'd hurt him if she touched his bruised cheek. His gut said otherwise. "That bail jumper I had to bring in? He tried to decline."

"Not politely, judging by your face."

Her attempt at a joke should've put him at ease, but the humor didn't reach her eyes. In fact, she was struggling to maintain eye contact with him. "You are correct." He nodded to the suitcase. "Are you heading to Massachusetts?"

"Yes." She hesitated for the barest of moments before returning to her suitcase. "My flight leaves at three. We can still sneak in a quick lunch if you'd like."

Her offer sounded like it originated from politeness, not desire. "Everything okay?"

She finally held his gaze, her eyes softening as she once again took in his face. "Says the man with the black eye and, I'm guessing, bruises I can't see."

"Nothing I haven't had before. It'll all heal." He stepped into her room, stopping on the opposite side of her bed to place the icepack on her bedside table before his fingers froze. "You didn't answer my question."

"I'm fine." She moved to her dresser and pulled out some clothing.

Her movement and tone defied her words. "You sure?"

With his challenge, her shoulders tightened. "I am."

He wasn't.

She'd slammed herself closed, and he wanted to know why. But he'd need to come from a different angle, because she was locked tight.

Niles leaned against the massive post at the foot of her bed. "Do you need a ride to the airport or does John have it covered?"

"I'm good. I'll drive separate and head there straight from lunch." She tucked things neatly into their spaces, then closed her suitcase and set it on the floor. "Ready?"

She wanted to pretend like everything was fine. He wanted her to tell him what was wrong. They hadn't seen each other since last night, so he didn't think her shuttered attitude linked to anything he'd done—he was simply the recipient of it. He didn't mind her struggles. He minded that she refused to share them with him.

He reached for her hand, and amazingly she let him take it. "I'm no mind reader, but it's obvious something's wrong. Tell me."

Her eyes, filled with shadows, captured his for one troubling beat. Then she blinked and something shifted. Her expression cleared of all emotion as if she had an off switch she'd hit. Oh, she tried to hide the change behind the huge smile drifting over her lips. Then tried to distract him by pressing her mouth to his. She slid her hands across his chest to link them behind his neck, pulling him close. The heat from her body warmed his sore muscles. She shifted against him. Her kiss didn't lack passion.

It lacked all feeling.

He braced his hands against her shoulders and gently pressed her away. He leaned down, his face close to hers. "As much as I enjoy kissing you, Everleigh, I want to know what's bothering you. I want you to open up to me."

"I did." She pressed in to kiss him again.

He leaned back, preventing her.

He'd wanted emotion. He got it. In the form of anger.

Her eyes flashed. "What is wrong with you? Most men I know would take kissing over talking any day."

"I'm not most men." He held his temper. She had enough for the both of them.

But then, surprisingly, she reined it in. Smoothed over the lines that had driven out from her pursed mouth and narrowed eyes. Resumed that flat smile. "No. You're not." She turned and picked up her purse. "We better get to lunch while we still have the time."

He blocked her escape. "I'm not going until we sort this out. I'm not spending the next hour sitting across from you pretending everything's okay. Let me in."

"Not you too."

He heard her mumbled words. "Me too, what?"

But instead of expounding, she shook her head. "I have let you in, Niles. I don't go around kissing just anyone."

"Which I greatly appreciate." He dragged his hand through his hair. "But I want more than the physical, Everleigh."

"We have more than that." Her fingers fiddled with the Rubik's Cube attached to her purse strap. "We flirt. We laugh. I genuinely have a good time with you."

"All things I enjoy too." He willed her to look at him, waiting patiently until she did. "But those are elements of a relationship. I want us to go deeper. You hold a part of yourself back. You were starting to let me in, but something happened since last night, and I'm on the outside again."

A long silence pulled between them. Then she sighed. "This is as much as I have to offer, Niles. I can't give you anything more."

He'd taken several punches today, but none of them hurt like the one she'd just landed.

Their attraction was strong. Their banter lightened his days. She was beautiful and smart, and Aunt Gertie loved her. He was halfway there himself. It would be easy to say what she offered was enough. But he'd settled once before, and he'd promised himself he wouldn't do that again.

"I spent a good portion of my life on the outside. My aunt loved me, but from a distance. So when Iris did the same, I thought it was natural." His voice sounded like it originated from outside his body. Maybe he, too, needed distance from this moment. A little separation from the pain he saw coming. "Like you, she kept me out and never fully gave me her heart. I thought our physical attraction was enough—that all she needed was time for us to grow closer, but we'd get there. I could be patient." He'd so convinced himself of that lie, he never saw the truth coming. "The problem with never fully giving your heart to someone is you make it easy to walk away when things get hard or your mood changes. That's exactly what Iris did." That pain healed, but he'd paid dearly for the lesson. With the cost so high, he'd vowed to use what he learned moving forward. "I won't do that again."

Her shoulders drew up in a sad sigh, then she pushed onto her tiptoes and pressed a kiss against his cheek. "I understand"—her fingertips moved to where her lips had been as she fixed a gaze full of regret on him—"but I don't open up any further than this." She stepped away and grabbed her suitcase from the floor. "I'll head straight to the airport then."

"Is my aunt going with you?"

"No. I'm going alone."

"Not even Brooke and Natalie?"

She shook her head. "I shouldn't be long, and Burt said he'd tag team with you to help Gertie while I'm gone. I figured you'd be all right with that."

"Of course." Though it did surprise him that Aunt Gertie decided to sit this trip out, along with Brooke and Natalie.

Something about this entire conversation felt off. He could press her, but it wouldn't get them anywhere. He wanted her to willingly confide in him, but she'd made her decision, and with it, stomped out any hope that wanted to linger.

When he remained silent, she turned and walked to her door. "Goodbye, Niles."

And he let her leave.

CHAPTER TWENTY-EIGHT

Archduchess Adelheid, age thirty
Rockport, Massachusetts, 1944

THE SEA ALWAYS BROUGHT HER such joy and peace. She needed both now more than ever.

Adelheid rested her hand on her still-swollen belly as she stood on the rocky shoreline, her face to the sunrise. Warm pinks and apricot tones swirled above the water, waking the sky. Sleep proved elusive these past months, and she'd become friends with the morning horizon. The consistency of dawn anchored her in a way she desperately needed.

Her fingers pressed into her abdomen. Though her womb had been empty for a week, her body remained soft and rounded. Marie promised they could stay here in her family's coastal home of Rockport until her heart and body healed. She hadn't the strength to tell her friend only one would recover.

She'd endured loss before but healing never arrived. Will's death seven months ago proved no different. The pain remained as sharp as the day she'd received word he was gone. In that moment her heart stopped, and she hadn't taken a full breath since. When she'd learned of their daughter's impending arrival weeks later, the only emotion that surfaced was a paralyzing fear. She no longer possessed the desire to love, not when she was intimately acquainted with the cost.

Hugh and Marie promised they would help her. They intended their offer to be one that allowed her to raise her and Will's child. They soon realized their aid would be in finding someone to adopt the baby. Adelheid staunchly refused any other option. She couldn't raise her on her own, even if she had the desire. But their daughter, created in love, deserved to be wholly loved. That part of Adelheid was irreversibly broken.

Someone wrapped a shawl around Adelheid's shoulders. "The Thompsons are here."

They'd arrived in town late last night, and Adelheid requested they come first thing this morning. The seven days she'd spent with her daughter in this home, hearing her tiny cries, seeing Will in the blue of her oval eyes, and even her own papa in the curve of her mouth . . . it all proved her decision to be the right one. The sooner she reached its conclusion, the better for them all.

Adelheid squeezed her friend's hand where it remained on her shoulder. "I'm coming."

Together, they turned toward the house. Picking their way across the rocks, they reached the damp grass that led to a screened-in porch. Inside, voices murmured and dishes clanked as Cook prepared a breakfast Adelheid wouldn't eat. Her body no longer provided for another life, so her missing appetite no longer proved an issue.

"What room are they in?" Adelheid asked.

"The front parlor."

She turned toward the stairs. "I will be there momentarily."

Marie's rounded cheeks lifted as her expression softened. "They're in no hurry."

But she was.

Lifting her skirts, Adelheid ascended to the third-floor nursery. She pressed open the door to find her daughter snuggled in her crib, the nanny rocking beside her in a wooden chair. The young woman immediately stood. "She's recently eaten. I burped her, changed her diaper, and laid her down to see if she'd sleep awhile longer."

"Thank you. You're free to go. I believe Cook could use your help in the kitchen."

With a nod, the girl hustled out the door. Adelheid watched her daughter cooing in the crib. Her wide eyes roamed the room. Too intrigued by the world around her, she wouldn't fall asleep anytime soon. While that would have proved easier, her daughter deserved a proper goodbye.

With a deep breath, Adelheid crossed to the crib and scooped her into her arms. Then she settled them both into the rocker the nanny had occupied. With a press of her foot to the floor, she set them in motion.

"Little One, I want you to always know that this was for your best." Adelheid blinked, surprised to find wetness in her eyes. She'd truly believed she had no tears left. "You deserve so much more than what I have to offer." No child should spend their life longing to be loved. Her greatest gift to their daughter would be ensuring that didn't happen to her. Even now, her broken heart couldn't muster what she knew she should feel. Only what she knew she should do.

She held her close, inhaling her sweet baby scent. Will would have been an amazing father. He'd reminded her so much of Papa. Loss and uncertainty had touched too much of her life. This time she'd give her heart away rather than having it torn from her.

Standing, she took a fortifying breath before she walked to the door and descended one floor to her bedroom. She gingerly laid her daughter on the bed, then moved to the wooden box on her dresser. Carefully she opened it and lifted a secret compartment to reveal an extra space in the bottom. Encased in the same hatpin from her childhood, the Florentine Diamond glittered from the black velvet interior. Adelheid removed it, then walked to her armoire. From it, she removed a letter she'd written last night along with the yellow blanket she'd crocheted over the past six months. Woven into the stitches were her and Will's initials.

She returned to the bed and wrapped her daughter in the blanket, then tucked the diamond and letter into the pocket she'd stitched, securing it with the pearl button she'd added. Picking up her daughter, she nestled her nose beside her tiny ear. "My prayer for you is that you shall never want. For comfort, shelter, or love."

And she'd done all she could to ensure that prayer would be answered. Through giving her to this couple, she hoped to guarantee love. In this final hiding place of the diamond, provision for all her needs.

Arms full, Adelheid walked them to the parlor. As she stepped through the door, a young couple turned from where they stood in front of the fireplace. Sam Thompson was tall and thin, much the same build as Will. But where Will's hair had been chocolate brown, this man's was blond. Leah

Thompson stood beside him. Short in stature, her sweet nature filled the room. She'd wrapped her blond locks into a braided bun and soft tendrils curled around her face. Their eyes held tentative hope.

They had nothing to fear. She would not change her mind. They could give her daughter what she could not.

Adelheid walked straight to Leah. She pressed a kiss to her daughter's forehead before slipping her into her new mother's arms.

Tears slid down Leah's face. "Has she a name?"

"Vienna. Though if you'd like to change it . . ."

Leah shook her head. "Vienna is beautiful." She peeked up at Adelheid. "This way she'll always have a part of you."

Vienna stretched in Leah's arms, then nestled into her hold. Adelheid pointed to the blanket. "There's a family heirloom tucked inside the pocket. It was meant for me to wear on my wedding day." She swallowed around the sudden tightness in her throat. "Should you ever need anything at all, that will provide for you."

Sam wrapped his arm around his wife's waist. "There is nothing more that we could need, but if there were, God will provide."

He didn't say the words with any haughtiness. Rather, a peaceful trust rang through his voice and stance. Sam stood secure in who he was and who his God was, making Adelheid even more sure of her decision.

"There's also a letter. You may decide when or if to give it to her."

Leah pulled her loving stare from Vienna. "'Thank you' doesn't seem like enough."

"I am the one who should be thanking you." The air grew stifling around Adelheid. She needed to leave. "I wish you safe travels." Turning, she raced from the room.

Soon after, Marie found her along the rocky shore again.

"They're gone," Marie spoke softly. "They're taking the train to Buchanan, Virginia. Sam's been called as a missionary to the people in the mountains there."

Her daughter's life would be so vastly different from the world Adelheid grew up in.

For that, she was thankful.

CHAPTER TWENTY-NINE

Three days in Rockport.

Three days of ignoring her ringing phone and buzzing texts.

Three days of fruitless searches among the cobwebs in a dank basement.

Today something needed to change.

Everleigh pushed open the heavy door that permitted access to the storage room of what was once Dr. Warren Fairchild's practice. Two of the walls held small rectangular windows that let in slivers of light, illuminating dust that danced on the air and covered the contents of the room. Someone had added metal shelving throughout the space and packed every square inch with old medical equipment and boxes upon boxes of files.

No doubt that someone was Dr. Fairchild's son, who'd graciously given her access to the space. His father had willed the building to him since he'd followed in his footsteps and also gone into medicine. It had functioned as a local medical clinic until a decade ago when he'd decided to change careers and pursue his lifelong dream of owning a small-town café. Now the upstairs hosted a popular coffee shop and bakery with such amazing scones Everleigh might very well have gained five pounds in the past three days.

That was the only thing she'd gained.

She didn't especially feel like counting her losses, but her buzzing phone ensured she couldn't forget them.

Glancing at her screen, she saw Natalie's number flash again. Niles had stopped calling after he left two voice mails. The first explained in great detail that he didn't appreciate her lies by omission when she neglected to inform him that Natalie, Brooke, and his aunt weren't accompanying her because she hadn't informed them she was leaving. Or told Natalie and Brooke about her findings. He'd threatened to fly them all out there.

His second voice mail said the only reason he wasn't was because they all were willing to give her space.

He must have agreed with them because he hadn't called again.

Neither had Brooke or Gertie.

But Natalie continued to leave messages letting her know that when Everleigh was ready, she'd be there to talk things out.

Too bad, but Natalie was going to be disappointed. There was nothing to talk through. It was the same old song, different verse, and she was done singing it.

Everleigh flipped on the light switch and crossed the dimly lit space to the shelves that held Dr. Fairchild's old files. Whoever moved them hadn't given any thought to keeping them organized. Different years and dates were mixed in with random patients, nothing alphabetized either. The only order Everleigh had been able to find in this search was to start in one corner and slowly work her way through every piece of paperwork. She'd made it two-thirds of the way through the room. With a sigh, she grabbed another stack of folders and sat at the desk she'd cleared off the first day.

Two hours into her search, the scent of the day's soup and bread special pulled her attention from the current book. She rubbed her sore eyes. Maybe this was a fruitless effort. She had to be crazy to think she could come here and find information that proved, yes, Adelheid had a daughter named Vienna. But she couldn't let go of the feeling that she was on the right track, and if she left this room without looking at every single piece of paper in here, she'd always wonder.

Besides, where else was she going to go? She was under no illusion that Gertrude would ask her to stay on after all of this. She didn't have another job to return to or anything to pull her back to Kenton Corners. Staying here made the most sense. Either she'd leave with a new lead on the diamond, or she'd accept Uncle Maddox's offer to help her find a new place to stay. His had been the only texts she returned.

Thirty more minutes, then she'd break for lunch.

Twenty-three minutes later her breath hitched in her lungs.

Was that . . . ?

She traced the name on the birth certificate in front of her.

Vienna Hayes Thompson.

Everleigh sat back in her chair. Took a deep breath. Leaned forward again.

Hayes was William's surname.

And the birth date listed: 8/31/1944. That fit.

Sam and Leah Thompson were listed as parents, but she knew in her gut this little girl was Adelheid and Will's child. The birth certificate might have been doctored to cover up that fact, but it was the only thing that made sense.

Her mind spun, and while she couldn't answer all the questions bombarding her, she'd just found an answer to a huge one. Vienna was indeed a person, and she could very well have the Florentine Diamond or know its location.

Everleigh jumped up from her chair, excitement buzzing under her skin like it did when she was close to solving a puzzle. Adrenaline took hold and she grabbed her laptop from her backpack, her next step as familiar as her own name. Finding information and knowing how to connect it to her next piece of the picture came easily. She fired up Google and headed to a paid site where she could locate addresses, birth and death certificates, even criminal records with only a name. She purchased a subscription, then her fingers flew across the keyboard, entering Vienna's full birth name and date.

Within seconds a marriage certificate popped up on screen. Vienna had married a Roger Rydel. Knowing her new surname, Everleigh checked next for a death certificate, and when none popped up, she searched for a current address and exhaled as one popped up.

Serenity Falls, Virginia.

She not only had a name, but a next location. The strongest lead they'd found yet. Only . . . she peered around the empty room. The silence pressed into her with a force she hadn't expected.

Flicking her gaze away from her phone, she pulled up the Expedia site before her common sense caught up with her. She could finish this alone. If the diamond happened to be with Vienna, she'd bring it back and ensure everyone received their payment from Caspar. She harbored hurt but no ill will toward Natalie and Brooke.

Then there was Niles. For the life of her she couldn't seem to get a read on her heart when it came to him.

All the while, a sliver of guilt over pursuing these answers without Gertrude wiggled in.

Instead of facing the choices in front of her, Everleigh found a flight and booked a ticket to Virginia, determined to run before all her emotions could overtake her.

⇢ ⇠

After an evening plane ride to Roanoke, Virginia, followed by a car ride to Serenity Falls, Everleigh made it to her new hotel room. She dragged her suitcase inside and did her best to shut out the guilt following her since she'd left Kenton Corners. The closer she came to finding Vienna and the diamond, the worse she felt.

She didn't want to see anyone. She also didn't want to rob Gertrude of this moment. Somewhere along the way she'd made a heart connection with Gertie, but it wasn't only that. Gertie was a fellow puzzler who'd been collecting clues to this one particular mystery for years. Everleigh knew what it was like to have done the work of connecting all the pieces, then someone came along and placed the last one. If she saw Vienna without Gertrude by her side, she'd be guilty of the same thing.

With a groan, she settled onto the lumpy bed. This place wasn't nearly as nice as the hotels they'd stayed in up to this point. That's what happened when she hopped off the company payroll. She'd bankrolled this entire trip, and her pockets resembled those tiny ones on jeans that could barely hold a penny, whereas Caspar's ran deep.

Picking up her phone, she ignored her days' worth of unreturned text messages. No new ones had accumulated, well, except for spammers. Each time one dinged, Everleigh's heart jolted into a fast rhythm, until she realized it wasn't Niles. She didn't need the reminder that she missed him, because the weight of his absence pressed against her daily. Really, though, what more did they have to say to each other? They wanted different things.

She dialed Gertrude's number before she changed her mind. Three rings in and she answered. "About time you called."

Unable to read her phone screen, Gertrude had given everyone their own ringtone. "How are you, Gertrude?"

"Indignant."

She'd expected as much. "I'm sorry I left without you." Might as well hop right to the heart of the matter. "I would like it if you could find a way to come and meet me." As Gertrude started to respond, Everleigh qualified her request. "This invitation doesn't include Niles, Brooke, or Natalie."

"Burt can take me." She offered a simple plan without arguing. "Where are you?"

"Buchanan, Virginia."

"I'll be there tomorrow. Think you can pause your Lone Ranger antics until then?"

With her promise, they disconnected. Everleigh emailed the necessary information to Burt. Within the hour he returned her email with Gertrude's flight information. He'd been able to secure them a direct flight, first class, arriving tomorrow at eleven in the morning.

Everleigh settled into bed for the night. Her phone dinged a text. She picked it up.

Uncle Maddox.

> Sorry Palmer caused you more trouble.

Everleigh typed back.

> Not your fault. I knew what I signed up for.

> Doesn't make it any easier.

> I'm not used to things being easy. Why start now?

Three dots appeared. Disappeared. Then a meme of a man playing a violin filled her screen.

Ha. Ha. Ha.

Seriously though, you okay?

It's all good.

Standard answer.

Because it's true.

Try again.

What did it say that her strongest relationship was with someone she rarely saw? Maybe there was something wrong with her. She knew he would just keep pushing, so she typed.

Just tired.

Never was that statement so true. Exhaustion pulled at every part of her. How did one rest a soul, though?

Those dots went through another round of appearing and disappearing. Finally,

Get some sleep. I'll check in
with you tomorrow.

Sounds good.

Good night, Sunshine.

She may or may not answer the next day, but she wouldn't tell him that. Everleigh texted her own good night then plugged in her phone. She'd call

Vienna in the morning, and if all went well, by this time tomorrow she'd have helped Gertie solve a lifelong puzzle.

Now, if only she could solve her own.

Nowhere near ready for sleep, Everleigh stared at the ceiling as she wrapped the scratchy hotel blanket around her. Pieces of her life lay scattered about. She couldn't connect them into the old picture anymore, but they also didn't form a new one. It made no sense. What had always seemed like such a perfect fit for her, no longer did.

Huffing, she stood to pace. She had a feeling a long night stretched ahead, and she worried the only person finding answers tomorrow would be Gertie.

Though she prayed she would too.

CHAPTER THIRTY

VIENNA HAYES THOMPSON RYDEL LIVED in a tiny log cabin along the banks of the James River. The Blue Ridge and Allegheny Mountains soared on either side of her home, their hills bursting in shades of emerald green against a sapphire sky. What Vienna lacked in interior square footage, she made up for with her views.

"I wish you could see this," Everleigh said as she parked her car.

Burt had delivered Gertrude to her at the airport before hopping a return flight home. After a quick lunch with minimal conversation, Everleigh drove herself and Gertrude straight here. Neither of the women could stomach any further delays.

From the passenger seat where she'd rolled down her window, Gertie inhaled deeply. "Between the pines I smell, the rushing water I hear, and the warmth of the sunshine, I can imagine it's beautiful."

It only felt right, coming to the end of this mystery in such a magical place. When she'd spoken with Vienna this morning, the old woman quietly listened to Everleigh's tale. How Gertrude had searched for years, wanting to finish this hunt for the sister she'd started it with. How they'd come into contact with a mystery man named Caspar. How that led to visiting places she'd only dreamed of seeing, and how they'd met such helpful people along the way. Rafael. Jerrick. Fleur. And how, for reasons they'd expound on later, they thought her parents might be connected to the story as well.

When she'd finished, Vienna didn't confirm or deny her relation to the Habsburgs—or if she had the diamond.

She did, however, warmly invite them to her home.

Everleigh helped Gertrude from the car. "Nervous?"

Gertrude leaned on her cane with a small laugh. "Excited. Nerves don't do anyone any good. I can't change what's about to happen, but I can be hopeful for answers. No matter what they may be, I've enjoyed the journey in getting here." She gripped Everleigh's hand where she held her steady. "I've enjoyed getting to know you."

"And I, you." As she said the words, she realized she meant them.

They neared the cabin and the front door opened. An elderly woman stepped out. Even far past her youth, Vienna's long face and rounded chin resembled that of the pictures Everleigh had seen of Archduchess Adelheid. As did her apple cheeks and still-brown hair—Everleigh doubted she dyed it. Her wide eyes belonged to her father, Will. Everleigh recalled how filled with life they were in the picture of him and Adelheid.

She had no doubts. This was their daughter.

"Welcome. You must be Gertrude and Everleigh." Her alto voice held an accent that sounded Southern but with a twist Everleigh couldn't place. She immediately felt like they should be sitting on her front porch drinking a sweet tea.

Vienna invited them to do exactly that.

Once they were situated, she and Gertrude on her porch swing and Vienna in a nearby rocker, Everleigh spoke. "Thank you so much for inviting us here today."

"I feel I had to after hearing your story." Vienna held a hatbox in her lap. The cream cardboard was covered in florals and worn in places. She opened the top and pulled out a photo album. "I wanted to show you my parents."

She appeared in no hurry to talk to them about the diamond, and Everleigh sensed she wasn't a woman easily rushed. The slow, easy rhythm of her rocking chair seemed to set their pace, and Everleigh downshifted to match it.

Reaching over, she took the book. Gertrude leaned in close. "Narrate it for me."

Everleigh cracked the book open. She peeked from the first black-and-white photo over to Vienna. "These are your parents?"

"Sam and Leah Thompson. They raised me in this cabin. Daddy was a missionary, but I daresay it was Mama who filled their revival meetings.

She could bake the best pies in the county." Sweet memories played wistfully across her face. "They'd come hungry for a slice and leave full of Jesus."

"She sounds like a wonderful woman," Gertrude said.

"She was."

Everleigh flipped through the book, describing the photos that told the story of Vienna's upbringing. The day her parents adopted her. Building this cabin. The small tent where her mother taught children to read during the day and her father held services at night. Vienna transitioned from an infant to a child to a beautiful young woman. There were only a handful of pictures, but each one showed the love between her and her parents. The first photo with Vienna alone appeared to have been taken when she was in her late teens or early twenties.

"That was taken shortly after my parents passed away."

Everleigh's hand stilled against the plastic covered page. "How old were you?"

"Nineteen. They died on the mountain, coming home from praying with a family whose child was sick. That child was healed. Mama and Daddy went on to heaven."

Gertrude shifted, reaching out her hand toward Vienna's voice. "I'm so sorry for your loss."

Vienna accepted her touch, gently returning the squeeze. "It was a long time ago. I suppose you've realized, too, that life is filled with all kinds of moments. Joy, laughter, grief, tears. They balance each other. I wouldn't appreciate the sweet moments nearly as much if I never knew the painful ones." She released Gertrude to set herself rocking once again. "Our God is good. All the time."

"All the time, God is good," Gertrude responded with the familiar refrain.

"What did you do after they passed away?" Everleigh asked.

"Keep flipping those pages and you'll see."

She'd gone on to college. Visited the ocean with friends. Earned her teaching degree. Returned home. Taught first grade at the tiny redbrick school in Serenity Falls. Met her husband. Had three children. Directed the Christmas plays at her church. Won blue ribbons with her mama's pie recipe. Become a grandmother. Buried her husband. Purchased horses and rode them. Become a great-grandmother.

Vienna Hayes Thompson Rydel had led a full life.

An hour filled with memories later, Everleigh turned the final page. A gasp slipped out of her lips before she even fully processed what her fingertips touched.

Gertrude straightened beside her. "What?"

She gingerly lifted the paper from the book. "It's Adelheid." The photo was on a page torn from some book. Adelheid reclined on a stool. She wore a dark, fitted silk gown with large poofs of tulle stretching from her shoulders. Her hair was styled in a short, waved bob reminiscent of the 1920s, and she held a pair of white full-length gloves in her hand. It was a familiar picture that Everleigh had seen many times during her internet research of Adelheid.

Everleigh returned the photo to the book and met Vienna's twinkling gaze. The old woman sipped her sweet tea. "When Mama and Daddy passed away, I couldn't go through their things. So I closed up this cabin and lived in a small apartment in town. Then Henry and I married and bought a home near the school. He taught me not to grieve the past, but to celebrate our here and now. He convinced me to come here each summer. He boxed up Mama and Daddy's things and put them out in the shed for me, and we got busy living life." She nodded to the small building a few yards from her home. "Our children loved it here, and we built our own memories. When Henry passed, I decided to move out here permanently. I was so busy enjoying my kids and my grandkids that I didn't think to go through that shed." She patted the hatbox in her lap. "But seasons change and this one provides me with a few more quiet days. Imagine my surprise when I decided to tackle that shed one day and discovered where I came from."

Beside her, Gertrude had gone still. She had to be wondering the same thing as Everleigh. Was the Florentine Diamond in that old, cardboard box?

Vienna slid the top off and lifted out a soft yellow baby blanket. Next, she lifted a folded sheet of paper. She settled both on her lap. "That picture was tucked in here with all of this. I added it to my photo album because she is a part of my life. If it weren't for her, all those other pages wouldn't be filled."

Questions filled Everleigh's mind, but none felt appropriate to ask. Instead, she settled in and allowed Vienna to continue her slow unraveling of her story.

She unfolded the one-page letter. "I'd like to read this to you."

Gertrude pressed in as if to ensure she didn't miss a word.

Vienna lifted the reading glasses that dangled from a beaded string around her neck. She slipped them on her face and held the letter close.

> *Darling Vienna,*
>
> *I gave you up so you would have a life I could not provide. When your father passed away, something broke inside me. A piece that had been weakened through all my years. I possess the ability to clothe you, shelter you, educate you. I could provide a life of traveling the world and tasting riches you may now never know. I could do all of these things, yet none of it would matter, for I could not give you the one thing you needed most: love. So I give you to someone who can.*
>
> *I also give the diamond that I would have worn to marry your father. It only seems right that you should have it now. Should you ever be in need, this will provide.*
>
> *Humbly yours,*
> *Adelheid*

Vienna folded the letter and returned it to the hatbox. "Immediately after reading this, I researched her to see if she ever married or had more children."

"You wondered if you had siblings," Gertrude surmised.

Vienna nodded. "But she never married."

A hummingbird darted to the feeder on the corner of the porch. Everleigh watched it flit and dodge around the red container. A beautiful creature that never stopped moving even to fill its emptiness. She blinked to Vienna. "As far as we can tell, she never had another relationship at all. She stayed busy helping her mother and traveling for family affairs."

"That's what I discovered as well." Vienna wiped condensation from her glass and took another sip. "It's interesting, isn't it? We both experienced loss. We both made ourselves busy. She was busy building walls while I was busy building my life. She wanted to close herself off, and I wanted to experience as much as I could. Why do you think that is?"

Everleigh had no clue. It was a mystery she'd love to solve but didn't know where to start searching for the answer.

Vienna stopped rocking. She set down her tea. She stretched the yellow baby blanket over her lap. One small pearl held a pocket closed, the letters *W* and *A* embroidered in white on either side of the shiny button. With hands covered in age spots and wrinkles rounding each knuckle, Vienna opened the pocket and slowly pulled out an item. Small diamonds sparkled in the sunlight, set together in a rounded section that widened then narrowed again before another section began. Everleigh immediately recognized the piece from pictures they'd studied. Even knowing what would come, she sat in disbelief. As the fourth section pulled free from the pocket, Everleigh's breath halted.

The Florentine Diamond. Arches of additional tiny diamonds surrounded the massive gem, making up the fourth and final link to the hat ornament.

"Gertrude," she whispered as she grasped her hand.

"It's here?" Gertrude squeezed Everleigh's fingers.

Vienna stood and brought it to them. She placed it in Gertrude's free hand. "You've spent a lifetime seeking this. I believe you should have a chance to hold it."

Removing her grip from Everleigh's, Gertrude carefully cradled the hatpin. Her fingers traced the piece, coming to rest on the diamond whose story had dominated nearly all of her life. "I don't mind that I can't see it, but oh do I wish my sister Amelia could." She blinked rapidly, no doubt trying to prevent tears from falling, but one managed to escape.

Vienna returned to her seat. "Ever been told that a diamond is simply a lump of coal that did well under pressure?"

Everleigh nodded at the familiar saying, but Gertrude chuckled. "I always hated that saying. Diamonds aren't made from coal."

Vienna smiled. "No, they are not. They are related, but not the same." She set to rocking again. "Coal is made from carbon and dead plants. It holds on to all the dead things, and it turns black. A diamond, on the other hand, is made from pure carbon. When pressure hits, it shines. It has clarity. It still hardens, but it hardens into something beautiful that captures light and then throws that light all around.

"And diamonds come in all sorts of colors, like that one you're holding, because sometimes there are tiny impurities that pop up. They change the diamond, but in the end, they only make it rarer. Special."

Vienna was tossing her the clues to the mystery she'd proposed only moments before.

"I like to think I'm like that Florentine Diamond."

And though she left it unsaid, Adelheid had become the coal. That didn't mean she'd been harsh or even that she hadn't loved her daughter. By giving her up, she'd demonstrated a love she hadn't believed herself capable of. It simply meant she'd allowed the circumstances of life to rob her of living a full one. A faceted life filled with clarity and color.

Something began to crack open inside Everleigh.

Vienna continued, "I opened that hatbox two years ago. I've prayed ever since then about what to do with that diamond. I don't need it. My life is already overflowing with treasures. But I sensed God asking me to hold on to it until he told me it was time to let it go. When you called yesterday, I felt him telling me that time had come."

Gertrude leaned back in the swing as if undone by the reality that her decade's search was ending here on this porch in the middle of a small town in Virginia. It would take time for them all to digest this moment.

A moment Everleigh had stolen from Brooke and Natalie.

She'd need to face that hard truth later.

"You're really going to let us take this?"

Vienna nodded. "On one condition."

"Anything." Gertrude spoke before Everleigh could. Though the same response rested on her lips.

"Don't tell people about me. I enjoy my quiet life, and I'd like to keep it that way."

"You don't want people to know you helped find this lost treasure? There could be a finder's fee." If there was, she wouldn't take it from this woman.

Vienna's face lit with a peace that had to originate from deep inside. "Oh, I know most call that a treasure, but to me, my treasure is captured in that book you're holding. All the years spent with my friends and family. Relationships made. Love soaked up and spilled out. They've filled my heart so full, there's no amount of money or accolades this world could give me that would ever be better."

For where your treasure is, there your heart will be also.

The verse from Matthew rang through Everleigh's mind. She'd never seen it so exemplified as in the woman in front of her. And she'd honor her wishes. Her wheels started turning about how to answer the multitude of questions coming their way. They'd figure it out.

Together.

Having agreed to her terms, they all stayed on the porch. Vienna told them more stories. Gertrude held tight to the diamond. And Everleigh worked to solve the new mystery in her mind—was she coal or could she choose to be a diamond?

CHAPTER THIRTY-ONE

EVERLEIGH STARED OUT THE WINDOW as they descended from the clouds. They'd be landing in Chicago in twenty minutes, nearly a week after she'd fled by herself. Hopefully, the damage her actions caused could be overcome.

"You've been awfully quiet." Gertrude spoke to her right.

Gertrude had sprung for first class tickets for their flight home, declaring at her age she'd earned the right to splurge. They'd agreed not to speak one word about their search or the diamond during their public travel. Gertrude secured the piece in her carry-on which they didn't allow out of their sight. They'd prayed their way through TSA, thankful for the ease of the pre-check line, and miraculously made it through without a hitch. It definitely helped that their outbound travel was through a smaller airport.

"I'm just tired, I suppose."

"I bet." Gertrude removed her other earbud. She'd been listening to an Agatha Christie novel. "It takes a lot of energy to always hold people at arm's length."

Everleigh opened her mouth to fire off a sharp quip of some sort, then stopped. "Yeah," she admitted, "it does."

"I'm guessing that Vienna's diamond talk got you thinking."

"It did."

Gertie set both earbuds on her iPhone. "Mind if I add my two cents?"

Every puzzle or mystery Everleigh ever solved involved collecting loads of information, clues, and pieces. She'd study them all to see which were pertinent and which she could ignore. She'd do the same here.

"Please do."

"One thing that Vienna and I share in common? We're both on the far side of life."

She tapped Gertrude's hands. "Would you stop with the 'I'm ancient' bit? Age is just a number, and yours is low."

"I assure you"—Gertrude returned the tap—"age is not just a number. My bones feel every one of my years."

Everleigh *pfft*'d her.

"Either way, my age says I've been on this planet longer than you, which means I've accumulated a lot of knowledge."

"And I thank you for sharing your wisdom with me." She'd done so numerous times, and Everleigh appreciated those moments.

"See, that's what I want to talk with you about." Gertrude's voice lowered, denoting a move from teasing to seriousness. "Everyone makes the little old woman the wise one in books or movies, but let me tell you, I'm not. But I do have hindsight and that lends to wishing how I'd have done things differently." She twisted in her seat to fully face her. "I've not been sharing my wisdom with you, Everleigh, I've been sharing my wishes."

The ardency in her voice. The ruefulness on her face. They heightened Everleigh's attention, pulling her further in as Gertrude continued. "I was like that lump of coal. I let too many things cut me off from what really mattered. Adelheid, me, you . . . we're all alike in that way. Our catalysts might all be different. Our reactions not alike. But our outcomes were the same. We don't let anyone close."

The plane jostled, and they gripped their seats.

"You okay?" Everleigh held Gertrude's hand until the turbulence passed.

"A few bumps aren't going to stop me." She maintained their shared touch as she talked on. "You keep on pushing people away, one day you're going to wake up and realize you gained your distance but lost yourself in the process."

Everleigh stilled as the echo of the words she'd read in Royalston rolled over her. She'd never told that part of Luciana's journal to Gertrude. Chill bumps peppered her skin, as if God had used Gertrude's voice to turn up the volume on what he was trying to tell her.

Oblivious to Everleigh's churning emotions, Gertrude went on. "Wishing about the past is wasted emotion if it doesn't lead to transformation in your present." She pressed into Everleigh's personal space. "Change your life, sweet girl. Make it count so you aren't left with memories filled with more remorse than love. You'll have experience, a life chock-full of rich moments built with friends and family. Wishes that you went out and made come true."

Gertrude quieted. Then with a nod, she settled into her chair, their hands still clasped. "We'll be landing soon."

The Chicago skyline filled the landscape outside her window. Everleigh had boarded this plane wondering if she was coal or a diamond. Gertrude's words sealed the conclusion she'd already reached. They also gave her hope for change. There was only one thing strong enough in her life to help her do that. Only one thing that could overcome her weaknesses, her habits, her fears. One thing that could truly take this heart change from a wish to reality.

A person, not a thing. And he was the one piece that could solve every puzzle in her life. He held all the answers.

She sat straight.

God.

He was the answer to Uncle Maddox's riddle. God was simultaneously something she could never solve and yet the one solution to every question and empty place in her life. She didn't need to figure him out to trust him, because God wasn't an enigma to solve. She could spend a lifetime delving into the mysteries of him and never find every answer. Yet he knew every single thing about her, and he still desired relationship with her.

She wanted the same thing with him. Because what she did know about him said he could be trusted. Sometimes to remove the hardships. Sometimes to walk her through them.

And that he loved her oh, so much.

Everleigh closed her eyes, lifting a prayer as the plane lowered. She handed God every anxious thought. All her insecurities. Each aching wound. And she watched as he began to piece together a new picture for her. One he'd been holding all along but she couldn't see because she'd been too intent on creating her own. His was so much more beautiful, and she could only see the border. The rest would come together slowly as she walked out the changes he'd enable her to make—if she continued to trust in him.

She would. And no doubt there'd be other course corrections along the way. She was far from perfect, but she determined here and now to keep pressing into the one who covered those imperfections with his grace.

As the plane bumped along the tarmac, Everleigh opened her eyes. She wasn't the same woman who'd boarded this plane. She wasn't the same woman who'd flown away several days ago. All change required was the determination to be different. But the evidence of that change would take time to be seen. With God's help, she could develop the effort and patience she'd need for the process, because it wouldn't be easy, but it would be worthwhile.

They taxied to the gate and the door finally opened. Everleigh grabbed their bags from the overhead bin and attached them together so she'd have a free hand available to guide Gertrude.

"Ready?" Gertrude asked, though the sound of that one word encompassed more than simply disembarking this plane.

"I am." Everleigh moved them out the door. She leaned toward her friend as they walked up the Jetway. "Thank you, Gertrude."

The old woman answered with a nod and a smile that spoke volumes.

They made it to Everleigh's car, exited the airport, and headed toward Halstead Manor. She'd texted the crew, including Niles, that they needed to meet. She hadn't called because she wanted to speak to them all in person. There was so much to tell everyone, but Everleigh's apology pressed strongest against her lips.

She only hoped they would accept it.

CHAPTER THIRTY-TWO

Everleigh climbed the steps to Halstead Manor, recalling the first time she'd stepped foot inside. So much had changed in the past six weeks. They were changes she wanted to keep. Still, her stomach twisted. Owning your stuff brought freedom, but—in her case—it also brought nausea.

Luckily, just as they'd arrived, Uncle Maddox sent a return text to the one she'd sent him giving the solution to his riddle. His words of reassurance and promise to pray helped settle her stomach. Some.

She pressed open the door for Gertrude. "We'll go to the left," she instructed.

Everleigh stood on her right, allowing Gertrude to skim the wall on her left. Surprisingly, Gertrude moved without her normal pause. Her confidence spoke of familiarity, which Everleigh attributed to a growing ease with her lost eyesight rather than the location, because Gertrude hadn't been here in decades. It was encouraging to see.

They stopped at the parlor. John perched on his desk, facing the open pocket doors. "Good afternoon. Did you have a good flight?"

A polite opening to their meeting. No surprise since they were the first ones here and small talk was really their only option at this point. "We did." She led Gertrude to the couch and helped her settle. "On time and smooth. Really couldn't ask for more."

John gripped the edge of the desk as he crossed his ankles. "Caspar would like us to call once everyone is here."

They trickled in over the next few minutes. Natalie first. Brooke next. Finally, Niles. Each greeted Gertrude, nodded a guarded hello to Everleigh, then took up positions around the room that kept them a safe distance away.

"Before we call Caspar," Everleigh began, nerves tightening her voice and cutting it off. She cleared her throat. "I have something I need to say."

The group turned their attention to her, caution in their expressions. Brooke stood with crossed arms and a tense jaw, while everyone else's stances seemed open to at least hearing her out. That bolstered her courage.

Hands fiddling with her Rubik's Cube, she plunged into her apology before fear replaced her wobbly bravery. "I'm sorry I ran off without you. You guys deserved to be there, and I kept you out of the loop. I went off alone because it's my default setting. But I don't want it to be anymore."

The tick of the grandfather clock reverberated in their maintained silence. Palms wet but mouth dry, Everleigh continued. "I know I'm not the easiest person to make friends with." An understatement she hoped to change. "I'm great at all the surfacy stuff, but I put up huge walls when it comes to anything deeper. I wanted you to trust me, when I was unwilling to trust you with every part of me. And I am sorry." Tough words to say, yet they felt immensely right rolling off her tongue.

This fresh start required everything out in the open, so she held nothing back. "I helped Constance Quimby stash her money away from her son."

"Everleigh, you don't have to—" Natalie began.

"I know." She held up her hand. "I want to." They'd already demonstrated in so many ways their desire to be friends. She'd been the one to remain closed off. No more. "Palmer Quimby is a selfish drug addict who Constance tried to help multiple times, unsuccessfully. He was siphoning off her money to support his habits along with his wife's."

Brooke scoffed. "I've only met him once, and I believe that."

He did know how to make an impression. "Constance worried about her grandchildren. She wanted to restructure her will so everything went to them once they reach the age of twenty-five, but if Palmer caught wind of what she was doing, he'd contest it and try to have her qualified as incompetent. And her lawyers had become more loyal to him because they believed he'd be inheriting her fortune soon."

The attention in the room remained on her with Brooke still closed off and Niles impassive, but Natalie gave her an encouraging smile. One out of three was a start. "I put Constance in touch with my Uncle Maddox, and he set up an Offshore Asset Protection Trust for her in the Canary Islands where he lives. It's incredibly hard to trace, and with the laws structured how they are, Palmer can't legally touch it or contest it. But he can try. I stayed quiet because I didn't want to give him any idea where the money had gone. The longer he was in the dark, the better."

That wasn't the only reason, though, and she was going to own all of it. "Plus, I thought I shouldn't have to defend myself to you before you'd defend me to others."

Brooke rolled her eyes. "We didn't ask for answers so we could defend you."

"We asked"—Natalie joined in—"so we could know and support you."

"Yeah." Everleigh blinked rapidly. "I get that now, and if you'll give me a chance, I really would like to try to be friends. You guys mean a lot to me." With uncertainty accelerating her pulse, she nervously turned to Niles, who remained disturbingly silent. "More than I expected, and I don't want to lose you."

He didn't move. Not even a muscle on his face twitched.

Brooke, however, shifted. Her hands gripped her hips, and her silvery eyes kept their cool edge.

Finally, Natalie broke the silence. "I said I'd be here to listen when you were ready to talk, and I meant it." She tucked a wavy piece of her hair behind her ear. "I don't like what you did, but I understand a bit better now why you did it, so thank you for sharing." She paused, as if choosing her words carefully. "I'd like to try and be friends, too, and I think you honestly meant your apology."

"I did. I do." Everleigh added every ounce of conviction she could to her words.

"Then I forgive you." Natalie stepped over and engulfed Everleigh in a hug as she spoke. After a second, she motioned for Brooke to join them. "Brooke?"

Brooke flicked her gaze from Natalie to Everleigh as indecision rippled across her face. Everleigh couldn't blame her. Especially as Brooke put words to her feelings. "I appreciate the apology, too, Everleigh, I really do, but what you did was messed up. Keeping the information about your suspicions on Vienna from us was wrong. And okay, we got past that and didn't follow you to Rockport because we could tell you needed space. But we never once thought you'd retrieve the diamond on your own. Ditching us on that? It hurts."

"I know." She hadn't then, not fully, but she did now.

"Do you? Really? Because friendship isn't my strong suit either, but I started to let you in. Then you cut me out. Now my knee-jerk reaction is to cut *you* out." Each word arrived with more force until Brooke abruptly stopped. She peered up at the ceiling, a weighted pause settling between them. Finally, with a long sigh, she returned her gaze to Everleigh's. "I suppose I'm working on changing, too, though, because I'm not going to do that." Brooke had no problem speaking her mind, after she thought through exactly what was on it. "Our friendship took a hit and it's going to take time for me to trust you again. I'll need to see actions, not just hear words. But I'm willing to try if you are."

Everleigh nodded. "Absolutely."

They both stood there awkwardly until Natalie snagged Brooke and dragged her to their side. "A great place to start is with a group hug."

Brooke groaned but stepped into it. "Is this going to become a regular thing?"

Timid laughter released from Everleigh as she embraced the moment. Group hugs were new to her, too, but she could get used to them. Just, "Maybe we save them for special occasions."

"You'll be amazed at what I can qualify as a special occasion." Natalie gave another tight squeeze then lifted her head from their small huddle. She bent and nabbed Gertrude from the sofa while calling to the guys. "Come on. Not all the group is in here."

John sighed but walked over.

Niles remained against the wall. Everleigh lifted her head and latched on to his gorgeous brown eyes. "You coming, Yogi?" She waited a beat, then, "Please?"

The edge of his mouth tipped up, and he slowly shook his head. Pressing off the wall, he strolled toward her. She turned from the group hug to meet him halfway and slip into his embrace. He wrapped strong arms around her. "You make it very difficult to stay upset with you."

She tipped her chin up to capture his full attention. "I'm sorry I walked away. I can't promise I'll never make you upset again, but I do promise not to walk away again. To stay and talk things through even when it's hard."

"That mean you're ready to let me in? All the way?"

She nodded. "I might need a little space sometimes to regroup, but I will always come back around and work through the tough conversations."

"Deal." He brushed her hair behind her ear, his fingers lingering there. "So you really want to be friends?" He repeated her words from minutes earlier.

"I'd like friends to be where we start."

"And where we finish?"

His touch. His nearness. She leaned into him and the promise of what could be. "Anywhere that's together."

"Has he kissed her yet?" Gertrude's voice broke in.

"No," Natalie answered. "No, he has not."

Everleigh lifted her lips till they nearly touched his. "Don't want your aunt upset."

"Everleigh." The way he said her name, with a tempered craving that hinted at a voracious appetite, curled the most delectable warmth through her. "I will never need an excuse to kiss you."

And then he did.

＊ ＊

Unfortunately, more kissing would have to wait until later.

Everleigh and Niles sat beside his aunt on the couch. Natalie reclined opposite them in the leather club chair, while Brooke settled on its arm. John returned to his perch on his desk's edge to dial Caspar.

Phase one of her apology was over, and while it had been a success—her lips still tingled at the memory—phase two would be more difficult. She'd not only robbed the people in this room of a moment they'd worked hard for, but she'd also put her job in jeopardy. If Caspar decided to dock her pay, she'd understand. She'd promised not to go off alone, and she'd broken that promise. It was her bad decision to own, and it might turn out to be a costly one.

Caspar eventually answered. "Hello, everyone."

"Hi, Caspar." They responded in unison.

"John tells me that you went on a fact-finding mission on your own, Everleigh."

The benefit to his computerized voice was it remained emotionless. Therefore, she heard no condemnation. Interestingly enough, she didn't feel it from him either.

"I did. And I apologized." It had been hard, but also freeing. Reconciliation was coming. "They accepted my apology, and I hope you will too. I know you wanted us to all work together, and we told you we would. Unfortunately, old hurts and habits got in my way."

"Your propensity for being alone?"

"Yes."

A familiar pause preceded his response. "You seem to have decided that's not what you want any longer."

They all shared a glance and then Everleigh faced the phone as if Caspar stood in the room with them. "I have."

"Then you've found something more important than the diamond." No, the computer couldn't convey emotions, yet the more he spoke the more she heard pride. Encouragement. Happiness.

Her nerves began to settle as she realized that was all he had to say on the subject. He was moving forward, so she could too.

"You did find the diamond, didn't you?" Though phrased as a question, Everleigh could have sworn Caspar spoke it as a statement to which he already knew the answer. She had no clue what he looked like, yet she could picture him smiling.

All eyes latched on to her and Gertrude. Everleigh moved to stand behind her older friend. "We did."

Much like when Vienna had revealed it to them, the air seemed to still as the others took in this news. Gertrude reached into the bag she carried and pulled out the silk cloth they'd wrapped the diamond in. With painstaking care, she unfolded the edges. She held the hatpin up for them to see.

Sunlight hit the jewels, casting rainbows onto the surfaces around them. The Florentine Diamond sparkled brightly, its size still breathtaking no matter how many times she saw it.

"I want to thank you, Caspar." Gertrude's voice shook with emotion. "You've given me a gift I can never repay."

"Gifts aren't given with payment expected. They're free."

For once, Gertrude remained speechless. Everleigh suspected it wasn't for lack of words, but due to her fighting back tears.

"The only stipulation given by Vienna was she remain anonymous. She doesn't wish to be linked to the Habsburgs, both for her own privacy and for Adelheid's sake. She wants to honor the decision the Archduchess made when she gave her away."

Brooke's brows pulled together. "She doesn't want to know more about where she came from? Or to connect with the rest of her family?"

"She has her family. Three children. Seven grandchildren. Two great-grandchildren." Everleigh recalled one of the last photos in the album where Vienna was surrounded by all her loved ones. "She's content."

Brooke absorbed the info, though it didn't seem to alleviate her confusion. If anything, it appeared to agitate her more.

Unable to see her discomfort, Gertrude moved the conversation forward. "I'd like to finish this by bringing the diamond to the Austrian government. Is anyone opposed to me setting that up?"

"I'll have a plane waiting to take you."

"All of us?" Everleigh asked.

"Yes." Caspar didn't hesitate. "Let me know when you plan on leaving."

"Tomorrow?" Gertrude asked.

Everleigh consulted the room. Everyone nodded.

"Tomorrow it is," she confirmed.

This time, they'd reach the conclusion together.

CHAPTER THIRTY-THREE

FOUR DAYS LATER, GERTRUDE RECLINED on an iron bench tucked away in the gardens of Schönbrunn Palace. They'd quietly handed off the diamond to the Austrian government, who had placed it on display at the summer palace for a few months before they'd move it to its permanent location within the Hofburg.

The team had taken a photo with government officials near the glass case that housed the Florentine Diamond and received thanks, handshakes, and a small monetary gift from some of Empress Zita's grandchildren who attended on behalf of the family. That celebration remained private so they could protect Vienna and her wishes. To the world, the credit for finding the Florentine Diamond would remain anonymous.

Afterward, the women, along with Niles, John, and his wife, decided to hike the hill behind the palace that led to manufactured Greek ruins and a breathtaking view of the city of Vienna. Gertrude convinced them that she'd be content to sit on a bench and wait for them. Hidden down a side path with ivy-covered arches for shade, she inhaled the scent of roses on the late spring day. They didn't have to tell her a cloudless sky hung above, because she'd felt the sun's rays as they'd strolled. It felt good to rest and have a few moments to savor these past few days.

For years she'd hunted the diamond. A part of her never thought this day would come. She guessed that's why it was so hard to believe it had.

Something crunched across the gravel path. The rolling sound cut off as whoever it was stopped a few feet from her. A familiar scent lifted on the air, one that filled distant memories yet confirmed current suspicions.

The voice that accompanied the scent sounded older, raspier, yet remained the same tone and cadence. "Hello, old friend."

She couldn't refuse the smile that lifted her lips. "Hello, Jerrick." Gertrude turned toward the voice. "I wondered if you'd come."

As children, she, Amelia, and Jerrick had raced across the grounds at his grandparents' home, Halstead Manor. Jerrick Forsythe, the friend who'd first enticed them with stories of the Florentine Diamond. It was in the past few weeks she'd discovered he was also a Perez. A piece of this mystery that had only raised more intrigue, especially with the name *Caspar* also in play.

His hoarse chuckle lent to ease rather than surprise that she recognized him with no introduction. "I'm sorry I didn't see you in Lekeitio."

"I assumed you had your reasons. Quite possibly to do with Caspar." Though she hadn't seen Jerrick since the 1970s when his grandparents passed away, he always had intention behind his actions. She doubted he'd changed. "Are you related to him, or does he work for you?" Because once upon a time there'd been a Caspar Perez, and while he'd long since died, that didn't mean another couldn't share his name. She strongly suspected that was the case here.

"When did you realize our connection?" He skirted her question.

"I didn't. Not right away, though the name definitely piqued my interest." It brought her back to her days in the FBI. "Then Everleigh revealed her first meeting was at Halstead Manor, the very place we'd played and where you'd told me about the Florentine Diamond."

"Among other treasures."

She could imagine the smile on his face. "Yes, among other treasures." Something else she'd been thinking about these past weeks. "At that point, I assumed it could be possible the Perez family was involved and perhaps the Forsythes knew more than what I'd always deemed were simple childhood stories. But I never imagined your families were tied so intricately. Not until Madeira when Rafael mentioned both you and your mother by name and that she was a Perez. While I still had no proof you both were who I'd once known, it was the only thing that made sense. Jerrick. Luciana. Halstead Manor. The Florentine Diamond. All of them together were too big of a coincidence, and I'm not one who believes in coincidences."

"You never were."

If he knew that, then, "You didn't intend to hide from me?"

More hoarse laughter. "No." He coughed before continuing. "Like you adeptly pointed out, with all those ties coming to light, it would have been impossible. But I thought you'd enjoy more than one mystery to solve."

He'd always been the one to spark their adventures and craft clues when they were children. Back then, she'd thought him full of imagination. She'd come to realize that much of what he spoke about originated from the true stories of his family. No matter the influence, they'd shared some of her favorite days.

A wave of nostalgia washed over her. "That I did. It made it all the sweeter when Esmerelda gave us the picture with Adelheid and your mother. When Everleigh described Luciana's birthmark, it was like placing the final piece of a puzzle. I was positive then that she was the Luciana I once knew as your mother."

"I wish I could have been there to see your face."

"And I wish I could see yours now." She reached out her hand toward where she'd heard his voice and found his arm. Wrinkled like hers, she traced it to his fingers and gave a gentle squeeze. "I'm glad you're here."

He returned the pressure. "I started you and Amelia on this hunt when we were children. I wanted to help you finish it."

Memories that had hovered ever since she first suspected his involvement rose to the surface again. Long summer days playing with Amelia and Jerrick. The tales they'd spin of missing treasures. The quests they'd pretend to go on to find them. Now, her sight was gone, Amelia was gone, and it seemed Jerrick's ability to walk had left him. "What happened to you, my friend?"

She heard the effort in his words as he spoke again, softer this time. "ALS."

"I'm sorry." Her heart hurt for him, remembering the vibrancy of his youth. Although, she supposed, they'd both slowed with time. "How are you feeling?"

"Tired. Everyday tasks are becoming harder. Some days more so than others."

"Yet, you came to finish this with me." His offering somehow meant even more. "Amelia would have loved to be here with us." She'd been

Jerrick's friend first, and her younger sister had dragged her into their world. Gertrude forever remained thankful she had.

"I was sorry to hear of her passing."

"When did you hear?"

"Years later." He paused for a moment. "I would have helped sooner, but I was not in a place to until now."

She needed no details to understand. His last name might be Forsythe, but he also belonged to the Perez family. His family had gone quiet even before she'd retired from the FBI. She'd heard rumors but didn't need to know specifics about their silence. "Your past caught up with you."

"It did." Birds called from the trees around them. "Truthfully, I'm sorry I ever started Amelia searching for that diamond as children."

Gertrude stiffened. "Her death, it wasn't because she went after it, was it?"

"Nothing nefarious, no. But I shoulder the blame because I told her of it. I encouraged her."

"We were children."

"You were the sisters I always wanted, and I failed her. You."

It hit her then, his reasoning behind suddenly showing back up in her life. "You're trying to right your wrongs before you pass away."

"Yes," he conceded. "Facing my own mortality has made me face other things as well. I owe much to many. You were simply the first."

She could understand that. Her loss of sight brought to light much in her own life. At first she'd felt weighted down, until she'd fallen into the arms of Jesus and allowed him to carry her. "Be careful not to carry burdens that don't belong to you. Amelia's death was not your fault."

"I have made my peace with God. I know he holds my burdens." Even in his rough voice, she heard the same stillness and rest she'd found. "I simply wish to help others now any way I can."

"You've more than done that here." Even if she hadn't found the Florentine Diamond, her life would have remained full. But what Jerrick had done was help her write a most beautiful ending to her story with Amelia. She could close their book with a satisfied sigh and hold it dear to her heart. "How do I thank you?"

"I hadn't intended to ask you for anything." He hesitated. "But I'm afraid I must."

"Of course." She hadn't seen her friend in over forty years, yet their connection remained strong. Especially after the gift he'd just given her.

"I might, in the near future, need your contacts and expertise."

"As a private investigator or retired FBI agent?"

"You're wise enough to know that answer."

She did. She was also extremely curious, though she had a feeling based on his ambiguous responses that any answers would need to wait. "You'll have my help. Whatever you need."

Footsteps dug into the gravel, slowing as they neared. A male voice she didn't recognize spoke. "It's time to go, or we'll be late for your meeting."

"One more moment," Jerrick requested. The man must have nodded because Jerrick continued. "You should know, there's further need of the girls' assistance, and Caspar will be calling them again. You should also know, someone was watching Everleigh, but he's taken care of that."

Gertie gripped his hand tighter. "If he's taken care of it, why are you telling me?" She paused. "Ah, my expertise and contacts?"

"Yes. Although that wasn't the favor I was referring to earlier, those could be of great use here as well."

This time, she couldn't quiet her curiosity. "Is it safe? The girls working for him again?"

"Life is never completely safe. I believe we both know that." He drew in a breath. "But working for him is the safest place they could be."

She trusted he spoke the truth. "Thank you for keeping me in the loop. I'll keep my ear to the ground."

Whoever stood nearby cleared his throat. "We really need to go."

"All right." Jerrick's wheels crunched as he turned directions, gently breaking the hold she had on him. "It was good to see you, Gertrude. Good to see Amelia's son as well. He looks like her."

"Her spitting image."

"You've raised him into a fine young man. Better than I was at that age."

She wished she could take the credit. "He practically raised himself. He resembles Amelia in more than appearance."

"He's a lucky man."

"I'm the lucky one."

The space between them filled with tender reminiscence. She wished she could see Jerrick's face. Instead she envisioned the familiar smile he wore. "I'm ready." He spoke in a soft, coarse whisper. The travel and talking had clearly tired him out. She had so many more questions.

"Will I see you again?"

"We never truly know what the future holds."

How incredibly accurate, especially in this moment. She'd love to believe his reappearance in her life wasn't a onetime occurrence, but the only predictability in life was that it was forever unpredictable. "Then goodbye, old friend."

"Goodbye, Gertrude." And Jerrick rolled away.

⇾ ⇽

Spring erupted over Schönbrunn Palace in a colorful palette that only God himself could create. Everleigh stood at the top of the hill with the breathtaking view of Vienna spread in front of her. The vibrancy of reds, yellows, and oranges played against the pastels of greens, purples, and pinks, breathing life into what recently had been dormant. It was as if he reached down and gifted her with a picture of what he'd done in her life. She still grappled to take in this day she'd experienced. The past two months, really. Arms wrapped around her, embracing her from behind, and she leaned her head against Niles's solid chest.

"Happy?" he asked.

"Very." Even more than that. She was content. She couldn't remember a time when she'd been so at peace. Seemed dismantling her walls hadn't left her open to hurt as she feared. It opened her to love, because there was a difference between being guarded and being imprisoned. Walls that guarded kept you safe, while still allowing the good things inside. But, if you weren't careful, those same walls could change into ones that imprisoned. Those kinds of walls held a body captive. Demolishing them had set her free. "You?"

"I suppose." Laughing, he arched away from her jab, nabbing her hand as he moved. He tugged her close and pressed a kiss to her lips.

"This is getting old," Brooke grumbled as she, Natalie, and John, holding hands with his wife, Hattie, approached.

Niles paused his kiss only long enough to toss out a, "Get used to it."

Natalie turned to Brooke. "Don't worry. They're in the infatuation stage. No one can sustain that."

John held up his and Hattie's entwined hands. "We are."

"You've been married a few months," Natalie said. "You're on a delayed honeymoon. You're still newlyweds."

"Which is why I'm taking my bride back down this hill and to the zoo to see their panda." He smiled down at the petite brunette. "She has a thing for pandas. I have a thing for her."

Tenderness turned her eye roll into a look of adoration.

This trip was the first time they'd met Hattie. Everleigh quickly learned that while Hattie didn't use many words, she spoke her love for John loudly in every glance she gave him. And the words she did use were carefully chosen. Hattie didn't waste a moment but filled them with intention. Everleigh could see why John had fallen for her.

They made plans to meet up for dinner and said their goodbyes.

Lines furrowed across Brooke's forehead as she watched them leave. "How long did it last with you and Mason? I need a timetable here."

"For us? Till he said, 'I do.'" Natalie attempted the words lightly, as if meant as a joke, but her downcast eyes spoke of heartache.

Everleigh tapped against Niles's chest, then cut her eyes toward Natalie. He released her. "Think I'll go people-watch for a bit." He lumbered off to gaze over the gardens.

"Speaking of Mason," Everleigh began, "he didn't want to join us?" They'd invited him to come for the long weekend, so he wouldn't have to miss as many days of school.

"He had tickets to a White Sox game." Natalie tucked her hands into her pockets. "They're playing their best season. Haven't lost a game yet."

Brooke scoffed. "I would pick Vienna over baseball every single day."

"Me too." Natalie nodded. "We like different things. It's okay."

But her body language didn't support her words. Mason hadn't simply picked baseball over Vienna, he'd picked it over his wife. It was hard enough to envision him missing the opportunity for a trip like this with her. Nearly impossible to believe he'd choose his favorite sports team's win over celebrating his wife's win.

Pulling in a deep breath that straightened her shoulders, Natalie switched topics. "I still can't believe we're here. That I actually held the Florentine Diamond."

"A part of me wishes we'd have held on to it." Brooke honestly admitted. "Or at least that we were more vocal about finding it."

"That accomplishment would definitely boost your résumé," Everleigh noted.

"Very much so." Brooke slipped her sunglasses over her face as she stared out over the city. "And it would stick it to my competition."

She didn't say Storm's name, but it hung in the air nonetheless.

They strolled toward where Niles sat on a bench, people-watching. White gravel made paths between the bright green grass of the palace grounds. Red flowers created scrolled patterns in mirrored sections. Hedges blocked off hidden floral corridors accessible by wide, ivied arches. While hundreds of visitors milled around the area, the massiveness of the gardens made it feel as if only a few people explored the paths.

Everleigh placed a hand on Niles's shoulder. "We should get back to your aunt." She cast a glance out over the grounds.

"Yeah." He stood. "I was trying to pinpoint where we left her, but it's tucked into those hidden areas so I can't see her."

"Knowing her, she's probably chatting with anyone who walks by."

He chuckled. "I'm sure."

As the four of them started down the hill, Everleigh's phone vibrated, displaying an unfamiliar number. She would have ignored it, but investigators and lawyers were still calling with questions about the Palmer situation—most of whom she referred to John, who was representing her. He'd also assured her, like Uncle Maddox had promised, that she had nothing to worry about.

"Hello?" she answered.

"Enjoying the palace grounds?" Caspar's computerized voice spoke in her ear.

Everleigh jerked to a stop and put her phone on speaker. "We are." She motioned to everyone. "It's Caspar."

They circled around her, questions in their eyes. He'd already had John deposit their paychecks into their accounts, and they'd had what they'd assumed was their final meeting with him in Gertie's suite last night. "It's beautiful here." They'd told him their plans to sightsee today.

"I'm glad." When he paused, she heard unfamiliar noises in the background, along with the usual clicking sound. "I had thought our time together was coming to an end, but there is another item I now have a desire to find. Are you interested?"

Everleigh looked around the circle, meeting Natalie's wide eyes, then Brooke's smile, and ending on Niles's nod. Because, of course, wherever she was going, he was coming along. "I think so," she said. "Can you give us a few more details?"

"Tuesday morning at Halstead Manor. Until then, enjoy Vienna."

The call disconnected.

"Looks like we're stuck together for a little while longer." Brooke spoke first.

Natalie perked up. "I'm good with that." The past couple of months seemed to have revived her. They also seemed to highlight issues she had with her husband. Everleigh hoped this new quest wouldn't deepen the rift.

They resumed walking on their way to collect Gertrude. Brooke and Natalie on her left. Niles on her right. He reached for her, entwining their hands. She was sandwiched in between people who two months ago she didn't want to allow into her life. Now she couldn't imagine life without them.

Natalie sidestepped a giggling toddler running from his parents. "What do you think Caspar's going to send us to find next?"

"I have no idea." Brooke wrapped a strand of hair around her finger. "I'm almost as curious about that as I am his identity."

"Whatever it is," Everleigh said, "I promise not to go rogue. We're a team."

The more familiar the word became, the more she loved it. Especially as Natalie grinned her way, and Brooke playfully nudged her. Whatever their next adventure led to, it wouldn't beat the treasure of the friendships she'd found.

Walls down. Heart full. Love brimming. Everleigh stepped forward.

Sometimes wishes did come true.

ACKNOWLEDGMENTS

Finishing this book came at a difficult time in life. It was on the heels of my mom's passing and while we were cleaning out a lifetime of love and memories from my parents' home so my dad could move. A huge thank-you goes to my siblings who allowed me to go MIA for a bit of time while they shouldered the brunt of the work as I neared my deadline. Your gracious gift of time and space provided me the ability to shape this story into something I could place into readers' hands. Love you all.

And, of course, to My Love and my kiddos. They put up with a lot while I live in my story-worlds. Messy house. Take-out. Distracted wife and mom. I am so appreciative of how you all love me, even if you sometimes think I'm crazy. ☺ You are my biggest blessings in life.

Then there's also my writing-world friends who saw this story in its roughest shape and offered kind—and honest—feedback, brainstormed solutions, or talked me off emotional cliffs. Joanna and Ashley, thank you both for your constant support of me and my work. And Jess? I honestly don't think I could write a book without you. I am constantly in awe and filled with thanks for how God pushed us together and has used us to sharpen each other in so many ways. You truly are my iron.

Janyre Tromp. Thank you for what seemed like a simple inquiry one day asking what I was working on, then being able to hear something of worth in my ramblings. I am beyond thrilled to not only be at Kregel, but to be working with you. You pushed to make this story better, yet you never compromised my voice. You're a gem. ☺

Linda S. Glaz, agent extraordinaire. Thank you, thank you for your constant belief in me. But most of all, thank you for your love for Jesus and always encouraging your writers to pen the stories he's given us and let him worry about where to place them. You balance pushing us to be better writers with reminding us not to compromise. And you do it well. Thank you.

My Jesus. My all in all. Thank you for the gifts and talents you've given me. Using them is my honor and draws me closer to you. My prayer is that they draw others closer to you as well. All for your glory.

AUTHOR'S NOTE

SEVERAL YEARS AGO I HAD the opportunity to travel to Vienna and tour the palaces there. I heard all about the royal family, and their story intrigued me. I never thought, however, that I'd weave it into this tale.

And though there is much history in this book, I did put my own fictional spin on nonfiction elements. For the sake of storytelling, I condensed the years of upheaval between 1918 and 1921. During that period the emperor and his wife left and returned to Austria several times in hopes of remaining as sovereigns. Ultimately, they were forced to flee and abdicate the throne—though Empress Zita refused to use that terminology. Rather than show their back-and-forth travels, I chose to begin the story with elements of those years wrapped into one opening.

Bruno Steiner was a real person, as was the debate over whether he stole the Crown Jewels or if they stayed with the royal family in exile. The Florentine Diamond remains the center of that mystery. Playing with the unanswered questions was sheer entertainment (and at times torture) for my writer brain.

The places Everleigh and friends visited are actual locations Zita took her children during her years away from Austria. Some I've visited, others I have not. I did have the chance to go to Royalston, Massachusetts, where Calvin Bullock, Hugh, Marie, and their children Fleur and Fair all lived. William Hayes, however, was a fictional character created as my imagination ran with what I thought might have happened to the Florentine Diamond. His relationship with Adelheid and their daughter, Vienna, all originated with me.

This was my first story that allowed me to incorporate my love of history, but it won't be my last. It was fun to place my own creative spin on a mystery that is still alive today. Any inaccuracies spotted in this book are all mine. And if you do spot any, I sure hope they don't take away from your joy of reading the start to the Treasures of Halstead Manor series. Until next time . . .

SNEAK PEEK

The Novel Adventures of Natalie Daughtry

Luciana Perez, age eight
Lekeitio, Spain, 1922

Luciana Perez rolled over in bed and reached in the darkness for *Alice's Adventures Under Ground*, which Papi had left on the small table beside her. She'd wanted to continue imagining herself alongside Alice chatting with the mouse, but Papi had said he had a visitor who would not be put off. If only she had one of the new electric lights Papi had added to many of the rooms downstairs, she could try to read another chapter herself. It would take some time, however, for the lights to be installed up here. But there were electric lights in the library.

Nabbing her beloved book, she stood and tucked the worn pages under her arm, then crept across the floor. In the hallway she looked to the nursery, where she could hear Mama's whispers to baby Paloma as she rocked her. Luciana turned the other way and tiptoed down the stairs, avoiding the squeaky step at the bottom.

She stole across the wood floor toward the library, where a light stood beside the cushioned window ledge she loved to cuddle up on. Mama had even left a blanket there for rainy days . . . or cool nights like this one. Summer was nearly over and soon she'd have to open the only type of books she didn't like: schoolbooks.

Her lips scrunched up at the distasteful thought.

As she pressed forward, her eyes caught on the cracked-open door just beyond the library. Papi's study. Voices drifted through the tiny opening. Luciana tipped her head, moving closer so she could peek inside.

"My work with Empress Zita is none of your concern, nor should you make it anyone else's."

Luciana perked up at Papi's mention of her new friend's mother. Only days ago, while playing with Adelheid, Luciana had learned that Adelheid's mother gave some of her jewels to Papi. Neither she nor her friend understood why. Luciana's Papi tended grapes in their vineyard. What would he want with other people's treasures?

She pressed closer to listen for anything she could tell Adelheid or that would feed her curiosity.

Another man whose back was to her responded. "It is my concern when you refuse to pay me. This is not what we agreed upon." He sounded similar to when Papi read *Alice's Adventures* and pretended to be the mean Queen of Hearts. The man's deep pitch caused her to shiver with a different fear than Papi's villain voice produced.

But then Papi spoke, and the strength and calmness of his tone erased any worry she felt. "It's not, and for that you should be thankful. What you brought me is fake." Papi stood in front of a painting of people strolling through a park. After a moment, he turned toward the stranger. Luciana pressed against the wall so Papi didn't see her. "A very well-made reproduction of Seurat's work, but a fake nonetheless." His footsteps echoed through the room. "If you would like me to fully uphold my end of our agreement in light of this knowledge, I still can."

"N-No, sir. I'm fine." Suddenly, the stranger sounded like the frightened subjects of the Queen. "I'll go."

"Ah, yes, I thought you might. However, before you leave, there is something I need you to give me."

"Yes?" The word cracked as he said it.

"The name of who made this." When the man didn't answer, Papi continued. "I assure you, if you're wondering who you need to be more concerned with angering, it is me."

Luciana flinched. Of all the voices she'd heard Papi use, she'd never heard that one. Cold and hard like the jagged cliffs outside.

The man spoke a name Luciana wasn't familiar with, but Papi seemed to be. Then he scurried toward the door. Luciana ducked into the library, her pulse skittering fast. Of all the stories she'd longed to hear tonight, this had not been one of them.

※ ※

Present Day

No one had prepared Natalie Daughtry for this season. There'd been bridal showers and baby showers and crazy amounts of advice on how to navigate the past years, but people had been conspicuously quiet on what to do once you raised your children and your marriage sputtered into complacency. So here she was, taking a job at a bookstore to fill the minutes, hours, and days stretched out in front of her.

Of course, work at a bookstore with the eccentric owner Harry—complete with unkempt white hair and a love for colorful plaid suits—wouldn't be all bad . . . especially since Harry had added an automated espresso machine at the rear of the store near another sitting area. He hoped patrons would stay for a while and become so ensnared in the book they were reading that they wouldn't be able to leave without purchasing it. Seemed to be working. The method was responsible for the last four books Natalie added to her bookshelves at home.

The bell over the door jingled, and Natalie peeked around the romance section to see a tall, middle-aged man with light brown skin, black hair, and dark eyes enter. He looked like someone who frequented gyms more than bookstores, but who was she to judge her fellow bibliophiles?

Harry had gone to the restroom, so Natalie greeted the man. "Good morning, may I help you with anything?"

He looked up from the thriller that had caught his eye on a table by the door. "Just browsing," he said, his eyes squinting as he studied her. "Have we met?"

"Not that I know of." She was good with faces, even better with names. Mason always relied on her to supply them because they frequently slipped his mind. This stranger wasn't anyone she recognized, and Kenton Corners was small enough that she'd become familiar with most people. Though there was no way she knew everyone.

His perusal of her intensified. "I'm sure I've seen you someplace." Then he snapped his fingers. "Halstead Manor, right? You've been out there?" He must have seen her confusion as he quickly added. "I was recently there with a crew doing some work for . . . John, I think his name was?"

A few weeks back there had been a group packing up as she'd arrived. They'd been fixing siding on the house, but she'd been so focused on what had been happening with Everleigh that she hadn't given them much notice.

"Yes, right." She held out her hand. "I'm Natalie."

"Matt." He clasped her hand. "That manor's a pretty interesting place. Does it belong to your family?"

"My boss, actually."

He looked around the space. "This owner owns the manor too?"

She shook her head. "Nope. Different boss."

"Oh." He nodded before holding up the book he'd been checking out. "Happen to have any other titles by this author? I love her signature twists and turns."

Natalie was familiar with the name. "Sure. Follow me."

They chatted while he chose which book he wanted for his next read, then made their way to the front counter. Harry was waiting and helped Natalie ring him up. As the door closed on his exit, Harry turned her way. "Stupendous, Natalie! Not even on the clock a half hour and you made your first sale. Nicely done. Nicely done."

She often wondered if Harry even realized he often repeated himself. Some people were likely bothered by it. She found the trait kind of adorable. "I'd like to take all the credit, but I think it helped that he knew me. Or at least said he recognized me."

"Hmm." Harry squinted toward the front window at the man's retreating back.

"Apparently, he's seen me out at Halstead Manor. He must be a part of Stew's Crew. They've been working out there recently." At least, that's whose van had been in the driveway that day.

Harry shook his head, causing his white hair to stick out further. "I'm acquainted with all of Stew's boys, and he's not one of them."

"Unless he's new."

Again, he shook his head. "I had them out just yesterday to fix the awning over my door, and I chatted with them while they worked. That man isn't part of the crew."

Natalie stared at the door he'd exited, her curiosity peaking. The only people she'd bumped into at Halstead Manor besides her new friends had been that work crew. If Matt wasn't one of them, how did he know her and her connection to the manor?